RED ROAD GREEN

A story of

Jonathan Franklin

RED ROAD GREEN © 2022 JONATHAN FRANKLIN

SPARSILE BOOKS LTD

For Annabel

and

*for Zébel, agent of FUNAI, who did his
best to protect uncontacted tribes*

and

*for those Indians whose homeland and livelihood
have been obliterated by unnecessary invasion.*

B R A Z I L

N
↑

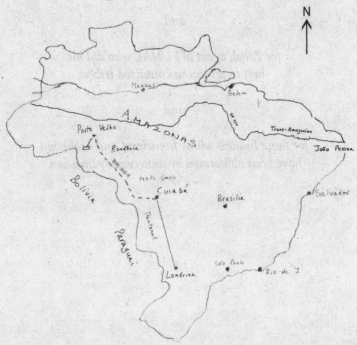

Manaus

Belém

A M A Z O N A S

Porto Velho

BR 319

Trans-Amazonian

João Pessoa

Rondônia

BR 364

Mato Grosso

Cuiabá

Brasília

Salvador

Bolivia

Paraguai

Paraguai

São Paulo

Londrina

Rio de J

———— Paved 1,500 Kms

– – – – Dirt & Mud 1,462 Kms

———— Paved and unpaved

SOUTH WEST AMAZON

*Between 1960 and 1985 two million people struggled up
Highway BR 364 into the Amazon in search of a better life;
the largest migration in the 20th century outside war.*

*This is the story of a young woman and a young man
who went up that road before it was paved.*

*Amidst the greens of the Amazon
and the flames of its destruction
they tried*

ZONI

'Indians! Indians!' came the voice, and again more strident, more frantic, 'Eeeendiaaans. Eeeendiaaaans...'

Silence.

She stopped cooking, wiped her hands down her skirt, picked up the baby with one sweeping grasp of both arms and hurried out of the hut to find her brother. She heard pounding feet.

'Two Indians,' he gasped, 'quick, get pans and sticks and bang them together. Come on all of us. There may be more. We must scare them off.'

'Maybe we're in their territory?'

'Come to hurt us?'

'All of us together. You too Idi. We must try to show more than we are.'

'*Tá bom*, for you Romi I will, but I can't leave him for long.'

Idenea[1] put Zoni back in his play-pen and pulled the mosquito netting over. 'Be good my Baba boy, I'll be back soon.'

He started pushing his favourite tractor about. She'd often left him on his own while working in her orchard close by.

She grabbed a wooden spoon and a frying pan.

All five rushed off banging and shouting and spread out as best they could. Soon the fallen branches hid one from the other. She should have worn trousers; bare legs and a skirt were not right for clambering over fallen trees and through spiky undergrowth. She halted to catch her breath beside the dark green wall of tree trunks, some forty metres high. She was about two hundred metres from their two huts, on the edge of the clearing.

A chill ran up her legs and the hairs on her arms stood up.

'Romi, where are you? Romee...?'

Unwillingly, as if pulled by an invisible magnet, she turned her head to her left. A man, close up beside a tree, different from any man she had seen before, stood completely still, his body weight evenly balanced on both legs. He was staring at right angles to her

---

1 Idenea is pronounced Idy-nay-ya

in the direction of the two huts, quite oblivious of her. A headband of parrot feathers circled his black hair and a belt of woven fibres gripped around his waist. Otherwise he was naked. He held a wooden bow taller than himself and a couple of feathered arrows in his right hand.

As she stared at this red-brown man barely ten metres away, she stopped breathing and was deaf to the whistles and whoops from the jungle and the distant pot-banging. Alone with the Indian, beneath the canopy of trees. All her weight on one leg, the toes of her other foot just touching the ground, quite still, her body suspended. Her lungs forced her to breathe violently inwards. At this sound, he looked at her.

His brown eyes, framed in gently slanting sockets, locked onto hers. His expression disinterested, his mouth set and calm. He was smaller than her, with broad shoulders and his biceps accentuated by straps of dried palm leaf. She stared at him, her lower jaw slack and heavy. She could hear her own quick breathing. He was as he was, at ease in his own. She was still standing on one leg.

In that short moment before they had time to react, a cry from the direction of the huts, a cry that every mother recognises: the scream of her own child in distress. Two sharp screams of, 'Mama, Mama,' broke her trance. Then again, 'Mamaaaa...' a hysterical scream and no more.

Her legs were already running.

'Zoni,' she yelled as she dropped the frying pan. 'Zoneee, hold on, *meu querido*. Mama is coming.'

She ran towards the first tree trunk, sawn and ready for sale, its top level with her shoulders. She clambered up the trunk. On the rounded top, without looking, so great was her haste, she jumped down into a jumble of broken branches. Badly grazed and bruised, she scrambled out ripping her skirt. She pulled at her flip-flops to keep them on. She craned her neck to see over the mass of horizontal tree trunks and slashed vegetation.

'*Oh meu Deus*, Zoni, why am I so far away?'

She straddled the next trunk, but this time lost her balance and fell onto the thorns of the spiky Tucuma palm tree, some of the thorns longer than her forefinger. She didn't feel, didn't notice the blood oozing from the punctures in her skin. She blundered from side to side. Clumps of knee-high razor grass, encouraged by the light let in by the felling, had invaded open space between the trunks. She ran and jumped like a hurdler, the sharp edges of this stiff stemmed grass sliced at her legs and arms. Her lower body and arms black with ash, her skin red with blood, she stumbled up the short slope to the main hut, her lungs retching with pain.

Empty play-pen. The carefully arranged mosquito net cast to one side.

'No!' she howled.

She ran into her bedroom. Nothing. Nobody.

'My baby.' She screamed at the jungle, to the mule, to the sky, to the sun. 'Romi! Where are you? Help, *Oh meu Deus*, help me.'

Romi was on his way back up the path with Juca, Bosco and Carlito, when he heard his sister's cry. He ran the last few metres and found her kneeling face down with her hands flat on the ground.

'What's happened, Idi, your body, so much blood?'

'I was beside an Indian. He was looking over here. I heard Zoni scream. I ran. Zoni's gone. Stolen. Romi, *Pelo amor de Deus*, for the love of God, please…Find my baby.'

1

TO CUIABÁ

The Perfect Peace Motel — O Motel da Paz Perfeita.

The Madonna was no bigger than a child's hand. She wore a tiny gold crown and held baby Jesus in her arms. Idenea Saladini was staring at her as she swung from the rear mirror of the bus as it rolled along the gravel road to Cuiabá. The Madonna was a miniature copy, even to the blue dress, of the small statue that she used to pray to every day in the jungle. And Idenea was praying to this one.

'*For the love of God, why do I do this? Praying again when I know that the Holy Mary doesn't give a shit about me. Que merda de vida.*'

She'd been on highway BR 364 changing buses from village to village for three weeks, taking casual jobs as a waitress. She scratched her head. If only she could wash her hair. The sadness in her chest weighed heavy. Would Cuiabá be any better?

The driver's flesh bulged out from below his shirt and over his belt like bicycle tyres. He wedged his sunglasses onto his head but they slipped over his eyes on a film of sweat. He'd let her on for free at Rosario Oeste as long as she cleaned the bus of chicken shit and scraps of food. She picked up sandwich crusts and stuffed them into her mouth. Her baggy t-shirt, her flip flops, a ten cruzeiro note and a plastic bag with a small wooden doll were all she had.

At a filling station, her bladder aching after so long without a stop, she went behind the kiosk to piss. Black vultures were pecking about on the rubbish. Their wings flapped up the sour smell of rotting fruit skins, curling her nostrils. The sun stared down.

The bus driver came up behind her as she crouched and groped at her breasts.

'I'll have some of that as well.'

'Go to hell you bastard,' she yelled, pulling up her pants and kicking at his shins.

He stepped back at the sight of the red scars on her legs swearing, 'Filthy bitch'.

He was holding the bus door for her when she came back. 'You're in trouble, aren't you? Go and find the restaurant *O Boi Gordo*, the Fat Bull, and tell Mano that Horatio sent you. He'll help you. He's a small fellow and talks like a machine gun.'

At the bar in the bus station, she scanned the menu board looking frantically for something to eat she could afford. Piped music churned out. Dogs wandered over to the newly arrived bus and lifted their legs on the big wheels. A radio blasted out football commentary. After a small plate of rice and beans she put just one coin back into her pocket. The woman who served looked her up and down and added a lump of meat.

Idenea kept chewing so the taste of the salty grill would last longer. She set off to find the *Boi Gordo*. She recognised some of the road signs, when she and her family had passed through this colonial town of Cuiabá on their way north three years ago. Then, there had been horses and mules, now cars rushed and honked their horns. A driver shouted as she crossed the road. 'Hey, lanky girl, get in with me!'

A traffic policeman showed her the street. Mano, short for Emanuel, shook her hand. 'You're in luck, I've just opened up and need a waitress.'

She looked up at the sky. 'Me, in luck?'

He pulled some notes out of his back pocket.

'Go next door and get some new clothes.' He looked up at her with excited brown eyes. He was so small she could see over the top of his bald head. 'Off you go! Tips can be good.'

She chose some blue jeans and a white t-shirt from hanging rails pushed onto the pavement. Looking in the shop mirror. 'Is that me? *Oh meu Deus*.' She rubbed off the sweaty grime that streaked her face.

She counted her money each week. At night, on her wooden bunk with a radio blaring over open walls, she would cry into her pillow. Stroking the rough cotton, she conjured up the smell of her baby, the velvety softness of his hair.

'Wait for me please, *meu querido*, I'll be back soon to find you. I'll work and I'll work till I have enough, I promise.'

Most days she served a small dark girl. She was with a different man every time. That day the man jumped up shouting '*Filha da Puta*' and left without paying.

The girl beckoned Idenea.

'Don't worry, I'll pay,' she said with a smile. 'It happens all the time. You're new here, aren't you? I'm Ana.' She held out her hand. 'You look so sad.'

Idenea warmed to Ana's comforting smile. 'What do you mean, it happens all the time?'

Ana hesitated and lowered her brown eyes. 'I work as a hostess at Ludo's in the Perfect Peace Motel in Coxipó. Ludo looks after me. I come from a favela in Salvador and have no family. You and I could be friends. I get so lonely.'

'Me too.' Idenea smiled, her lips twisting as she did.

Ana said, 'Somebody tall and gorgeous like you would do so well. And those eyes of yours...'

'Doing what?'

Ana sighed. 'The man who walked out said why couldn't I be tall like you. Come and meet Ludo. I'm sure he'd find a room for you.'

Idenea leaned forward. 'Room? You mean working as a whore? Are you crazy!'

'Money.'

Ana squeezed Idenea's hand. 'I pick and choose. Look, I pocketed three hundred cruzeiros a couple of nights ago just for talking, nothing intimate. For me it's a job. I can't do anything else.'

Idenea pulled her hand away.

'Intimate? I can't do that, it's disgusting.'

Ana sat back, her red lips half open, appeal in her eyes. 'You don't have to say yes all the time. We could be friends...'

'No?'

'Think of the money,' Ana insisted.

Idenea shook her head. 'It's shameful.' She hesitated. 'I have to think. It's all too quick for me.'

12

'So is the money. Here, let me look at your hands.' Idenea placed both hands on the table.

'I'll give you some cream to soften them. Look, it really helps.' Ana laid her chubby brown arms on the table and stretched all ten of her soft brown fingers beside Idenea's scab-covered knuckles. 'See what a little money can do?'

Idenea leant forward and lowered her voice. 'Tell me about the money.'

Two days later she hugged Mano as she said goodbye. He smiled sadly. 'You're in a hurry, aren't you? What a shame.'

When Ana picked her up, she laughed. 'I've never been in a taxi before.'

The driver tried to catch her eye in the rear-view mirror. 'So, you two pretty ones live there, do you?'

Idenea shrank back into her seat. 'What am I doing, Ana, I must be crazy?'

'Look, here's a present.'

Ana slipped a bracelet of purple amethysts around Idenea's left wrist. 'You and I are not going to be alone any more.' She kissed her on the cheek.

'Ana, you sweetheart.' Idenea lifted her wrist with rapture in her eyes. 'Things are going to be all right, aren't they?' She rubbed the bracelet with her thumb.

Ana pointed at a row of single-storey buildings at the end of a dust track. Above a wooden gate, in lettered neon lighting, shone *Motel da Paz Perfeita*, the Perfect Peace Motel, with a flashing pink heart at each end. Ana sat Idenea down at a table under a slatted bamboo roof beside the main building. She ordered two cokes and some chips. Idenea drank in quick sucks through a straw. Ana walked off to a bar where a dark haired man was serving. She beckoned Idenea and introduced the man as Ludo. He was as tall as she was with a broad chest and his dark hair cut short.

'Hi, Beautiful,' he said smiling, 'Ana has told me all about you, looking for work?'

Idenea smiled grimly. He asked her many questions as he showed her the saloon bar with its small round tables and a television on a shelf amongst bottles of whisky and Pinga rum.

'This is where I will introduce you to my clients.' He never stopped smiling but, Idenea was sure he didn't really want to be her friend.

'Your accent tells me you're from the south like me so you'll understand when I say my cut is fifty percent of your earnings, right?'

She nodded and slipped one arm through Ana's. Her stomach tightened as she looked around the empty white room. How could she sell herself?

She told him about the scars on her legs.

Lips pressed thin together, he said, 'Well, turn the light off so they can't see. And here, wear this round your neck at all times.' He handed her a plaited cotton necklace with a wooden cross. 'It will protect you from the nasties. Anybody hurts you and they're Ludo's enemy. A few broken arms around town show I mean business. And take my advice. Don't wear high heels or you'll embarrass the men.'

Ana fingered an identical cross around her neck and smiled encouragement. 'Come on, it'll be all right.'

Idenea tried to smile.

Ludo pressed his lips tighter and gripped her free arm. 'There are plenty of lost people like you in this town so do what I say, understood!'

As Ana showed her round, she kept her eyes fixed to the ground. Her room was Number 5 down an open-air corridor beside a grass courtyard with a pond in the middle. She put her few clothes on the only chair and the wooden doll her father had carved for her on the bed. The sheets smelled of washing powder. She could not sleep. As she closed her eyes, she saw her old house and the mango tree with their mule tied to it and their dog, Bolo, chasing chickens. And there was her mother's voice and the smell of wet coffee bushes.

14

Her first client was the sixteen-year-old son of a friend of Ludo, desperate to prove himself. She could have felt sorry for him, goaded on by his father to have his first experience, if he hadn't swaggered and exaggerated so much. She kept her t-shirt on. He was more nervous than she. She didn't know how to deal with his clumsy antics and pushed him away. He went into the bathroom and she heard him groan as he masturbated. He threw more money on the bed than she could earn in two weeks as a waitress.

The following night would be different. Ludo had told her he was an important client, a big cattleman who liked blonde girls.

'You'll have to sharpen up on last night my girl, understand?' He took her hand. 'I can see you're not a true blonde, but you'll do.'

He led her to a table where a tall thin man wearing a wide felt hat above a short black moustache sat drinking pinga. She hung back, one hand on her stomach as if to hold down the rising panic in her gut.

Ludo pulled out a chair. 'Senhor Machado, this is Idenea, our new girl.'

She sat down, eyes to the table.

From a narrow sun-lined face he looked her up and down. 'Fresh? Good for you Ludo.'

Ludo walked away. She continued to stare at the table. She slid her hands under her thighs. Machado got up and walked noisily in high boots over to the bar. Maybe he only wanted to talk about cattle. That was okay, she knew about cattle. He put a glass of orange juice in front of her and filled his own with pinga.

'Drink.'

Still looking at the table, she forced a quick thank you but didn't touch her glass.

'Go on. Do you good. Where are you from?'

She told him.

'Speak up girl. I can't hear you.'

'Near Londrina, down south.'[1]

He drank.

'Yeah, I know. Good land for coffee. Up here it's cattle and more cattle.' He coughed.

He was bored. He swivelled round to watch the television above the bar and shouted, 'Yeah! Yeah!' at a football game. She saw the back of his hat and watched his hand grip his glass. She sweated cold. Men and girls were laughing and drinking at the bar. Ana sat at one end with another cowboy, one arm round her dark brown shoulders. She waved at Idenea, then saw who she was with and mimicked disgust and mouthed between scarlet lips, '*Cuidado*. Watch out!'

So much noise.

Machado turned back, his voice slurring, 'Want another drink? Here have some pinga.' She shook her head. 'You don't say much do you, my girl?'

His head bent back as he drank and his hat fell off. He had a browny-white bald head, a rim of straggly black hair over his ears. Blotches marked where the sun had burnt his neck. He banged his glass down and pushed back his chair.

'Take me there! I'm off soon.'

She hesitated and looked around for Ana. She wasn't there.

A strong hand on her shoulder. 'Get on with it or I'll call Ludo.'

She stood up and headed along the passageway. Yes, he was drunk. His boots trod heavy behind her. In the room that she was beginning to keep neat and clean as some sort of home, a cold numbness wormed into her stomach. She took off her skirt and pants and stood naked from her waist down beside the bed. In spite of the heat she shivered. All she could think of was how quickly she could get this over with. He kicked the door shut.

Like a big cat he was right in there. She turned off the light, a glimmer still edged beneath the door. He steadied himself against the wall.

He flicked the light back on. 'And the rest?' he growled. 'Strip girl, I want you stripped.'

'Please. No.' She raised her hands to her shoulders to cover her breasts. She struck at his groping hands.

'You're strong, aren't you, *Puta*.'

She struck at him again. 'You can't treat me like this.'

He flinched at the blow. '*Puta*, you forget who's paying for this.'

16

Her promise to her baby flashed into her mind. He forced one arm behind her back and ripped off her t-shirt and bra. He shoved her backwards. She closed her eyes and heard him at his belt. His boots on, bruising her legs. She cried out. He thrust a hand over her mouth. Her breath in short puffs through her nose. Smell of stale pinga, smell of stale sweat. He called out, '*Puta*' and slammed the door behind him.

From down the passage the tramp of his boots and, 'Ludo, Ludo? That new girl of yours? No good. Get rid of her.'

She lay quite still hating herself, hating everything. Dirty, dirty. She struggled to her feet. There was a roll of notes on the bed. She locked the door, turned on the shower. Scrub, scrub, wash it off. How could she have ended up in a place like this?

Where was her husband, where was her baby?

A light tapping on the door. She pulled Ana so close that the tears on her cheek wet Ana's neck. They sat on the bed. Ana held her in her arms.

'It's all right, my love, I'll show you a few tricks that'll help you.'

She grasped one of Ana's hands and with her wet cheek still on Ana's neck and as if confessing said, 'I need money to find my little boy. I promised. But Ana, the shame.'

Ana levered their bodies onto the bed side by side. 'Ssshh, let's sleep now. I'm not going to leave you tonight. Things will be better in the morning.'

In the morning she gave Ludo his fifty percent.

'You look miserable,' he said counting the cruzeiro bank notes. 'You'll get used to it. Settle in and count the money.'

Zebu.

Five hundred head of white Zebu cattle jostled and surged forward.

Robert Jenney rode as back man in a gang of six. Up since five they had done four kilometres and there were two more to go to the corral, with the midday sun high above. Robert's job was to keep the

17

stragglers in line. His face white, his ears and nose clogged, sweat mixing with the dust crusted his shirt. He spat to one side.

The lead peon cowboy, whipstock across his saddle, straw hat tilted back, led the wedge-shaped column that stretched for 200 metres behind. Sitting straight, he jogged deep into his saddle. His marchador horse trotted with its front legs and walked with its back limbs. Along each flank of the column, fifty metres apart and ten metres out, two cowboys kept the herd together. Their whiplashes trailed in the dust beside their horses' hind hooves. They goaded and whooped in high-pitched cries. All had ·38 revolvers strapped around their waists, except Robert Jenney.

He'd had enough of guns.

Bobby, as everyone called him, all of six feet tall and his horse more of a pony, stretched his legs straight down from his western-style saddle, slotting the toes of his boots into cup-shaped leather stirrups close to the ground. He sat to the trot. The hooves of his horse beat the ground. Large green mosquitoes spiked into the hogged mane. He was thankful for his knee-length boots and long shirtsleeves. His jeans, heavy with sweat, chafed at his knees.

Ari, Bobby's cattle manager, outrode to the right, a blur in a balloon of dust. He rode differently to Bobby; his leather-clad legs angled forward from his saddle, heels down, spiky wheeled spurs jutting out. Rawhide reins in one hand high above the pommel, he reined back and forth. His horse frothing at the mouth flung its head side to side against the jab of the curb. His other hand, wedged on his hip, held the short wooden stock of a Mato Grosso cattle whip. His black moustache just visible beneath a wide straw hat.

'I tell you,' he would laugh, his breath whistling through his near toothless gums and his arm around Bobby's shoulders, 'I've ridden till my leathers stuck to my thighs.'

Ari was the son of cattle drovers who herded young steers from the west towards the fattening pastures and the distant markets in the east. Sometimes up to 500 kilometres over weeks. Ten kilometres a day was good progress with six or seven hundred head in hand. Home was a circle of hammocks with an old tarpaulin stretched over. Ten hours droving by day on slippery red mud during the rains and in a cloud of thick red dust up your nose in the dry. He was a tall man with black grizzled hair and a potbelly like a bowler hat; a descendant of slaves mixed with gaucho blood from the south. In the saddle at the age of four, the master of a long whip at twelve. But he knew his business even though he couldn't read or write, just able to jot down the weight of a bullock on a ripped-open cigarette pack. 'I know my cattle,' he'd say and cuff Bobby on the shoulder. '*Sim, Senhor*, I do, *Filhos da Puta*, Sons of bitches!'

After, in the nearest bar, sweat and red grime soaking their clothes and congealing their hair into rigid sticks, he'd bang a bottle of pinga down in front of Bobby and order a beer for good measure.

Ari leaned forward over his horse's neck and lifted up the short stock of his whip. A wide circle with his arm sent six metres of rawhide whirling above his head. Eight steel rings, woven into the lash next to the stock, balanced and increased the power. He shot the whip straight in front, *crack*! He pulled it back over his head and six metres directly behind and beyond his horse's tail, *crack* again! Then, still in rhythm and with ever increasing speed forward again and *crack*!

'*Vai! Vai! Filhos da puta.*'

The nearest beasts swerved back into line.

Behind and out of the dust jogged the camp-boy with hammocks, rattling water tins and cotton bags full of pork fat and farofa manioc flour.

Their job was to buy two hundred head from this Pantanal herd for trucking 1,500 kilometres to the north, which would take a good two weeks, over mud and dirt roads to the Fazenda Rio Largo ranch in Rondônia.

The cattle kicked up the dust. Calves scurried about bleating for their mothers. The breed is originally from Nellore in India. All are white with hanging dewlaps, black eyes and round humps on their backs. Their long legs keep the bulls' genitals from knocking into prickly pears, damaging fertility. They don't moo like European cattle, but cough like big cats. In the early days, Bobby found their swaying white humps unnatural as if a batch of giant caterpillars might suddenly erupt from them.

Young bullocks mounted the backs of heifers and other bullocks. Their hind legs scrabbled to keep up. Losing balance, they dropped back onto all fours. Dark brown shit slipped down the backs of white legs. No steam. At first Bobby hated the sharp stench but now, he happily inhaled the heavy smell thick with dust. They trotted and ambled through open country dotted with palm trees and large copses of scrubby green jungle. Mud lines on the palm trunks marked the height of the annual flooding. Above, black vultures followed, circling round and round, their wing tip primary feathers like spread fingers.

These five hundred were part of a herd of about six thousand. Nobody was sure of the exact number. The cowboys had driven them up from the rising waters of the Pantanal flood plain. Once a year tropical rain surges down the Paraguay river breaking its banks and submerging an area nearly half the size of France; a haven for a multitude of birds. When the flood retreats, the cattle are driven back to refreshed Mimosa grass.

A couple of steers dashed out to one side.

'Look out, Ari! There's a rogue breaking your way.'

It was the same one that had tried several times that day. Ari spiked his horse into a gallop. The steer jigged sideways. Ari's right arm rose in one fast forward motion. The narrow thong of fresh yellow rawhide at the end of the whip sliced the steer's right eye clean out. He always boasted to Bobby how good he was with that whip and had tried to teach him to use it. Impossible. All Bobby could do was bruise the back of his head with the flying steel rings. He cheered in admiration and cantered over. The steer fell back to a walk and halted, shaking its head, its right eye dangling from its socket. Ari wound his whip around his waist, pulled his lasso off his pummel and roped the steer easily around the neck.

'*Meu Deus*, Ari, that was something. I believe you now.'

'*Tudo bem*, Chefe,' Ari laughed, 'I told you I was good, ever since a boy. These wild Pantanal cattle need a lesson. That bastard didn't know Ari was here. It won't come out again.'

He pulled a knife from his belt and chucked it to Bobby. 'Here, Chefe, cut it off.'

Bobby cut the eye free and dropped it into the dust, a treat for a following dog, and wiped his bloodied hands on his jeans.

'Jenney, you must turn yourself into Macbeth.' The voice of his school master came back to him. '*No, this my hand will rather the multitudinous seas incarnadine, making the green one red*.' Don't you see Jenney he's all ready half mad. So, try it again and go mad yourself.'

Bobby wiped his hands even harder on his jeans till there was no blood left on them. Quieter now, the herd plodded on. The one-eyed steer edged back, shaking its head as blood slid down into its mouth.

'We'll be forced to buy that one, Ari, you'll see.'

Ari's chuckle whistled through the gap in his front teeth. 'Sure, Chefe, we can eat some of it tonight. And tomorrow they'll sun dry what's left.'

Bright green parakeets burst from above and darted overhead. Bobby dropped back to his position and the dust. Approaching the corral, more cowboys rode up, broad grins and moustaches. Mongrel dogs, big and small, prowled behind.

Built of rough-hewn timber, the corral was in three squares; a large collecting ring led through to a smaller one for branding and on to a bigger holding pen. In the branding ring two stout lashing poles stuck up out of the gravelly ground close to a lean-to with a tin roof. Branding irons lay beside a mound of white ash.

Ari rode up. 'Action now, Chefe.'

He pulled a short whip from a saddle strap. He jogged off. Bobby unrolled his own. He could lash and crack this whip at full length. Ari had seen to that. Double wooden gates swung open. A bull's skull and horns topped each side post. Men yelled, dogs snarled, whips cracked, cattle groaned, Bobby's pulse pounded and half an hour later the herd was corralled, any loose ones quickly rounded up. Inside, the cattle relaxed. Bobby breathed sun-baked dung. A small metal windmill on top of a wooden scaffold pumped water into troughs along the perimeter.

Their horses tethered under a tree, the men slapped backs and swaggered awkwardly in high-heeled boots over to a hut for water and stewed sun-dried meat, rice, beans and coffee. Bobby walked with a light easy stride, his body lean, his back straight, wiry and athletic. He squirted the remains of his leather water flask down his throat. Behind, two cowboys roped up the one-eyed steer, drew knives and slit its throat. Jets of blood pumped out. First it collapsed to its knees then rolled to one side. The dogs, snapping at each other, lapped at the red. Overhead more and more vultures spiralled upwards.

While the sun sank in a blaze of orange behind the waving palm leaves, Ari bargained for the young heifers and cows in calf. He crouched on the ground, his back against the hut wall and drew numbers in the red earth with a short stick. He laughed, he swore and shifted his hat from side to side. He yanked and stroked at his black moustache saying he'd never seen such rubbish in all his life. Pedrão, the foreman, told him to go to hell and find better.[2] Long silences. In the end the ready cash belted around Bobby's waist did the talking: half now, half at load up.

That night they ate tough steaks cut from the one-eyed steer, grilled in the open, and downed neat pinga. Dogs edged towards the smell and fell upon cast-off bits of gristle. Ari and Pedrão told ever longer stories of droving and of huge jaguars killing cattle. 'Remember that monster cat with the short tail bitten off and the laughing horses with no lips. Yeah, those greedy piranhas!' The men asked Bobby about the Beatles and the Queen. Slung in their hammocks, Bobby blew out the one candle.

'Ari?'

'Yes, Chefe?'

'We're going to make this work, aren't we, Ari?'

'What, Chefe?'

---

2 ão at the end of a noun or adjective means big/large

'I mean the whole damned project, all ten thousand head of it. I'll get there. We'll get there. Won't we?'

'Of course we will, Chefe. Now go to sleep.'

Ari snored loudly.

Sleepless, and worse, worrying that he couldn't sleep, Bobby gazed up at the leaves of the palm roof. Even after three years always the same faces, always the same words from his Colonel.

'I'm transferring you out east to the 2nd battalion in Malaya.'

Always his same reply. 'What, throw me out of the army, sir?'

And his boss, Alistair, in London shaking his hand. 'I want you out in the Amazon right away.'

There was the three-year plan. In the first year five hundred hectares of jungle cleared; by year three two thousand hectares all fully planted up with grass and one thousand five hundred head of Nellore cattle. The four men at that meeting in São Paulo had been Luiz Antonio da Costa, his son Luiz Geraldo da Costa, Alistair Atkinson of Atkinson & Atkinson of London and himself, the newly appointed manager of the Fazenda Rio Largo Cattle and Agriculture project.

Alistair was trying to diversify out of Africa and Asia, and into Brazil; the country of the future as Luiz Antonio da Costa had persuaded him.

Alistair liked Bobby's army background and in spite of the cloud that hung over him, damned bad luck as he called it, he wanted to help him. He was sure this ex-army captain would do a good job in a tough enterprise like this.

Bobby rolled over face down into his hammock.

Was he doing a good job? *Was* he?

And there was his son Michael, with his wide eyes asking why he was going away. And with her hand on his shoulder, his estranged wife, Beatrice, her dark hair down onto her shoulders.

Squirrels rustled in the rafters.

That bloody school question. The sheet of white paper taunting him with its emptiness, to explain why he'd chosen Hope instead of Faith or Charity as his life's creed for his last essay before leaving. His teacher, Mr Doggard striding about. 'Choose Jenney, choose. It matters.' His family motto; *Dum Spiro, Spero*. While I breathe, I hope. What choice did he have? All that certainty.

The weariness in his limbs finally closed his eyes.

He woke to the rose of dawn and to *Bom Dias* in gruff voices and the smell of wood smoke and fresh coffee, the men's faces losing their greyish shine with the glow from the east. The dogs stretched and sniffed at scraps in the embers of the fire. Ari and Bobby made up one branding team and two ranch cowboys the other. One of them stripped to the waist, his black skin gleaming in the early sun, wore a tight leather skull cap from the northeast state of Ceará. Several more men sat on the corral fence to watch.

One jeered a friendly, 'Let's watch the blondie.' And another, 'On you go, Blue Eyes, let's see if you can take it.'

Fazenda Rio Largo branding irons with their big 'L' brand mark poked out of a heap of burning logs. Whips cracked. Ten animals bundled through. Ari lassoed the first heifer. Together they dragged it bucking and leaping till its head jammed against the nearest lashing pole. Bobby looped his lasso and placed it on the ground to catch the heifer's back feet. He heaved with all his strength, the noose tightened and the heifer thumped down onto its side. He grabbed its tail and threaded the lasso between the hind legs and pulled upward. The heifer snorted and writhed but couldn't get up for, unlike horses which rise front feet first, cattle rise back feet first.

'Good, Chefe. Hold the bastard still otherwise the iron will smear.'

Ari stamped his foot hard onto the supine heifer's left flank and pressed the glowing red 'L' brand into its lower thigh.

The heifer bellowed and tried to kick. Bobby pulled its tail with all his weight. His arms ached. Ari held the iron, one second maybe two, three millimetres deep, not more or he'd wound and blow flies would come. Singeing grey smoke and the smell of burning hide stung into Bobby's throat. Ari jumped back. Bobby let go. Ari released the head. The heifer bounded into the air. Two cowboys drove it into the holding corral.

Ari swore, '*Filho da puta*, what a dump. Why don't they have a branding gate?'

Bobby's back and chest ran with sweat.

The third beast, a young steer, on the ground and pinioned, Ari called out, 'We'll need meat up there won't we, Chefe? Let's keep this one and fatten him up.'

Bobby nodded. Ari drew a slender knife from his belt, grabbed the steer's scrotum and cut a slither of skin from the underside. With three fingers he slid out one testicle. He scraped gently, careful not to cut the holding membrane and artery, until the dark shiny oblong lay in his hand. The bullock panted and heaved. The second ball out, the scrotum shrivelled up with an ooze of blood. On release, no bucking and leaping only a clumsy, hind legs apart, stagger.

Ari beckoned. 'Hungry, Chefe? Need more strength? Wait here.'

He stuck both balls onto the L of the branding iron and held them over the fire. Minutes later. 'Here, Chefe, watch out it's hot.' His laugh hissed through his teeth. 'Good for your own performance. You'll see.'

'I'm sure you're right, amigo.'

Bobby rolled the burnt brown ball gingerly between his thumb and forefinger, bit and chewed.

Ari chewing and grinning. 'Well, Chefe?'

Bobby swallowed and spat. 'Next time, Ari, they're all yours. Maybe they'll fire you up. I hate kidney and this tastes much the same.'

A raucous shout from the watchers. 'Give the gringo water, he'll need it.' Bobby took the offered leather flask and squeezed a curving stream into his mouth.

On the morning of leaving, with the L of Fazenda Rio Largo still festering but well cauterised onto two hundred left flanks waiting for the long truck drive north, Ari chucked a bucket of water over Bobby and he did the same back. A quick coffee.

'Freshen up, Chefe, we're off to Cuiabá today so stop fussing about yourself. Beer, good grub and the girls. I'll arrange everything. You'll see, blondes, mulatas, blue eyes, brown eyes and the bodies, whoah!'

With a circular motion of both arms he roared with laughter. His face, the colour of old mahogany, close up to Bobby's who gripped his arm with an urgent strength as if pleading with Ari to sort out his life for him.

Room No 5.

Into Bobby's battered jeep. Ari had promised to give him a good time in Cuiabá and Ari keeps his word.

'Stop, Chefe,' Ari cried as his head banged on the roof. 'Chefe, *pelo amor de Deus*, stop. Get me a horse.'

'Move over, Ari.' Bobby elbowed Ari's ample backside off the brake lever. 'I can't drive with your butt all over me.'

Yellow woodpeckers swooped up and down in front of them.

After four hours pitching and lurching, they unfolded themselves stiffly out of the jeep and checked in at a hotel in central Cuiabá. Old colonial buildings, a tall church spire, narrow cobbled streets and a fish market down by the slow brown river. Bobby breathed in the sweet smell of cooking sugar. He had been away from people for too long.

Ari lumbered about in his high-heeled boots. He shouted at the cars and buses, '*Filhos da puta*. This is the end of the world. Where's that place I've heard of, with the tender meat, beer and girls?'

Several bars later they returned to their hotel. Ari by now was swearing at everyone. Nobody took any notice. That made him even more irritated. Bobby asked the manager for a good place for the evening, his thigh-clinging bell bottoms so clean beside Ari's grimy leather chaps and Bobby's stained jeans. The Rolling Stones blared out *Honky Tonk Woman* from a couple of speakers on the wall above a bright poster of the smiling Brazilian football team after their 1970 World Cup triumph. Ari winked at the manager and then winked again, all the while moving his hands and arms suggesting bodies and round shapes.

The manager looked at Bobby in despair and said with a sigh, '*Calma*, cowboy. There's a bar on the edge of the bush in Coxipó about three kilometres from here. The Perfect Peace Motel, and...' He pointed at Ari, 'mind you behave yourself out there, cowboy. Get me? It belongs to a friend.'

Ari drew his chest up. 'I'm a cattle dealer not a cowboy.'

The manager shrugged. 'As you say, *tudo bem*.'

Half an hour later they were drinking beer in the Perfect Peace Motel. Bobby ran his thumb up the ice-cold mist on the outside of his glass. He let the cold linger in his throat and ordered another and then another. Their table stood on gravel beside an open-sided saloon attached to a long bungalow built in a square. Above them bamboo canes lashed together kept the sun and rain away. Bare bulbs on fly-blown plastic wires hung down.

'Clean eh, Boss? No dust.'

Ari liked to call Bobby both Chefe and Boss.

Bobby nodded as he licked the froth from his lips.

Two moustached men with broad-rimmed hats pushed back on their heads, their elbows on the single plank of a bar, sat drinking and laughing with a couple of girls. One girl with white lipstick wore a white leather miniskirt above short white boots that stood out against her dark skin. The other, paler and tubby, sat cross-legged on a high stool with a tight red miniskirt, red lipstick and red high heels that she swung back and forth on her shiny red toes. They drew on their cigarettes and let the smoke curl away through pouting lips. A haze of smoke drifted below the ceiling. The theme from the latest Novela sang out from a television perched above the bar.

Ari pointed and winked. 'Look over there, Boss, see. Ari was right.' He gripped Bobby's shoulder. 'It's good to be together, eh, Chefe?'

Outside, the dense night sky stretched all around, punctured by the silver stars of the southern hemisphere. Reaching his arm upwards Bobby could stir his hand into that black velvet, stroke the folds of darkness, catch some and smooth the softness over his face and eyes. He needed that caress. They were on latitude 15° south, roughly a thousand kilometres below the equator. Sweat lingered on their skin. Wet patches darkened their shirts.

Ari ordered a bottle of pinga and gulped down two small glasses. He poked at his teeth with a wooden pick and grinned. 'Beer's too weak for a real man.' He sucked through his teeth. 'Pinga is good for here.' He put the palm of his hand between his legs and jerked vigorously upwards as he drained another glass. He gasped and croaked. 'Look, I know.'

'Over there, Boss, look!'

He beckoned at the waiter. 'Hey, where are some girls for us? My gringo friend. He needs cheering up.'

The waiter hesitated. 'But, Senhor, they only go by prior arrangement or with friends of the management.'

Ari stood up steadying himself with both hands on the table. 'What do you think my friend has come all the way from England for, to play football, to drink your beer? No. Go and find two, otherwise I'll complain to your boss.' He winked at Bobby.

A few moments later a dark European-looking man with an aquiline face introduced himself. 'I'm Ludo.' He spoke Italian Brazilian from the south. 'Senhor, my girls do not go with just anybody and besides, you're drunk.'

Ari lifted his eyes slowly upwards, 'Senhor Ludo. Find a pretty girl for my friend. I promised him and Ari keeps his word.'

Ludo glanced at Bobby and walked off.

Bobby pushed his chair back. 'Ari, I'm not up for this. Let's go.'

Ari chuckled. 'Now, now, Chefe, sit down and leave things to me.'

'And your wife?' Bobby ventured.

'Listen to me, amigo, a man needs a wife, a mistress and a girlfriend. Anyhow my wife is a good woman. She looks after my two beautiful boys.'

Stroking his week's stubble and looking forward to lying in a bed for the first time in two weeks, Bobby wondered how it was possible to deal with so many women at once. From the back of the room two girls approached, one tall and blonde, the other of medium height and dark. They were holding hands and chatting together. The dark one was laughing, the tall one unsmiling. Both wore identical wooden crosses around their necks. The dark one waved at the two girls at the bar. The tall one walked in an ungainly way, like a boy, one foot directly in front of the other. Her legs seemed to go on forever. It was the length of her, slender not frail, her arms long and, although covered, Bobby sensed they were strong. And it was she who stopped in front of him.

He stood up and eased a chair back. He placed the chair carefully and pushed it forward as she sat down. He turned to one side in sudden shyness and with an unfamiliar feeling in his chest.

'*Olá, boa noite*,' the shorter, darker of the two, said with a bright smile.

Ari, on his feet, called for the waiter. 'Well, you two pretty ones, what will it be, beer, pinga, whisky?'

The shorter laughed gaily. 'Whisky for me, Big Boy. Thanks, you're a good one.'

'Whisky it'll be, my girl. What's your name?'

'Ana.'

'Good, Ana. Waiter, a whisky and another pinga for me. And for your friend?'

The taller, unsmiling one, said orange juice and looked across at Bobby, her eyes blank. Ari put his arm around Bobby's shoulder.

'There you are Chefe, two girls. Forget the cattle for now, just look at these two lovelies.'

Bobby didn't look and edged to one side of his chair, his back stiff and straight. 'But, Ari, we have to talk about our cattle...'

'Chefe, for the love of God, relax.'

'Please, Senhor,' the taller said, 'come on, please, at least look at me.'

Bobby turned and lifted his glass in front of his mouth to hide the flush on his cheeks. She crossed her legs, uncrossed them and

29

crossed them back again while sliding her glass from one hand to the other. She looked straight at him, her mouth slanting downwards in a twisted smile. He lowered his glass.

'That's better, if I can't see your face how can I understand your funny accent?' She paused and in a tired flat voice, 'Anyhow your talk is boring. Where do you come from? From the south like me, I hope? What's your name?'

He tried to smile. 'Call me Bobby. And my funny accent is because I'm British. Now, please, you tell me *your* name.'

She hesitated, fiddled with her glass, and spoke so quietly that he could only just hear.

'Idenea.'

'What a beautiful name.'

'Yes, I think so too.'

Her blonde hair hung down over her shoulders, her natural brown showing at the roots. Her face was oval with wide-apart clear grey eyes. She wasn't obviously pretty like her friend Ana. She wore no make-up, just big grey eyes. He smiled at such simplicity and willed for her eyes to come back to his. She was handsome, that was it and with an easy charm; that boyish walk as she had come up to the table, the way she spoke as she looked at him, her head at an angle with an innocent hesitation. 'Look,' she seemed to be saying, 'I will go forward. I'm up for it.'

Ari shoved at Bobby with his elbow. 'Watch out, Boss, she's after you.' He sprawled his arms across the table pushing his glass towards Ana.

Idenea's smile twisted again. 'I haven't been asked about my name before.'

His eyes didn't leave her face as she spoke.

'My father was called Adonis. Then after an attack of the pox his friends nicknamed him, Idé the Beauty Gone. And my mother was called Neapolitana like the pretty girl on an Italian ice cream sales board. She wanted me to be pretty as well.'

'Like who?' he interrupted.

30

'Like the pretty ice-cream girl, don't you see?' She said crossly. 'Twenty-two years ago. Yes, I really am twenty-two not eighteen like the other girls around here claim to be, the liars, just to fool the men.'

She frowned at the girls at the bar. 'So, my parents made my name out of theirs, Idé and Nea, so I'm Idenea, get it? The night I was christened, my mother placed a chicken's head and a candle at the corner of our road.'

'Why that?' He leaned forward.

'My mother said she had black blood, so if she didn't do a little Macumba, spirits would come in the night and steal her baby and bring it up in the coffee fields.' Her chin in her palm, she stared at her glass held in her rough-skinned fingers and chipped red finger nails. She looked up and this time he was sure her eyes were shining.

'What am I doing, talking like this?'

He said gently, 'That's all right, my life hasn't been easy either.'

She played with her glass. 'I was thinking that maybe spirits taking me away in the night to the coffee would have been better. *Oh meu Deus*.'

Eyes wide-open, she gazed blankly over his shoulder. 'Life has treated me hard. You cannot imagine how hard, you *Bobo de Inglês*.'

One of her sleeves slipped up exposing white scar lines criss-crossing the skin of her arm.

He pointed at them. 'How did you get those?'

'Don't look at me like that!'

'Sorry!' he exclaimed. 'I don't understand what you are doing in this place and...and those scars?'

She pushed her chair back and in a tight angry voice, 'That's my business.'

'Please don't go. I'm going back north in a couple of days so please stay.'

She dropped her shoulders and turned to her friend, Ana, who shrugged helplessly at Ari. He was staring into the bottom of his empty glass.

She put her elbows back on the table. 'Do you know what your name Bobby means?'

'Yes, I do. Bobinho means a small, silly boy.'

31

'Well then, I'll call you Bobinho[3], all right, *tudo bem*?'

And like a shaft of sunlight in a jungle clearing after rain, she brightened.

'Come on, let's go and dance. I want some fun for a change. Poor Ana. Your friend is drunk.'

Bobby jumped up, paid the bill and slapped Ari on the back. 'See you in a couple of days, amigo. Don't forget we have the cattle to load up? I'm going dancing.'

Ari, with his head and shoulders on the table and with his eyes shut, didn't answer.

Bobby gestured at Ari. 'I can't leave him alone like this. He would never leave me.'

'He's fine. Ana will see to him, won't you, Ana?'

Ana smiled reassurance.

Outside into the dark, the lights from the bar shone onto the earthen road in a square of red. Rain clouds spread across the stars.

'*Vamos*! I love to dance.' Her laugh was hesitant, as if out of practice.

She strode out in front, her hand out backwards encouraging him to keep up, leading him down to where the road slid into shadow and towards the distant beat of drums. Catching up, he was again struck by the way she moved, her legs seemingly out of proportion to the rest of her body, her bright green skirt reaching over her knees, her shoes flat heeled, even more like a boy's. Abruptly, she put her arm around his shoulder.

'We're going to have fun. I want to see a foreigner dance. It will do you good, loosen you up.'

He caught his breath, conscious of a joy he had forgotten possible. Her arm rested on his. All he had done was pay the bill and look at her, more out of curiosity than desire, but now he couldn't take his eyes off her. She was different from the other girls in the bar. Here,

---

3 inho at the end of a noun or adjective means small/sweet/charming

stuck out in the middle of raw Brazil; on the edge, the swamps, the wide rivers sighing and the chattering jungle hidden in waves of darkness.

He quickened his pace and glanced sideways, hoping to catch her eye. They ran a few paces, hand in hand giggling like children. A couple of cars passed, honking their horns. In front a beam of light sliced into the night sky like the probe of a gigantic searchlight. And from it the beat of drums.

Beside the road, some five metres from the edge, a single strand of cheap barbed wire sagged in long loops attached to tree trunks and crooked posts. A white cow stood motionless, silhouetted against the blackness.

'Look, Idenea.' He pointed. 'That's the Nellore breed Ari and I bought today for trucking up north, to our place near Mutum in Rondônia. We bought a couple of hundred head.'[2]

She stopped and pulled at his hand.

'Where?' Close to shouting, she repeated, 'Where? Tell me, right now, *where* did you say?'

He stepped back. 'It's where the ranch is. We're taking cattle up there. What's wrong?' He tried to find her eyes in the darkness.

'My family.' Her voice dropped to a whisper and stammering, 'That was our home, my life - that - is - what - happened.'

A car hooted them out of the way.

He placed a steadying arm on her shoulder. 'Tell me about that later.'

She began to move rhythmically. A few more paces and she was in full samba swing. She turned to him, smiling and teasing.

'Okay, *tudo bem*, my foreigner, *vamos pular*, let's go dancing.'

And she grabbed his hand and danced towards the sound of the band. Again, he wondered what this lovely girl with the sad smile, one moment awkward the next graceful, was doing here pulling at his arm. Was she a professional call-girl, eager to take advantage of cattle ranchers and gold prospectors? No. Maybe, like him she had been drawn to this new frontier.

The dancehall was a circular wooden stockade built from tree trunks sunk vertically into the ground and strapped together with steel cables, the top of each pole sharpened to a point. The light from inside burst upwards picking out the wings of thousands of insects like sparks from a fire.

Crude paintings hung on the outside walls; bulls chasing cows and giant guitars with their players, mouths open in silent yells. Two swing gates, each with a steer's horns for a push bar served as the entrance. On each side of the gate, life-sized dolls dressed in black leather, their legs astride gaudily painted Japanese motorbikes.

The beat of the drums hammered at their ears and thrilled with anticipation. Moving to the rhythm, Idenea pushed on the bull's horn.

'It's Saturday!' she shouted. 'Much samba. Let's go.'

Her eyes bright, she mouthed the words of the song that blared out from inside. A big man, eyes white in his head, demanded money. Bobby handed over some crumpled notes. And they were in. The weight of the noise slapped them in the face. He breathed in the heat, the noise, the cheap perfume.

From a brightly-lit stage, the band boomed and rushed its music through four giant loudspeakers. Spotlights flashed colour beams lighting up shiny faces in blues and reds. Bare-chested men and bikini-topped girls served drinks behind a bar. Around their necks a bull's horn pendant, the size of Bobby's hand, swung from side to side on loose chains.

'I've never been to a place like this before!' he cried out.

She jived towards the middle, the dancing mass jumping up and down on the earthen floor, squashed right up to the edge of the wooden walls, arms in the air, hands pointing upwards, quite uninhibited and free. Everyone was singing the samba song, 'Portela, Portela...' Men's biceps showed through cotton sleeves and girls' breasts outlined under sweat-damp t-shirts. Then she was gone. Uneasy for fear of losing her, Bobby, never much of a dancer, edged and bumped self-consciously between the closely-packed bodies. Again, it was her height, her long uplifted arms. There she was, turning round and round on the spot, wiggling her bum so incredibly fast, singing and pumping her arms, jumping, twisting. She was quick and graceful, her eyes half-closed, lost in the beat.

For a moment he stopped his awkward swaying about and watched her, so different to anyone he'd seen before.

She opened her arms and beckoned him over.

'There you are, Bobinho. Come on, let's see you dance.' She locked her hands behind his neck, and to the rhythm sang out, 'There – Now – Look, *This* is how. Watch me.' From under her arms he breathed in her sweat, sharp and alive.

Keeping her eyes level with his and her hands behind his neck, she danced, her body vertical from head to foot, her t-shirt wet with sweat. Her breath brushed his face. To every beat of the drums little by little she edged closer, all the time holding him with her eyes, smiling her twisted smile. And he flattered himself that she seemed happy because of him.

'Wonderful,' he said and put his hands on her hips.

'Ah, so you do like it, my foreigner?'

She pulled their dancing bodies together. She placed her forehead on his and, closing her eyes, continued to move in time to the beat, up and down, so close that her breasts fixed to his chest, her belly and thighs to his. His awkward movements only added to the friction between them.

'What are you doing?' he said out of breath, pushing her away to see her face.

She opened her eyes. 'Do you like it? It's one of my tricks. Ana taught me.'

'Like it? You're driving me mad. See what you've done to me.'

She looked down, still dancing and seemingly disinterested laughed, 'Good, all good.'

The professional, he thought with hurt pride. She was only here for the dancing. Well, if that's the life she'd chosen, to hell with it, he'd go with the craziness of the night. He put his arms around her waist and pulled her to him, stopped her moving and kissed her quick on her lips. Then, pushing off, he twisted into that wild circle of heat and noise. Out of stubborn curiosity he glanced back to see if his kiss had pleased her. Did she care? She was staring at the ground her lips in a twisted smile, a look he was beginning to recognise.

'Well, Bobinho, you did like that, didn't you?'

And in an instant his English reserve melted away. They danced, never far from each other. She showed him the rhythm and the way to keep it. When she pulled him back into that taunting closeness he just had to wrap his arms around her, try to kiss her. Sometimes his lips touched hers for the briefest second but when he really tried, she pushed him away and he missed altogether.

Suddenly he blurted, 'You're beautiful, Idenea.'

'Me beautiful? Never.'

Surprised by his courage he said it again, 'Yes, you really are beautiful.'

'Ssshh to that.'

At the bar they paused to recover. She handed him a short glass with a slice of lemon and pineapple sticking out. He coughed and spluttered. She laughed in his face and patted him on the back.

Above, insects darted in and out of the funnel of light as if from nowhere and burst out like fireworks as they whirled and spun in a silent storm.

A drop of rain splashed onto her forehead.

'We're going to get wet,' she laughed.

Big drops bounced on the dusty floor. A white flash of lightning blazed, changing faces from brown to white. Flash after flash. A crash of thunder. Shrieks of laughter followed by a frantic burst of vigorous dancing as all the lights went out and the band stopped dead. The rain drummed on the ground and on the bar's tin roof, soaking everyone in seconds. Bobby looked at his watch. Midnight and three hours gone.

An outside generator coughed into life. A light flickered. The crowd of dancers, steam rising from their bodies, pushed out through the gates. Cars revved up, motor bikes roared off into the dark, headlights tunnelling through the dense downpour. Cyclists, heads down, pedalled away. The players dragged their instruments under cover and Idenea and Bobby were alone.

'Come on, don't stand about, Bobinho, let's run for it.'

Running, slipping, they headed down the road. After a hundred metres, thick red mud covered their legs, soaking his trousers. Their hair lay flat to their scalps. Hers stuck to her shoulders as well.

'Look at your trousers!' she yelled.

'Look at your legs!' He shouted back. They splashed on.

Halfway to the motel, the same Nellore cow was still standing in the same place beside that single strand of wire. She hadn't budged. A white mongrel dog had joined her. Two figures, one small, one large, heads down, alone and white against the black edge of the trees, rain sheeting down their flanks and darkening the white.

On arrival, out of breath and panting, he gasped, 'Where do you think I'll find a taxi at this time of night?'

Idenea, expressionless, 'Don't be silly, tonight you stay with me.'

He didn't answer.

'This is where I live.' She took his hand.

Men and girls were still leaning over half-empty glasses at the bar, the television showing a Western. There was no sign of Ari or Ana. One of the drinkers cried out, 'Good for you Blondie, give it to her,' and banged his glass on the counter. Bobby, all of a sudden full of doubt, hesitated. Paying for sex? But there was something different about this strangest of girls.

She led him out of the bar towards the dark outline of a long bungalow set in a square. The rain had stopped just as quickly as it had started, but great lumps of water still splashed down from leaves and the roof edge, sparkling in the dark. By the light of a couple of dim bulbs, a small pond glimmered in the middle of a grass courtyard.

Idenea opened door Number 5 down one side of the passage. She turned on the light and arced her arm around.

'This is my home,' she said flatly and locked the door. 'I have no other way.'

They stood still, both hesitant, eyes to the ground.

'Wait here, I'm going to wash off this mud.' She disappeared. 'You come after me okay, *tudo bem*?'

A shower started up and, through the frosted glass, he glimpsed her tall figure undress and then step out of sight. Alone, he felt as nervous as though he'd never been with a woman before. The last time, in a room with flowery wall paper, where he'd gone to prove he was still capable, had left him wandering about the streets of Soho in a self-hating daze.

Her voice from the shower, 'I'll be there in just a moment, *tá bom?*'

'Fine, fine.'

He looked around the room.

A small double bed, what the French call d'occasion, stood out from the wall. A wicker chair, a small chest of drawers, a bedside mat and a table with a cassette recorder and a pile of tapes all crammed next to the bed. The walls were white with cheap nylon curtains covering the French windows that gave out onto rough grass. He turned slowly, taking in one by one the possessions that made up her life. A roughly hewn wooden doll lay on the seat of the wicker chair. The doll, about double the size of his hand, lay on its back surrounded by red bougainvillea petals. Each petal had been arranged edge to edge to form a perfect circle around the doll.

What is this? he thought. Such care.

On the wall opposite the bed hung a picture of an Amazonian Indian in a feathered headdress. He was staring into the middle distance as if waiting for something to appear at any moment from an undefined elsewhere. Behind the Indian's head, a red macaw sat in the branches of a vivid green palm tree. At the bottom of the picture in bold yellow letters, '*Vejo no horizonte a força da minha tradição* - I see on the horizon the power of my tradition'. The Indians he had seen before had been lost and out of their world, dressed in shorts and dirty t-shirts, idling outside bars seeking any sort of menial work and, more often, alcohol. But he'd never met up with one in his jungle home.

The bathroom door opened. Idenea stepped out wearing only a short towel folded tightly under her armpits, her legs stretching down in shadow below. Her hair hung in damp tresses onto her shoulders.

'Go on, Bobinho, go and wash that mud off,' she said unsmiling and practical. 'And hurry up.' A nervous smile crossed her lips.

So, he wasn't the only one.

In the shower, the red mud slid away and he looked down at his body. 'Come on, wake up for God's sake, don't let me down.' His throat tightened as he wound his towel around his waist and stumbled back into the bedroom, his heart banging in his chest.

The bedside lamp cast a glow over half the room. She was sitting in shadow on the edge of the bed. He hesitated. She stood up, her towel still wrapped around her.

'You're nervous, Bobinho, aren't you? I can feel it. I'm new at this game as well.' She threaded her fingers through her hair. Her eyes seemed to plead for his understanding. 'We'll try together, won't we?'

She pressed a button on the tape recorder. The same samba song of an hour ago filled the room. She raised her arms and as before put her hands behind his neck and started to dance, not to every beat, but to every other, slowly but with the jerky energy of samba. She placed her forehead on his and closed her eyes. A few beats and her towel fell around her dancing feet. With his forehead pressed to hers, he could only glimpse the roundness of her small breasts below. With a quick movement of one arm she flicked off his towel and kicked the two to one side keeping her forehead tight on his.

'Dance, like I showed you,' she whispered.

There was no sound except for the music. Their naked bodies only an inch or two apart, his hands heavy and shaking he placed them on her hips and drew her to him moving to the rhythm. Her skin touched warm under his fingers.

'You haven't been with a woman for some time, have you?'

He lowered his eyes. And she knew.

She dropped a hand and eased him up towards her belly button and with a forward push held him there. He sought her mouth in frantic need. She let him kiss her again and again but she gave no return, keeping her body tight to his, beating to the rhythm. She pushed him backwards onto the bed. She was flat on top of him, so fast he couldn't make out what had happened.

'Let me see you,' he whispered.

'No!' she said sharply and pinned his arms down with unexpected strength.

Still flat on top, she eased her knees up beside his hips, frog-like. Placing herself, she pushed hesitantly downwards. In spite of his own disarray, he sensed that like him she was unsure of herself or, more likely, unwilling. She put her hands on his shoulders and sat up.

'Well, Bobinho, I've got you now,' she teased, grinning, triumph in her pale eyes, her hair falling over his shoulders.

He couldn't answer, as if there was a pad of wool in his throat. He reached up to pull her down and kiss her. But she was having none of that and shoved him away with determined arms. She rocked back and forward. Her smile no longer a twist and her eyes open and frank.

'You're feeling stronger now aren't you, my Bobinho?'

He couldn't hold back the longing inside. He wrapped his arms around her, kissing her neck as he sprang into her again and again.

He flopped onto his back sighing, 'Thank you, thank you, you're so lovely' as if the past three years were tumbling out of his chest one by one. He closed his eyes.

'Thank you for what?' She put her hands on her hips. 'Stop calling me beautiful, *tá bom.*'

She took his hand. 'It's late, so stay here with me? You're different.'

She stroked his head. 'Why do you smile so tenderly at me?'

She turned and lay with her feet beside his head, her body running lengthways towards the end of the bed. Chin between her hands, she stared up at the picture of the Indian. Only the white-curtained French windows broke up the blank wall space. There was no bustle here. It was out of time.

He could hear her mumbling, 'Give him back to me.'

'What are you saying?' he said.

Still mumbling. 'I don't know if he is my friend or my enemy. If I could only read into those eyes...'

He knelt beside her. Violent sun had browned her skin, burning it deeply and bleaching the hairs white. Many insects had bitten and the skin, in self-defence, had turned slightly leathery and pimply in texture. He stroked down her back. On her thighs and legs, the tips of his fingers touched ripples like corrugated paper. Some were pink and angry.

As he touched, he was sure the pain of his own bullet wound had been nothing compared to these. An urge to protect this girl seized him. He imagined knives and whips.

'Has some bastard beaten you up?'

'No, Bobinho.' A quick scornful laugh. 'No, those are from thorns and spikes in the jungle near Mutum.'

She rolled over onto her back, unmindful of her nakedness, and smiled shyly up at him. There were no marks on her breasts nor on her neck. Her torso was firm with muscle. Her eyes sought his for assurance that he could accept her. She lay still and innocent under his touch.

'Of course. Now I get it.' He smiled.

'Get what, Bobinho?'

'The way you crouched over me like a frog, so no one can see, right?'

As he said no one, a twinge of jealousy touched into his chest. 'One of your tricks as you put it?'

'Yes, sort of. I'm not like the others. They all boast how many men. Even Ana counts as if it's a game with a score. For me it's horrible.'

She turned towards him. 'I like your smile.'

'I like yours too.'

'I'm so angry and want to shout out at the whole world. But you listen. All the other men around here just talk about themselves. I curse myself every day for the mess I'm in.'

She swallowed at the air and slumped down beside him.

'Ludo told me to invent something to hide my scars. Like a frog. That's all I am now, a frog. And now you're revolted, huh?' She reached for a sheet to cover herself. 'I'll get dressed.'

Vejo, no horizonte a força da minha tradição

'No, no, stay as you are. I'm used to things like that.' But he was lying and deeply bothered.

He touched a stretch line running down from her belly button. 'And you've had a baby too, haven't you?'

'Okay, clever boy, you're not so innocent, are you? Yes, my son Zoni. He's two years and two hundred and sixty-one days old today, and not with me, my poor baby. Gone, taken, out of my life. *Meu Deus*, how I miss him. I think of nothing else. Sometimes I wish I were dead...'

She sat up and wrapped both arms around her knees. She closed her eyes as a high-pitched keening poured from between her lips as if she would cough up her lungs.

'That's him,' she whispered pointing at the wooden doll on the chair surrounded by the bougainvillea petals. 'I give him fresh flowers every week. One day I'll find him.'

'Where is he?'

'I don't know.'

He put his arm around her shoulders. 'I have a son as well but I know where he is. You don't, that's terrible.'

She looked at him with a wild look in her eyes.

'Now, Idenea, you tell me why you're here.' He hugged her to him. He dried her cheeks with the edge of his pillowcase.

Several minutes passed as she struggled with her breathing.

'Why am I talking to *you*? I hardly know you.' She pushed at him in irritation.

Shutting her eyes, she gripped his hand. Then very slowly. 'I am alone in this world. I have nothing and worst of all no baby any more. Oh, m*eu Deus*, my baby.'

He touched her hip with the back of his hand.

'I want to know everything right now about you and that Indian. *Everything*.'

She stared up at the ceiling and in a whisper, hesitantly and in short bursts.

'Oh, Bobinho. We were coffee farmers in the south, then three years ago we went north...'

2

IDENEA

—Father was shouting.

Trotting towards us.

Waving a piece of paper.

Me and my favourite brother Romi piling up dead coffee bushes killed by frost ready for burning.

43

Chico, my younger brother, raking over the few beans we'd managed to harvest that year on the old tiled square.

We looked after a thousand bushes on an estate owned by foreigners.

Coffee is always with me.

Father was so excited. *Free land.* Government giving us *free* land. Read it. You're the best reader, Idi.

My beloved school teacher always said I was a good one.

The paper had República Federal at the top and I smiled at Father's thumb print smudge of a signature.

You, Adonis Saladini and family of Aldeia São Antonio in the state of Paraná are awarded 100 hectares in the Territory of Rondônia in the municipality of Mutum.[3]

Father butted in. You see, I was right. This shit can go to hell.

He was always saying he'd worked since he was fourteen. After two years of frost he wanted out, away from dead coffee.

I read about money, loans, 100 hectares and the last paragraph telling us to go to the Ministry of Agriculture in Porto Velho within three months.

Father hugged us. See. *Free* from big agro business, *free* from frost. We'll have enough to eat. He patted our mule. No more carrying bags of coffee beans for you old friend and I nearly sold you for food.

Romi asked where Rondônia and Porto Velho were.

Up north, my son.

Father pointed vaguely across the lines of brown sticks. In the Amazon. We'll soon find out. Let's tell Mother the good news.

He legged onto our mule, his long legs flapping. Mother pleased? She so cautious, especially with money.

The nasty foreman, who was always saying I had sexy legs when I was up a ladder picking coffee, told us only quarter wages for no harvest. That broke Father's heart. And I was so proud of my cropping records.

Romi said we must find a map.

Father, tall like me, waving his arms this way and that at Mother outside our house. Freedom, Our Own, Plenty of Food, several times. My mother Tana, short and dark, her red scarf tight on her head, stroking our mule under the mango tree.

Bolo our black and white dog wagging his tail. We were best friends. Mother shaking her finger. And you believe the Government, Adonis? She only called him Adonis when cross with him and that was often. We wouldn't be living here sharing water with five others if they'd built those promised houses, would we?

I'd never heard bad things said about our house with the red cement floor full of holes that Mother and I swept every day. I liked the tiles above me as I lay in bed in my tiny room and Father's snoring coming over the wooden walls. I didn't mind. And the banging of pots next door and the laughing and quarrelling and the smell of everybody cooking rice and beans were all part of me.

And, Adonis... Mother one hand on the cross around her neck, where's the money to get there? We're down to one chicken a week for the five of us? How, Idi, how?

I said for Father to explain. Father beamed at me. Good girl. Let's go inside. I've been in a queue for a whole week to get this piece of paper.

Mother warmed up some rice and chicken bits. Father's hands, hard-skinned and crusted spooned out far less for himself than for each of us. Our plates were soon clean. Only six chickens left in the yard. We caught a few fish in a pond but we were hungry. Mother taught me to be careful.

Well now, my dearest ones. Father's thin pocked face smiled so kindly. My friend Matéus told me about this great opportunity. He said we must impress the government and have enough people for clearing land with axes and saws. And there's only me and the boys, that makes only three and I'm getting on.

I can work, I said. You persuaded me to leave school to keep the coffee records. I'll come with you.

Mother gazing out of the window. My dear girl, we are women and this is man's work. Anyhow, it's too far for me. But Mãe, I said, I'm up for it. I can grow fruit and vegetables. It will be exciting, a better life, plenty to eat.

Romi and Chico said it was too risky and mad.

Listen, I'm your father. I've got nothing to offer you here, nothing. I'm old for a venture like this but for you it's a future. I don't want you to hang around here and fall into alcohol and nothing. We've had a hard life, haven't we, Mother? Don't you see I'm doing it for you children and...

I'm coming, Father, I'll persuade them. Romi nodding. Both my brothers were always rather scared of Father, but not me. I loved him for his strength and enthusiasm, so I was sure this would be a success and I wanted to be part of a new world.

Mother crossly, Adonis, we'll talk later.

Father said the two cousins Bosco and Carlito were out of work. They can come and Bosco's a good worker and we're all Saladinis. I saw Romi stiffen. He hated Bosco. An accident with a cart had broken Bosco's ankle and he always blamed Romi for his short leg. Father told Romi to forget it as we needed all the muscle we could find. And, Idenea, my dear, why don't you arrange things with Valdo? That will make six men so eight of us in all?

Arrange things, how? I asked.

Simple, my dear. Marry him. He can ride a mule and use a hoe, useful, huh? And you seem to like him.

Chico laughed, he drinks too much.

Father quickly, there'll be no chance for that up there. Anyhow our Idenea will stop that, won't you?

Valdo to be my husband? Two days before he'd been kissing me. He was so sweet, my coconut boy. I called him Coco because of the way his brown hair stuck up. I'd kissed him back, his hand on my breasts. I was so excited but afraid of anything more. He'd come over on his old scooter. He loved motorbikes and hated the five kilometres on a mule to see me on Sundays and Saints' days. He said I was the reason for the scooter and took me to the back of a clump of trees and we so nearly did it.

Mother kept saying she'd have no unmarried daughter with a baby, thank you very much. I was nineteen and boys said I was a pretty picture. So why not? Much younger girls were married. So would Valdo ask me himself?

Romi held my hand. Although older, he's small and dark like Mother. I can see his soft brown eyes.

Dear sister, are you sure about Valdo? He's like me and Chico and can hardly read or write. Will you like him being less than you?

I said that I'd teach him or do it myself.

That night I heard Mother's voice over the wall and with Father repeating, We're going, we're going. Long pauses. Finally Mother saying it could be better to be poor on our own land than on somebody else's and here there was less and less food. So that was that, we were going. My heart jumped. But Oh *meu Deus* would Valdo come? I tried to sleep. I always worry about everything.

Father said Matéus would find us an old truck if we gave him a small share in our new farm. He'd tell Bosco and Carlito and he'd look out for Valdo.

Chico, tall and blonde like me biked off and brought back an atlas from the one-roomed school where I had learned so much. I'll never forget my teacher's hug when I left to help with the coffee. I looked down the track and heard Valdo's scooter and he was holding me, all excited. Your father has told me everything. We must get married. Mother let him kiss her cheek. But I could see she was unsure.

I rushed out to find my best friend, Rosa. We sat on the old wall under a tree swinging our legs and giggling as we always did when watching the boys play football on the coffee square trying to catch their eye. And how we'd be, a teacher, a film star, a model, a mother. Nothing like hoping is there? And the Kiskadees in the branches above crying their *Bem te vi*, Good to see you, call. We held hands and couldn't stop laughing and crying at the same time. I loved my friends.

I'll miss you so much, Rosa said again and again. It's like you're going to a foreign land.—

Idenea breathed deeply and grasped at Bobby's hand.

—The priest would scold us if we didn't go to Mass in the village half an hour away on the mule. So, all my friends were next door. If Father couldn't take me to school in the cart, I walked. I am so full of memories for how hard-working we were. And there were always those Kiskadees in the trees with their sharp cries. I was so young.

I put my arm around Rosa. You'll be with me when I get married won't you, my darling Rosa?

Yes, yes, and I'll do your hair and your lipstick. I know how much you like it. And I'll tell Valdo to be good to you, otherwise I'll kill him. We hugged and I said I'd write.

Romi drove up in an old Mercedes truck with our mule and cart tied on top. Father could only drive a cart.

Father leapt out. *Olha*, look, he said proudly pointing at dents and scratches. There's our flying angel to freedom. I told him about Valdo and he hugged me tight. I had never seen him with such energy. Romi and Chico discussed how to build a platform for the mule and our few things.

We were ready in two weeks. Romi and Chico fixed a wooden tail board to the back of the truck and painted on it in red letters *Esperança nos leva pra frente*, Hope takes us forward. Everybody would see and know. We packed our clothes into old coffee bags.

My wedding. I counted the hours. Mother made sweets and friends brought more. Father nailed corn cobs on the trees next to our house saying they'd bring many babies to work up north.

I borrowed a white dress, too short, so I sewed on a matching hem and washed my hair twice. And what was it going to be like with Valdo? I'd often looked between my legs with a mirror and wondered why men wanted that so much. Mother caught me at it once and gave me hell. But she told me that it would hurt and there'd be blood. I laughed.

Romi drove us up the dust road to the Estate church. I was behind the cab in my white dress, my hair flowing in the sun, my lips painted red by Rosa. I'd put a red hibiscus in my hair as well. The brothers shouted at everybody we passed, Look at our truck. Valdo wore a suit that was much too big for him, his shirt and tie didn't fit properly and he'd flattened his hair with water and that made him look even smaller than me than usual.

Father held one of my arms and Rosa the other as we walked into church. Don't be nervous she said, but I was. Not everyone could fit in. There was so much chattering that I'm sure nobody heard Valdo say I will or me say I will. He smiled so sweetly at me.

Everything was going to be all right.

I prayed, as I always did, before the blue statue of the Holy Virgin holding the baby Jesus on the altar. I prayed so hard. Holy Mary, bless me. Holy Mary, bless our marriage and dear Holy Mary bless this life that's coming up, please, please.

We drove back, me in my white dress, waving at everybody. I ate so many sweets at our party. I love the eggy chocolaty *brigadeiros* best. The boys drank beer and pinga. Rosa never left my side and we danced together. Father toasted me and Valdo and then said, To our new farm *Fazenda Boa Esperança* in Mutum in the Amazon. So that was it, the Farm of Good Hope. How exciting. Everybody cheered. I choked on the pinga. We had presents of towels, a crucifix, saucepans. My grandmother gave me a notebook. Write about yourself up there, my dear, you'll have plenty to tell. I still write and think of her when I do.

Father gave us a wooden doll he'd carved himself. To encourage you to have children, he said proudly.

Then Bosco—Angelico—limped up dragging his bad leg. He shoved his angel face right into mine. He stank of pinga. You should be mine, he said, you know that, don't you? I wasn't in church so I didn't hear you swear to be with Valdo forever...so for me you're not married, see? We'll all be alone up there, huh? I pushed him off. I hated the way he was with me.

I looked for Valdo, I could hear noisy singing in the dark. Only six hours before we were to leave. I lay on my bed. I so wanted Valdo to take my dress off and make love to me and for me to hold him tight. It was my wedding night, *pelo amor de Deus*. I could hear Father snoring. With the pinga and all of that day I fell asleep.

Father was shouting at everybody to get up. Valdo face down beside me. Smell of pinga, he didn't budge. I wasn't cross, there was still today and tomorrow. Father, bang, bang at the door again calling at Valdo to help load up and for me to help Mother with food. I shook and shook him. He stumbled out dropping his suit at his feet. I had no time to change.

Father said cheerily that I looked pretty in my white. He handed me two frames of photographs. One of him and Mother on their wedding day and the other of his father and mother soon after they had arrived in Brazil. He said we couldn't leave them behind. They were part of us.

Bosco came up all red-eyed as I put some leftover sweets in a box with cold rice and beans.

Still a virgin, huh? he sneered. Let me know if I can help.

I ignored him, the bastard.

There were no shadows in the pale dawn outside our house. I clambered up behind the cab. Mother was standing in the doorway, Valdo behind her.

Father called at her to get in. Mother didn't move saying that she wasn't coming and that we were all crazy.

Valdo said Mother was right. He didn't look at me.

I can still see Father leaping out of the truck and dragging Mother into the truck.

I jumped down as well and grabbed Valdo's arm asking him if he was going to leave me a virgin. He followed, his head down. Bosco laughing.

Romi revved the engine. I looked back at our little wooden house with its blue shutters and the mango tree in front and the two orange trees behind. My home for all my nineteen years. *Meu Deus* so many salty tears in my mouth.

Romi drove with Father and Mother up front. The rest of us plus cousins Bosco and Carlito O Lentão, the Slow, as he was called, in the back with everything. We flopped onto a couple of mattresses. The mule wedged between two poles so close I could stroke his nose. My tears soon stopped. The boys said I looked odd in my white dress and sang, *All in white to the north goes Idenea, all in white so she goes.*

Valdo told them to shut up. But it was quite funny really. *Meu Deus*, on a promise from the government and me in my wedding dress on top of a truck. And still a virgin.

We only did a hundred kilometres that first day. Father said the truck must be nursed along. The first night at the back of a petrol station we ate what Mother had brought from my party. The boys stretched our orange tarpaulin, the only new thing we had, out from the truck as a tent.

With frogs croaking nearby, me and Valdo had to lie close to my beloved parents. I kept looking towards them. We tried to keep quiet and wait till everybody was asleep and fumbled about. I wondered after what the heaving blankets must have looked like and all the noises from underneath. In spite of all his boasting he hadn't much idea. He poked and pulled at my wedding dress. I didn't care. It was all new and exciting—like our journey.

How it hurt, I couldn't believe it. I did cry a little and wondered if I'd had the wrong man forced on me by my father. So that was it. All that talk, not much fun. But we learnt to be together and I became fond of him in spite of his laziness and his drinking. In the morning I was all awkward and saw my own blood on my dress. I tried to hide it but that shameless Bosco jeered at me.

Well not so white does our Idenea go north, not so white does she go

Bastard.

Valdo dug out some clothes for me. Romi coaxed the truck along, never too fast in the heat. We prayed it wouldn't break down but it did. While Romi hammered about in the engine, covered in steam, we rigged up the tarpaulin for shade. The further north we went, the hotter the sun. We soon tired of telling the same old stories.

At night, me and Valdo lived in our own small world curled up on a mattress as far away as possible. We camped at the back of petrol stations amongst pigs and chickens looking for scraps. Mother and I cooked rice and beans. Bolo scrounged for his meals.

We met other families heading north. An old bus with three families, dogs, goats, mules, stopped beside us. On good days we did three hundred kilometres. In Cuiabá, Father pointed at a sign post;

BR 364 Porto Velho 1,462 kilometres.

He was so full of hope and said we'd do it in a few days.

We should have turned back right then. That's easy to say now. Ten kilometres out of Cuiabá, the dirt road began. It was October with the rains beginning and the surface slippery mud. It was easy to skid and fall flat on your face.

Out of the scrub into the jungle, holes, bigger than our truck, holes the size of lakes full of water. Romi couldn't handle this to begin with. We got bogged down in a line of trucks and buses and we waited for two days in front of a hundred-metre hole. We nearly gave up. A saint of a driver took all the cargo off his own truck and, with just a bare chassis and a rope attached to the back, he charged the flooded hole. Great bow waves shot up and brown water covered his windscreen. The truck bucked and reared, wheels spinning, water flying everywhere. Boys red with mud ran beside yelling *Vai! Vai!* We cheered wildly when he got to the other end. He pulled us through one by one with his winch and hawser, each of us carrying some of his goods. I told him he would go to Heaven.

He hugged me. Isn't that where we're going anyhow? he said.

I hugged him back.

Our turn, we walked knee-deep in mud beside. Father led the mule in the edge of the trees. There were moments when the truck nearly turned over and with that days of sorting out.

It began to rain every day, quite different from what I knew. The sky, bright blue one moment with round white clouds high above and hot as hot below. Clouds rise up, dark at the bottom, white at the top. So tall the white bit that they seem to reach up into Heaven for ever. The darker bottom goes darker and darker, the wind gets up and the noise in the distance like tearing paper. I didn't know what it was first time I heard it. Crrrrrrrrrrrrrrrr, far off to start with, then closer over the trees.

The first drop falls onto you as big as the end of my finger, then another and with the tearing noise all around, drumming on the leaves. Sheets of water. The splashing on your head, in your ears, in your eyes, in your mouth. Drink as from a tap. You smell wet and earth. One moment I could see someone close by, the next moment hidden by a white shroud as vertical wave after vertical wave of water drifted through.

The first drops throw up the dust in furry water balls, like caterpillars, then another and another until whoosh, water everywhere. Reddy-brown mud sprays up as high as my knee. The road seems to float in the bouncing red water. Deep channels carve into the side of the road, such is the weight of water. The force of God.

Then as if God has given a signal, the white veils retreat over the trees, the sound becomes fainter and fainter.

The first time it happened, I felt I was at the beginning of the whole world.

Many laughed out loud. I did too but later the laughter became a cry of despair.

Then the clean-up. Although the sun was hot, steam rising from the surface of the road, it never fully dried before the next downpour. The further north we went the more it rained and the worse the road got, with holes and ruts as far as you could see—all flooded with water. Jeeps and trucks sinking in. Sometimes we had to push ours from behind and the wheels spitting out over our bodies and faces, only the whites of our eyes left showing.

One day our truck was being pulled through a very long hole, Romi trying to keep it steady. Bolo sitting beside him and barking. The truck sinking, the cab first, down, down. Were we to lose everything? Romi really worried. Even his ankles covered in mud. The slippery, filthy muck had actually got into the cab. Two days to clear up.

At night, we dropped down at the side of our truck and slept covered in mud, too tired to wash.

The best way to get clean was to stand in the heavy rain, take off my clothes and wring them out. One time, hands came feeling around my waist, touching my breasts. Valdo? No, it was that brute Bosco with his angel face leering at me. I screamed at him to fuck off. Valdo came running and threatened to beat him up. Bosco just sneered, the bastard. He made me feel so dirty.

Our travelling seat of mattresses was red with slime. We had no hammocks then, so we fixed up a tarpaulin tent on top of the truck. That worked and the rain sloshed down the sides. We unloaded the mule every night to let it eat. Father always said mules were tougher than horses.

The boys soon got bored of watching parrots and fooled about in the back. I leant on the wooden crossbar behind the cabin with my head on my hands, staring ahead for hours. The road ran straight red like a line of blood, slicing forwards. The bulldozers had only made bends around hills and rivers. They hadn't worried about ownership, there wasn't any, only the State and the animals. I didn't know about Indians then. At times we'd cover so little ground, a hill in the distance one day, the next seemed just as far away.

I made up a game called Hope. The long straights were my life, you see, going forward and being positive. The bends were my Hope chances. I won or lost points on what I saw around a bend.

I counted what I saw. Plus points were...one point for a man, two for a woman, three for a child, my highest award was four for a baby, two for a hut, two for a cow, half for a chicken and then one for a flight of parrots, they were so cheerful.

Minus points were two for an abandoned truck, four for a deserted and burnt-out hut, for a grave...six, and one for a vulture. Lurching slowly around a bend, I would hold my breath in anticipation. Some days I won, others I lost. It was those black vultures that used to beat me, hundreds of the ugly brutes. I didn't know then how useful they are. I so terribly wanted things to work out. For me it was Hope that counted always. Now I don't know any more.

Aaah, how we ever got there I'll never know.

I believed in God then and used to pray. Get us there, dear God, please get us there. But I reckon God thought I was a waste of time.

There were stretches where only one truck could pass, the other side of the road sucked away by so much water and the surface spun off by heavy wheels. Stuck in a queue and standing behind the cabin I saw along top of truck after top of truck, tail end to tail end for hundreds of metres, people chatting in the mud below, boiling up rice, making coffee and waiting. Often an abandoned truck on its side, wheels removed, showed where somebody had given up, all their belongings gone. Some had built shelters within the wreckage and had been there for months. They stared at us desperate, all hope gone from their eyes. I turned away and for the first time, fear in my heart. Parrots flew over screeching away and columns of vultures marked rubbish or something dead.

Romi started to crouch over the steering wheel as if hugging it. Every now and then he'd say, *Can you hear that*?

What? Father asked sharply, what are you listening for?

The engine. Romi replied flatly.

Something wrong?

I don't know. There's a noise, listen.

No there's nothing. There can't be anything wrong, it's a Mercedes.

Romi insisted, I don't care. I bet it's never been on a road like this before. Listen, can't you here the rattle?

I said. Stop scaring us, Romi. *Pelo amor de Deus*, we can't break down now, we've come too far.

He kept saying, It's there and it's new.

From then on he drove with his black hair drooping over the wheel, listening, listening and often with a voice close to panic he'd say it was getting worse.

I tried to ignore him and although I did listen to the engine, I couldn't hear anything.

We'd stop in a village and there weren't many, just our road running through with new wooden houses on each side. A woman with a small child asked if we were going south and could we give them a lift. They'd lost two children to disease and wanted to go home. The skin on her husband's face stretched tight. Fear hit me again. After that I began to notice many people going in the opposite direction. We waved one time. They didn't wave back. I didn't look any more

We lost our exhaust in one of those goddamn holes, bust off in the mud. After that we Saladinis really did roar along.

Five weeks later not one as Father had said.

Porto Velho was much smaller than we had expected. We'd imagined it as some golden city with cinemas and shops.

I'm going to buy a motorbike and lots of beer, said Valdo.

I scolded him and said I would be happy with soap and a new dress.

Bosco jeered, Me, I'm going for a big jeep.

Bastard.

Romi said quietly, Showing off again, eh Bosco? Always at it aren't you? All I want is to sleep in the same place for a few nights.

And Mother, You two stop quarrelling and being idiots. There's no money so be sensible.

She only thought about money.

Father just smiled, he knew it was empty talk. Valdo kept quiet, he was homesick for his family back south and kept peering into the jungle and asking what animals roamed about in there.

The red road turned to black tarmac, the truck steady, we sang samba. It was midday, the sun bit fiercely at our heads, no more trees

56

for shade. The roads criss-crossed at right angles. Old cars and trucks ripped to bits lay to one side. Hand-painted boards announced, Come to this hotel or to that garage or to this churrascaria. Outside town the huts roofed with palm leaves, the centre of town filled with white-painted brick houses with tiled roofs and patches of green in front. No traffic lights.

Down near the river were three steel water towers with domed tops, yellow diggers and tractors all over the place. By the port the streets were old and cobbled. And the great wide river, boats tied to the bank and beside it rusty tin sheds with rusty steam engines outside. Why that town was there, probably mad like us. Black vultures circled overhead and sat on the wooden fences or lumbered about in the trash.

Father pulled out some papers and told me to find out where to go.

All sorts of people, brown, black and others from the south like us and trucks, battered buses, old taxis and smart government cars. There were carts and mules with one rider, mules with two riders, normally both men, the women on the ground, chickens and goats. Children ran barefoot chasing dogs and rolling old bicycle wheels with sticks. There was purpose in the air. We stared at these people and wondered if we were going to be like them.

The Ministry was a smart green building set back from the road in a garden and, to my surprise, there was that clapped-out bus with the three families amongst all the other trucks like us. The river glinted in the distance. A queue led to a desk with a big man surrounded by piles of papers. Father took me along to take notes. At least we were out of the sun. We shuffled forward hour after hour sitting on our heels with our backs wedged against the wall. Flies everywhere.

Finally our turn. The big official in army dress, fat and important, with a small electric fan pointing at his face. He asked many questions. He looked hard at Father and then, with a humourless expression, pulled out a folder that had *Mutum* stamped on it in big black letters.

You're lucky to be allocated here, he said aggressively.

He rubber-stamped each page in green with the word *Protocolo* and wrote the number 921 at the top.

Come back in two months.

He spoke roughly as if we were servants.

Make sure you bring this ticket with you or you'll get nothing.

He passed over a ticket with 921 stamped on it and a green leaflet.

Colonising the jungle by growing food. Your Future. The Government is here to help.

Father, in disbelief, two months, what do we do for money?

The official pursed his lips. Next, he said, beckoning at the queue.

We walked, our lives in *his* hands.

Luckily Mother had chatted to the family in the next truck. She told us about an open patch of scrub close to the river where other people had stopped. Some had built wooden shacks and had been there for months. That night we lay side by side looking up at the underside of our orange cover. Father said we had to get jobs and for the boys to bike into town and find work. Me, Mother and Father set up a tent with poles from the bush.

Father built a shack for us newly-weds out of packing cases so we could be alone. Dear Father.

By midday our bodies ran with sweat. We found a track to the river. I washed and washed. That big Madeira River with its circling rounds of water passing slowly by, always changing, surging up from the bottom into whirlpools running in a dirty brown flood to the Amazon. So much water, so much power.

Father told me to read the leaflet.

Bosco teased.

Read on, read on, what Idenea can't read nobody can read.

Filho da Puta!

It was friendly and full of pictures.

The Government welcomes you to this new territory, it said. *You are a lucky family, the government has provided you with land and money to grow crops and animals. There will be an immediate payment to help you start up. If you need more, come back and ask for it with a full written justification but remember the Government is generous.*

Something like that anyway.

So much money, Father interrupted, we'll be rich.

Your land is covered with mature jungle. This is a precious natural resource. You will receive 50 or 100 hectares. You must not clear trees on more than half. Your property will be one of several in your location. Take note of the attached map...

But is the land good? Mother nagging.

It must be, it's got big trees, answered Father.

The Government has built an access road and each property will run beside this road. Your number will be on a marker post at the front, the land is yours to work and when you have repaid your loan, the land will pass to you and your children for ever. Aaaah for ever!—

Idenea pushed herself up onto one elbow. With her forefinger she stroked a line from Bobby's chin downwards.

'The map was like this. Main road in the middle, access tracks like these.' At each rib she slipped her finger to the right and to the left.

Unlike the night before, he was no longer nervous.

'Bobinho, you asked me to tell you everything. Now is not the time to make love.' She laughed, 'I'll soon put a stop to that.'

She ran into the bathroom, came back with a towel soaked in cold water and draped it over his waist. His eyes followed her every move.

'That'll work, you'll see,' she said playfully. 'Well now, while that's working, I'll see if my friend is about.'

She opened the curtain and peered out into the sharp midday heat of the courtyard and tapped on the window, her body silhouetted against the bright light.

'Come on, where are you?'

A young Marsh deer poked its nose through the curtains. She stroked it between the ears.

'Meet my friend, Doçinha. A cowboy friend of Ludo's found her caught in wire. I tell her how I will find my boy Zoni one day. She stands quite still and listens to me, even at night...Aaaah so.'

'Well?' Turning her full nakedness. 'Has it worked?' The towel lay flat across his belly. She smiled, an open smile, no slant any more and straight into his eyes.

'No wonder the boys thought you were a good catch, Idenea.'

'Bobinho, stop that silly talk, the liar that you are.' Even so, she glanced shyly at him.

'It's the way you are,' he said, 'so different. The way you talk with such candour.'

'I've been called pretty but never beautiful.' She said beautiful, looking at him with that new open smile on her mouth and in her eyes.

Down the passage, a woman's voice shouted. 'Get out you *Filho da Puta* or I'll call Ludo and he'll break your shit of an arm.' A door banged.

'Oh that's Abadia.' Idenea's smile faded. 'She's always screaming and shouting. Poor girl.' She paused and took his hand. 'Do you still want me to go on?'

'Yes. Yes. I've been on my own for so long as well.'

She smiled with a sweetness as if they were old friends. 'You listen and that comforts me. Maybe that's why I like telling you.'

'And I seem to recognise the place you describe,' he said, 'it sounds so familiar.'

She pointed towards the picture of the Indian. 'Soon he'll tell me where he is. You'll see.'

She lay down beside him.

—Father, bursting with enthusiasm, started counting on his fingers what we would need on our 50 hectares. Axes, saws and so on. Mother kept butting in with how much for food.

Father's answer was simple. Add it all up and we'll ask for it like the leaflet says. We'll check prices in the local shops.

That evening the boys biked back in wild excitement.

This is boom town, my husband cried, chucking his bike to one side. He pulled out a fat round black fish and proudly presented it to me. It's a tambaqui. My new boss says the river's stuffed with them. I got a job helping fishermen deliver around town. This one's a present. They admire us for getting here. The town is full of new people: planters, farmers, cowboys, gold prospectors all muddling about with the old-time rubber and nut traders. They say the Government is pouring money in.

He became more and more excited. And there's gold in the river. God willing, we're going to get rich, *ricos amigos*. Romi and Bosco found jobs as well didn't you?

Suddenly all was possible. Bosco to work in a bar. Romi in with builders and new houses under a government scheme. Chico and Carlito in a sawmill.

Mother said, Adonis, you and Idi go get work as well so we bring in as much money as possible for by the good Lord I know we're going to need it.

We ate fish that night, our first fresh food for a month. I teased Bosco with, So in your bar you can ogle the girls all day long, huh? He sniggered back, Was that a joke, eh? There're only men around here. No women in this end of the world that's for sure, just you, just you. The idiot.

Father got a job as a waiter. As for me, after asking all over town, a schoolteacher told me that the army needed somebody who could read and write. So there I was, a receptionist in that big green building surrounded by a high wall with barbed wire on top and the national flag flying above. I felt very lucky. I had to fill in forms and answer questions about safety, even about snake bites. The young soldiers were polite and never molested me. The commander was a jolly colonel who always said hello. They all wore t-shirts with—*Foi bom que voce veio*. It was good you came.

In just one week we made more money than ever before. Mother nagged and nagged till we handed over three-quarters of our wages. No one knew where she put them. Valdo and Bosco liked staying out late drinking, so it was hard to get them to hand over. And *pelo amor de Deus,* did they drink.

At night Valdo held me telling me that we were going to be rich.

I was pleased for him and his funny coconut hair.

But that Ministry leaflet bothered me and I had seen the jungle pass by, tall and dark and full of noises. It couldn't be easy for simple people like us, least of all for Valdo.

Once a week I went with Father and Romi to chase after our Protocolo 921. Standing forever in a queue, only for that big official with funny coloured curly hair, Captain Dias or the Chefe, to tell us to go away.

Valdo and Bosco wanted to stay saying we were earning so much so why go into the jungle, the unknown.

Mother kept quiet. Secretly she agreed with them. But I would follow Father. He was a man of the land not a waiter. We couldn't live on the edge of the river forever.

Finally after two and a half months, Captain Dias instructed all the family to turn up. He shouted *Family Saladini? In here now.*

He was pointing at a map with *Federal Land* printed across the top. He didn't shake hands. We sat on a bench. A girl of my age typing at the back.

Now listen to me, family Saladini, and listen very carefully.

I noticed he had a squint and I couldn't make out where he was looking. He jabbed his finger on the map. Your plot of land, number 921, now remember that number, is here. Down this federal road, turn off in Mutum village onto the access road and you're at the end, 15 kilometres from the village. Get in there now. There's a map and instructions in the folder here. Who can read?

Father put his hand on my shoulder.

That Captain thrust a folder at me. Take this and do as instructed. You can only cut down half of your jungle. Federal Law, understand? And no Castanheiro[4] trees, right! On he went. Do as I tell you. Think of me as the cow that produces the milk for your existence. I say this to all settlers. Some listen, some don't. Those that don't, regret it.

Now off you go! I'll visit within a year to check on your progress.

We filed out like naughty children.

---

4 Castanheiro; a Brazil-nut tree, forbidden to cut down.

We left camp. It was an early Sunday morning. We passed a column of children all dressed in white shirts stepping out, one behind the other, to a marching tune that came from a new chapel. They were so innocent, so full of hope...

Nobody sang. The sun beat down. With all the extra weight, the truck lurched. Soon we were back in cursed mud with a hundred and fifty kilometres to go and heavy rain every day. The further from town, the worse the road with all of us and the mule on the ground pushing, pulling, unloading and loading, goaded on for that bright future.

The jungle was closer now, no bulldozed margin. Flocks of parrots hurried over. I saw my first macaw flying steadily on its way, red and green. The blue ones came later, so beautiful, so straight in flight. Never far from the big river, we crossed smaller rivers on bridges made of concrete and steel with railway lines in the middle. I had no idea why. Knowing came later.

Romi didn't bother to listen for engine trouble any more. Yet another massive hole had ripped off our new exhaust. Black smoke spat out under the engine as the road opened up and we rolled in short sharp jerks into the village of Mutum. A couple of dozen houses on white painted stilts stood in a clearing. Some had palm leaf roofs, others corrugated tin.

We set up camp and fell into the bar, *Bar da Amizade* in large white letters above the entrance, for a coke. We didn't care about the cost. Something big was about to happen. We had to spoil ourselves. It was a shop as well. Sacks and dusty tins everywhere On the floor funny looking grey balls with holes through the middle.

Heat fell on us from the tin roof.

The owner was a small, fat man with fair skin and red marks on his forehead from too much sun.

So you're new, eh? he said, cheerfully. Well, I look forward to serving you. Bébé's the name, my pleasure I'm sure. He laughed in high pitch. Later I learnt that his nickname Bébé was because he looked like a baby. He chuckled knowingly. We settlers must help each other.

A pistol in a leather holster stuck out on a shelf behind him. Valdo had seen it as well and looked at me in surprise. Our gun, which Romi thought he was going to protect us with, was somewhere in all the mess on our truck.

Valdo pointed at it and asked what it was for.

Oh, keeping baddies away, Bébé said, pushing over more cokes. Snakes, drunkards, Indians, jaguars. We get all kinds through here. He giggled again his horse-like whinny. A man of the world like me has to be prepared.

I was sure he was only thinking of making money out of us.

Indians, jaguars? Father hesitantly.

He laughed. This is deep jungle. The next village is a good sixty kilometres away. You might see a jaguar on the road at night or tracks in the mud. They don't bother anyone. As for Indians, several half-castes wander in and out and the boys from the Indian Protection Agency say there could be a small tribe behind where you're heading.

Father asked him if he had seen any real Indians? Are they good people?

Never seen a pure blood, he said. One time I know I was being watched. I felt it on the back of my neck. Makes you go cold, creepy to think somebody you can't see is watching you.

He leant over the bar with a knowing look. I used to rubber tap, that's how I got going up here. I went far into the jungle. Trees and trees and insects and wild rubber all over the place and maybe Indians. Nowadays my lads tap for me. There's the result, look.

He pointed at the grey balls with holes in the corner. Rubber is valuable. One of my tapper lads disappeared last year. His mate swore an Indian arrow must have killed him. No proof, no body. Look, there's no law here, no police. The army comes charging through sometimes on the way to the Bolivian frontier searching for drugs. That's all. I look after myself. All you can do here is survive.

A woman, of much the same size as Bébé, came and stood beside him. She smiled at us. That smile changed everything in the room. Father beamed back. We all felt much better. Here was someone I could talk to. She had dark brown-reddish skin. She was the first mixed blood Indian I had ever met.

She said, I'm Juliana, his wife. *Bemvindo*, Welcome to Mutum.

Bébé pushed a list of what he sold across the bar. Crazy, crazy, I thought. But where else could we go? That night we got drunk. Bébé kept pouring out the pinga. Even Mother got tipsy in spite of her money worries. We played pool in the corner. There was another truck driver together with his woman sleeping in the cab parked beside us. Written on their back board was *Com Deus voce vai longe*, With God you go far.

Mother didn't say a word. She was scared stiff. We fooled about and laughed the hysterical laugh of the truly worried.

Early morning, Bébé pointed down the road. There's a sign on the right after twelve kilometres with the lot numbers marked on it. The entry road is three kilometres long. There are other settlers, some have been there two or three years. *Boa sorte*. See you soon. And he laughed, again the squeak. Apart from his stinking breath, there was something syrupy about his wish to please.

We reached the sign. A shower soaked us and after that the mosquitoes and those little black biters borrachudos hit us. My neck looked as if someone had cut my throat. The access track that Captain Dias had called a road, what a joke, ran off at a right angle. It was narrow, all mud and gravel, with the jungle right up on each side. We crawled forward, unable to hear anything above the roar of the engine.

We passed through a homestead, a mule tied to a tree and a couple of children playing on the ground. There was a pink bougainvillea growing up the side, a small corral, a few cattle. Black charred stumps stuck up out of the green. On a board was *Fazenda do Bom Futuro* in white letters. Some kids rushed up, scattering chickens and shouting. A woman came out of the hut and waved. She smiled and I smiled back. My heart lifted. Their name was Baldoni, and had come from the south like us.

We didn't dare stop for fear of never getting the engine going again. We started to sing, with relief perhaps, at seeing a cheery family doing all right. There were other small settlements every quarter kilometre, a hut, a couple of cows, a few papaya trees—that's my favourite fruit. We passed on belching smoke.

The path narrowed even more. In front was a rough track with the trees pushed to one side. Romi stopped, searching for a way forward. A man emerged from a thatched hut.

Father shouted, where to for lot 921?

The man I knew later as the skinny one, Magrinho, shook his head and pointed at the blocked path. Through there maybe, he shouted back at us. Then he did an odd thing. He made a thumb's down sign, thought better of it and still pointing in front shouted, To the end, keep going. Good luck. I'll ride in and see you. He passed his hand over his brow wiping at imaginary sweat.

The nervous liquid feeling in my stomach was back.

Chico and Carlito jumped down and started slashing forwards with their shiny new machetes. Valdo didn't. There were hoof marks on the ground but no tyre marks. By the looks of it a machine had been through sometime ago. On and on, slower than a walk, the truck pushed and grumbled on. The two boys did their best. Branches dragged at the truck as we forced our way, the upper branches, like a roof, hid the sky. I couldn't see more than fifteen metres on either side.

We passed two deserted huts. Then another with some maize. A scraggy man in a straw hat beside a dark woman in ragged clothes carrying a baby stood in the doorway. They said they were hungry and could we help. Father said we had to keep going to make camp before dark, but we gave them some rice and beans. The man smiled his thanks. He couldn't have been more than thirty and had no front teeth.

He said that they'd been there two years and that the soil wasn't very good. We were the last they'd seen. Hope you get in all right, he said. Come and visit, we like to talk.

Another five hundred metres of slashing. A big tree blocked our way. Just visible, nailed to the trunk was a dirty white board with

921 painted in black. Huge brown tree trunks rose up on all sides. Creepers trailed within touching distance, everything in dim shade.

Romi switched the engine off.

Idiot, why'd you do that? shouted Bosco banging the top of the cab in panic.

Well, said my brother, quietly, we can't go forward and we can't go backwards so that's it. We're there, Lá…Lá.

There wasn't a sound. No one said a word. The engine gurgled and stilled. The jungle seemed to hold its breath.

Quiet, it said, who are you?

I wanted to reply, Look at us. Please admire us for getting here. Then the frogs started, Ooaaght, tic tic tic ticup tic. Birds high up began whistling again. A group of parrots screeched and peered down, somersaulting around. The mosquitoes were on us in seconds. Every living thing had paused to watch until our noise had stopped and gone from their world.

Try to imagine us in front of that tree. We were the foreigners for sure. I had a big hole in my stomach. Aaaah so…

So, this was it. Oh, dear sweet Jesus. Just us, the trees and a dark green mass all around. Our future home. Because of the dark or more likely the damp, it was cooler. Some relief at least.

Father's calm voice. Out we get. Let the mule down so he can eat, poor devil. You boys make camp. Mother start cooking supper and me and you, my girl, will put up the cover and get some bedding together. It'll be damp on the ground.

Later I asked him how he'd felt that night. Pretty good, nervous yes, but that's what we'd come for, wasn't it? No complaints.

I would have done anything in the world for Father.

As the light began to go, we stretched our cover from one side of the truck to the nearest trees. Mother and I cooked and our paraffin lamp gave out a flicker of a light. Nobody said much. Crouching under the cover, eating supper, Romi said, we're young and strong so cheer up everyone. We can do it.

We all laughed, tension forgotten, mighty pleased with ourselves. We slapped and swore at the mosquitoes and laughed ourselves stupid telling stories about our old home.

There wasn't a moment's silence. The croaks, the whistles, the animal calls were so foreign. As I lay on the mattress beside Valdo that night, I thanked the good Jesus and I thanked the truck. I patted the mud-covered wheel behind my head.

Well done, clever old girl, I whispered, you made it.

I didn't know the truck would never move again as it sank into the ground, its engine torn out for use somewhere else, its lights ripped off to light up a settler's hut. But that night I knew we'd done it. Got there. Aaaah, *chegado*. Aaaah so—

Idenea swung her legs off the bed, sat up, and stared at the shimmer of heat in the courtyard. Her back, long and slender, cast a shadow over the white of the sheets. She was as still as a statue silhouetted against the light.

Bobby touched her arm. 'You can't stop now'.

She pulled her knees up level with his hips, her face half hidden by her hair. He could just make out the shine of her eyes.

'*Tá bom*, if that's what you want.' She flicked the words out with her tongue. Gone the languid murmur, her eyes straight at his elbow.

—Next morning, as the dense green softened, we looked at each other, mud covered, spotted red with bites. We peered up at where the sky began, a good forty metres above. Not a word from anyone.

Mother got a fire going and made some coffee and heated up some rice. The clinking sound of tin plates and men coughing were out of place.

Not much good for football, laughed Valdo.

We'll see, we'll see. Father was always positive. Come on everyone, let's get going. Remember this is our land, our *Fazenda Boa Esperança*.

I prayed and prayed. I didn't know what an odd lot we were. I listened to the jungle in the same way as I always did later on. I lay with my eyes wide open. Not a moment's silence. I often shouted out at the noise to try and stop it. That never worked. Noises so close.

With the heat towards midday, the hoots and screams fell away. It was a rhythm that I later came to know really well. Suddenly there would be no noise from any animal, just the flickering rustle of the leaves high up. The whole jungle seemed to stop and turn in on itself, hold its breath, exhausted, all energy drained by the sun above. I imagined the monkeys and the birds, all with their tongues hanging out, gasping, no umph left to call or scream, a stop in their day...silence. And then after an hour or so without warning...Boom like a clap of thunder and they'd all be back at it again, barking and crying. I would drift into a doze, my upper lip wet with sweat and my eyelids weighed down by the damp. At first I tried to fight through it but it was better to lie in my hammock and wait...I couldn't...I just can't...just can't...

'And then?'

Under her hair, her eyelids, as smoothly as stage curtains, drew shut. Her breathing purred in her throat.

He folded his arm around her head and kept it there as the heat closed his eyes.

3

FAZENDA BOA ESPERANÇA

The Saladinis threw themselves into the work. This was new and there was no boss to satisfy. At first, the truck and all their belongings, Bolo and their mule as well, occupied an area not much bigger than the truck with its front bumper half a metre from the soaring tree and the number 921. Adonis, gripping a machete, slashed into the green leaves and branches.

'Come on everyone, let's find water.'

The boys and Idenea followed, swinging their machetes with enthusiasm. Not so Valdo, he stayed with Mother Tana as she began to sort out the camp.

Idenea walked back. 'Here's yours, Valdo,' and handed him a machete. 'Vamos, let's follow Father.'

Valdo didn't move, looking at the ground. 'What about snakes?'

'Yes, yes I know. Use your machete if you see one.'

'And the spiders?'

'Oh, come on.' She grabbed his hand and pulled him forwards.

Cutting through the undergrowth and parting the low-hanging creepers, they found a stream that ran around a gentle rise in the forest floor.

'Our base,' declared Adonis, 'let's get stuck in.'

All six men and Idenea, with axes and machetes, cleared enough room to pitch the cover into a more permanent tent. They fooled about hardly noticing the rubbing of the axe handles and the punctures in their legs from spiked foliage. Soon all had changed into long trousers and boots. Valdo didn't mention spiders or snakes again but Idenea noticed he always worked behind one of the others.

Adonis strode about. 'We're here to stay. *Olha*, Look, our own land, it's ours, really ours.' He picked up a clod of earth, kissed it and rubbed it between his hands.

Idenea and Mother Tana wedged the cooking stove in one corner of the makeshift tent. Two days later, they had a place to eat and sleep. Their hands were half-raw and their necks bled from bites but nobody complained. They winced from the sting of the raw alcohol that they rubbed on to toughen the skin of their hands.

Mother Tana placed her small wooden shrine in another corner, put the bright blue and white doll-sized statue of the Virgin Mary inside and crossed herself. Later, on Sunday, she lit a candle, stuck it in soft wax beside Mary and said, 'All of you now, bow your heads, cross yourselves and say Ave Maria at least twice. You'll see how she'll help us, bless her soul.'

At night Idenea and Valdo sat close together joking about how they were going to build their own hut away from the others.

She smiled shyly. 'It'll be on stilts with its own steps, a window and a thatched roof and... and a baby.'

Valdo stroked her arm.

'A baby?' sneered Bosco, 'what's the use of that?'

He had been ogling at her body trying to figure out exactly where her legs began and how her breasts would look out of her t-shirt. She turned away.

'I want a beginning, I want a baby,' she said softly,

Bosco grinned. 'That's easy, let me know any time you need a good firm start up, I'm always ready.'

In the darkness, broken only by the yellow of the kerosene flame, no one smiled.

Valdo jumped up. 'Leave her alone, can't you. She's my wife. You're her cousin. Show respect.'

Bosco laughed sharply and raised his hand. '*Calma*, I can have my jokes, can't I?'

Mother Tana, keen to avoid a row, interrupted, 'We need the sun to dry our clothes and heal our wounds. Knock that one down.' She pointed at the tree that had blocked their way and whose canopy spread over their camp.

That tree was about forty-five metres high and took the men three full days to cut down. On day one they chopped and slashed aimlessly about to clear enough space for the fall. On the second, impatient for a result, they set about the main trunk. Four-metre-high buttresses rose out of the earth and angled into the trunk, three of the men side by side fitted easily between two of the buttresses. They hacked at these with the energy that accompanies doing something new, shouting encouragement to each other; the new yellow axe handles rising and falling. In their innocence they started to cut and hack in at ground level.

On day three, when the axe cuts neared the centre, the tree that had withstood this onslaught without any sound or movement, suddenly creaked and shuddered. The men stepped back a few metres, their bodies oily with sweaty grime. A short gust of wind settled it all. The tree lost balance and with the uneven weight distribution of its extended branches began to twist. The remaining fibres snapped, cracking like rifle shots.

'We're too close!' yelled Adonis.

As they ran, the tree hesitated as if unable to decide which way to fall and then gracefully turning vertically on itself began

71

to lean over, slowly to begin with and then in a rush. The lower branches pushed smaller trees effortlessly downwards breaking their stems with multiple sharp reports. As the crown stretched out and downwards rushing to the ground, it collided with two other substantial trees, thirty centimetres in diameter at least, snapping them in two with a deafening din of splintering wood and thrashing leaves.

The men gawped at the violence. The upper branches mingled, shoved and pushed with others to form a writhing mass as if some green-scaled monster was erupting out of the ground. The trunk, parting from the cuts at the top of the buttresses, jumped upwards into the air as the full weight of the tree plunged outwards and then in slow motion, arched back banging into the earth sending tremors up Idenea's legs. It continued to move, its branches wrestling with each other. There was a cracking and a pushing downwards. The overall sound was an extended sigh. The tree lay down and was still. Parrots screeched and fled.

Silence. Then everybody started jumping up and down, punching the air with their fists, boasting to each other of their individual prowess.

'Ayee! *Olha*! Look at that. Our first. We did it!'

They took a week to cut off all the branches. The forty-five-metre trunk stretched out like a giant's pencil. Strips of skin hung from their hands.

Comparing blisters Valdo said, 'Look at mine, I bet they're the biggest and, *Meu Deus*, do they hurt. Let me see yours, Bosco.'

Bosco, hands behind his back. 'I say, toughen up, you Coconut, and learn the rhythm.'

Their skin took months to harden enough to withstand the constant chafing of the axe handle. Before the arrival of chainsaws, cutting and felling became such an effort that they quarrelled as to who should do it and resorted to lottery to decide a weekly rota. Adonis tried to keep order, reminding them of how much they had to do but soon his calls of 'Let's get stuck in' were ignored. As well as starting her plantation, Idenea slashed and cut with the men. She grew strong and capable.

Days of toil turned into weeks of hard struggle chopping and clearing. Adonis couldn't work all day and would flop into his hammock at eleven. Even the younger ones stopped for three hours over the midday meal. Their bodies grew lean and sinewy.

After a month they had a clearing about the size of four tennis courts.

When Idenea eagerly showed the first egg from one of the chickens from the south, Mother Tana hard-boiled it and with her sharpest knife cut it into eight pieces so that everyone could have their share. She sliced from shiny top to shiny white bottom and then across, making sure that each section held some yolk. She placed all eight pieces onto a tin plate and handed them with a quiet concentration as if they were a communion offering.

'Look at that,' Adonis exclaimed. 'Our own food, it makes the rice and beans taste better.' He laughed and carefully fingered the tiny white morsel onto his fork.

That night Mother Tana, kneeling in front of her shrine, gave thanks for this first home-grown food. Other firsts had arrived in the rough hessian sacks: cockroach slivers and their eggs mixed in with the cheap rice and beans. Soon after, Idenea's early morning job was to pursue and sweep up the cockroaches. Some had plain shiny brown shells, others dark cross bands on the shiny brown. The crackling sound of stamping on one gave her momentary satisfaction. Then on to hacking and hoeing in the red earth set aside for their orchard. Brushing her sweat-laden hair back she could feel the hardening of her hands against her cheeks.

The first casualty came when an ocelot pounced on one of the laying chickens.

'Murder!' shouted Tana at the forest wall.

Bolo barked on and off for hours staring into the jungle where the wild cat had run, the chicken flapping in its jaws.

Every day Idenea watched and measured the maize seedlings as they sprouted out of the ground and would soon become bread on the table.

Eventually the boys biked out to the distant village. They asked Mother Tana for money saying that it was good to get about and meet the neighbours.

'Our money is precious,' she said and then relented, reasoning that to hold back would cause a row. 'Off you go then and see you behave yourselves.'

All five young men biked away with a 'See you later' over their shoulders. A drink, playing pool and possibly a girl, even if the bar was fifteen kilometres away, spurred them on. Two days later, sick and drunk, they pushed their bikes back up the track. Tana scolded, wiped her hands on her apron and thumped the table. Idenea was just glad to see Valdo back home.

Bosco and Valdo riled as Mother Tana scolded.

'Look,' they argued, 'we met a man who said he'd buy our trees. He said he'd lend us chainsaws and everything. That's lots of money for us. We will eat better. He'll come and see what we're up to. And he said the land is bad up this end. So, what do you say to that?'

No answer.

As the rainy season was on them, they hurriedly built a hut with the old yellow cover as a temporary roof, stretched over poles hacked out of the jungle, and lashed bamboo canes for the walls. When heavy deluges sheeted down, the drumming on top of the cover was so loud that sign language was easier than shouting. The rain splashed in from the sides. They ate from a table made by Adonis and Romi from old boards from the truck. They slept side by side in hammocks, away from the ants, slung between poles strong enough to bear their weight. Each hammock draped with a white mosquito net.

Soon after, at Adonis' suggestion, they built Idenea's longed-for hut on stilts about thirty metres away from the main hut. It had a bamboo floor and woven palm leaf for roof and walls. She and Valdo moved in amid laughing and teasing. Inside for a bed was a foam mattress on split bamboo canes held up off the floor on logs, two hammocks, two chairs knocked up from scrap wood and a tiny table from packing cases. They continued to eat in the main hut and washed and bathed in the stream fifty metres away.

For the first time since leaving home, Idenea hung up her mirror. It was so small she could only see half of her face at one look. Left half, smirk at it, move sideways for the right half and smirk again. Horrible, she'd mutter at the red bites, ugly, ugly. Putting on her favourite lipstick was even more difficult. She eked out her last stick over three weeks and then rarely looked in the mirror again.

They made love often, breaking quickly apart. She kept a bowl of water close by to pour over their heated bodies.

'I want a baby. We'll call it Amazon, *tudo bem*?'

Bosco soon came to know the reason for the bowl of water and seeing her filling it in the stream jibed, 'At it again, eh?' and slapped the palm of one hand onto the upturned fist of the other.

'Nothing to do with you,' she snapped back, flushed with embarrassment.

'Wish it was,' he grinned his angelic smile and slapped palm on fist again.

Best of all was slipping away unnoticed to the stream and making love in the running water. After a few times, Idenea said that she was sure someone was watching. She would stop, hold still in the stream and peer intently through the brown tree trunks.

'It's just a curious animal wandering about,' Valdo mumbled and pulled her back to him.

'No, no. We're being watched. Could be Indians?' Her skin pimpled cold and she pushed him away.

Adonis cut three short boards and painted in uneven letters *Fazenda* on one, *Boa* on the middle one and *Esperança* on the third. He dug two poles into the ground on each side of the entrance track, strung a wire between them and hung the boards across.

'Now we have a proper entrance,' he said proudly.

By the time they had cut the jungle back thirty metres and extended the main hut to allow for a separate bedroom for Adonis and Mother Tana, Christmas was on them. Mother Tana killed one of the five precious chickens, stuffed it with manioc flour and chopped dried meat. By midnight on the 24th they were all drunk on pinga. They laughed and sang, 'We're here and we're as happy as can be.'

Romi shouted at the tops of the trees ordering Papai Noel to come down with presents. Idenea vomited and staggered off to bed, thinking that this was no way to make a baby.

'I've got a cold, it's like flu,' Adonis announced one morning, as the early mist rose up dividing the height of the trees in two. 'I'll stay in today.'

He lay in his hammock, pushing himself sideways back and forth with his foot against a pole. By midday he felt dizzy, unable to focus on anything. By evening he was soaked in sweat.

'I'm freezing,' he whispered to Mother Tana. 'I'm aching all over. Somebody is hitting my head with a hammer. Give me a blanket.'

Mother Tana had brought a thermometer in her medicine box. 'Forty degrees,' she said screwing up her eyes.

He was shivering uncontrollably as she helped him onto their foam mattress. She rolled him over and covered him with a blanket.

She fetched all the coverings she could find: blankets, towels, old rice sacks. But still his teeth chattered and he mumbled in short bursts. Only his head showed from under the covers. His eyes shone upwards, unnaturally bright.

'*Meu Deus*, my eyes hurt so much, and my legs.'

She bathed his forehead. 'This isn't flu, Adonis, you've got malaria and I don't know what to do.' She raised her voice, 'Idenea, read the guide book, we should've thought about this long ago.'

'*Malaria*...'Idenea, after fumbling at the pages, read aloud, '*is a complicated disease contracted from the bite of a female Anopheles mosquito.*'

Her lips moved along the words. '*Symptoms are a high fever; shivering one moment from cold and sweating profusely the next from excess body temperature. Go to a doctor and ask for the recommended pills. These are named Aralem and Rezoquim. Above all drink as much water as you can to prevent dehydration. Eat fresh fruit. With the right medicine expect a slow recovery after ten to twelve days. There will be considerable loss of weight. This disease can reoccur. Try to avoid baring your skin. Cover up. Take extra care between 6 and 7 in the morning and again between 5 and 6 in the evening. These are the dangerous times when the malaria carrying mosquitoes are more prev –a - lent.*' She pronounced each syllable twice, 'prev –a - lent.'

Mother Tana gestured at the doorway. 'Quick. Go to Mutum. Find some medicine. Someone told me there's a bark with a name like Jesus that's good to chew. Off you go, I'll take care here. Get pills as well. Quickly now.'

Idenea and Valdo were gone in ten minutes.

Two hours later, with a jerk of his arm, Adonis threw off his covers one after the other.

'Too hot, too hot,' he groaned, 'water, water.'

Soon he was naked, his skin wet with sweat beading down his rib cage. He sat up, tried to walk about to cool his skin but could only stagger as strength fell away and his muscles failed. His urine ran dark yellow. Soon after, he was pulling the covers back on as his body stiffened to the first spasm of a deep shiver. Even as he shivered, sweat continued to ooze out of him. A day later his temperature was 42°.

'Heavens Father, how thin you are,' Romi exclaimed, leaning one hand on the mattress to bathe his father's face. Liquid squeezed up between his fingers out of the mattress.

The round trip to Mutum and back took Idenea and Valdo a day and a night. Valdo had to push the cart from behind while she pulled at the mule's head. Covered in mud and out of breath they burst into the *Bar da Amizade*. Frantic, they begged for pills, please, please anything.

'*Calma*.' The owner, Bébé, held up his hand. 'Sim, Senhor, I've got pills, lucky for you and even luckier yes, I believe in Jesuit bark myself. I often chew it, it's raw quinine. A man of the world like me. Wait here.' He rummaged about in the back room and reappeared with ten small white pills and a few fragments of reddy-brown bark.

'Take one pill a day and chew the bark.'

He demanded far more money than they had. They hesitated. He smiled. 'That's the price. Yes, it's expensive. Take it or leave it.' His smile a smirk. 'Take it or die.'

Idenea noticed the heavy smell of his breath again. 'We haven't got that much with us. We thought you'd be kind and...'

'As I'm a man of the world...' Bébé shrugged and leant over the bar, 'who wants to help poor settlers. Go on then, hand over what you've got and bring the rest later. But you get nothing more from me till you pay.'

Idenea recognised his whinnying giggle and knew she did not like this man. They walked back to the mule and cart.

She scolded Valdo, 'He ripped us off. Why didn't you help me argue with him?'

'Hey.' He turned on her. 'You can't talk to me like that. Wives down south don't talk like that to their husbands. Life is different up here. He's got to live as well, doesn't he?'

She slapped the reins along the mule's back. 'Well, somebody's got to make a stand.'

That night they slung their hammocks between two trees.

'The ants won't get me up here,' she said defiantly to the blackness and to the whooping of the night animals.

Next day they trotted up the short slope to find both parents in and out of coma.

'Oh dear Jesus, you as well, *Mãe*? Here take these pills, chew this bark, quick, quick.'

She tenderly held her father's head as she helped him to swallow a pill.

Adonis struggled up onto one elbow, 'Thank you, *a minha linda*, my beautiful.' She bathed his brow. And to her mother gently, 'Now you, *Mãe*, swallow and chew on this bark while I wash your arms.'

Each child took it in turns to sit beside the bed and watch helplessly as Adonis's fever reached 42° and then 43°. He could hardly move. Their cries brought Idenea running. They pleaded for water but vomited within seconds. And the smell: an insidious invasive stench seeped from the stricken bodies and the sodden mattress. She could smell it outside. She washed their clothes again and again but the stench stayed, so ingrained was it in the fibres, rancid like rotten butter mixed with the acrid whiff of spent cordite and old sweat.

Twelve days passed before their fevers dropped and they could stomach a little rice and water. Neither could walk properly or do any light work. When Adonis pulled his old trousers back on, he had to punch three new holes in his belt with a nail. Mother Tana's smock dress fell down over her body like an old sack. They'd lost four to five kilos each.

Adonis summoned enough strength to kiss his wife weakly on the cheek. 'We're alive Tana, my dear. We must thank God for that.'

Towards the end of April, the rains eased. Valdo and Bosco led two men on mules up to the main hut. They had machetes slung on their saddles and Taurus ·38 revolvers in leather belts around their waists. Five or six cartridges showed, one or two live, the others empty pushed in to impress. One of the two was Bébé from the bar and the other a timber man they'd met when playing pool and drinking.

The timber man was fat and jolly with short legs and a drooping moustache. He swung off his mule and shook hands with all the family.

'*Madeira*, Wood, that's my business. Call me Senhor Madeira, everybody does. Makes it simple, you see.'

He strode over to a felled tree that had cost the family so much effort and slashed at it with his machete. With his hands on his hips, he laughed and his belly wobbled. 'Good, Good, I can take these and those two over there.'

They inspected the length of each tree, clambering along the top of the trunk. Progress was slow with Senhor Madeira poking and slashing as they stumbled amongst the hacked-off branches. He blew out his breath ballooning his cheeks.

'Phew! Look at that. Wow! Heavens above. What difficult access. You're right in the jungle here, aren't you?'

He showed them how to identify the trees by their bark, the form of the trunk and the shape of the leaf.

Bébé followed behind, panting and sweating. He could only speak in short gasps.

'I'm a man of the world' gasp, 'I'll arrange a truck' gasp, 'when the roads dry.' And addressing Romi, 'Listen to me, Saladinis, it's going to cost you.'

Sitting in the hut around the wooden table, a tin cup of coffee in each hand prepared by Mother Tana, they struck a deal. Idenea wrote it out as Bébé leant over her shoulder. She recoiled at the smell of his breath. Apart from his breath it was his exaggerated desire to please that so irritated her. He giggled and squeezed her arm.

'It's okay, my dear, I won't hurt you.'

Mother Tana nudged her husband. 'That's not much for us, it's a bad deal.'

'It's money though, my dear, isn't it?' Adonis sighed, 'and you're always complaining the cash box is nearly empty. *Vamos*. Come on everybody it's a start, and with us two half sick all the time, we need every penny. What do the rest of you think?' His eyes shone out of sunken sockets, the fever loosely gone.

Romi shrugged. Bosco insisted it was a good deal. Valdo said he didn't know. Chico and Carlito said nothing.

'*Olha*,' Adonis argued, 'we eat the same thing every day. The new chickens are still too small. God gave us this land, not just the Government.' Tana cast her eyes down as he spoke. 'God is showing us how to survive. We need the cash. There's no going back.' His eyes shone brighter. 'Our future. At least hope for one. We have to survive. Don't you agree?'

Each Saladini nodded and repeated 'To survive' one by one.

'Let's sign then. Idi give us the agreement. Come on everyone, where's a pen? Everybody sign, we're all part of it. I'll fingerprint.'

'Woah up,' exclaimed Senhor Madeira.

'Yeah,' Bébé agreed, 'there's no need to sign anything. We're among friends, aren't we? Let's just get on with it.'

Adonis read out what Idenea had written.

'A hand shake is good enough for me.' Senhor Madeira shook Adonis's limp hand.

Idenea caught Bébé's eye. He was smiling but at her glance his smile faded to a sneer and then to nothing. Even in that heat she felt the palms of her hands go cold. She called to Bolo. He padded up to her side wagging his tail. She stroked his head.

Outside a Screaming Piha, a Piscoteiro[5], so tiny in size so loud in voice, pierced all other sound with its Whoooeuh… whee…wheeuh. Once, a pause and again strident and wide awake, 'Wheeeup'.

'That bird, that bird,' she murmured.

Senhor Madeira stood beside his mule, hands on hips, chin out. 'Good luck, Boa sorte and good work. We'll all get rich from this accursed forest, you'll see. Remember mogno, mahogany, is red gold in foreign places and cereijeira, cherry wood, is yellow gold right here. Ciao and be happy.'

---

5 Piscoteiro means a wolf whistler, the nick name given to the Screaming Piha.

Bébé mounted his mule, jabbed his reins around and without a farewell followed down the track.

'Our lives,' muttered Mother Tana watching them go, 'will be completely in their hands. Don't you see, they'll control our money, make slaves out of us? And we have nothing signed.' Her brown pupils no longer framed in white but in fever-stained yellow moved accusingly from one to the other. 'Even you, Idenea, fell for it. Be warned all of you, watch out. We have to fight and even more so now with no contract.'[4]

She walked up to Adonis. 'You showed them how desperate we are. You were too keen and easy.'

Adonis raised his eyes in mock despair. 'We'd be down south and starving if I hadn't agreed.'

She turned away. 'Well I don't see much difference, we're still hungry.'

The wind, gentle after a short sharp shower, tilted and tipped the leaves high up in the canopy, nudging them to spill their tiny pools of water to the forest floor below.

The next morning, Idenea rushed out of her hut.

'Mama, I'm going to have my baby. There's no more bleeding.' She threw her arms around her mother who had to hold onto a post to keep her balance.

'My own little jungle baby.'

Valdo held her hand proudly. Adonis hugged her.

Romi and Chico said, 'Well done, sister.' Mother Tana kissed her and set to for the midday meal with a song on her lips, even the rice and beans smelled better.

'We'll go for a check-up as soon as we can, won't we, *meu bem*?'

'Where?' Idenea asked pressing one hand on her stomach and waving the other at the jungle. 'Down that road over the holes? Not me. No, I'm having my baby here.'

That night they drank to baby Amazon and their new life. Even Bosco smiled. So that old Coconut could do it, the lucky idiot.

Four months later her pregnancy hardly showed from her lean body. She stroked the slight bulge of her belly over and over again, skipped and jived to music ringing out from the pocket radio, which the men had dangled from one of the posts to follow the blaring of football commentary. Her energy high, nothing was too difficult, not even hoeing in the heat, and her parents' malarial weakness didn't bother her any more either. Having babies was the beginning of a better life. She glowed. Her orchard was sprouting and the papaya trees had already grown two metres with promise of her favourite fruit. She thought only of her baby.

Adonis proudly kept the official stamped document, proof of their holding, in a plastic folder under his bed. By now the two buildings, the main hut and Idenea's smaller one on stilts, had palm thatched roofs and walls. Inside, hammocks swung from post to post with the mosquito netting folded in during the day. With the dry season on them they'd swept a yard around the two huts of about ten-by-ten metres of trampled red earth. Beyond, where tall trees had recently stood, was a mixture of quick-growing secondary vegetation, short-thorned Cansansa, yellow prickly pear and the razor grass Capim Navalha.

The men had pushed their way into the undergrowth and within two hundred metres had identified trees that fitted Senhor Madeira's description. They hacked a rough pathway for Bébé's truck, which at the first visit brought in two old chain saws and fuel for a week.

'*Sim senhor*, okay, okay, *tudo bem*. I'll be back in a week to collect the first logs. Get to it, there's much money coming your way. You'll see, Ciao.'

Mother Tana, her hair tied tightly in the same old red scarf, and Idenea, one hand stroking her belly, were watching from the main hut.

'Maybe we were wrong, *Mãe*. Look, the promised saws are here so maybe money really will follow. And that Bébé wants to help.'

Outside the men sawed and slashed, preparing for the first log collection and the arrival of money and survival. A log might take two days to prepare with the struggle to clear for the fall of the tree. After slicing the felled tree into five-metre lengths the men would lean against the log in silence, waiting to regain their strength. If one of them started to walk back to the hut complaining that he was tired, the others, infected by a common lassitude, would follow, slashing through the head high debris left over from the morning's work.

As collection day approached, a sense of expectancy grew. Parrots, chattering to each other, flew across the tiny clearing. From their height, it showed as a ragged hole as if a meteorite had bombed in, layering the trees in random directions like in a game of giant poke sticks. The narrow entrance track, covered by the overhang of branches, was only just visible from above like a snaking line of red crayon. Macaws clambered in the branches, biting at fruit. Black vultures lumbered about on the ground near the chickens or sat halfway up a tree peering down with naked grey necks and lidded eyes. At times they rose up above the trees with heavy thrashing wing-beats to circle endlessly above the tiny settlement, ever searching for scraps. Bolo chased them whenever he could summon up enough energy to jump up and yap at their tail feathers.

At every meal time one of them would angrily question whether Bébé would ever come.

'Of course he will,' Adonis insisted. 'The saws are his and worth much money.'

Romi laughed, 'Well, mine is always stopping and there's only enough fuel for two more days. Then what?'

'Courage my son.'

A week passed. No Bébé.

'We have to eat less,' Mother Tana said as she dished out ever smaller helpings. 'The young chickens aren't ready and Idenea's corn's not ripe yet. Here, you boys have more and you as well, Idenea. And for baby. Father and me can do with less.'

Bolo was chasing a vulture that had dared to amble towards the hut.

'There's nothing much for Bolo either, let alone for that ugly bird,' laughed Idenea stroking her growing belly.

Bosco was picking his teeth with a fork. 'That bastard Bébé is not going to keep to his contract, I can feel it. So then what do we do with no money, no nothing? Why aren't your vegetables ready, Idenea?'

'Soon,' she said slapping at a mosquito. 'The bugs have eaten so much but you'll see something very soon. So till then, why don't you go and hunt?'

'With what?'

'I don't know, but that's what real men do.'

Bosco laughed, 'You want a real man, is that it, eh?'

Idenea put her hand on Valdo's shoulder. 'You know what I mean.'

'Stop it,' cried Mother Tana, 'fighting won't bring food.' She clattered the empty tin plates together.

'Come on.' Romi stood up, his jeans with a rip down one side. 'Bébé must come soon. He promised.'

A week later than agreed, they heard the rough coughing from punctured exhausts twenty minutes before two trucks swayed up the uneven track. The younger men ran to meet them. Bébé drove one while a dark-skinned man with a tight blue forage cap, pulled down to ears that jutted out over sun-glasses, drove the other.

Bébé's revolver belt wedged up his sagging stomach. They recognised the other driver from the bar. He wore a grimy green football t-shirt with 10 stamped on the back, faded yellow shorts and flip-flops. He had short straight black hair and dark brown hairless skin. A medallion hung around his neck.

Valdo approached him. 'You go for rubber, don't you? Those large grey balls in the bar are yours, aren't they?' They shook hands.

The driver nodded. 'Juca's the name.'

'Let's go. Vamos!' said Bébé aggressively. 'Quick. I can't hang around all day. Where are the logs? All of you now, load up.' He marched about muttering under his breath, sweat already heavy on his brow. 'Stupid settlers. A man like me...'

Old Bad Breath, thought Idenea as he stamped by without a greeting.

With short straight poles angled down from the truck's chassis to the ground, more poles used as levers and with the help and pull of a steel-roped winch, the Saladini men and Juca loaded four five-metre mahogany and cherry logs over six long hours. Bébé stood about shouting orders. Nobody took any notice. Mother Tana dished up coffee, water, rice, beans and shaki[6]. Idenea and Romi measured the logs with diameters ranging from one metre to one metre thirty. When done, all were streaked with grime, their shirts sticking to their bodies, everybody full of bad temper.

'And now the money, please,' Adonis called out. Too weak to work, he had only been able to watch the men, but now as head of the family he came to negotiate. The men ran up expectant, rubbing their hands up the legs of their jeans.

Bébé opened the side door of his truck's cabin and dragged out sacks of rice and beans, tinned vegetables, packs of shaki, bottles of pinga, jeans and a couple of boxes of 20 bore cartridges. He pulled out some bank notes from his back trouser pocket and slapped them down on the table. His eyes moved from side to side under the rim of his hat.

Adonis turned to Idenea. 'Count it, my dear.'

Half an hour later Idenea, who had noted many of the shop prices in the big town and at the bar, placed her carefully written reckoning on the table.

'What you're offering is not enough.' Adonis grimaced and with a deep sigh, 'This is robbery.'

The family muttered among themselves and shuffled uneasily.

Unmoved, Bébé placed both hands on his hips. 'Count yourselves lucky. Here's food and some cash as well. A man of the world like me keeps his word. See.'

Bosco pushed Bébé angrily on the shoulder. 'Shit man. We work and struggle and now you cheat us, eh? Come on pay up, you *Sem Vergonha.*'

Adonis stepped up to Bébé, as firmly as his weak legs allowed.

_____

6 Shaki; dried, salted low quality cow meat, mostly fat and often shrink packed. Staple food for agricultural workers in the interior.

'Father don't.' Idenea ran to his side and put her arm around his emaciated waist. 'You're too weak to fight. Leave that to us. Go on, Valdo, you do something.'

Valdo smiled sheepishly and looked to Bosco.

Bébé stepped back out of the hut and let his right hand fall onto the butt of his pistol. He let it rest there. He was in control and he knew it. The loaded trucks stood a few metres away. Juca smiling a humourless grin sat in one of the driving seats, the door open, engine running.

Bosco sidled up to Romi and whispered noisily, 'Where's our pistol?

Bébé jerked his chin in the air. 'Pay attention to me, you lot. How much do you think these goods cost me? How much to get them out here and how much do you boys owe me in the bar with all that boozing, yeah?' His beady eyes settled on Valdo and Bosco.

'You're lucky, that's what you are, that a man like me bothers to come out this far at all. Yes, you still owe me, sure you do but I'm patient. Take your time, I can wait, I'm generous. Meanwhile I advise you to accept what I've so kindly given you and get back to work.'

'You say we still owe you?' Mother Tana cried out shrilly. 'Not true. Give us what we agreed in cash. You're charging three times more than any shop. I can see what you're up to, making us your slaves and in debt forever.'

'Now you understand me, you old bitch,' Bébé replied in a quiet voice, 'this is how things are around here. Be grateful.'

They watched in silence as the two trucks crawled away down the pathway belching black smoke and rolling from side to side under the weight of the logs.

Mother Tana was crying softly into her scarf and muttering, 'I told you, we will be slaves, slaves...'

'I'll show him.' Bosco ran to the back of the hut, rummaged around and finally pulled out an old Taurus ·38 pistol, put a bullet in and chasing after the trucks, his gammy foot dragging behind, he fired into the air yelling, *Filho da Puta*, you bastard.'

As the noise of the retreating trucks gave way to hooting and whistling from the trees, Adonis said, 'Real life starts now. If we reckon it's been hard so far, we were wrong, very wrong.'

Romi shook his head. 'But Father, you could have been tougher with him. I mean we could have stopped the trucks.'

Chico nodded. 'I agree with Romi.'

Bosco was still brandishing his pistol. 'He had one of these at the ready and we didn't.'

'Now listen to me, boys.' Adonis turned back to the hut. 'I may not be as strong as I was, but this is for me to decide.'

This was new, thought Idenea, her brothers arguing with their father. She stroked her belly. 'I'll protect you, my little one. Don't you worry, you'll see that Mama does.'

As the rains slackened, felling became easier. Cotton wool clouds drifted across blue skies and the humidity level fell. The sun's glare became sharper and dried out the slashed undergrowth so Idenea could burn it, leaving the red earth ready for the maize, melon, squash, tomato and other seeds they had brought with them.

She worked long days in her plantation watching her belly grow. Tying up the tomato plants was her favourite chore, keeping the books her least. Tana wove a wide-brimmed hat from palm leaves to shield her daughter's face from the sun, rising up barely above the tree line by eight in the morning and not sinking down below again until five in the afternoon. The water levels in the streams and rivers fell and cracks appeared in the exposed earth, the surface turning to dust. Leaves high up clattered together as the jungle dried.

Every ten days or so they loaded up four logs and with that came the inevitable rows and threats with Bébé. Juca was easier. Although he worked for Bébé, he'd say 'Poor innocent bastards' as he drove away.

When Idenea wrote out the figures, the debt to Bébé was always bigger. 'Father, it's not possible, either our logs are too cheap or the goods we're paid in are too expensive.'

'*Calma*, my girl, we eat twice a day and that's enough. We need to buy a cow or two once the grass is up; that'll improve our lives and be something to look forward to.'

'It's not that Father, I'm happy in myself. Bosco doesn't bother me any more now that I'm pregnant and Valdo doesn't bring back so much pinga from the village. He says he wants to be a good father. No, it's the size of our debt. My figures show we are doing better than the debt says.'

'She's right,' said Mother Tana, 'something's wrong. I'm sure of it.' She wiped her hands vigorously on her dress, pulled at her red scarf and kicked at Bolo. 'What it is, I don't know.'

Get your burn done before the end of July, they'd been told.

In early July, in preparation for planting grass seed for their cattle pasture, they burnt the undergrowth and branches. There were several abandoned mature trees, worthless to Senhor Madeira, lying full length on the ground. Do your burning after a small shower for a more intense burn. With pieces of old truck tyre wrapped in sacking then dipped in diesel oil and lashed to stout bamboo canes, the men lined up along one side of the clearing. They fired up the oil-soaked rags and pointed the flames to the ground. A hard sun shone down.

The men pushed in with their torches. Within fifteen minutes, mounds of flame joined together. An hour later a wall of leaping flames about four metres high moved across the clearing, fanned by the wind. The crackling of the flames and the explosions of bursting matter smothered all other sounds. At first, the men followed a few paces but soon stopped and just watched, their lungs heaving for cooler air.

The men yipped and cheered.

A cylindrical column of white smoke climbed over two hundred metres up into the blue sky above plot 921. Back towards the road several kilometres away, more plumes of smoke and flying ash showed that other settlers were burning their jungle as well. These columns of white moved gradually upwards and as they rose they leant away from the wind and soon, high up, they mingled together forming one dense layer that dimmed out the sun's rays. Not far behind the Saladinis' relatively modest column, a much larger mass of smoke billowed up into the blue casting a broad shadow on the green below.

The burning season was in full swing.

For a small fire the Saladinis' was a success. When the bulk of the flames had died down, only thick branches, trunks and standing palm trees still flickered with fire. Black ash showed where leaves had burnt, white ash where a branch or a thicker stem had disintegrated. The acrid smell of burnt wood pricked into everyone's nostrils. Where the flames had invaded the edge of the jungle, the green leaves had shrivelled and hung lifeless ready to drop at the first gust of wind. The damp in the ground had prevented the fire from penetrating more than a few black-stained metres.

No parrots flew back over the clearing that evening. No macaw swung in the trees for days after.

That night at supper, the single oil lamp in the centre of the table was not the only flame that lit up the begrimed and glassy faces of the diners. Only thirty metres away, a geyser of fire would leap into the air out of the smouldering ashes, dance wildly up and down throwing bright orange flashes into the dark and then subsiding back down only to leap up again as more and more combustible material flared up. Out in the middle, barely a stone's throw from the hut, a brilliant yellow flame hissed upwards from a trunk scattering sparks like a huge roman candle, the flames feeding and crackling

on the dry creepers that still clung to its sides. The smell of burning
wafted in and infected the taste of the rice and beans. The whites
of the human eyes showed bright, and the firelight went deep into
their eyes and ignited red embers. Their skins gleamed oily black in
the glow of the lamp. The glare of the flames picked out the cords in
Adonis's neck. The night shifted restlessly about the hut.

They talked in short bursts. 'Get the grass planted then cattle',
'And milk', 'When did we last eat a fat steak?', 'Only a few chickens
left.'

Silence as they watched the orange-dotted blackness. The soft
breeze peeled off the top layer of ash exposing red embers that
glowed like molten lava below.

Romi spoke. 'Think of all the big ranchers and their fires near
here. I've seen some big fellows driving about. We're doing okay.'
He rubbed his blackened face. 'What I need is a girl and a football.'
Everybody laughed, reassured.

A gossamer layer of morning mist rose slowly up from the ground.
At first only the tops of the trees, leaves tinged pink in the early sun,
were visible. Rising on upwards, this soft pale veil divided the jungle
wall in two. In the upper half the treetops seemed to float on this
fine white gauze and appeared separate from the red earth and the
dark round trunks in the shady underworld below. The capuchin
monkeys were calling to each other, their throttling cries beginning
gently and then swelling to a throbbing chorus that crowded out
all other noise in a pulsating wave of sound, louder, quieter, on and
on. This was the magic hour. The heat was to come.

It was a Sunday. Mother Tana lit a candle and knelt in front of
her shrine. As she prayed over her rosary a shadow darkened the
china figure of the Virgin Mary and her baby Jesus. Adonis was still
asleep and Idenea not about. The boys and Valdo had biked to the
village the day before to play pool and drink. She worried about all
this drinking, the pinga was so cheap. She worried about everything:
money, food, life, their future in what she'd come to call their 'Insect

Hole'. Fortunately, Idenea was too far into her pregnancy to risk any excess of alcohol. She'd brought her up as a sensible girl, but she must, must, go to the big town for a check-up. Would she go? No, however much she nagged at her. *Tudo bem* was always the reply. Tana loved these private moments with her daughter, watching her stroke her belly and murmuring, 'You'll see *Mãe*, my baby will be so beautiful.'

Mother Tana, worrying away at her rosary beads, still hadn't noticed the Virgin Mary darken with shadow.

'*Bom Dia*.'

The brusque voice cut into her prayers. Still weak from malaria, she struggled to her feet to see the heavy form of Captain Dias from the Ministry leaning on a post right behind her.

'So, what are you all up to then, huh? Half-asleep? Don't you know there's work to do?'

He was wearing a camouflage-style shirt and cap. She remembered him well, the cross-eyed squint, hectoring voice and the sheer bulk of the man. Odd though, the army uniform, she thought.

Twenty yards behind was an open jeep with the driver leaning on the wheel. It was Juca again, the driver of Bébé's logging truck with his golden medallion swinging from his neck. He was chewing gum and must have turned off the engine and coasted the last few metres to allow Dias to surprise.

'So here I am. Me, Captain Dias. I've come to check on things as I said I would, remember?' He looked around him. 'Where are the others, your family?'

Adonis, disturbed by the loud voice, pushed through the mosquito-netted door of their bamboo-walled bedroom and stood beside his wife. He nervously wiped his brow with the back of one hand and put his other around Tana's waist.

'Good morning, Captain, good to see you. The boys are in the village,' he mumbled, half awake. 'It's Sunday.'

'I know that. Now, listen to me. Our projects are urgent. Remember how lucky you were to get one.' Captain Dias pushed in under the roof, his army shirt sticking darkly to his chest.

Idenea, hearing an unfamiliar voice, came over. A simple cotton slip plainly showed her rounded belly. Her hair hung in long unbrushed tresses.

'Baby, huh?' boomed Captain Dias, looking sideways at her through his squint. 'Well, well, more mouths to feed, better get on with it then, hadn't you? Now, Senhor Saladini, show me what you've all been up to, *tá bom*?' He pointed his forefinger at Adonis. 'My time is precious so let's get going. Vamos.'

Adonis sipped at his coffee and offered a tin mug to Dias who waved it away. Father and daughter showed the Captain around. The blackened branches still reeked of burn. They told of their difficulties and of the risk of malaria. Dias grunted as Idenea told how she had rushed to the village to find medicine. Adonis explained how they had done a deal for logs with a man called Bébé in the village.

'Good, good, selling logs, huh? I know him, he's a man of confidence.' Dias hauled his heavy body over a log.

Idenea resented the way he paraded about with his hands on his hips as if he owned the place. An hour later back in the hut Dias, panting and soaked with sweat, took off his forage cap revealing the chequered orange and black colour of his curly hair.

'Now pay attention, you Saladinis,' he began, 'this isn't enough, not nearly enough. You've been idle.' He jabbed a forefinger at the three of them. 'I want to see more clearing, more planting. The government has so generously provided this land. Get on with it. Why only two huts? There're several of you, aren't there? Build more. I want the place to look established, understood?' He poked his finger at each of them. Because of his squint, Idenea wasn't sure to whom he was speaking.

'Well, Senhor.' Adonis, humble as always, could not help saying Senhor. 'We believe we've done well, selling our timber and clearing and burning two hectares and me and my wife with malaria. It's hard work and life's expensive. Everything costs double or three times more. We're in debt to that man Bébé and it gets worse all the time and our money's nearly run out.' Exhausted by the effort of explaining so much, he paused for breath. 'And the land isn't much good either. Look at our maize, it's the first year and ought to be good but it isn't.'

Dias ignored the last statement.

'So, you owe Bébé money, do you, huh?' He clicked his tongue. 'That's your business. What I'm saying is that you haven't done enough.' He was watchful and ringed with trouble.

Dias faced Adonis abruptly. 'Where do you keep your land titles?'

Surprised by the sharpness of the demand, Adonis replied without thinking, his humble automatic response to authority taking over. 'In our store box under our bed.'

'Get them.'

Idenea felt a shiver go down her spine and cried out. 'Don't Father, don't give them to him.'

Dias's tone casual and patronising. 'How do you know what's good, you idiot young girl?'

'I know,' sticking to her reasoning, 'that those papers confirm our ownership. They give us rights. I've read them.'

'So you can read, can you? Yes, I remember you now, quite a little Miss Sharp, huh?'

Back to Adonis. 'Get them out old man or I'll make life difficult for you. I need to change something that will be better for us all. And hurry, I have to check on other settlers.'

'No, I won't,' Adonis said quietly, 'my daughter is right.' He smiled at Idenea with defiance in his eyes.

Dias grasped Adonis by his shirt and shoved him towards the inner bedroom. 'Get them.'

Idenea ran over and wrestled with Dias's arms. 'Leave my father alone, you bully!' she yelled. 'Can't you see he's weak from malaria. Come on, Romi, Chico, help me.' And she remembered they were far away.

Dias swung round and with all his weight propelled Idenea across the room. She tripped on a table leg and fell to the ground.

'The baby!' cried Mother Tana and rushed over.

'It's all right, Mother.' Idenea pushed herself up. And to Dias, 'Go away, you brute, leave us alone!'

Adonis stumbled into his bedroom, glanced back at Idenea and rolled his eyes as if to say what else could he do?

'Father, don't give them to him.' She looked around, searching for a weapon. Where were the boys' machetes? That would make the brute think.

Dias plucked the envelope with the land titles from Adonis's hand and slotted it into his shirt pocket. He elbowed past Mother Tana and Idenea.

'Now listen to me. Until you've done much more and I mean much, much more and I'll be the one to decide what that is, you don't get these back.' He spread his arm round the whole clearing. 'This place, here.' He gestured at the ground, 'is Me. So get on with it, make it look like you've been here a good six years, understood?'

'Give them back, you thief,' screamed Idenea. 'They belong to us.' Unable to fight, tears stung behind her eyes.

Ignoring her, Dias lumbered back to the jeep.

Idenea hugged one of the posts until a kick from her belly forced her to caress it with both hands. 'How can I fight with you inside me?'

Mother Tana knelt in front of her shrine, the candle still alight, and picking up her rosary mumbled, 'Debt, debt and more debt, titles gone, freedom gone.' Again and again.

Back at the Ministry of Agriculture and Land Reform in Porto Velho, Dias, the Captain or the Boss elbowed his way through the swing doors. Such was his hurry that one of the doors flew back and hit his shoulder.

'*Merda*,' he swore at the jab of pain.

He knew his desk would be piled up with reports about land. Who owned it, who didn't and what would he do? Sure enough, there they were with Urgent or Very Urgent stamped across them.

He switched on the fan. It rattled and swayed and with difficulty managed to move a small amount of muggy heat from one side of the small room to the other where it still remained muggy. He pushed past a couple of filing cabinets and edged his heavy frame behind his desk. No pictures hung on the grubby white walls.

How could he be expected to think straight in such heat? He was certain those bastard fascists of soldiers up the road had air conditioning cooling their smug faces. A big change was going to hit them very soon, he was sure of that. His bulky body writhed in irritation. He rubbed one hand over his crinkly hair, his fingers passing over dark yellow curls on one side of his head and then on into black curls on the other. An albino. His genes hadn't made up their minds.

Saladini he had written across the top file. Difficult family, especially the girl. After all the arguing with her, no wonder he was so late.

A brown envelope with Ministry of Agriculture in black letters on the front lay on his desk. That's odd, he thought as he ripped open the envelope. Out fell a thick document with a short note pinned to it.

> *Brasilia. Dear Friend, The big boys here are beginning to become excited about land in your area. I recommend you run through this Decree Law [enclosed] once again. Make sure you take full advantage of any opportunities.*[5]

There was no signature, but he recognised the hand-writing of Pedro, his friend from the old days when all had seemed possible. They had trained together in East Germany and even now after the '64 coup and the unassailable command of the Military, they, the old disciples, still quietly strove to keep the flame of the Cause alive. He picked up Decree Law 4505, the Statute of the Land, and breathed in satisfaction. Land reform. But reform wasn't good enough, it just played with the problem. Seizure, that was the way for the people.

Pedro had underlined, *'Promote social justice—redistribution of land—by confiscation for social interest'*.

He sat up straight, feeling much better, and scuffed at the dried mud on his army camouflage trousers that he wore to command respect. His imagination ran wild with excitement. At last, all that training might come to something and he was ready, always would be.

He had been christened Ananias Silenti Barbosa as had his father and grew up in a favela above Rio. At eighteen he'd won a scholarship to university in Rio. *Meu Deus*, how he'd struggled. Less than five percent of his year's intake could have been considered black or mulato. So, he took to dyeing his hair all one dark colour and wearing a woman's nylon stocking over his head at night to try and straighten out the frizz. Later, when he gave up trying to change his looks, he regretted the fool he'd been and how he'd betrayed the Cause.

He discovered Communism. He hung a portrait of Marx above his bed. He defied the police and during the notorious March of the Marbles was so badly hit on the side of his head by a police truncheon, that his left eye was permanently damaged leaving him with a squint and a walleye. He was thrown into gaol for several days without charge. He could only think of revolution.

Then the Military took over. Hopes dashed. There had been the tap on the shoulder and intense talk with a younger student. And to East Berlin. Why had he been chosen? Was it the colour of his skin and his simmering rage?

There, snow outside, in their dingy bedroom beneath a single bare light bulb and heating for one short hour, he and Pedro would argue late into the night.

'Who are you praying to?' Pedro would ask sarcastically when he heard mumbling in the cold shadow.

'To Marx. Oh, shut your stupid mouth, Pedro.' And he would pound the wall beside his bed with his fist.

On leaving, they were told they would be contacted for Work Opportunities back home. 'Be negative to cause unrest. Remember, you are the shield and the sword for the Cause, for World Socialism.' They were told to change their names. Ananias changed his last name to Dias.

He leant back in his chair. The fan blew hot air. He smiled. Yes, maybe now, at last, he could be the shield and the sword.

Two weeks after his return, the same young student tapped him on the shoulder. He was to join the Ministry of Agriculture in Rio.

Mercedes Batista, a woman clerk working in the archive department, placed a pile of folders on his desk. They were cases of small subsistence level farmers losing their land to neighbouring large landowners. Her father was one of them.

She had a tight sinewy body, danced in the samba school Portela, had naturally curly black hair and always a slash of red on her lips. She'd come to Rio to live in her aunt's two-roomed shack in a favela. She told how her father had been pushed out by force. As she raved about these injustices her nostrils flared.

'I'm all with you,' he would say.

He told her about the Cause. She taught him untiring aggression. They rarely laughed. Some of their friends considered them dangerous, others as true carriers of the torch.

When they married, she declared, 'I want lots of babies who think like we do.' They tried and failed and tried again. She had four miscarriages in two years. She resorted to Macumba with its dances and chanting. Even sacrificing chickens failed to produce the longed-for baby.

And then the Military began its purge. He had to keep moving further and further away to the west. She hated the heat and the insects. In the Mato Grosso there was no relief and in Rondônia it was even worse with the threat of malaria.

One day, quite suddenly, she announced that she was going back to Rio.

He was distraught. 'You can't leave me out here all alone.'

'Then, take me somewhere cooler and where we can have a real influence on the lives of poor people. Besides, we have no children to keep me here.'

Captain Dias sighed and opened the Saladini file. He had to deal with that one immediately.

'Food for baby, food for me,' Idenea chanted as she swung her hoe into the earth. The heat didn't bother her any more and to sweat she had to work hard.

Hardened blisters on her hands scraped her cheek as she brushed her hair back. She secretly admired the growing muscles on her arms and legs. She smiled to herself, 'I'll show those men'. Valdo liked them too and squeezed them when he wasn't away in the village drinking too much. Sometimes the boys called her to help with the heavy work, to hold or to pull on a rope.

Pregnancy increased her determination. Even after a swarm of green locusts had devoured every heavily-laden tomato plant, leaving her without a stalk or a single green leaf, she remained cheerful. She'd tried beating at them with her broom but there were just too many whirring and clinging into her hair with long spiky green legs. But her favourite papayas and watermelons were thriving.

During the rainy season from November to April, when mud prevented the entry of the timber trucks, they felled and sliced up the saleable trees ready for collection. The younger men had quickly recovered from their first bouts of malaria and found renewed energy in the cooler, damp weather.

Adonis had argued in favour of buying a few head of cattle, a milk cow or two and some pigs. Fresh meat, fresh milk for us and the baby, he'd insisted. That will do them good and fight malaria so they'd been told.

'Where's the money coming from?' fussed Mother Tana. 'How much do we owe that rascal Bébé?'

Idenea spent a full day adding and subtracting. Her figures showed that they owed more than two months' log value.

Romi and Bosco on mule and bicycle drove in eight head of cattle: two mottled brown cows, three white bullocks and three white heifers. On the back of the mule tied into a sack with only their heads sticking out squealed four black piglets. They'd done a deal with Bébé and Mr Madeira against future log supplies.

'It took us two days to drive them up the track,' they announced proudly.

Bolo chased the cattle. The pigs, with grunts, saw him off, tail between his legs. The mule hated the pigs and sidled up with the cattle. There was plenty to eat for the cattle that first year, the grass sprouting green in the ash.

The family celebrated their arrival with pinga and walked around the hastily erected pen of wooden stakes, staring with pride at the thin bony animals and toasted, 'To a big ranch. To fresh meat. Fine looking, aren't they?'

But their debt was greater than ever. Idenea knew it, Tana knew it. The men hated discussing proof of ownership and facing up to the truth that they owed more than they had in the whole world.

One night after a log collection Mother Tana said, 'We're trapped, aren't we?'

Adonis sighed and struck his forehead, 'Come on, Mother, we're alive.' Nobody else said a word.

Idenea felt the stabbing pain of the first contraction as her womb extended and started to expel the baby inside her.

'*Mãe*,' she cried running over to Mother Tana. 'It's coming, look.' She pulled up her shirt for her mother to feel. Her belly had changed shape.

'*Boba*, silly girl,' Mother Tana scolded, 'you should've gone for a check-up long ago as I said. Come on, let's get some things together. It's your first so it'll be slow. We'll take the mule and cart and then the bus. I had you in a hospital, safe and sound and that's where you should be right now.'

'No, no, I'm staying here. I want my baby in the jungle with the trees all about me and the monkeys crying, not in a grubby bed in a dirty clinic. I'm strong, just help me, *Mãe, tá bom*?' She gasped and clutched at her stomach. Mother Tana called her irresponsible but Idenea wasn't listening and by the time the next contraction came, nobody was going to persuade her to travel a hundred and fifty kilometres over potholes and ruts.

'All I have is a small bottle of disinfectant,' said Mother Tana, crossly. 'I'll need hot water so over here in our bed, not in your hut.'

'No, I can sit back in a chair or lie on the table.' Idenea giggled enthusiastically. 'It will come easily, I know you will, my little Amazon baby. No, no I'll lie in a hammock.'

By late afternoon, at that magic hour when the sun has lost its heat and lights up the jungle in amber yellow and the call of the birds has begun to change, Idenea was having contractions every half-hour. She groaned at the unexpected pain as each one wrestled with her insides and then let her be for a time, only to gather more power for the next. In a tight semicircle around her the men watched, their eyes on her body and their ears ready for every groan. They sang folk songs from the south. Even Bosco joined in. Valdo gently swayed her hammock to and fro.

Mother Tana shooed the men away. Disappointed they shuffled off into the darkness. 'You, Valdo, stay here with your wife. Adonis, go to bed.'

The single flame of the kerosene lamp made unsteady brown shadows in the gloom. The pots and pans glinted with faint reflections. Idenea's face shone sweat from pain and effort. She called on the Virgin Mary in the corner to help. She pushed violently at her belly.

'Come on, come on, my little one, get moving' and 'Dear sweet Jesus, make it all right, please, please no trouble. I'm a good girl, I promise you I really am.'

'I'm not having my baby in a hammock.' She clambered naked onto the table. Her waters burst as she legged up and streamed onto the earthen floor.

There was no moon just the stars pin-pricking the black above. The single tiny kerosene flame, swaying from side to side in the feathery breeze, cast a feeble orange glow over the twenty-year old girl lying on a table. She spread her legs and placed the back of her heels against the sides of the table and thus spread-eagled she wedged herself. Valdo splashed water on her forehead.

The dull light of early dawn painted the hut and the figures inside a greyish brown. The pain was so constant now that she

101

had become accustomed to it, as if she didn't exist away from it. She moaned softly to herself and to the baby inside her. 'Come on! Come on!'

The sun rose and the midday heat oppressed the clamour of the jungle into silence. Only the dry leaves in the tops of the trees whispered and rustled. At that hour, in that heat, when all physical effort seemed impossible, Idenea pushed her baby out. She cried out as she did so. She couldn't help it. A long high-pitched scream, not just rent from her by the sharp pain but from triumph and for joy. Her cry spread around the clearing and into the trees, drowning all other sound. The capuchins snapped their mouths shut, stopped fidgeting for a moment and peered down at the two thatched huts.

She smiled ecstatically as she took the sticky purple ball in her arms. She touched the umbilical cord that was still part of her and slipped her thumb and forefinger along the slime and blood up to her baby's stomach.

'Valdo, quick, get me that sharp knife. Put it into the fire and wash it.' He did as she commanded. 'That's it, good. Now you hold the baby and I'll cut.' She gripped the umbilical and with the hot knife sliced it close to the baby's belly.

Mother Tana looked at her naked smiling daughter prostrate on the table, her wet baby in her arms, her thighs blotched with blood with the umbilical hanging down between them and thought to herself, 'You're a strong one my girl, aren't you? Much more than me. So God be thanked that he made you so.'

When the afterbirth finally came out, Mother Tana threw it outside where it landed in a shiny pink lump close to the side of the hut. Minutes later yellow and white butterflies were all over it, their wings fluttering up and down, settling still for a moment and then up again, brilliant against the red earth. Little Amazonas, Zoni for short, as his mother had already nicknamed him, was as alive as the butterflies dancing on the wet placenta.

When Mother Tana and Adonis fell to malaria again, already weak, they took longer to recover. Adonis thought he would die. Idenea heard them mumbling incomprehensible words, twisting their heads from side to side. She shook them till they regained consciousness.

Using some of their precious savings, they made the four-day round trip to see a doctor in the big town.

'I don't guarantee your life if you catch this sort again,' he warned, 'You've got the dangerous Plasmodium Falciporum. Spray the inside of your hut and put up netting and stay indoors in the early morning and late afternoon.'

'We do, we do,' wailed Mother Tana.

'Well, try these pills as well then and drink milk, eat fresh food and citrus fruit, *tá bom*?' He patted them kindly on the shoulder and showed them out.

'Next please.' He looked glumly at the line of people sitting on the two long benches and crouched against the wall. He frowned. Some were shivering, others showed open sores as big as your hand.

The queue never ended, day in, day out.

But the mosquitoes were everywhere, particularly at night and out of the sunlight when egg-laden females succeeded in penetrating the poison-free margin of the sprayed netting nailed up at the doctor's suggestion. Mother Tana and Adonis were unlucky. They collapsed in trembling fits of hot and cold onto their sweat-soaked bed. This third attack came when Zoni was about a year old. Both fell ill together again.

Idenea did her best for them. Outside, she swore at the sky, at the trees, the rain, even at the monkeys. Inside, her parents mumbled in delirium. She knelt in front of the statue of the Virgin Mary. 'Dear Mary, look after my parents. Please save them.'

One morning as the cries of the animals and birds intensified and the family were eating breakfast of maize bread, eggs, rice and dried fat, Mother Tana said sharply, 'We're going back south, if not we die. Adonis that means you and me.' Lines of weariness around her eyes and mouth, her breasts weighing down in little hammocks. 'And you Idenea, don't try to change my mind. We're too old for this struggle.' Her lips trembled. 'And leaving my only grandchild...'

Three days later the family plus Zoni and Bolo stood outside Bébé's bar waiting for the daily bus to Porto Velho. The buses were old. Mercedes engines kept them going. Hard wooden seats had replaced softer, padded ones. Passengers included chickens, pigs, goats, sheep and the occasional parrot or macaw. The drivers were always in a hurry trying to make up for the delays caused by breakdowns, floods and mud.

Daily was ambitious. Often no bus might come along for days and then two could arrive together, sometimes one towing the other.

The bus that picked up the Saladinis had a large celestial comet with a line of golden stars streaming out behind and the name COMETA painted along both sides. Dents and scratches had obliterated many of the stars. Mother Tana and Adonis kissed and hugged their children and cousins before clambering aboard and squeezing onto the furthest back bench, wedged in beside a couple of chickens in a bamboo cage. The smell of human sweat and fresh animal dung hung heavy inside. Only Bosco remained dry-eyed. The others wept.

The driver was a short man. Black curly hair poked out of his open shirt and over his ample belly. A toothpick stuck out from each side of his mouth and jerked up and down when he spoke.

'Jump in, my children. I'm Paulo and we're late and my woman's waiting for me. Vamos.' His eyes flashed across the rear-view mirror. Sweat rolled down his forehead. Loud pop music interrupted by football results blared out from a tiny radio swinging from the rear-view mirror just above his head. A small metal cross dangled beside it.

The Saladini children were left wiping their eyes in a spray of gravel as the bus accelerated away. Idenea continued to wave Zoni's hand at the cloud of dust.

Romi turned to her. 'I know what you're thinking, Idi. Who will be the boss now? Me, I suppose?'

Bosco sniggered. 'With no titles there's nothing to be boss of. Anyhow I'm the oldest and the most experienced.'

Romi retorted sharply, 'I'm the elder son and the title is in Father's name.' His eyes followed the heavy limping gait of his cousin. 'Come on, Bosco, you work well, we all work well together in spite of our quarrels. Don't let's start another one now.'

'Yes,' Chico joined in, 'we need all the hands we've got to get those titles back.'

Bosco beckoned towards the bar. 'Come on, Valdo, let's have a drink.'

The road ran close to the Madeira river that flowed to Porto Velho and eventually north into the Amazon. Bridges, built over seventy years ago to carry steam locomotives, now carried road traffic. Wooden planks ran parallel, separated at wheel width running approximately where the old steel rails had previously lain.

Paulo enjoyed timing each trip. When he beat his own record, he awarded himself an extra beer. Depending on the rain, the surface of the road changed by the day so he could never be sure.

Gripping the wildly gyrating steering wheel he pulled himself up out of his seat half standing, half crouching, by balancing himself with his left foot under the clutch pedal and with his right foot on the accelerator. His arms bent at the elbow and his backside projecting backwards as if standing up in the stirrups of a cantering horse, he rode the bus, glaring fiercely through the windscreen as the front wheels sank and crashed into the first hole. As the wheels leapt out of the last pothole, the whole bus shuddering from end to end he yelled, 'Yee hah! Ride him Cowboy! Yahoooh...' The toothpicks jerked up and down between his teeth.

Some passengers shouted, 'Yee haaah' in chorus with him. The road straightened out and headed towards one of the longer bridges. Paulo knew that this bridge marked the halfway point. A glance at his watch pleased him.

About thirty metres over he saw a truck approaching from the other end. He braked quickly to judge who was closer to the middle, so who would cross first. The balloon of dust that had boiled behind carried on and covered the cab, blinding Paulo's vision in a swirling cloud. Thinking of a possible record time he drove on guiding his wheels carefully on the runner planks. Twenty metres through the dust cloud, he realised the oncoming truck was much closer to the middle than he was. He swore. It was up to him to back off.

He rammed the gear into reverse. The wheels careered off the runner planks. Now, only the cross-timbers supported all four wheels. Two metres below the river. His left-hand side wheels were only centimetres from the edge of the bridge.

The passengers sat in tense silence. Mother Tana and Adonis couldn't see out either side and were unaware of any danger.

Paulo revved the engine and slipped the clutch to secure a steady grip. An unexpected jerk caused his right foot to slam down onto the accelerator. This extra surge of power flipped the wheels into a violent spin. The crossbeams underneath snapped. As the first one broke, the spinning wheels sought to climb up onto the next and then the next as each one broke one after the other, creating a hole as big as the back of the bus. Paulo lifted his foot off the accelerator. The bus began to slip backwards, breaking the remaining beams one after the other like match sticks.

'What's up?' a voice cried out. Another, 'Oh dear sweet Jesus.'

For a few seconds the bus see-sawed slowly back and forth. Someone moved or the fuel sloshed to one side. With a crash of rendering wood, the bus plunged backwards into the water, its rear half disappearing below the surface, before bumping to rest on the river bed. Brown wavelets covered the painted orange comet. The front wheels hit resistance in the upper timbers holding the bus close to the vertical. The rear wheels, with the engine still in gear, churned the water into a muddy froth.

Screaming, the passengers fell backwards on top of each other. Paulo turned off the engine. The thrashing of the wheels quietened.

'Get out quick. God help us. Children, where are you?'

Mother Tana and Adonis tried to stand up, but tumbling bodies knocked them down. All their strength had drained away weeks before in malarial sweat. More people fell down kicking and lunging on top of them.

Paulo managed to pull a couple out. Those higher up in the bus jumped into the river and swam to the bank. Others escaped through the windows. Two small children unable to swim were swept down river. Piranhas attacked their bodies so fiercely their parents had to look hard at their chewed-up faces to identify them. Five bodies bobbed and rolled on the surface at the back of the bus. Beside them floated half-dead chickens flapping weakly. A goat floundered about snorting brown water out of its nose.

Idenea wanted Zoni home in bed before dark. Still wet eyed, she'd bought a cheap plastic toy for him and a comb for herself in the bar. How was she going to look after her hair now that her mother was gone?

'Get on your bikes,' she said flatly to the others and tied Bolo to the back rail of the cart and jumped up. 'It will be dark if we don't hurry.'

All nodded except Bosco who tugged at Valdo's arm. 'We're staying for a drink, aren't we, Valdo?'

Idenea, with the rawhide reins in her hands. 'I'm your wife, Valdo, remember. You're supposed to be with me.'

Valdo smiled weakly, raised his hand in salute and then slipped through the beaded curtain of the bar, grumbling that they didn't come there very often.

'We'll be back tomorrow,' Bosco called out, 'and remember you lot, I'm the Boss from now on.'

Romi and Idenea walked and biked the fifteen kilometres at the mule's pace.

Romi said, 'The titles are in Father's name, so logically we, his three children, take over from him, right? Bosco's a bastard for trying to challenge us.'

'But how do we get our titles back from that squint-eyed captain?'

No more talk, they had the ruts to negotiate, their wheels wobbling from side to side. Bolo trotted under the cart out of the sun. They shouted greetings to the other settlers as they hurried past.

Arriving in the deserted clearing was eerie. They had never left it on its own before. There was no smoke from the cooking fire. Zoni's tame monkey jumped off its pedestal and ran in circles as if relieved that no hawk had grabbed it.

Zoni started to whimper. Romi leant his bike against a post. Idenea heated up some rice and beans left by her mother. But there was an emptiness to the familiar setting, no Father to keep their spirits up, no Mother Tana to warn of unwise dealings. As she fell asleep that night, holding her baby's hand, she knew she was alone and now the lynch pin of the family.

'Romi! Romi! Romeeee! Ideneaaaah...Cheeco!'

Valdo was pushing his bike up the track with violent jerks, his cries piercing the pink of early dawn. 'There's been a terrible accident.' He ran to the hut.

Idenea, used to Valdo's cries of panic at anything unusual, said with a shrug of her shoulders, 'Go on then, what's happened this time?'

'They're dead. Tana and Adonis are dead. In the bus. I've seen their bodies. Come quick!' He dropped down onto a bench and started to retch and sob.

'Quick. Quick.'

When the bodies of Mother Tana and Adonis had arrived at Bébé's bar the evening before, Juliana, Bébé's wife, had laid them out side by side on a table in a nearby hut. She lit four candles and placed one at the head and one at the feet of each body. In the morning she put new candles, crossed herself and whispered a prayer. Jim Bladel, the missionary from the south Carolina Baptist Fellowship came across and said how sorry he was. The news had spread fast. Jim was seated beside the bodies when Idenea and her brothers rushed in.

Nothing could prepare them for the sight of their parents stretched out on a table, their faces white, lips purple, hands stiff, their clothes rigid from the water.

Juliana waited half an hour before saying softly, 'You have to bury them today. The heat. And you ought to tell the police and get a death certificate.'

'What police? What certificate?' Romi cried out between stifled sobs. 'There aren't any.'

Idenea held her father's skinny wrist and her mother's claw of a hand and through uncontrollable weeping, 'I'm not having them buried here. They come back with us, to be beside us always.' She rubbed her face on her t-shirt sleeve. 'We need a priest.' Little Zoni was pulling at her legs and yelling.

'I can do you a proper Christian burial,' offered Jim Bladel. 'I'll be your priest.' They had no choice. Jim had arrived two years before with enough money to build a small chapel and a hut for himself. His job was to persuade and baptize souls into his church. He was a tall gangly man with close-cropped hair and strode busily about the village in a clean white shirt. He would be away for days on end looking, as he would say, for people to save for God. When he succeeded, his bank balance grew.

Six hours later, under the chatter of a flight of green parrots, the bodies of Mother Tana and Adonis were lowered side by side into a single grave thirty metres from the main hut. Romi and Chico had hacked through the volcanic shale beneath the six inches of topsoil. Romi had never dug so deep before, only tilled and scraped away at the top to plant maize and tomatoes.

Jim Bladel read the burial service in Portuguese in a broad southern American twang, out of place and incomprehensible to the listeners, their heads drooped over the grave looking down at the two bodies still dressed in the clothes in which they had died. There hadn't been time to knock up any coffins. Even Bosco wept as Jim Bladel said, 'Earth to earth'. Idenea had wrapped the heads of her parents in clean cloths. They all helped to shovel the gravel into the grave.

'I wish we had one of our own priests,' Chico said under his breath.

'I'm here for you,' replied Jim in his slow drawl. 'It's God's calling, life-fulfilling. Call in at my blessed chapel in the village. You can't miss our smart yellow hut with our message that God is always with you written over the door. I'm here to show people the way'

Idenea watched him as he spoke, intrigued by his accent and good intentions.

Romi and Chico hammered together a wooden cross. Idenea painted Adonis on the right-hand side and Neapolitana on the left and Saladini 1901 - 1966 on the vertical. Juliana and Jim Bladel stayed overnight. Nobody spoke much at dinner. Idenea tried lighting a candle on the grave but the wind blew it out. Juliana cuddled and joked with Zoni. 'Be a good boy or the monkeys will get you.' He squirmed on her lap.

Idenea and Valdo built a bamboo play-pen for Zoni inside the main hut.

'You're too big now for Mama to carry all the time, my little Baba, so be a good boy and play in there while Mama works nearby, otherwise Mama will be cross.' She tickled him till he laughed.

On that first Saturday after the burial, the tone of conversation around the midday table was uneasy. The pinga bottle was passing round when Valdo started the trouble.

'I want money to go to the bar, to get away. Hand over some cash, Idenea. Don't be so mean. You'll come with me won't you, Bosco?'

'She'll only hand out cash when I say so,' interrupted Romi, 'and that's when we fully know our money situation, debts and all.'

'Who are you to decide?' Bosco blurted out as he shovelled rice and beans into his mouth, chewing and pointing with his fork. 'I've had enough of you and your big ways.'

Romi had been anticipating this challenge for several days. At Idenea's suggestion he had taken to sitting at the head of the table in his father's old place.

'Bosco. You may be the oldest here but we three children inherit the titles to this land, and I'm the eldest of the three so I will be in charge. You came up with us to escape the south, right Chico, right

Carlito?' Romi folded his scabbed-covered fingers into a double-handed fist under his chin and looked directly at Bosco. 'If you don't like it here you can always leave.'

Bosco leapt to his feet, his eyes shifting from one to the other. 'I have more farming experience than the lot of you put together. Your father said I was to teach you how to sow and look after animals, remember? So I'm the natural boss.' He looked around for approval, his angelic face twisted in fury. He picked up a table knife and shook it at Romi.

'Take us or leave us,' countered Romi, 'and put that knife down.'

The others, with the exception of Valdo, nodded. He didn't like quarrels, especially with Bosco who was a good drinking companion, when he wasn't leering at his wife.

'Valdo,' Idenea snapped at him. 'You are part of the family and my husband so support us.'

Valdo looked away.

Bosco's voice rose. 'I'll settle this now.' He ran to his clothes box underneath his hammock and flung up the lid. He scuffed about inside. 'Where is it? This will sort you lot out.' He looked back at them seated around the table, at first with a wild grin of triumph and then with acute chagrin.

'If it's our pistol you're looking for?' Romi's voice was steady. 'I've put it in a safe place.'

Bosco spun round, ran and stumbled across the hut floor, picked up a table knife and threw himself at Romi, one arm around his neck and the other jabbing with the knife at Romi's chest cutting the surface of the skin. They fell to the floor kicking and rolling from side to side.

Chico sprang to his brother's help, pulling at Bosco's arm and shouting, 'There is no law here. We have to live together, so for God's sake stop it.'

Held firm by the two brothers, his arms pinned into the small of his back, Bosco spat out the words, 'I'll leave this *merda*. I'll make money with rubber, you'll see.'

Romi's t-shirt reddened with blood. Carlito O Lentão just stared. Idenea grasped Zoni to her chest and moved to one side.

'You're behind all this you *puta*, Idenea!' yelled Bosco, 'only you knew where I kept that gun, you spying about all day. I'll have you one day.' With a final curse he relaxed his muscles. The brothers let him go.

'Let's try and work something out.' Romi spoke in short gasps, trying to recover his normal quiet manner.

Bosco opened his arms as if to embrace all his efforts of the past months. He started packing a bag. 'Valdo,' he said, 'let's just go to the village for a drink.'

'Come on, Bosquinho,' Romi said, still breathless. 'Oh, all right. Idenea find some money for them, it's Saturday after all. Let's talk things over again in a few days.' He sat down with a sigh. 'I've had enough of quarrelling.'

Bosco fetched his bike, his bag tied on the back. Valdo followed behind. They paused in front of the hut.

'Romi,' he called, 'sorry for the fight, I lost my temper. You're right, families must stick together. I'm going to go tapping latex with Juca. Valdo's coming to help me talk to Bébé and arrange things, aren't you, Valdo?'

Valdo raised his eyebrows in surprise. Weren't they going just for a drink? 'Give us enough cash for a beer or two, Idenea, won't you?' he asked sheepishly.

Coming up behind her brother, Idenea said quietly, 'I don't believe Bosco is sorry at all. He's got some scheme cooking with that truck driver, Juca.' She hadn't been into her parents' room since the burial. She knelt down and pulled out the tin money box from under Tana's side of the bed.

'There's practically nothing here,' she cried out in surprise.

Jumping up, she ran forward shaking the few notes and coins in the bottom of the tin. 'There's only half the last timber delivery. Somebody's been in and robbed us.' She looked accusingly at Bosco and shouted, 'You again. Give it back, you thief.'

Romi and Chico rose angrily to their feet. Romi hissed painfully through closed teeth. 'We don't want another fight, we've had enough. If it's you, Bosco, give it back now.'

Bosco pulled the long dagger from his belt that he used to cut meat and trailing creepers. He pointed it at Romi and let his bicycle clatter to the ground, wheels spinning, his voice strident. 'Fuck you! *Vai tomar no cu!*[7] Touch me and I use this. I swear by God I will.'

The brothers hesitated. Idenea tried to catch Valdo's attention but he avoided her eyes and stayed beside Bosco's bicycle.

'Go and cool off in the village, Bosco,' Romi said with a resigned shrug and headed back to the hut. 'As for you, Valdo, decide what it is you want.'

Bosco and Valdo pedalled away down the track and were soon dwarfed by the trees.

Idenea put her hand on her brother's shoulder. 'Where did you put our pistol, Romi?'

'I buried it at one end of Father and Mother's grave but I can't be sure that nobody saw me.'

'Good thinking.' She gripped his arm. 'It's up to you and me now, isn't it?'

Romi nodded. 'We can't go back. But how are you going to manage Valdo?'

'It's his drinking I can't handle.' She sighed. 'But it's Bosco, I don't trust him. Taking money is bad enough, trying to be the Boss is worse. Why does he say he'll come back? I'm sure there's something going on.' She drew a half circle with her big toe in the red earth and finished it as a question mark.

Of a sudden, a rough whirring noise. A single engine monoplane only twenty or thirty metres above tree level flew straight towards them. It banked sideways, the engine straining in a steep curve. As quickly as it came it disappeared over the top edge of the jungle before returning, only this time so low that the faces of the pilot and passenger were visible.

Idenea waved Zoni's hand at the plane as it rose up over the trees for the second time.

'Look, Zoni, see the two men in the plane. They're looking at us.'

---

7 Vai tomar no cu; Go get buggered.

And it was gone, the noise of the engine sucked into the cushion of damp leaves.

'Who was that?' said Romi, dazed.

Idenea shook her head again and stared after the sound of the engine. 'There you are, something else we don't know.'

Late that night in Bébé's bar, four men sat on rough wooden stools. A single candle flickered amongst the empty beer bottles and cigarette ends. A couple of truck drivers were playing pool in the lower part of the room. A bare bulb covered in fly droppings lit their game. Round balls of latex stacked in one corner. Mosquitoes whined around the men's bare skin. Large beetles, disorientated by the light, flew from one side of the room to the other bumping into the legs of a chair or table before falling to the floor on their backs. Unable to fly, their black hairy legs waved feebly in the air. Tiny red parasites covered their bodies. The players cracked them under their feet. Outside in the dark a small generator puttered away.

Valdo was slumped over the end of the bar, muttering to himself and shivering with malaria. Bosco and Juca sat on stools, their hands around bottles of beer held between their thighs. Bosco was red with mud. He hadn't washed since the fight with Romi earlier that day.

Juca wore clean jeans and a bright blue open neck shirt. His golden chain hung around his neck. His black hair, sleek from a shower, stuck flat to his skull. On his feet were shiny black raised-heel loafers. This slick dressing belied that he was a man of the forest, a rubber tapper. The balls of latex in the corner were his. He walked far into the jungle identifying wild rubber trees and tapping into them with V shaped cuts that drained the white sticky gum into small tin cups strapped to the trunk. He would return three to four days later to collect. He smoked the raw latex over a fire trenched into the ground, folding and pulling the rubbery substance around a wooden pole until it formed and solidified into a ball the size of a ship's buoy. He worked alone, spotting signs of snakes, jaguar and deer. He recognised the tell-tale marks of an Indian tribe that lived beside an uncharted river. Occasionally he saw an Indian. He never bothered them and they ignored him. Sometimes a collecting cup went missing and he liked to think of it being used as a drinking mug deep in the forest. He never told anyone.

Born in the territory, a rarity amongst so many immigrants, Juca had Indian blood mixed with black and European from earlier migrations that had given him a mahogany skin with little body hair except on his head. Some people called him *Bugre*, Indian. He could disappear without trace within a hundred metres of Bébé's bar. When he smiled, and he smiled often, two lines of dark empty gums split behind his lips. Sucking raw sugar cane had removed his front teeth leaving his eye teeth protruding like small fangs. He worked on and off for Bébé, tapping rubber and collecting logs. He moved restlessly about with no particular base. Home was the hammock he carried on his back. That had changed when Captain Dias told him that he needed men of the earth like him to colonise this great territory.

'Look here,' Captain Dias had said, 'I'll put jobs your way from time to time. Check out our projects, talk to people and that sort of thing, *tá bom*? Maybe I get you some land one day?'

'Land of my own? *Tudo bem*, Boss.' Juca had replied, flattered and calling him Boss for the first time.

'But that's just between me and you, right?' Dias had jabbed his forefinger at Juca's chest. 'Tell anyone and I'll drop you.'

Bébé sat behind the bar facing Bosco and Juca, his peaked cap pushed back over his head. Smoke from three cigarettes curled upwards. The talk was of land. 'I own land; I've got cattle; I'm a man'.

Tonight's talk was of the Saladini's fazenda.

Bébé spoke quietly as if he was afraid someone might overhear. 'So now with the parents gone, that plot's up for grabs, eh? What about squatter rights?' He looked at Juca. 'It could be a good opportunity. There're big buyers around here so we've got to move quick. You could be useful, Bosco. You're always saying how hard you work and that you don't get enough.'

Bébé breathed in heavily. 'Why they stay on beats me. They're just coffee pickers from the south, not jungle men like us. We've got to destroy their will to stay before somebody else does.'

'It's that girl, Idenea.' Bosco puffed smoke at the ceiling. 'Like I told you, Juca, she's the problem. She believes in what they're doing like her father. She even called her kid Amazonas. But I'm sure her two brothers don't have their hearts in it. Not like me.'

He turned towards the mumbling figure of Valdo. 'And that's her useless husband. She should've been mine, not his.'

Bébé chuckled knowingly. 'Their land isn't much good, is it? But then land is always land, isn't it?'

'Not good?' Bosco said. 'What the fuck d'you mean? It's from the Government. It must be good. Why get us all the way up here if it's shit?'

'Forget that, Bosco. You don't think they've surveyed every square metre, do you? Nobody knows what's good and what's bad except those who work on it, right Juca?'

Juca nodded. He blew smoke through his toothless gums. 'You'll have to scare them out though. You can't starve them, they already grow enough to eat, pretty good really, considering.'

Bébé pushed at his cap. 'Yes, Bosco, you're in there with them. Why don't you put pressure on them?'

'Maybe I am, maybe not.' Bosco kicked at the bar.

'Carmen.' Bébé called over his shoulder. A girl in her late teens pushed through the beaded curtain from the back.

'Yes, Father?'

Maria Carmen, like her mother Juliana, had a face akin to an Indian, unlike the narrower features of her father. She wore her short black hair gripped to her head with shiny white plastic combs. She smiled shyly at Juca. She knew him from his many visits and looked forward to them. Juca, empty-gummed, smiled back.

'Carmen, be a good daughter,' Bébé ordered sharply, 'Fetch me the Saladini account. Quick, off you go.'

Minutes later. 'Look at that, so help me God. They owe me four months log delivery. That's more than the land's worth. Even more now without titles. The Boss did well.'

116

'Boss?' Bosco alert as ever.

Juca's hand tightened around his glass. His flirtatious smile at Carmen fading. So, here's another one with the Boss.

Bébé coughed. 'Captain Dias.' He studied the Saladini's account with exaggerated attention.

'It was Dias who stole our titles,' Bosco said, eyeing Bébé. 'That's who you mean, isn't it? He said we had to make our land look more established like we'd been there seven years. *Merda*, we've worked like dogs.'

Bébé and Juca exchanged glances. Bébé faked a yawn. 'It's late now. But I say we carry on with the logging, start a rubber trail through their plot. Juca, you take Bosco with you. This could be something to work for together, eh boys? Bosco, you could help, don't you see? It'll take time. At least that's on our side. I'll keep the accounts.' He belched loudly and slapped his stomach. 'Bed now you lot.' He pointed at Valdo. 'And him? I'd get rid of him, Bosco, if I was you. Send him back south.'

Outside in the branches of the overhanging tree, a colony of golden-backed orioles squabbled together, tight in their lozenge-shaped nests, confident that the human presence would protect them from raiding monkeys and toucans.

Bosco humped Valdo onto a plank of a bunk out the back. Staggering to his feet, Valdo vomited over the floor and over Bosco's shirt.

Bosco peeled off his shirt in disgust. 'You stupid coconut!'

Bosco lay down on a straw mattress next to the retching Valdo, his head buzzing. If only he could force those two shits of brothers and this drunken idiot Valdo to leave, then he'd try and convince Idenea he was the best to look after her.

Get the titles into his name. Heh, heh, come to think of it no need to do that, same family name. He'd have Idenea for himself and the land. Images of Idenea naked, washing herself in the jungle stream before his eyes. The force of his ejaculation convinced him of success.

Frogs croaked from the jungle edge that reared up in black shadow a few metres away.

Juca lay folded down in the length of his hammock, his eyes wide open. What if Dias really did get him some land? Maybe the Saladini's if only they would leave? Or, he could squat and claim for himself. Take Carmen with him. He saw himself riding amongst his own cattle and there was Carmen smiling up at him with their baby in her arms. Land and a girl. That could be him one day.

Bébé, lying beside Juliana inside their mosquito net, lay staring up at the rafters. More land would give him status and wealth. He had to get rid of those Saladinis. Only four of them left. Why should Dias have given a Government grant on troubled land? It had to be all right.

The next morning, Bosco took Valdo to the clinic in the big town and fixed him up with a job at the sawmill where he and Juca delivered their logs. 'Here's work and money for you and less malaria, right? I'll watch out for you on the farm, you can trust me.'

Valdo, through yellow eyes, smiled weakly. Bosco would try to get her, the bastard. Thank God Romi and Chico were there to watch over her. 'Respect her, Bosco, she's my wife. Leave her alone or by God I'll, I'll...'

'Of course. Sure thing.' Bosco smiled his angel's smile and slapped him on the back.

A year on.

Idenea stood in front of the thatched hut she now proudly called her home. She held the hand of her eighteen-month-old baby boy, Zoni. In red plastic sandals, he was learning to walk. Close by, in opposite directions, marched two columns of black leaf-cutter ants. There was a business-like manner about these columns, one moved clumsily with the weight of a leaf larger than itself, the other swift and free. Little Zoni watched them intently, eyes down, treading warily. He knew what could happen if he broke their trail, not as bad as the tiny hot-biting red ants but still nasty.

'Mama. *Formiga*...'

'Leave the ants, *Querido*, or they'll bite you.' She lifted him up and hugged him. He wriggled.

Formiga, after Mama, was his first word. She had already started to teach him to count, numbering the parrots as they flew over and reciting the alphabet picking out objects, A for *Árvore*, B for *Bolo*.

'You'll be the best-educated boy in all the Amazon, my darling Baba. You'll see if Mama doesn't make you so.'

She played games, running around the yard, splashing in the stream pretending to be a piranha. Bare armed, clad in a simple white t-shirt with a grass-coloured cotton skirt and rubber flip-flops, she had grown accustomed to the constant insect attacks. She still wore her hair long. With less physical work to do now she had Zoni to care for, she sometimes toyed about with her hair, up and down, plaited or turban shaped studying the result in her tiny mirror. She'd call out, 'Isn't Mama fine today?' He was more interested in chasing beetles with a stick or playing with his pet monkey.

Her eyes followed the two tracks that led out of the yard through the rough jumble of twisted and half-burnt branches. Purple flowering bougainvillea climbed up the side of the main hut, its walls of split canes lashed together with creepers and open squares for windows, white with netting. The jungle was a good seventy metres away and their clearing big enough for eight football pitches.

With the two milking cows and half a dozen skinny bullocks came extra chores, daily milking and constant fencing work. Fear of another visit by Captain Dias and the desire to have their land titles back drove them on. The yard around the huts was bigger and with daily sweeping she could walk about in her flip-flops without cutting her legs or brushing against a poisonous caterpillar. At night though, the clouds of mosquitoes forced them to wear clothes and hide behind mosquito netting or within the smoke radius of their fire. To her surprise neither she nor Zoni had caught malaria, unlike the others.

'Come on, Zoninho, let's see how the flowers are. We'll do drawing today, *tá bom*.' She led him towards the cross that marked her parents' grave. Several bright red flowers grew beside it. 'Look,

Father, look what we've done. It's yours as well. Aren't we clever?' She put her hand on the cross. 'Look Zoni, red for love.'

From habit she glanced towards the other end of the grave where she knew Romi had hidden the ·38 Taurus revolver.

She sniffed Zoni's hair and nibbled a chubby arm. His round face topped by dark brown hair was like his father's. He stretched his arm impatiently towards his monkey as it pranced about pulling at its tethering cord.

'Shoo off, silly monkey,' she said, 'it's lesson time not monkey time.'

Zoni grabbed a wax crayon and drew a wobbly circle. She patted him on the head. There were moments when time rushed past, so new was every experience, others when time stood still in the trembling heat as before a rain storm. She sighed, proud of what they had built with their own hands. Pretty good really, she thought. Then as quickly as those thoughts had come, sadness drove them away. She slapped her forehead in desperation. And the debt.

After lunch, lying in her hammock while Zoni slept, she was looking forward to writing up her diary in the notebook her grandmother had given her. A pile of old comics and cheap fashion magazines that she'd picked up in the village lay in one corner. She hadn't looked at them for weeks. Writing about her daily adventures and her attempts at drawing were far more fun than looking at clothes she'd never wear. To draw, she used wrapping paper and any old pencil.

Valdo's last visit had been four months ago, long after his second attack of malaria and his move to the big town lifting and sorting heavy planks of hardwood all day. Sawdust flew everywhere and stuck in his hair making him look even more like a coconut. He could not work for more than an hour at a time and would lie on a pile of planks covered in a skin of sawdust. To begin with, he had visited Fazenda Boa Esperança every Saturday afternoon and stayed overnight. The twelve-hour trip tired him as much as his work. Soon every week became a fortnight and then three weeks. Each time, as he drew near to the familiar track, nausea gripped his stomach. The jungle and everything in it, was enemy.

Zoni would run to meet him with cries of, 'Papai. Papai.'

Safe inside the hut he played with Zoni, chasing him, telling him silly stories about the south. Idenea laughed. But they did not touch each other, even to hold hands. They hardly spoke and when they did the conversation went nowhere. She so wished things could be better.

One Sunday, she'd been hanging up some washing when Valdo came running with Bolo at his heels.

'Come quick, Idenea, there's a snake making a funny noise with its tail.'

She dropped a pair of wet jeans.

'You've left Zoni alone with a snake? Are you mad?'

She sprinted to the tool shed, grabbed a machete, and at a run pushed through the netting into the hut. From outside Valdo heard two violent metal clangs. Idenea came out holding Zoni in one arm and the machete in the other. She was breathing heavily. 'It's dead, it's in two pieces so it must be dead. At least go and throw it away.'

He turned away. 'I can't. I'm sorry, it's no good, I can't.'

'Well then, hold Zoni.'

A minute later, with the broad end of her machete, she pushed out two lengths of rattlesnake. The two segments, roughly twenty centimetres long each, were still writhing, the mouth open and the two white upper fangs biting, biting.

Breathless she said, 'Now give me Zoni and throw these bits away.'

'I can't,' he murmured.

'Oh, *meu Deus*, then I will.' She fetched a shovel, pounded the two pieces till they stopped moving, shovelled them up, strode over to the rusty oil drum for burning house waste and chucked them in. Bolo followed her, wagging his tail. She rubbed her hands on her hips. 'There, that's done. Now give me Zoni and let's get on with it.'

She avoided his eyes. Zoni had kept quiet all the time, one moment circling his arms around his mother's neck, the next around his father's.

A week later a letter arrived.

Porto Velho.

Dear Idenea,
I am not good here
I am very sorry
I go back south to my family and my people
I find work and earn money
Then you join me, tudo bem
Look after Zoni. Tell him his father sends him a kiss every night
I will try to send letters to this sawmill
  Maybe I come to visit you
  Your husband Valdo

Bosco couldn't prevent smirking when he had handed it to her. 'Wipe that grin off your face, Bosco, you've read it haven't you?' Later she read it twice to Romi, tears in her eyes.

Romi took her hand. 'He was never as strong as you, Idi. And you knew that right from the start.' He kicked at the ground. 'Perhaps we'll all go back south one day. Maybe it was just Father's dream or Government madness? Remember when I cut through the topsoil for the grave? Look at the quality of the maize this year, puah!' He kicked again. 'And maybe this merda of a place doesn't even belong to us anyhow.'

'Don't say that.' Idenea looked up at the underneath of a black rain cloud. 'We mustn't panic. We've done so much. The Indians manage all right so why not us?'

'They're different.'

She raised her hand towards the jungle. 'I wonder how different they are to us I mean...in there?'

A young cockerel crowed, a familiar reassuring sound, his neck arching, one leg lifted, still for a second.

'Back south,' she thought wistfully.

She paced back and forth and then wagged her finger at Zoni. 'This is home now, my baby, and you're part of it.'

Macaws, bright red and green, clambered in the tops of the nearby trees, biting at fruit and nuts and cackling together. A screaming piha whistled.

Juca arrived carrying a small canvas bag over one shoulder, a string hammock over the other and a rusty, single-barrelled, hammer action 20 bore shot gun in his right hand. Bosco followed behind with another ·38 pistol that he wore jauntily around his waist as if to challenge Romi. He had three or four live bullets in the magazine, the other half-dozen cartridges in his belt were spent.

With Juca leading, they trekked into the jungle, never in a straight line, circling around tree trunks and buttresses, avoiding the spiked palms. Great branches and looping vines hid the sky. They walked in a twilight world of shadowy greens, gently waving huge leaves where birds and animals ignored them. A sun bittern displayed its circular chequered wings and stalked stiffly away. Howler monkeys looked down from above. A blue butterfly as large as your hand swooped and curved in front of them.

Juca had shown Bosco how to identify the wild rubber trees, how to carve the V-shaped drainage cuts. At night they slung their hammocks between two trees always beside a stream, lit a fire, heated up rice and beans, manioc flour, dried pig fat and waited till Juca reckoned the latex had run. They talked about land and sex, Juca about Carmen, Bosco about Idenea and his desire to own land especially Fazenda Boa Esperança. Juca, swinging in his hammock, kept quiet and smiled his toothless smile.

They filed out a couple of days later with the smoked ball of latex on a pole slung between their shoulders. Bébé sold these balls on to travelling agents from rubber factories. He divided up the cash: the majority for himself, wages for Juca and Bosco and a small commission to the Saladinis. 'For allowing my boys to work on your place', he would say. Juca knew Bébé was cheating him but he didn't argue at the low pay-out. With land and Carmen at stake, he didn't want a quarrel.

Bosco only came to work on the fazenda when he wasn't tapping rubber. He would greet Idenea with a cheerful *Bom Dia*.

She didn't lift her head. He made sure the others felt his presence and talked about, *our wealth*.

'What wealth, eh?' questioned Romi, 'We owe too much.'

'There's money in rubber, see.' Bosco replied with a wink pulling at one ear lobe and slamming a wad of notes on the table. 'See I'm part of the team again.'

Chico gawped at the money and pushed past his brother. 'Heh, let me come with you.'

The next time the three of them set off, as Juca said, 'For a long trip.'

'That wasn't clever of you, Romi, to let Chico go,' Idenea chided as she watched the three disappear. 'Now there's only you, me and Carlito to do all the work.'

'How could I stop him? Anyway, the money will help.'

Four days passed. The trio did not return. Five days and still no sign. On the seventh only Juca and Bosco appeared, dirty and hungry.

'We lost Chico,' Bosco blurted out. 'He vanished. We've spent three days looking for him.'

'It was you,' Juca said softly, 'who lost him, Bosco, not me, you. You went off with him on your own against my advice. You should have taken care of him.'

Bosco limped up to Romi. 'Chico was there one moment, gone the next. It's thick jungle. I yelled and yelled for him. I ran to find Juca to help. We both searched everywhere.'

'It was your fault.' Juca's voice flat, without emotion. 'You idiot.'

Bosco's eyes were half-closed with exhaustion, his breath in short gasps.

'Indians! Juca, you said they were close.'

'Did you see any Indians, Bosco?' Idenea stepped forward. 'No? You're lying. Where's my brother? Why didn't you stay with him?' Her face red with anger, her grey eyes shining. She pointed at him. 'Find him, you bastard?'

'No fighting.' Romi cut in. 'We must get help. Where's the Guide book? Quick find it.'

Idenea ran, fetched the booklet from her hut, fingered about and read, You must immediately report any contact with Indians to the Indian Protection Agency.

That afternoon they all went, dog, monkey, the cart, all of them, straight away.

Quiet settled over the clearing, no shouting, no bangs. The jungle wall seemed to have edged back closer to the centre of all that human effort. Nature was already seizing back what she had yielded up amidst so much noise and violence.

Half a dozen vultures dared to sit on the roof of the main hut. One plucked up courage, dropped to the ground and ambled clumsily into the hut to snatch a bone. Above, his mates craned their grey skinny necks downwards and in moments all six were on the ground squabbling over grains of rice. The Capuchin monkeys didn't bother to look towards the hut for entertainment any more. One adolescent strayed along a branch away from its mother's arms. A Caracara hawk dived and grabbed it. A sudden downpour of rain spattered onto the leaves deadening all other sound.

The National Indian Foundation, FUNAI, was housed in a square of run-down bungalows on the outskirts of Porto Velho. There was a school for Indian adults and their children who had survived the destruction of their homeland and hadn't fled into what little remained of the forest. José Magalhães, the senior protection agent, had agreed to talk to the Saladinis. He was asking for details of Chico's disappearance when the door burst open and two policemen pushed in and seized Bosco.

'You're wanted for questioning.'

Bosco pointed at Idenea. 'This is your doing, you bitch.'

The policemen dragged him out.

Idenea hugged Zoni and said quietly to Romi, 'He's such an idiot, I haven't seen a policeman in months.'

Romi shrugged. 'Maybe he's done something we don't know about.'

Military Police Headquarters. Date Oct 15th 1971.

Incident: Temporary Arrest for murder. Suspect - Snhr Bosco Saladini.

Report written by Lieutenant Wellington Irineu Bentes.

CONFIDENTIAL. This morning Captain Dias, the head of the Land Agency telephoned this Command to report that a certain Snhr Bosco Saladini may have committed murder near Mutum in a small settlement 165 kilometres from here within the Command's authority. Captain Dias said that his source of information was reliable and that the suspect Snhr Bosco was in the FUNAI office with the rest of his family. Captain Dias strongly recommended that we arrest Senhor Bosco Saladini and bring him in for questioning.

In the interests of good relations between the Military Government of this Territory and the Ministry of Agriculture and in particular the Land Reform Agency, the Governor, Colonel Delgado, recommends that this Command cooperates whenever possible. The Command therefore took in the suspect for questioning. I attach my report.

Present:- Suspect; Snhr Roberto José Saladini, known as Bosco. Interviewing Officers; Lt Wellington Irineu Bentes, on secondment from Central Command Brasilia and Sub Lt Mario Petronilo Alves.

Report written by Lt W Bentes.

Suspect Snhr Bosco looks nervously about the room. He demands to know why he is here and plays difficult when we take his finger prints. He is dressed in shorts and a t-shirt and is extremely dirty with several abrasions on his skin. He limps when he walks.

Questions [Q] by the officers; Answers [A] by the suspect with observations by the writer.

Q. Name please?

A. Roberto José Saladini, known as Bosco.

Q. Address?

A. Plot 921 Mutum, Fazenda Boa Esperança.

Q. Profession?

A. Farmer and pioneer.

Q. Senhor Bosco, you are suspected of murdering or causing bodily harm to your cousin Senhor Francisco Saladini. Which act is true, murder or bodily harm? Why and where?

A. No, no...nothing, *nada*...not me...Chico disappeared...terrible...Who accuses me? Tell me.

Obs. Suspect is sweating profusely. He sits on his hands, shifts his body about and looks all about. He appears to be a typical settler from the south.

Q. Our information is very reliable. You said, 'Not me'. What does that mean? Where is Chico? If you did not harm him, who did? Were you alone?

A. I don't know, Yes, No...No I mean I was alone...Juca was there, I mean Juca wasn't there. We were three...rubber tapping...and there were Indians nearby...so Juca said...I never hurt anybody.

Q. Indians? Never hurt anybody? Our informant tells us you attacked your other cousin with a knife not so long ago. Do you have a gun, is it legally held? Explain yourself.

A. Why? Yes. Why? No. I mean Yes for self-protection against animals and things, anacondas, jaguars...snakes...never fired...you can count the bullets if you want.

Q. Who is Juca?

A. Me and him go rubber tapping together. We earn money. Chico asked to come.

Obs. Suspect has difficulty talking.

A. Juca said there were Indians nearby, he showed me signs, he says they are quiet people. Chico disappeared into the trees...maybe Indians hurt him...maybe saved him...I don't know. I swear, I swear by God. Why should I kill him, why?...other people get lost in the jungle, don't they?

Obs. Suspect is no longer frightened, is clever and realises that there is no evidence so will play this interrogation to the end.

Q. Not so easy to lose one among three of you when calling out to each other all the time is it? Tell us what happened.

A. Already have...he's lost that's all. You must believe me.
[Extract finished here].

Report and summary of the interrogation of Senhor Bosco Saladini accused of murder.

It is impossible with the limited resources available to investigate a rumour of a suspected murder so far away. As it is, let me point out, we are unable to make any impression on the trafficking of drugs through the territory by road from Bolivia or by private aircraft, let alone check out the possibility of a distant murder. We often hear of murders that we do not have the resources to investigate.

Suspect Snhr Bosco Saladini was dismissed without charge.

I shall be investigating the source of the informant.

The suspect is told to legalise his gun or hand it in to the Command within 15 days. This is unlikely to happen.

It is the writer's opinion that the suspect knows much more than he is prepared to admit and knows what happened to Snhr Chico. Also it is doubtful that there are Indians so close by that are unknown to FUNAI. I will recommend that their representative, José Magalhães, investigates.

After dismissing Snhr Bosco, the writer challenged Snhr Juca, unofficially of course. He objected to all my questions. He said he'd heard a gunshot but that it might have been a breaking branch. He is arrogant and needs to be watched.

End of report. Signed Lt W Bentes.

The Saladinis returned as they had come, by bus. Idenea asked the driver to go slowly. He nodded, familiar with the accident that had killed Mother Tana and Adonis. Some said a hundred died, others fifty. Some that the driver was eaten by Piranhas, others that, at a full moon, he can be seen running along the road at night waving his arms.

Bosco sat tight beside Romi, his eyes closed, feigning sleep.

Romi said, 'You were lucky they didn't arrest you, Bosquinho.'

'I told you he's lost or killed by Indians. It's obvious.'

In his heart Romi was a little afraid. There was so much talk of Indian aggression, whether real or imagined he wasn't sure. He'd never seen one. His fear was infectious. Idenea clasped Zoni closer to her chest as she looked out of the window at the blackness and worried whether Chico was still alive.

Bosco, eyes tight shut, hissed, 'It was you, Idenea, who told on me, wasn't it?'

'Idiot!' She spat at him. 'How would I know how to contact the police? I was on the fazenda. You tell me what's happened to Chico? That's what I want to know. He's my brother.' She started to cry.

The bus lurched slowly through the night, headlights criss-crossing wildly from side to side; one moment on the red of the road, the next painting the tree trunks white.

Juca was swearing quietly to himself. That bastard Lieutenant Bentes treating him as an inferior with those nasty questions. Oh well, he thought, it must have been the Boss's idea to put the police onto Bosco. But how odd of the Boss to do something like that. Maybe Bébé's plan of heaping debt on them until they ran would work better. It was that girl in front of him; she'd never give up, tough bitch that she was, but he admired her for that. His thoughts moved to owning land and to Carmen.

The bus rattled on.

Unlike Idenea, they hadn't seen any Indians and were coming up the track banging their pots to a samba rhythm. The humid air trembled with the manic screeching of the cicadas

'No Indians, huh?' Bosco was saying. 'Maybe we did scare them away.'

'More likely they went their own way,' said Juca with his inscrutable smile.

Seeing Romi pulling a sobbing Idenea to her feet, they ran up.

'Zoneeee, he's gone,' she screamed, shaking her head from side to side. 'Romi, where is he, *pelo amor de Deus*? Please find my baby!'

'He can't have gone far, Idi, he's only small. We'll find him. Don't worry.'

She flung her arms around her brother's neck. 'Don't you see, he's been taken. Look at the mosquito net. He couldn't have done that, he's not big enough.'

He hugged his sister tight. 'We'll find him, Idi, don't you worry.

'Your legs, Idenea,' said Carlito O Lentão, 'all those...cuts...and blood.'

'Who would steal a baby boy?' said Bosco.

'I don't know' Her sobbing dragged at her lungs. 'Indians. They were there, so couldn't be anybody else.'

She pulled out of Romi's embrace and ran towards the jungle, her ripped dress flapping behind her and began to shout, 'Zoni, where are you? Come to Mama!'

Romi examined the dusty ground for footprints but Idenea's frantic pacing had scuffed the dirt around the pen. In the pen was the wooden doll that Father had carved for Idenea and the bright green plastic tractor that Zoni pushed about in the gravel chirping, Vroom Vroom.

Little Zoni had been at the heart of their family, the reason to keep going. Romi had to keep the family together. His stomach, lead heavy, sapped at his strength. In God's name what were they doing up here?

He gripped Juca's arm. 'Juca, you with your tracking skills, if it's Indians, you'll find him, won't you?'

Juca leant one arm on a hut post and said quietly, 'Not Indians, they've got enough problems of their own.'

Romi kicked the ground. 'Are they trying to scare us away?'

Bosco, with his back to them, was staring over the top of the elephant grass. He heard Romi call at him for help.

'Bosco! Come and help.' Romi shouted again. 'Don't just stand there.'

Carlito O Lentão had walked a few paces towards the jungle and was calling softly, 'Zoni, it's time... for our ball game. Come on. Be...be a good boy, it's me Carlito.'

Bolo had trotted after Idenea. He turned and ran back to the huts, barking. He stopped at Romi's feet and barked more. Then he turned and scampered off to find Idenea again. He circled her legs, still barking. The pet monkey ran round and round its tethering post, until the length of chain ran out and jammed its head against the post. Caught, it could only flick its tail.

Bosco didn't move. He was smiling. So, what would happen now? He turned and seemed to grin at Juca, as if to show he didn't care. Whether a smile or a grimace, Romi saw it and with his body stiffening, he strode over to Juca.

'What's up with you and Bosco?' he shouted into Juca's face. 'Go on, tell me, what is it?'

Juca leant further back onto his post, his lips stretching over his gums into a flat smile. 'Ask Bosco, maybe he knows something that I don't.'

Romi spun round and in one springing jump threw himself at Bosco. His right shoulder caught Bosco's chest and, catching him unawares, pitched him to the ground. Romi jumped astride him and pinioned his arms. Juca didn't move.

'Go on, Bosco! Out with it!' Romi was pushing Bosco's arms behind his head.

Bosco spat into Romi's face and kicked with his legs. Romi held his grip, his hair flopping over his eyes.

'You bastard, Romi. Papa's boy. Fuck off. I wouldn't limp if it wasn't for you.' He gasped for breath. 'You only stay here for your father's sake and for that sister of yours.' He kicked and kicked. 'Get out before malaria kills you.'

'So that's it, is it, Bosco, let you take over the fazenda? Steal it like you did our savings, eh? You with this new mate of yours, Juca? What did you do to Chico? Lose him on purpose, murder him? Juca said he heard a gunshot.'

Romi hissed the last words through his teeth, saliva dribbling from his lips. 'You and your stupid schemes. That cart of coffee? Overturned, all your own fault, crushed your own shit of a foot. Father wanted to help you. God damn you.'

Then, as if the whole effort was too much for him, he loosened his grip, sighed and stood up. He turned his back and walked towards the hut, his arms hanging loose by his sides.

'Dear God, what's the point of all this?' In a daze he looked about. 'Idenea, where are you...?'

If he had glanced behind him at that moment, matters might have been different.

Bosco jumped up, pulled out his heavy skinning knife and hurled it, not as a skilled knife thrower, but as if chucking a stone. And he threw with all the fury of humiliation. The butt end struck Romi at the base of his neck, the blade spun and cut his left cheek.

Bewildered, Romi stopped. He raised his left hand slowly to the wound. Blood ran down onto his t-shirt. He picked up the knife and tossed it into a guava bush in the orchard twenty metres away. Turning, he gaped open-mouthed at Bosco. His quiet good sense left him. He started to sprint towards his parents' grave and the hidden gun.

'I'll finish with you, Bosco. This time with a bullet, you'll see.'

Bosco had no idea what he had intended by throwing his knife except some sort of revenge. But now, he had to act. He hobbled to the guava bush and grabbed the knife.

Romi reached the wooden cross, fell to his knees and scrabbled in the earth, splitting his fingernails. Blood from the cut in his cheek dripped onto his arms. Yes, the gun was there. He ripped open the plastic bag. Still kneeling, he aimed at Bosco, now just a short running five metres away.

'You son of a bitch, Bosco.'

He pulled the trigger. A sharp click. Nothing. '*Merda*'. Of course, idiot, how could he have forgotten? He had unloaded it to prevent rust jamming the bullets in the chambers.

'*Merda.*'

He lowered the pistol and covered his face with both arms. Bosco, knife raised, threw himself onto Romi, stabbing downwards. His knife pierced Romi's left shoulder above the collar bone and with his weight cut deep into muscle.

Romi cried out.

'That's for laming me, you daddy's boy and take this as well.' Bosco raised his right hand high again, the point of the knife directly above Romi's chest.

Juca grabbed Bosco by the shoulders and pulled him over backwards.

'*Basta*, enough, you fool. Do you want to go to gaol?' He rammed Bosco's hand against his thigh. The knife thumped to the ground.

'Juca.' Bosco groaned in frustration. 'Remember our plan.'

Romi stood up clutching at the deep gash in his shoulder with his right hand and at the cut in his cheek with his left. Blood seeped through his fingers and down his arms. Barely audible he said, 'Get me out of here.... '

'Where's Idenea?' he mumbled as he staggered over to the hut, leaving a trail of red. Lifting his head he shouted at the trees, 'Idenea.'

The capuchin monkeys stopped gathering fruit and peered down.

A hundred metres away, Idenea was shouting out, 'Zoni, I'm coming to find you'. She was waving one of his red plastic trainers in one hand. She'd found it between the buttresses of a tree, red and out of place like a paper-chase clue at a child's birthday party. There was joy in her voice. She ran in ever widening circles. She forced her way through the rough undergrowth, softly calling his name.

'Please dear God, tell him to come out.'

Romi slumped onto the wooden bench by the hut. The initial shock of the stabbing was wearing off, instead acute pain. He lifted his hand from the wound. Blood welled.

'I can't see properly,' he said quietly. 'Where's Juca?'

Juca ran over. 'Romi, it looks bad. I'll bind it as best I can.' He called out, 'Carlito, get the cart ready, quick.'

Romi, his face pale and his body slack, grimaced in pain as Juca began to bandage him with a ripped t-shirt. 'I'm all dizzy, Juca. Why are you doing this to me? I can't make you out, never could.'

'Don't worry yourself, Romi.'

As he bandaged, Juca was wondering where all this would lead to: him the good boy, Bosco the real *filho da puta*?

The black vultures that usually scrounged about near the pigs and chickens, squabbling over old papaya skins and chicken bones, flew up with laboured flaps to perch on top of the hut. They bent their scrawny necks towards the smell of fresh blood. Bosco sat cross-legged where Juca had thrown him, his face creased in hatred.

Carlito jogged up with the mule and cart.

Juca looked up from bandaging Romi. 'You come with us, Carlito, *tá bom*? Bosco can watch out for Idenea till I get back.'

Carlito kicked at the red earth. 'But, I…I…can't leave Idenea.' He waved his arms at the jungle shouting, 'Zoni, it's time… for our game.'

Juca levered Romi into the cart and jumped up beside him, 'Carlito, I need you, Romi could die. Run beside and help the mule.'

Romi's head flopped over his wounded shoulder. Blood leaked from his shirt down into his trousers. They trotted past the seated Bosco.

Juca called out, 'I'll be back tonight or early in the morning. Go and help Idenea. Tell her we'll go looking for Zoni.'

The jangle of harness faded away down the track, leaving the hut in the silence of the midday heat. One of the black pigs was already rooting about in the bloodied dust under the bench where Romi had been sitting.

Bosco hadn't moved. Eventually the force of the sun on his head drove him to his feet and he limped over to the hut. He went straight for a bottle of pinga, coughed and spat. He kicked at the rootling pig and sat down heavily on the bench. He drank again and laid his head on one arm across the table.

Outside, the cattle stood still in the glare. The only sound came from Idenea, a hundred metres away. One moment she was running, her arms waving wildly from side to side, the next standing quite still, listening and peering into the trees. She howled, she sobbed, her t-shirt and skirt so ripped that her bra and pants showed like a bikini.

She stopped by a tree. 'Romi, Carlito. Come here, I've found one of his shoes.' She waved the red trainer.

The short dusk was only an hour away, and after, the fall of dark. She blundered back into the hut.

'Where is everybody?' She collapsed onto the bench.

The beaded curtain to her parents' old bedroom parted in the middle. Bosco stepped unsteadily out, the bottle of pinga in one hand.

'It's me, Idenea. Just me.' His words slurring. 'I thought I'd give you a nice surprise. The others have all gone.' He sat down beside her.

'Gone?' She faltered. 'What do you mean, gone?' A chill tingled the skin of her arms.

'To go for help. They left me in charge.'

'Well then.' She forced herself to stand up. 'Come and help me find Zoni.'

He grabbed her arm. 'Not so quick, my princess.'

She wrenched her arm. But strong as she was, he held her fast.

'Let go of me, you brute.' She swung her free arm and slapped him across the side of his face as hard as she could. Startled and enraged by the blow, he rammed her arm behind her back, dropped the half-empty bottle and with the weight of his body thrust her against a post. She winced with pain and turned her face away.

'Got you, finally,' he snarled in her ear. 'You bitch. Now listen to me,' and he humped his body forward, expelling a rush of air from her lungs. 'It's me who should have you.'

'Let me go! You're hurting me...' She kicked back with her heels.

'Remember, I wasn't in the church to hear your vows.'

Bolo got up from his usual shady corner and wandered over to investigate. He glanced in the direction of the struggling pair, thought better of it and padded outside into the softening light where he licked his paws and lay down.

'Your shit of a brother and I had a fight. Juca has taken him to find a doctor.'

'You hurt my brother?' she cried out, struggling against his grip. 'You're mad.'

'No, just clever. You'll get hurt as well if you don't...' He paused to regain his breath.

His forehead was pressing hard into the back of her neck. He inhaled the smell of her skin.

'We can take over this farm together, own the land together. Juca and Carlito can work here. And, I'll fuck you every day till you make me a baby with two good legs.'

At this Idenea felt a new and insistent pressure against her upper thigh. Through closed teeth, 'Never. The titles are in Father's name, stupid. Let go of my arm.'

'What titles? They're nothing with all the debt. Anyhow my name's Saladini, the same as you. Can't you see?'

'No! No! Never, you crazy man.' Her arm was hurting. She started to scream, 'You bandit. Where's Chico? Where's my baby?'

'Only God knows where Chico is now.' He grinned. 'And your baby, that I really don't know.'

She sensed his grip slacken. With all her strength, she twisted around and knocked him off balance. For a second she was free but with one hand he held on to her wrist and grabbing at her with both hands, he flung her to the ground.

'Stupid bitch! You thought you'd get away? You can't see sense, huh? Well, see some now.'

He pulled her, struggling, across the earthen floor. On her back, her kicks thrashed useless in the air. He unhooked a rawhide tethering rope, bound her wrists together above her head and tied her to the leg of the table. He pulled out his knife and knelt beside her.

'See this bitch! I'll kill you like I should have killed your brother.' He pushed the point of the knife to the side of her neck. 'It would be so easy, there's nobody here.' His words thick with pinga, he sat back. 'And then all this will be mine.'

She closed her eyes.

'Well now,' he taunted. 'Look at you. Half naked and painted red and black just as I like. Go on, kiss me.' He leant down, grabbed her hair and forced her head backwards. With no strength left she was unable to resist.

Suddenly she thought she was going to die. She tried to calm her racing brain. What would become of Zoni if she did die? There was nobody else in the world to care for him. No, she was not gong to die. Instead she opened her eyes and moved her lips in a pretend kiss. Needing no more encouragement he slobbered over her. She jerked her head to one side and slackened her body.

'You can't do this, please,' she pleaded, 'We're supposed to be a family. Please let me go. I'm sorry for anything I've ever done to you. I'll go away. I'll leave right now.'

Surprised, Bosco sat back and started to caress her body. 'You're beautiful, Idenea. I'll show you how good I am. Then maybe you'll like me?' He ripped off her bra and groped clumsily at her breasts.

Revolted, she crossed her legs. She sneered, 'You stink of pinga. When did you last wash?'

Enraged, he jumped up, grabbed another coil of rawhide and tied her right ankle to a post that supported the roof. She gasped at the pain.

'You can scream as much as you like, the trees can't help you.'

'Bastard,' she hissed between her teeth, 'I don't scream.'

With her body stretched from table leg to post, he tore away the remainder of her dress and sliced off her pants with his knife.

She mouthed, 'My baby. I cannot die.'

He fumbled with his belt, pulled his trousers only half down, such was his hurry, thrust her free leg to the side with his knee and lunged forward.

Closing her eyes, she saw the branches of the trees, marvelled at their beauty and watched them bend gently in the wind. At her side she heard her own voice softly encouraging him, 'Maybe you are right' and 'Yes, you are good'. She continued to flatter in spite of the violent intrusion and the fetid smell of his breath up her nose.

It was all so simple, 'My baby without me is gone for ever. My baby.'

He finished, slumped across her, panting noisily. She edged her body sideways, pushed with her free leg and rolled him away onto his back.

'Untie me.'

He was too far gone to answer. She pulled at the table trying to reach the knot. But the table, where birth and meals had been, slid only a few centimetres. She tugged and tugged. She rested to regain her strength but exhaustion tipped her into a heavy sleep.

The clamour of night cries pulsed in the heavy air. Bolo hadn't moved. The monkey sat on his perch twisting his head from side to side.

As the glow of dawn began to hide the stars, the smarting of her cuts stung her awake. Her arms and legs were free. An empty rice sack covered her lower body. Bosco was holding one of her hands.

'Sorry, Idenea. Forgive me.' He sought her eyes. He stroked her hand. 'Please stay here with me. Everything will be good and everything can be ours.'

She rose up on one elbow, gasped in pain and, avoiding his eyes, stood up. She had to get away before he became aggressive again. But where to? The Indian agency in the big town? Quick, quick. They would know of the tribe. They would help. She stumbled over to her hut, dressed quickly, put her wooden doll, her small notebook, some clothes for Zoni in a plastic bag with a few bananas. She stumbled down the track. Bolo padded after her, her companion as always. She shooed him back. He lay down in the middle of the track with his head between his paws and watched her walk unsteadily away.

Bosco stayed seated at the table, hands clasped on his knees. She heard him yell.

'Ideneeeaaarh...'

She started to run. He'd never catch her with that funny leg of his. After half a kilometre she drank heavily from a stream and ate a couple of bananas. She sighed as the water washed cool over her cuts.

At each step her skin smarted, sometimes so sharply that she caught her breath. A bird above would see a small figure stumbling from side to side along the winding orange track. On each side of the track a flat blanket of heat covered a seething, ever wakeful wilderness. Chatter, chatter, all around the jungle stirred, green and red the flash of parrots and macaws.

She saw their mule and cart trotting towards her. She stepped behind a tree and watched Juca hurry past. She didn't hail him. She'd never been sure of that one.

A couple of hundred metres from the huts, Juca saw fresh jeep tracks. Somebody had taken a wrong turning. He trotted on. He found Bosco lying on the bench as if asleep. Idenea's clothes lay on the ground. He crouched down, fingered the rawhide rope still attached to the table, saw the cut knickers and realised what had happened.

'Where is she?'

Bosco didn't raise his head.

Juca rose effortlessly and looked out keenly over the tall grass. Everything looked good in the light of the early morning. He wasn't going to leave now with so much trouble about.

Much, much later, Idenea pushed through the beaded curtain of the Bar da Amizade. A couple of unshaven men playing pool looked up as she stumbled over to the bar.

'*Pelo amor de Deus*, Bébé, please help me.' She dropped her head and shoulders onto the wooden counter in front of him.

A click of pool balls and the two players leant on their cues, their attention on the mud-covered girl slumped over the bar. A beetle whirred, zigzagging through cigarette smoke and smacked into the wooden wall.

Idenea, her eyes closed, her breath coming in short rushes. 'My baby, help me.'

She felt a hand stroke her hair and heard Juliana's gentle voice, 'What is this, my dear, so much mud and all this blood?'

Idenea pushing up onto her elbows whispered, 'My baby.' Her eyes unfocussed searching back and forth, she grabbed Juliana's arm. 'Thank God it's you, Juliana. Zoni's been stolen.'

'Come now,' Juliana said softly, 'let's go to my house round the back.' She continued to stroke and led Idenea gently through the back of the bar towards the chugging of a generator.

Bébé, who had not greeted Idenea, opened a beer, smiled and said aloud, 'Well, now.'

In the corner of two mud brick walls under a tin sheet, electric wires fed into a shower head that stuck out on a pipe. An old bar of soap lay on the wet screeded floor. Juliana led Idenea under the shower. She turned on a tap. Outside the generator strained. Thin needles of water squirted down, cold at first, warming slowly as the generator recovered its regular beat. She bathed Idenea from head to foot.

At first, Idenea moaned at the sting of the water as it slipped down her sides colouring purple.

Juliana continued to bathe. 'Tell me what's going on. Yesterday, Juca and Carlito turned up with Romi bleeding from a machete accident. Ha! What a load of rubbish. I patched him up as best I could and sent him off with Carlito to find a doctor in the big town. There's been a fight, hasn't there? Juca asked me for some disinfectant and disappeared. And now you covered in blood, crying about your baby. So, what's up?'

'Indians stole him.' Idenea grabbed at Juliana's arm. 'I saw one right beside me.'

'Ssh, my dear.' Juliana continued to bathe, 'Don't be silly. Indians? Why would they do that?'

'Who else then?' Idenea shook her head in despair.

'We'll find him. You'll see.'

Juliana patted dry the split skin on Idenea's arms and legs with a clean towel. But all Idenea could say was, 'My baby, my baby.'

In the room that just fitted Carmen's bed, Idenea tried to lie on her side but she couldn't sleep in that position for the stinging from her cuts. She sat on the edge of the bed, pushing away the mosquito net to prevent it from touching her skin.

Carlito arrived by bus. He handed over an envelope.

'It's from Romi.'

Dear Sister Idenea.

The writer of this letter is a doctor. He stitched me up. He says I need special attention and risk dying if I stay here. I cannot write for pain. My money is nearly all gone. How can I leave you after so much? But I have to go back south. I can't stand it any longer. I don't have your strong will, Father always said that. I can't put up with violence. I don't have the courage to come back and find you. I am sorry. Bosco stabbed me. Beware of him. I try to forgive him. He always wants to have what he can't, the land and you of course. Join me as soon as you have found Zoni. The soil is no good up here and there's too much debt. Everything is against us.

Your loving brother Romi.

Forgive me, Idi, for leaving you. Carlito will help you.'

Idenea thrust the letter at Juliana.

'See, I can't stay here.'

She pulled at Juliana's arm. 'Who will help me? The police, the army, the Indian agency? I have no money. I can't think properly with my skin like this.'

Bébé was behind the bar, counting a pile of greasy notes.

'Bébé...' she began.

Idenea watched his boyish smile change to that bullying sneer she knew so well. He glanced quickly around to make sure no one was close by.

'I could sell you, you know.' His lips pursed together. 'Yes, and that brother of yours, the whole lot of you and make a profit. Get rich. I could sell you with the big debt you owe me and take your land as well for myself.' He continued to flip-count the bank notes.

'*SELL* me? Are you drunk?' Her mouth open in disbelief. 'I'm not a bag of rice.' What was he saying? She had to get away and those notes were the way.

Bébé with half-closed eyes. 'Yeaaarh, I'd get a lot of money for a young girl like you, a hard worker as well. Now let me see?' His voice dropped to a confiding whisper. 'How much do you really owe me? I'd take twenty percent off if your new owner paid cash up front. Business is business.'

She shoved her right fist between her teeth and bit her thumb. 'You think you own me, do you?' She whispered hoarsely. 'Your slave? Sell me to someone else?'

Bébé's lips pressed even tighter. 'Listen. For me you're just business. Out here, there's nobody. The stupid police and army don't exist. I helped you with malaria and buying logs. Now I want payback, you silly bitch.' He said bitch with pleasure. [iv]

Idenea's thumb began to hurt as she bit harder. For a moment she forgot the sting in her legs and arms. To be sold as a slave. Her teeth imprints showed white on her thumb.

'I heard all that.' Juliana ran behind the bar. 'You pig. You shameless thief.' She came up behind and snatched the notes out of her husband's hands. 'What did I ever see in you? Poor Carmen to have a father like you. *Que vergonha*.'

'Nobody else would take you, you half-breed Indian. That's why. Give my money back.'

Juliana thrust her hand over the counter, avoiding Bébé's lunging hands. 'Here, Idenea, take the money and run. There's a bus outside. Get your bag and go. Quick. I'll look after this brute.'

Bébé, wrestling with his wife, shouted after Idenea, 'I'll add that to your debt. You'll pay me back one day, I swear.'

Juliana, knowing that her husband was far too fat to clamber over the counter and chase after Idenea, cried out, 'Good luck, sweet girl. Get out! Off you go...*OUT*!'

142

4

THEIR EYES UPON ONE DOUBLE STRING

Bobby woke with a start. His right arm still lay across her shoulders. Her eyelids blinked open. At first panic and then a tentative smile as he stroked her brow.

'Bobinho,' she said in a sleepy drawl, 'I had such good thoughts, the first for so long.' She smiled.

His fingers traced across her forehead. 'There's more isn't there? What happened beyond that tree?'

She shook her head.

He looked at his watch. 'Come on, let's have some fun. You took me dancing and look what that led to. Let's go on the river. You never know, we might catch a fish.'

He jumped off the bed. 'And I bet I can dress quicker than you.'

Carried by his enthusiasm she jumped up as well, happy to be taken away even for a moment from thinking about her baby. Hopping about the room they pulled on their few clothes and reached the door in a rush together.

'I won.'

'No, I did.'

Half an hour later the taxi dropped them below the bridge beside the fish market in the old part of Cuiabá. Bare-chested men stood knee-high beside their canoes unloading their catches. On stone slabs inside the high-vaulted, colonial market hall, their wives chopped with heavy cleavers. Fish, still alive, flapped their tails as knives speared into their guts.

Bobby hired a dugout canoe. They paddled off down river, he at the back, she in the prow. They paddled past the last wooden shacks of the town. They challenged each other to see who the stronger paddler was. It's that hoeing and slashing, he thought as he struggled to keep up. Although nearly capsizing at every erratic plunge of their heavy wooden paddles, he managed to moor to an overhanging branch. He stripped to his pants and jumped into the shallows up to his shoulders.

He splashed water at her. 'Jump in, it's cooler in here.'

She hesitated, smiling shyly. 'It's different for me to...to undress just like that.'

'Don't be silly, we've just spent the last twelve hours side by side.' He splashed again.

She turned her back to him carefully taking off her outer clothes and levered herself over the opposite side into the water. He saw the scars on her arms and legs and wondered again at the cause and the pain.

'And the piranhas?' she said with only her head and shoulders showing and a hint of triumph in her smile.

'They only go for blood and those cuts of yours are healed, aren't they?'

'Yes.'

'So, the only ones you'll find near a big town and all the fishing are these.' He reached under the canoe with his legs and encircled hers. He pulled with his legs dragging her half under. She shrieked. The canoe rocked. She spat out water.

'Hey, Bobinho, I can't swim properly.'

'Here, I'll show you.' He dived under and eased her into the life-saver's position, his body under hers. 'Kick with your legs, you'll see.' She lay still and kicked at his word.

'It's fun being with you,' he laughed.

'You too,' she laughed back.

'Hey!' he said, 'you must smile more often. And how come you're so different?'

'What do you mean, different?'

'Well, I've never met a woman around here like you before.'

'Look.' She flexed her biceps and grinned provocatively. 'I lived with men.'

Tired of ducking and splashing they rested on opposite sides of the canoe smiling broadly at each other, toes touching under water.

'Where is your wife?' she said, gesturing at the ring on his finger.

He hesitated. 'In England with my son.'

'Does she know where you are?'

'More or less. She didn't want to be with me any more.'

'I'm sorry.'

'No need. It was my fault.'

'What's her name?'

He hesitated and quietly, 'Beatrice.'

'My husband, Valdo,' she sighed, 'he ran away.'

'Odd, isn't it?' he said changing the subject quickly. 'This village called Mutum. Your plot 921. It really does seem to be very near to our ranch. I know there's more than one Mutum but what a coincidence if it was the same.'

'No Bobinho. It's not possible.'

'I'm not so sure. Even in a huge country like this, old titles and state land overlap or at least the Ministry says they do. We've been trying to register our boundaries for two years. It's all damned politics.'

'Oh, Bobinho,' she sighed again. 'Land titles.'

He clambered back into the canoe.

'We must get back before the sun goes.' He held out his hand.

'What's that scar?' Her forefinger pointing at his right thigh.

'Oh that?' he said casually as he helped her into the canoe.

'Tell me how you got it?'

'An old bullet wound.' He turned his leg. 'See, in here, out there.'

'A bullet?' she exclaimed.

'Somebody who didn't like what I was doing shot me. Luckily, he didn't kill me. So, there you are, you're not the only one with scars.'

They paddled back, out of the current. She glanced back over her shoulder.

'You're still there aren't you?'

'Yes, still here.' His voice dropped. 'Watching you paddle.'

On shore they walked along narrow cobbled streets past old colonial porticos and rectangular windows with flaky blue and orange plaster. The falling darkness cast peaceful shadows. Heat radiated out from the walls. Radios clamoured out catchy tunes and every now and then a long drawn-out yell of 'Goooooal' told of a football shaking a far-off net. In one shop, they poked their fingers into the jaws of dried piranhas and gasped in feigned fear. He caught her hand and held it. She looked away to hide her smile. In a churras-caria overlooking the black sheet of the river, they ate grilled steaks from a Pintado catfish,

'Are you feeling better now?' he asked.

'For a little while, but I can't forget'.

Her happy smile, that he had come to like so much, fell back to a sad slant.

He reached for her hand. 'I've got things as well I've never told anyone. So, what happened beyond that tree with 921 on it? You promised...'

She took his hand between both of hers and told him: one moment proud as she described all the Saladinis had achieved, and the next in a halting stammer at the loss of her baby, of the Indian, of Chico. She skirted around Bosco but her voice faltered.

'And then what happened with him?' he insisted. 'Did he...?'

'No, Bobinho, I'm not telling.'

'You mean he...?'

She looked to one side and told of running away from Bébé.

'In the bus, I was in so much pain that I couldn't sit properly. I shut my eyes as we crossed the bridge where Mother and Father had died. At the Police Station in Porto Velho, I was told to ask the army as they knew about Indians. At the barracks, I pleaded with a sergeant. He spoke like men talk to women around here. I shouted and screamed. He started to drag me out, but then that nice-looking Colonel who I'd met when I worked there, appeared. I rushed up to him. He put his hand on my shoulder and called me 'my dear'. Indians you say? Are you sure? Maybe we can help but it will take a lot to mount a search operation so far away. I said that I'd get money. He smiled and told the sergeant to take details.'

'Did you go to the Indian protection people at FUNAI? I have a friend there.'

146

'Yes. They were my great hope, but the guard at the gate saw me off saying that his boss had gone up river and anyhow stolen babies weren't his business.'

'I ran from place to place. Every night I woke up choking thinking of my baby. I got a job in a bar. How I hated the rough men staring at my scars, so I bought a long-sleeved shirt with my first pay. Take a lot the Colonel had said. So, I had to work. After three months of little pay, I decided to go back south and ask my aunts and uncles for money so I could persuade the army to help me. I caught bus after bus and worked in bars for a day. Then I began to feel that if I left the jungle where my baby must be, I'd never come back. Then I met Ana. She told me about Ludo. And well...'

'That's who I am.' She stroked his hand.

Neither of them spoke for several moments. Bobby stared unblinking into her eyes.

'Extraordinary. It's just not possible.'

'What?'

'You're so brave.'

'What else could I do?'

'I know some of the people you mention.'

They flopped into the back of an ancient two door VW taxi with bald tyres. Her shoulder nudged against the side of his chest. The taxi lurched tilting her head further onto his shoulder. He edged his arm slowly, as if he didn't want her to notice, around her shoulders.

Smiling up at him, she said, 'You make me feel safe, Bobinho.' She curled her free arm over his chest.

'You make me feel good too, Idenea.' With a newly-felt confidence, he looked her in the eyes.

'Me?' She laughed. 'A simple girl from the south? You talk crazy, Bobinho.'

'You're special. You must believe that. You're honest. I always looked for that in the men I commanded. You aim at things in life, don't you? And hope that some good will come out of it all. You're a bit like me, different though. I often think I dance around as if I'm in a fairyland, round and round with hopes of all kinds. Then despair.'

'Aaah, tell me about your fairyland.'

147

He pulled her closer and kissed her between the eyebrows. He cupped his hand under her chin.

She closed her eyes and ran her tongue lazily back and forth across the base of his thumb. They did not breathe. Another lurch separated them. They gasped and giggled in the dark.

'I'm sad,' she whispered. 'I'll miss you when you go.'

'I have to go tomorrow, back north.' He had to tell her the truth. She'd been so frank with him. Her grip on him loosened.

'Our cattle don't arrive for a week. I'm meeting up with Zé, a friend at the Indian Agency, the one who could have helped you. He said he'd take me up an unknown river. He wants to contact a small tribe. I can't let him down.'

Her smile returned to its old twist. 'That Indian I saw. Maybe he comes from there, and my Zoni and where Chico disappeared?'

She sat up with a jerk. 'Where's my baby?' She slumped back, her head in her hands. 'It could be the same river, couldn't it?'

He touched her arm. 'It's too far away.'

'But it could be,' she insisted as the taxi stopped outside the Perfect Peace Motel.

At the reception Bobby rang the bell and asked for his bill. To Idenea, 'I'll be along in a minute.'

Surprise in her eyes. 'You staying another night?'

Barely audible. 'Yes, that is if you want me to?'

She stood quite still, her arms hanging loose by her hips. Several seconds passed while each held the eyes of the other. The dimples of a faint smile creased the sides of her mouth. She turned and stepped away down the passage.

'Well now.' Ludo was counting the notes. 'You like her, don't you? I can see it. She's tough but much bad luck. Take her away from here, she hates it. I only wanted to help her, give her some shelter and of course do business as well. She's still a girl and there's many a man without a woman up here. If you don't take her someone else will.'

Bobby winced at the thought of another man. He mumbled, 'It's complicated for me right now. I have to get back to the ranch. It's no place for a woman.'

Ludo shrugged. Bobby hesitated, glanced after Idenea then back at Ludo and frowned. He asked about an early morning taxi, and then remembered that he'd already booked the one that had dropped them off. Flustered, he stammered. 'How's business Ludo, good or bad?'

Ludo smiled. 'Now off you go to her.'

Bobby strode off, his head swaying the bare light bulbs as he passed.

Outside door Number 5, he put his hand on the door handle and held it there. He watched a pale green gecko on the wall for what seemed like several minutes. He breathed in deeply and turned the handle.

She was sitting on the bed and staring at her hands laced in her lap.

'Lock it.' She didn't look up.

Her voice quick and sharp. 'Why such a good time, then rush away? You won't take me with you, will you? I know you won't.'

In the silence that followed and although his mind was racing, Bobby still managed to reason. No, he couldn't take her, he'd promised Zé.

'Answer me.'

He didn't.

'Then what is it you want? Just my body?'

He covered the two paces between them as one and placed his hands on her shoulders. Angry, she pushed him away with her fists on his chest.

'What is it? Go on tell me?' She searched his eyes. No humour in them any more, instead a tight indifference.

He couldn't express what his heart so wished to. He could not mouth the words. His reserve simply wouldn't set him free.

'I...I...well, you see as I said, so much has happened to me. I'll tell you one day.'

'No, no, go on, tell me now.'

'I did say you are special,' he began. 'And that is much for me and...'

She loosened her arms and circled them around his neck like she had when dancing in the stockade. There was something more than a bullet wound about this man who was so drawn into himself. Smiling calmly now, she kissed his eyes.

'Then love me right now.'

She loosened the buttons on the front of his shirt. He slipped her t-shirt over her head and undid her bra. And she was smiling, facing him without any reserve. With his hands on her shoulders he held her at arms' length.

'Like them?' She teased, lifting her breasts. She whispered, 'it's your turn to begin. It was me last time, remember? Turn the light out. I'm still shy of my scars.'

'As I watched you paddle in the canoe.' He pulled her gently to him, 'I fantasised that if ever possible I would discover you from head to toe with my tongue without stopping.'

'Go on then, show me.' Her smile gone, she raised her chin and put a finger on her throat. 'Start here.' He kissed her neck and slipped the tip of his tongue along her collar bone, down the inside of her arm to her hand and then back again up and across both breasts.

'Yes, don't stop will you,' she whispered.

He knelt, his tongue touching all the time, around and over her belly button, no hurry and on to her hip and down the outside of her leg, over her knee and onto her instep. Resting and holding her right calf with both hands he smiled up at her.

'There you are.'

'You haven't finished yet.' Her hands dropped to his shoulders. She gently lifted his head upwards. His tongue back on her other knee followed the inside of her thigh to the centre. Her hairs still damp from the river lay pressed flat by her pants. Carefully he parted this triangle with his tongue. She pinched his shoulders with her thumbs and fingers.

'That's enough. It's too much. I want you with me, up here, all of you along me.' She sank onto the middle of the bed, her long legs falling effortlessly apart. As he leaned over her, she stretched out one hand and closing around him pulled him gently down. And he breathed in the intoxicating smell of her body. He didn't see the staring Indian. He saw the grey of her eyes and nothing else.

'Idenea, there's nowhere I'd rather be right now, with no other person. Clever, brave that you are.'

They held still, willing the moment to last. Later, neither could agree who started first. She raised her legs and crossed them over his back as the longing and the heat welled up inside her belly and then beyond control burned in wave after wave from her belly up to her neck along her arms and down her legs. She stifled her cries in the softness of his neck. Never leaving her, he kissed her over and over as all that he had became part of her.

Heat and sweat eventually separated them. They lay on their backs holding hands.

Had he found somebody like himself, somebody he could unite with in a shared hope and desire to go forward? He had tried before; so had she. Could they dare again or would it all pass in a day? For this moment he didn't care and let himself be one with her.

They fell asleep in that never to be forgotten, deep sleep of new lovers together.

At about four in the morning, Bobby awoke curled on his side. A few inches away, wide awake for some time, she lay facing him. Only their eyes bright in the semi-darkness.

'I don't want any money, *tá bom*?' she said sharply. 'I want you to take me with you.'

He hesitated. Sense of duty and now this new-found affection and fascination all struggled with his conscience.

'I can't. I promised to be alone. I'm sorry.'

'Then swear to me you'll come back. Ask about a missing child, about my darling Zoni.'

'Have you got a photograph?'

She shook her head. 'I bet you won't look, so take me with you. Don't you see what a chance this could be for me?'

'I'm sorry, I just can't.' He touched her cheek. 'Think of yesterday, and all the fun we had.' Seeing the soft brown hairs on the nape of her neck, his heart flooded with love for her.

Resigned, she smiled wistfully at him. 'And you Bobinho, about you I know nothing.'

They loved each other again. She pummelled his chest with her fists, fearful of this end that stretched out before her. That black shadow of despair she had dodged and pushed away so often over the past few months was back, edging around her, stealing her purpose and her hope. She could easily slip down, as through a trapdoor, into an unbearable pit of self destruction where, through a quick flash of panic, she saw herself wandering the streets, selling her body to any taker, day in day out. And now this man, who was tender with her, who cared for her. What could she do? When her passion started to rise, she forced it to arrive quickly.

She beat his chest crying out, 'Can't you see. I'm here...in this room?'

She burst into tears and turned her head aside.

He stroked her shoulder. 'I'll keep my eyes open, I promise.'

He dressed in an instant and left without another word. The taxi was waiting silently in the early morning mist. She heard the motor start up. She wrapped a towel under her arms and ran out.

'Make sure you look,' she called out at the dust ball. She kicked at the ground. 'And you, Bobby, you?'

The rising sun, a curl above the trees, marked the beginning of the day. A flight of small green parakeets chattered noisily overhead. The motel dog stretched in the dust. Soon it would be 35 to 40 degrees with the sun fiercer every minute. On the table below the picture of the Indian, she found a white envelope with her name written in neat italics. Two one-hundred-dollar bills fell out together with,

I will remember our two nights and day together. I hope you will. I leave these because you must have them. About myself, maybe I can tell you one day. B.

She knelt in front of the wicker chair and laid her head to one side on the seat with her lips close to the red petals that surrounded the wooden doll. Her breath caressed the image of her child.

Later she swore at the staring Indian. '*Filho da Puta*, it's all your fault.'

Bobby ran up the steps of his hotel in twos and ordered coffee, fruit and bread to his room. He stood long under a cold shower. He fingered the water back and forth through his hair, the rhythm of her telling singing in his head.

He grunted, 'My wound is nothing.'

When he'd paid off the taxi, he'd found a folded sheet of lined paper roughly torn out of a notebook in his back pocket. In forward slanting letters was;

See here,

It was so good to know you
like I've known you for a long time.

When some people go they leave behind Sadness Memories Nostalgia

This is one of those times I am sad to see you go
See you soon or never again
But don't go forgetting me,
you my leg of the bullet hole
How can I forget
Ciao Idenea
Coxipó da Paule Cuiabá

For the first time in three years, instead of avoiding his image in the mirror, he smiled at his soapy face. The line of a poem recited in class came back to him. '*Our eye beams twisted, and did thread our eyes upon one double string.*'

He took out a clean shirt, considered it for a moment, and instead of slipping it on, dressed in the same clothes he'd worn for the past two days. He strode down the passage and banged on Ari's door. No answer. He barged in. Ari lay on his back fully dressed, snoring loudly with one hand resting on the floor. He watched Ari's potbelly rise and fall. He smiled down at him and shook his shoulders.

'Heh, heh, Boss, let me be.' Ari sat up coughing and spitting.

'Great time eh, Chefe? Where've you been?' He scratched his head. 'Remember that girl, Ana? Girls always like Ari.' He heaved up and down with laughter, his breath hissing between his teeth.

Bobby put his hand on Ari's shoulder. 'We have to get organised. So come on, shift man.' Bobby smiled, cheery and light-hearted.

'Eh, Boss, you're in fine form. About time too, you and your black moods were getting me down.'

Bobby turned towards the glare of the window to hide the flush rising in his cheeks.

'Ari, just a small thing?'

'Yes, Chefe?'

'Remember when I was away and there was that squatter question and you flew around the ranch to try and check out our boundaries? What did you actually see below in those two clearings you flew over?'

'Well, Chefe.' Ari stopped splashing water over his face. 'Nothing much in the first one, just a palm leaf hut and a bit of a burn, probably abandoned.'

'And the other?'

'Eh well, bigger, still small but some grass and a few head of cattle and a couple of huts maybe. But Chefe, I can't think straight right now.'

'Any people?' Bobby with his back to the window and his face in shadow didn't move.

'Yeah well, I'm not sure.'

'Women, children?'

'Can't say really, flying too fast but there was a small child who waved.'

Bobby shook his head and said aloud in English. 'Too much of a bloody coincidence.'

'Come on Boss, it's you who's hanging about now.'

'You're right, let's go. Cattle up that goddamn road and into the ranch, so a week maybe. I'm meeting up with my Indian agent friend, Zé, at that fish bar over the river. See you there.'

In the bright heat of the street they parted with a handshake and a body hug. Ari edged his potbelly to one side for an easier grip on Bobby. 'God go with you Boss.'

'And you, amigo.'

Three hours later Bobby was staring out of the porthole as the plane curved upwards over Cuiabá, one wing leaning downwards as it turned north. He could make out the fish market below tucked into the curve of the river where yesterday they had hired the dugout. How long for a cork to reach the south Atlantic, a month, two, three, four, passing all those fish, the caymans and the millions of birds through the Pantanal flood plain? He craned his neck to try and pick out the Perfect Peace Motel.

As the plane reached the British Army recommended height of 800 feet for parachute jump training, he muttered, 'Go! Jump! Go!' He said it without thinking every time he flew; he'd jumped so often. He turned his head further but the plane's wing cut off his view. And he didn't know she lay on her bed crying her eyes out and praying to her God he would find her baby.

Still climbing, the plane flew up and over the dark red cliffs of the east to west continental rift of the Chapada dos Guimarães that divides the flow of the river waters; to the south to the River Plate, to the north to the Amazon. Once over, the cerado began with short trees and bushes. The pale lines of cattle tracks criss-crossed on the red earth. He could pick out the odd white and brown cow against the red.

Soon the small streams flowed into rivers and the big run of water to the Amazon began. He spotted a tiny palm leaf hut, a short path cut into the jungle, a square of maize, a dugout canoe. He pushed his head against the porthole for a better view. An hour-and-a-half and a thousand kilometres later over continuous jungle, the plane swooped low over the River Madeira and onto the new runway of Porto Velho. Out of the cool of the cabin onto hard black tarmac, the glare of the sun seared his face and the skin of his arms.

Through the temporary wooden terminal of a shed, a short taxi drive and he was back in the bustle of a frontier town. A town where, for nearly two centuries, the hope of riches had lured fortune-seekers to hunt for rubber, diamonds, tin, timber and of course, gold.

Bobby had allowed three days for his ranch business: be in touch with Colonel Delgado about title problems, run around for supplies, wages for the truck drivers, all done with enough money in his pocket. He imagined Idenea walking along these same hot streets but with little in her pockets.

Down by the river, he watched a pod of freshwater dolphins playing a hundred metres out from the bank, their sharp scimitar tails flicking out of the water, quite different from their cousins at sea. Behind him, grouped along cobbled streets, sprawled solid government buildings and new lines of half-built corrugated iron and plastic one-storey shops and offices.

He wandered back in the direction of the small railway museum passing two rusty steel water-towers with tops like coffee pots and Made in Loughborough cast into their steel supports rising up like fat totem-poles. He visited this museum every four or five months, pulled by a desire to see those sepia photographs, to look into those faces again. The museum, so proudly cared for by the town council, filled the old head office of the original Madeira Mamoré Railway Company. Rusting locomotives on rails that once ran 200 kilometres to the southwest and onto Guajará Mirim on the Bolivian border, were all that was left of a dream for the riches of rubber.[6]

The museum guardian shook Bobby's hand. 'Good to see you again.'

Bobby went straight to one of the cabinets full of letters and minutes of board meetings in Portuguese, Spanish and English. He studied the yellowing photographs of bearded white men in black top hats and frock-coats, feet astride a freshly laid rail track, with glum-looking Indians standing beside them. The absurd black clothes in such heat. At least the Indians were naked. Other photographs showed semi-naked black Africans. Those Indians who survived the work on the railway for a few months had soon fled back into the jungle, not strong enough for such labour. Only Africans from the west Indies could stand it.

This early invasion, even after the killing of so many Indians, only picked around on the edge of the forest. Now this new invasion, sixty years later, was a frenzied land grab comparable to the opening up of the American Midwest. For many of the poorer immigrants this might be their last chance ever to produce enough food to eat twice a day.

He stared into the eyes of the men staring back at the camera. Was there a triumphant smile from a face under a top hat? From other eyes, exhaustion and a resigned acceptance. He could see his own face reflected on the surface of the glass cover and wondered how his own eyes would have looked after so much hard labour.

A couple of months before, Bobby had sat next to a small dark man on a bus that had taken three days to cover 400 kilometres of the newly bulldozed BR 364.

As the bus bounced, bang and bang, Bobby and his neighbour collided in midair tumbling on top of each other. The man was smaller than Bobby, round and solid. He had an untidy black beard all over his face and had his hair back in a ponytail. His beady dark eyes were set beneath bushy black eyebrows.

Both apologised politely. 'Sorry, my name's Bobby'—'Help'—'Ouch'.

'Sorry, my name's Zé Magellan.'

At a roadside bar stop, Zé had pulled at Bobby's arm. 'Come on, out with it. What's a foreigner like you doing up here? Don't tell me you're another bloody missionary?'

Taken aback by the sarcasm in Zé's voice at the word 'missionary', Bobby had replied quietly while sipping at his glass of warm Coca-Cola, 'I'm a rancher. And you?'

'I'm an agent for FUNAI, the National Indian Foundation. I look out for Indians and try to help. I try to agree territorial boundaries.' He scowled. 'Where fucking possible,' and spat at the ground.

'Contact Indians, do you, huh? I don't agree with trying to influence primitive people.'

'So what do you know about primitive people, eh?'

Bobby hesitated. 'I've seen them in Borneo.'

'Borneo, why there?'

'British Army.' Bobby looked Zé straight in the eye. He didn't know what to expect; disapproval, admiration or a bored indifference? He wondered if Zé knew that Britain had helped Brazil in the early19th century, escorting the Portuguese Royal Family away from Napoleon and, much later, had invested in public services.

'Army? You?' Zé began to smile, his eyebrows lifting in question. 'With your accent, I thought you were from Santa Catarina down south. There're lots of Germans there with accents like yours. I spent my national service driving a truck in Rio. Silly for a shorty like me.' He laughed, pulling a toothpick out of his mouth. 'Difficult to see over the top of the steering wheel. You British are like us Portuguese. I'm of Portuguese descent, you know, with a bit of slave blood.' He pouted his fat lips. '*Pé na cozinha*,' a foot in the kitchen. We get around, don't we? Old friends, huh?'

Bobby laughed.

'I know about your empire. I'm descended from the great navigator Fernan Magellan, the first man to try to go around the world, not that he made it home, poor bastard.'

'Now where's that ranch of yours?'

'Mutum. Do you know it?'

'There's an unknown river near there, I need to check it out. There've been signs of Indians.' Zé put his hand on Bobby's knee. 'Come along with me? And we can talk. I'd like that, with a soldier.'

'I'd love to. I'm flattered.'

On arrival, their faces were so covered in red dust that their eyes shone out like a car's sidelights.

Bobby climbed the steps into the Suspendido Fish Bar; a construction of wood that stuck out over the River Madeira. Below, water swirled. Inside, you could eat well and drink even better. Part Indian and mulato waiters dressed in white jackets served caipirinhas, beer, grilled fish and steak. Their clean jackets civilising and out of place. When a breeze wafted in off the river, it was the coolest place in town: a refuge for miners and ranchers and even the odd civil servant. You could tell which by their dress; ranchers with high boots, miners with filthy broken finger nails, civil servant with a clean shirt. Many a deal was struck under the palm and tiled roof.

Bobby elbowed through laughing drinkers to the bar. One of them belched and slapped him on the back. He breathed in smoke and sweat. How he'd like to give her a good meal here.

He saw Zé sitting close to the river with a beer in his hand. Zé smiled and beckoned.

'Ready? Tomorrow we go,' he said curtly.

'I'm ready.'

Bobby heard a big voice booming for a beer. Surprised, he strode over and slapped Ari on the shoulder.

'Ari! You made it.'

'A man moves fast for a cold beer, Chefe. God willing, the cattle will be here tomorrow. Don't you worry, Ari's on top of it all.'

He pushed his hat back on his head. His tight leather trousers were red with mud, as was his rough cotton shirt. They ordered more beer as Ari told him not one of the pregnant cows had slipped a calf over four days of bumping and lurching. 'Tough brutes, those Nellore', he said draining half his glass with a couple of gulps.

'Come and meet Zé.' Bobby put his hand on Ari's shoulder and led him over to Zé's table.

A big man, with two shades of grizzly hair, sat opposite Zé with his back to the room. Ari and Bobby pulled up stools.

Zé gestured at the big man. 'This is Dias, the territory's land title watchdog. This is Bobby, a rancher.' Zé looked at Ari. 'And you?'

Bobby put his hand back on Ari's shoulder. 'This is Ari. Nothing happens without Ari.'

Bobby offered his hand to Dias. Dias clenched his fists on the table. Bobby had heard that he was no friend of the rancher. This was snubbing on purpose.

'What are you doing here?' Dias squinted at him as he sat down.

Bobby smiled in a friendly way. 'Farming. Opening up a ranch 150 kilometres down the road.'

'Yes, yes. I'm not a fool!' Dias was shouting. 'I mean, what are *you* doing here, you a foreigner? You shouldn't be here, this land is for us, not you foreigners. Haven't you messed up enough of the world without having to come here?'

Zé looked embarrassed. Ari gulped at his beer. Bobby looked down and studied the rippling patterns of the river through gaps in the floorboards. Shouldn't be here? Take a deep breath. How often during army training and then in battle had he been tested to the edge of self-control? He crossed his arms and looked up.

'We bring investment,' he began politely. 'We have local partners, we encourage employment, bring ideas, get on with things. But you obviously think there is something wrong with that?'

'You're a *capitalist*!' Dias spat the words at him. His heavy features darkening. 'Empire, exploitation. That's you. Here the land is for all the people, not just the few. Go back where you came from.'

At the bar the banter stopped, half-empty glasses held in midair.

Bobby felt every eye on him, his every word loud in the silence.

'Big and small can surely coexist,' he said. 'Help each other. Big brings money, small brings enterprise. Where I come from, we have many different people. It all seems to work out pretty well.' Bobby sensed general support from the bar.

'Where's your place?'

'Fazenda Rio Largo near Mutum.'

On *Largo*, Bobby felt a sharp kick to his shin. Zé was frowning at him.

Dias looked around seeking approval. Finding none, he turned back to Bobby, his wall-eye off centre.

'Good, so that's where you are, is it?' And to Ari, 'What are you doing with him, eh, cowboy?'

Ari, unperturbed by the superior voice, wiped froth off his moustache with the back of his hand. 'Earning a living. This gringo pays on time.'

He winked at Bobby.

Dias flattened his hands on the table and pushed himself up. The drinkers, still silent, made way as he thumped down the stairs and out into the night.

General conversation began again as a murmur.

'Always a bit of a bully,' said Zé, 'with his political ideas all those years ago, always angry. I used to march with him in protest against the Military. We wore hats with red stars. I had a picture of Ché Guevara on my wall. When I realised that I wouldn't get anywhere protesting, I took down the Ché picture and burned my hat. Dias said I was a traitor to the cause.'

'What cause?' Bobby said.

'To overthrow the Military.' Zé laughed without humour. 'Well, I hope your titles are safe.' He shook his head. 'That brute could cause you big trouble.'

Bobby shifted awkwardly in his seat.

Zé looked from one to the other. 'We're all in this *merda* together. We're lucky. Look at my poor Indians, poisoned and cheated.' He drew heavily on his cigarette and spoke slowly. 'I try to repair the damage ravaged on an alien people, and this bothers me. I'm also unwillingly helping remote people towards their own destruction and that is as certain as night follows day. And...' He lowered his voice. 'I can't face up to it. This agency is my job and I love it.'

He raised his eyebrows in question at Bobby.

'I, well? I must succeed.'

Zé pulled at his beard. '*Chega*! Enough! Off to bed. We're up early.' To Bobby. 'I'll pick you up before dawn. And don't on any account tell anybody, *tá bom*?'

'I'll be ready.'

The next morning, still dark, Zé wedged himself up on cotton-stuffed cushions so he could see over the steering wheel of his jeep. The faded initials of the National Indian Foundation FUNAI were stamped on the doors. This old *calumbeque* of a banger had often served as his bedroom up many a jungle trail.

He was wearing a pale grey denim hat, rather like a soldier's helmet, pulled down to his ears. His beady eyes shone out from an unshaven face. Beside him tall, fair and neatly shaven sat Bobby in khaki-coloured cotton shirt and trousers. There were a few badly mended rips in his trouser legs. Zé smiled approvingly. Strange fella, he thought.

Bobby glanced at his watch. The luminous hands showed 4.30 am.

'Great time of day, of night I mean.' Zé said cheerily.

In the back of the jeep lay a short aluminium canoe and an outboard motor with a long propeller shaft suitable for shallow water. Its back end stuck out over the tailboard. There were enough sacks of food for a week and a closed box that rattled at each bump. Bobby's neatly packed rucksack was wedged beside them.

'Better to go alone.' Zé had insisted, 'I don't want anybody to know where we're going.'

The air smelt damp and fresh. A lone dog, its skinny ribs picked out by the headlights, crossed in front.

As the jeep dropped off the end of the paved road, the headlights flashed onto the remains of rusting trucks and cars abandoned at the side of the road. Their drivers, brought to a final bone-shaking stop had walked off in despair, leaving them to rot. Some on their sides, their black tyres showing like the backs of giant woodlice. One or two had a palm leaf shelter over the back.

'What's in that box in the back, Zé?'

'You'll see,' Zé chuckled in excitement. 'Pots and pans, knives, hammers, axes, wire. To attract an Indian, show him we want to talk not kill.'

Zé wrestled with the wheel laughing at the vicious bumps. 'In a couple of hours, we'll be above the falls.'

'Say we see an Indian, then what? Will they be friendly or aggressive?'

'An arrow or two might fly about.'

162

'Arrows?' Bobby looked sharply at Zé, 'How do you protect yourself? With a gun?'

'I've never used my pistol yet.' Zé patted a leather holster in his waist band. 'I call out *amigo* in Guarani and stand still. If that doesn't calm things down, I get the hell out. The words of my other great hero, Marshall Rondon, 'Die if you must, never kill', are always with me. He was part Indian himself and this country's greatest explorer. And this territory is named after him in his lifetime, not bad, huh? He established the National Indian Foundation. Nowadays it's called FUNAI. I've never met true violence yet. Let's face it, the poor buggers have suffered. How do you think malaria got here? You and your wretched slaves brought it. The poor Indians suffer and the poor bloody monkeys as well.'

Zé turned off onto a rutted track as the first hint of dawn touched the tops of the trees.

'We must be near our place,' said Bobby, thinking aloud. 'It can't be more than eighty kilometres from here at the most.'

They took the battery out of the jeep and hid it fifty metres away, two wheels off and the nuts into Zé's rucksack.

'A fisherman might nick it. Look.' Zé pointed at a lone man standing on the edge of a rock a couple of hundred metres away, a bamboo cane in one hand. 'Good fishing here above the rapids. I expect he spent the night on the bank and lives in a hut nearby with wife and kids. Probably from the south, a charcoal burner and hungry as hell. Do you like fish?' They pulled the canoe out of the truck. 'He won't have checked if the land belonged to anyone, just set up on his own. Easy really. Cut four poles, dig'em in, cover with palm leaves, sling a hammock and there you are. Better than poverty in a city.'

'Gone feral you mean?'

'Yeagh. Once I met a man, as white as you, walking along a jungle path. He was naked, everything dangling about. He didn't know where he'd come from. He was friendly and I asked if I could help. He had red marks all over his body. He shook his head and carried on walking, barefoot. He seemed quite sane.'

'I met one or two like that out in the east who'd been isolated up a river for ages. They'd sooner fire a gun at you than say hello.'

'Grab the other side of the canoe, will you?'

They launched into the Madeira River, Zé with the water up to his waist, Bobby with it up to his knees. In the middle, some three hundred metres out, waves rolled and crested.

Heading up river they motored close in to the bank. Trees bulged over. Black cormorants vertical on the branches lifted off and dropped down low over the water. Some settled on the surface with only their heads sticking up, others dived. Kingfishers, as large as bantam chickens, flashing blue and green swooped down and up to perch and look again. Two black vultures circled above them.

'Not a pretty river,' Bobby called over his shoulder, 'but powerful.'

'Just you wait. It's one of the largest tributaries of the Amazon rising and falling more than fifteen metres every year.'

Zé steered while Bobby sat cross-legged amidships. Only a practised eye would have noticed the slate-coloured canoe and the two travellers, their heads barely visible above the gunwales, as it chugged up river. After four hours of steady progress, Zé turned left into the gentle flow of a smaller river about fifty metres wide. They glided in close to a sandbank where a cayman, mouth wide open, white teeth lit by the sun, lay basking. In the quieter stream the canoe gathered speed.

'Look at that one over there, Zé.' Bobby pointed. 'It's all skin and bones.'

'Yes, poor thing. Probably got a piranha stuck in its throat. It will die.'

Bobby stroked his own throat and imagined for a moment that it was full of bones.

In an overhanging tree, yellow-backed orioles cackled and fluttered. Their narrow-throated nests hung out over the water. If a fledgling were to fall; a boil of waiting piranhas. The black and gold adults flew out into the middle of the river squawked at each other, then flapped straight back to their nests, back forth, back forth seemingly all day, bicker, bicker.

'Look, Caciques? They nest above our ranch house'.

Zé nodded. 'We might see the rare red variety, very handsome. The Indians prize their feathers.'

A red-billed caracara hawk eyed them from the top of a tree, its head to one side. A grey heron, disturbed from fishing on a half-submerged log, lifted heavily off and flew with silent beats upstream. As the sun rose to midday, Zé steered near the bank in the shade. Bobby trailed one hand over the side in the tepid water. One moment he was staring at the brown water, the next at the green wall of jungle. As the heat softened his body, he pondered Idenea's story. He heard her voice, saw that twisted smile, the slow step by step telling. Ludo was right, they don't come like her very often.

And here he was, barely eighty kilometres from his own place. Could her plot 921 be next to or even part of his? If so, his partners would object to any trespass, that was for sure.

The sun flared down. The chug chug rhythm of the outboard and the humid heat lulled him into a numbed daze. He half closed his eyes. He sensed the curves in the river's course as the canoe wound back and around. He slipped down into the bottom of the canoe and laid his head on the cross-bench and looked upwards through heavy eyelids at the underside of the spreading branches.

Above, a labyrinth of creepers writhed together as they struggled to reach the light. He saw the confusion of his last four years in the maze of these twisting tendrils. At each bend in the river, the straight up darkness of the trees on both banks dragged his thoughts back to times he was fighting to forget.

The canoe glided out of the shade. The sun's bright heat burned at his skin. He sat up and splashed water onto his face. How could he find her child in this world of shadows and endless streams? No bars to hear gossip and no help from those invisible Indians. He dropped his hand back into the river.

They travelled all day; the general direction was south-east. In spite of Zé's cheerful comments, Bobby was unable to escape from the gloomy confines of his mind. At dusk they tied the canoe to the root of a tree. They pitched their hammocks between two trees and stuck short staves across and between the hammocks' support strings thus holding each end apart forming a rectangle the width and length of a human body. The mosquito net fitted neatly over this swaying bed and fell to the ground on each side without touching the sleeper.

Fire lit and after a meal of dried meat, rice and beans, they folded their nets under their bodies as they climbed into their hammocks. By careful positioning of hands and legs so that no skin touched the netting, no mosquito could puncture their skin. The two men lay silent, suspended above the ground. A few metres away the river shifted and gurgled. Fish broke the surface with a sharp splash.

Zé swung his hammock from side to side. He was quite sure that close by there were human beings exactly like him and Bobby except for their colour and isolation. Such was his excitement, sleep was going to be difficult. The embers of the fire flickered orange on the white of their hammocks; Zé's bulged down in the middle, Bobby's to the horizontal.

A quick breakfast of coffee and stale bread and they headed on. The prow of the canoe parted a dense shroud of mist that lay over the water. Zé steered close to the bank. His round denim hat was down to his ears and his dark glasses wedged on. Soon the sun dispelled the mist revealing the river in full width, the trees to their tops, a fishing egret sharp white against the dark water. Four green and red macaws flew over swearing at each other. Two black skimmers, white-bellied and red-billed, sped a few inches above the water, the tips of their lower bills slicing the surface.

Bobby pointed at a lone black howler monkey clinging to the trunk of a tree.

'On its own like that,' said Zé, 'probably got malaria, poor devil.'

They pointed at more and more. They did not speak, only smiled at each other knowing the sound of their voices could break the spell. By the time the sun was directly above, Zé had driven into six inlets. Each time the channel had ended in a lagoon thick with vegetation and no exit.

'We keep going, no going back.'

When the river narrowed to thirty metres and the water became shallow, he levered the long drive arm of the outboard upwards until the churning propeller broke the surface thrashing like a hooked fish.

An egret sprang off a half-submerged tree and instead of flying up or down the river, glided at right angles into a smaller stream. Zé followed. Low branches closed over into a greeny-brown tunnel. The current slowed. Vines as thick as anacondas grasped around the trunks of the trees. The water reflected black-purple.

Zé called out, more of a hoarse whisper than a call. 'Eyes open. Scan the banks for signs, foot prints, dug out canoes. Second nature to you, isn't it, soldier boy?'

Bobby sat up and scrutinised every metre of the sandbanks as they glided by.

The channel broadened and they sailed into a lagoon about three hundred metres across. Only the heads of fishing cormorants broke the mirror flat surface. They blinked in the bright sun. On one side trees with creepers hanging down to the water, on the other yellow sand banks running back towards the jungle.

'Piranha waters.' Zé announced with satisfaction, 'Grilled fish tonight. Right now though, we'll scout around.'

He kept the engine slow, adjusted his dark glasses and tugged at his denim hat. He savoured the magic of the moment. Here was a lagoon that nobody knew of, a lone fisherman maybe but even that unlikely.

He coasted close into the sandy beaches. More caymans basked on the rising banks. A flock of grey swallow-tailed kites hovered above the trees, their split tails spread wide. One and then another darted down hunting small lizards that lay on the broad leaves. High above vultures turned and turned.

'Cayman or canoe?' Bobby was pointing at a straight shallow score in the sand.

Zé cut the engine and nudged the prow onto the bank. They jumped out.

They peered down at the straight depression in the sand. It was about three metres long.

'Dug out canoe.' Zé claimed excitedly. 'Too long and wide for a cayman.' He wiped his dark glasses on his shirt. 'From now on we paddle. We mustn't scare them so we paddle slowly. We could be watched. And prepare to sweat, Gringo.'

Half an hour later, with sweat pouring down their faces, Zé, with a whoop of excitement, steered into a gently flowing channel not much wider than the length of their canoe. They paddled through a shadow world of tall trees and waving leaves.

Zé scanned the bank. 'This looks a likely place to me.'

They tied up to a tree sideways on, the drive arm levered up out of the water. Zé wandered in twenty metres or so flicking at low branches with his short machete. He cried out.

'Come here, quick. I've found something.'

Bobby ran to his side.

'Look, look a path.' Zé's black eyes shone at Bobby in triumph. A narrow well-worn path meandered through the trees beside the stream.

Zé gripped Bobby's arm. 'Do you think we're being watched?'

'I'd put that machete away, if I was you, Zé, right now.'

Bobby dropped to the ground. One second he was standing up, the next crouching, his body as still as the tree beside him. Only his eyes moved. From twenty metres away or unless you looked directly at him, Bobby had disappeared. He had moved as he had done so many times before, disciplined and careful, often in fear for his life. The words of his sergeant instructor at jungle school:

'Jenney, never do anything in a hurry in the jungle; stop, kneel, listen. A man in a hurry is a dead man.'

Zé dropped his machete and bending low stumbled over to Bobby.

'Seen something?' he whispered. Bobby mouthed 'no'. Completely still for several minutes they strained their eyes and ears. Zé couldn't control himself and kept looking from side to side. A screaming piha whistled, Wheee! Wheeeup! Wheee!

Bobby stood up. 'I can't feel or see anything. What about you, Zé?'

'You're a clever bastard, amigo, trained aren't you?' Zé pointed at the path. 'If I'm right this will lead to their village. We can't go there, not yet anyway. We'll hang up our toys and come back in the morning to see if any have been taken. Then hope for a contact.'

They strung a rope between two trees and tied on spoons, knives, pots, machetes and an axe. While they worked, they looked intently into the browns and greens.

'Why not all three axes, Zé?'

'I want to keep back two in case of a true contact. Axes are popular. Indians have no metal. Imagine us lot living amongst this vegetation without being able to cut anything. They fish and hunt with sharpened bone and hardened wood.'

Bobby thought of the chainsaws and bulldozers on the ranch.

Again, Whoooweeewheee-ep! a screaming piha whistled. A rumble of thunder in the distance. The two men, suddenly conscious of themselves, smiled at each other. They paddled back across the lagoon. Zé unravelled a circular fishing net with small lead weights around its edge and cast, fan shaped, over the water. He caught small fish for bait and soon hooked enough for dinner. The piranhas barked and snapped.

'Watch your fingers,' he said as he clubbed them to death before removing the hooks.

They pitched camp along the channel they had motored up that morning and soon had a fire going. Grilled piranha, although bony, tasted better than the dried salt meat of the night before. Sharing the same tree at one end of their hammocks, their heads only a couple of metres apart, and in spite of the rattling of the rain on the plastic sheeting they'd spread above their mosquito nets, talk was easy.

'If there are Indians here,' Bobby's voice quiet in the dark, 'what tribe will they be?'

'The Karitiana and the Karipuna are on this side of the river. We think they were brought in from further south sixty years or so ago to work as slaves in rubber and on the railway. Probably the majority died of exhaustion. Not strong enough, but we believe a few survivors fled into the jungle. Can't be sure, as they're not very keen now on the likes of you and me.' Zé paused. 'Also, there might be small settlements around here of unknown people who have never seen or been seen by modern man. By modern man I mean the unstoppable hordes of greedy bastards who won't die of a common cold or measles like these Indians will and they aren't even considered proper people.'[8]

The rain streamed down, the last flames of the fire sizzled and died.

'Who will you tell if we do make a contact?'

'Well? It's up to my boss.'

'And the missionaries?' Bobby said, rocking his hammock in irritation.

'You don't like them do you, Gringo? It's a free country for religion. They bring medicines we can't afford into remote places and that can help.'

Bobby butted in. 'And make money out of innocent people. Always so damn friendly trying to convert people for a dollar a head to send back to a mother-church. Uncontacted Indians should be allowed to stay in their lost paradise for as long as they want. Once contacted you unravel their society. So, don't bully them to a mad lifestyle they don't understand. That's what we learned in Borneo. They'll come in when they want to.'

Zé sighed. 'If you accept that Indian society will disappear and I'm trying to stop that, then maybe missionaries can help shattered lives.' He drew breath with a noticeable gasp and spoke brusquely. 'Millions of immigrants, like the multitude of stars in the night sky above, will be unstoppable. Many will die of disease but many bastards will hang on in. But my Indians won't. So, either we help them or it is death and their children's bones fought over by peccaries.'

---

8 Indians were made full citizens in 1988.

'*Death*,' he said again softly. 'If you don't find them, you can't protect them. Follow me?'

'Surely nobody should be allowed into this wild place.' Bobby continued. 'Let's not tell anybody.'

'Heh up, steady on, what about my career? This contact will be good for me. Promotion, in the local press, *Me*, José Maria Magalhães, discovers unknown tribe. I have to think of my little wife, Lala and our baby Jonala.'

'Now, you tell me what a professional soldier, a foreigner like you is doing up here? What's it like to be shot at? I can see all this is easy for you. Out with it, there's only the dark.'

'Too late.'

'No, it's not. You walk stiff so lighten up and tell me. I'm interested.'

'Oh, bugger off.'

'No. I bring you here, so you tell me.'

'Bargain, huh? But still bugger off.'

Silence in the dripping dark. Female mosquitoes, big and small, brown and yellow, swarmed onto the white netting frantically seeking the blood they needed to breed.

Bobby took a deep breath. 'I left my army under a cloud, understand. It was my own fault. I couldn't help it. I had family troubles at the same time and that's all I'm damned if I'm going to tell you.' He laughed quickly. 'You'd make a good interrogator, Zé. No need for thumbscrews with you on the job.'

'I want more later and I won't forget.' Zé murmured.

Take everything, we must be mobile, Zé said.

This time Zé in front with Bobby at the back. Zé's paddle flashed in the sun. The lagoon shone black and pink in the early morning, not a ripple ruffled the surface in the motionless air, not a fishing cormorant to be seen. Two Toco toucans, their bright black and orange bills out in front, beat rapidly across. The canoe knifed up a small bow wave.

They turned into the narrow stream. Zé knelt forward, a hand on each gunwale.

'Stop.' He signalled with a rapid downward movement of his hand and in a rough whisper, 'The axe and knives have gone.'

The canoe rocked as he scrambled to his feet.

There was a gleam in Zé's eyes. 'This is contact.'

Zé carried another axe to the rope, Bobby a couple of knives. Zé examined the empty hanging strings. He could not control his excitement. 'They've been unravelled, not cut. We hang more knives. I'll hold another axe in my hand and keep showing it all the time. We act normal, make coffee, see what happens.' Still in a whisper. 'Are you any good at tracking?'

They studied the ground beside the hanging rope.

Bobby pointed. 'Look. These are from the balls of feet. They're very faint but I'd say from a well-balanced step.'

'Very good.' Zé nodded approvingly.'

They tried to ignore the rope by looking in the opposite direction. Sun rays beamed down through the leaves and picked out shadowy shapes on the forest floor. Parrots cackled above. A Mutum bird whooomped and whooomped.

Zé whistled between his teeth as he bustled about. Was this an unknown tribe? Would they have to run for it? Or would he, Zé, be acclaimed as a modern explorer like his idol the great Marshall Rondon? His dearest wife, Lala, would be so proud and maybe his parents would finally accept his chosen career? His father had always chided that there was no money in Indians.

Bobby slung the hammocks in case of a long wait, stirred the coffee and hummed a favourite Handel tune. This was different to stalking terrorists, to planning an armed patrol. He stretched to full height.

At midday they lay in their hammocks, swinging gently from side to side, swapping jungle stories. They lay silent as the sun leant over.

A puff of wind, a rattle of leaves, both men pushed out of their hammocks. Bobby felt it. Zé felt it. They turned as one. Two Indian men were standing quite still about seventy metres away, their bodies half hidden by a tree trunk. They were a few steps away from the rope of tools and were looking directly at Zé and Bobby. They were of Zé's size and were completely naked except for a woven belt around their waists. Their black hair was cut in a circular pudding bowl fringe around their heads, their skin dark red-brown. Each carried a long slender bow.

For Bobby, there was the staring Indian on the wall of room No 5.

Zé mouthed, '*Raise one hand slowly, let it fall back real slow, walk back to the fire and fiddle about. In a moment I'm going forward with another axe, understood?*'

'Yes.'

Zé raised his hand. Bobby poked at the fire. Time stood still in the humid air. Zé walked back a few paces, picked up an axe and advanced with unhurried steps towards the two Indians. They hadn't moved since first eye contact. He stopped at the rope and offered the axe with a forward movement of his arm. He repeated this movement several times. The two Indians did not react. Bobby was right, they were barefoot. Zé reckoned they were in their early thirties. He smiled and took off his hat, letting his ponytail fall free. He swung the axe from side to side.

'For you,' he said offering the axe forward, 'to improve your lives.'

He tried a few Indian words that he knew for Hello and Good Day. With his confidence growing he edged forward until he could just make out the coloured markings on their cheeks. One of them shrank back behind his tree. Zé stopped, put the axe on the ground, stepped back and gestured with his hand.

'Take it.'

Bobby watched. Never before had he seen such an expression on a human face, was it innocence or was it calm indifference? One of them glanced furtively at his companion before stepping out from behind his tree, exposing all of his body, his eyes fixed on the axe. The other followed, bow in one hand, a dead monkey hanging from his belt. Cautiously they approached Zé and the axe.

173

At the moment when Zé and one of the Indians were holding the axe together, the Indian feeling its shaft and blade, Bobby heard a faraway noise. At first, he thought it was the buzz of one of those big black and orange bees, the size of your thumb, that fly so noisily in horizontal straight lines. If a human happens to be standing in the way, well, it's smack and the bee will either be clinging to your clothes or on its back on the ground whirring angrily. No, this buzz was too steady for a bee and dragged Bobby's attention away from the drama in front of him.

Oh no. Oh yes.

But there it was, the unmistakeable high-pitched rev of a speeding canoe. From the proximity of the sound, he could tell that the canoe was fast approaching the mouth of the inlet where they'd paddled in so quietly earlier that morning. The engine slowed and whoever they were, must be circling round and round. What could this be, a chance fishing party? Nobody else could possibly know about this place.

He glanced quickly over at Zé and the two Indians. Zé had a broad grin all over his face and the two Indians were smiling as well.

And then the cry.

'Zoneee...Zoneee...'

'God's truth!' Bobby swore.

He turned and raced along the river bank. It was her, that girl Idenea. How in God's name had she come here? Her voice again. 'There Juca, see there's another inlet. Go on, there's a canoe and, look, a man beside it.'

The canoe's engine dropped to a gurgle. Bobby hid behind a tree. What could he say to Zé before she saw him? Zé would think that he had told her where they were going.

'Shit,' he muttered as one of the Indians looked past him at the approaching canoe.

Bobby stepped out as Idenea's canoe bumped alongside. There were two other passengers, Ana, Idenea's friend from the bar, and the steersman. Bobby recognised him from Idenea's description as Juca. He was wearing a blue t-shirt tight on his biceps and a black forage cap with the peak reversed, his eyes hidden behind reflector lens sunglasses.

When the engine cut, the jungle was quite silent for Bobby. He looked up at the creepers hanging from the branches above. How lucky he'd been that Zé had trusted him. If Zé were to doubt him, he could easily fall back again into that sour old world of self-doubt and guilt.

Idenea hadn't recognised him yet, her eyes down trying to keep her balance.

'How in God's name did you find your way here?' He exclaimed, 'I told you I had to be alone.'

'You?' She blinked in disbelief. 'Bobinho?' She scrambled up onto the bank. They stared at each other.

'Our plot is near here...' she stammered. 'I had to come and look for my baby boy.'

He looked aghast. 'In this wilderness?'

She pointed at the steersman. 'He's a rubber tapper. He knows his way around and...' She stopped in mid-sentence, her body rigid, her mouth open, suddenly seeing the Indians.

'It's them,' she yelled, 'they've got my baby!' She sprang into a run. 'Zonee, Mama's here!' The Indians retreated into the shade of the trees.

'Please, please, my baby.' One flip-flop flew from her foot. 'Give him back to me.'

Bobby ran after her. 'Stop, you crazy girl.'

She ignored him. He sprinted and grabbed her by the wrist.

'Stop, listen to me,' he spoke firmly, 'your baby is not here. Try to see some sense for God's sake.'

'Let me go, you brute.'

Bobby held fast. She swung her free fist at his face. He caught it and held both of her arms. She struggled shouting, '*Filho da puta. Dog. Brute*'. She kicked wildly but his strength was too much, only this time it was the strength of the man who'd cared for her. She started to cry, a sobbing that changed to hysterical laughter as she collapsed to the ground. 'Oh what can I do? Please, Bobinho...what can I do?'

He let her go.

Zé stood quite still, his attention one moment on the screaming Idenea, the next on the disappearing Indians.

'The Indians have run off.' His face full of fury. 'You silly bitch, you've ruined everything.' And to Bobby, 'You know her, do you? I told you to keep this to yourself, you stupid bastard.'

Idenea, still on the ground, weeping silently, stared after the Indians.

Zé, axe swinging from one hand, stamped back to the canoes.

'*Vamos.*' He spat. 'All the whores in hell.' Then halting in front of the man in the blue t-shirt and dark glasses. 'Juca?' He exclaimed, 'What the hell are you doing here?'

Juca was leaning against a tree, one hand on the trunk, the other on his hip, one ankle cocked up against the other. He nodded and smiled through toothless gums.

'Well what do you know, Zé, how's life with you? As you know I tap rubber and she lets me work behind her plot. I'm just repaying a favour.'

Bobby came over. 'So, Zé, you know this man as well, do you?'

'Juca works for the agency from time to time. Born here, knows the jungle better than anyone else.'

Bobby shook his head in disbelief. 'So everybody knows everybody and we're up an unknown river. How..?'

'Simple really.' Juca spoke without emotion, his biceps relaxing. 'It's you, Gringo, shacking up with her, right?' He gestured at Idenea. 'She asked me to help her because you'd given her hope she might find her baby and Zé has often spoken about an unexplored river around here. So, I thought I'd have a look and get close to my origins, to the bugres you see.' He laughed without sound and blew his nose into the border of his shirt.

Zé raised his eyebrows in surprise. Bobby, embarrassed, glanced sideways at Idenea. He caught her eye and smiled quickly. She turned away.

Juca, enjoying the attention, stood onto both feet. 'I work on her place nowadays although I don't think it's hers any more as most of the family have left. I've often tapped for rubber on the other side of the big river.' He pointed at Idenea again. 'She's convinced Indians have stolen her baby boy. Impossible. A bad story. But she's no kitten this one...'

Zé raised an arm for silence. 'Snooping, that's what you're doing, Juca, snooping.'

Bobby close up to Juca. 'How far the other side of the river did you go?'

'Forty to fifty kilometres or so that way.' Juca waved his arm vaguely.

'Tssshh.' Bobby spun around to Idenea. 'So, your plot 921 is next to ours or on it. So, it *was* you that Ari saw from that aeroplane a year ago.'

Idenea sprang to her feet. 'It's our land. We worked do you hear? Not like an idle squatter waiting to be paid off. Tell me, Juca, why's it not mine any more? Romi will be back soon and me as well, so why isn't it mine?'[7]

'Just a hunch,' he drawled.

'I've had enough,' Zé grunted in irritation. 'I'll hang up some knives and come back in a week or two. And as for you, little mullata,' addressing Ana, 'you, who've said nothing, I bet you're as puzzled as me. I want explanations.'

He looked angrily at Bobby. 'You have much to answer for, young man. Now, let's get out of here.'

'I promise you I never told anyone.'

Ana pulled at Idenea's hand. 'I can't stand it here, the tall trees and all the croaking. Please, *meu bem*, take me away.'

The sun was way down as they paddled back into the violet blue of the lagoon. Above them parrots and toucans winged to their roost.

'Fish?' Zé called from his canoe. 'You or me Juca?'

'Never without one, Chefe.' He unravelled his throwing net.

They were stoking their fire with green leaves. Zé, silent. Gone the photograph in the papers; Young Sertanista, José Maria Magalhães, discovers unknown tribe. Is this the next Marshall Rondon?

'I want to know right now, how this cock-up happened. And you, Bobby, you let me down.' Bobby winced. And to Idenea, 'As for you, young woman, stolen babies, squatting and knowing this gringo. Go on explain yourselves.'

Bobby, in spite of Zé's accusation, was beginning to feel some inner peace again. Was it the orange of the fire or seeing this girl again?

'So, Idenea,' he said, 'you or me?'

She was crouching on a log as close into the smoke as breathing would allow. 'You tell him. I've had enough.'

Her eyes fixed on the red glow of the fire she was thinking of her failure to find her baby boy. She pulled her knees to her chin. He'd probably been eaten by a jaguar or swallowed by an anaconda. She hadn't looked at Bobby since he'd grabbed her wrists. But now this man was describing her life exactly how she had described hers to him. He spoke with such admiration. Could it be, that this man, whom she'd teased as being a silly Bobinho, liked her, truly did, this unknown foreigner? Little by little she turned her head so she could watch him. And she was charmed. She'd find her Zoni, sure she would.

'Meu Deus,' Zé coughed, 'you settlers get it thick. I thought my job was tough enough. All right, Bobby, forgiven, *tá bom*? But Juca you...' He pointed his finger at the swinging hammock. 'Stop following me about or you're out of a job, understood?'

Soon all five hammocks, five white cocoons, swinging gently.

Before the light of dawn crept through the trees, Zé was up. 'Come on everybody.'

The canoes slipped into the stream. Idenea and Ana eased their bodies downwards out of the damp so that only their heads showed above the gunwales. Bobby, sitting up in the other canoe, savoured the early cool. Birds, ghostlike in the mist, flitted across the bows.

They soon glided into the strong current of the Madeira river with four hours to go. The mist gone, Idenea sat up in the warmth of the sun and glanced across at Bobby. He caught her eye and smiled. He started to laugh, a belly laugh, bold and noisy. And like an uncontrollable sneeze, she couldn't stop herself from laughing back, all anger gone. Bobby flicked a handful of water at her. She splashed back.

Juca, steering alongside, frowned. This foreigner and that mad girl could wreck his plans for Plot 921. He'd have to tell the Boss. *Merda.*

Back in town with Zé's old jeep recovered, Bobby led the two girls over slippery cobbles to his one-roomed wooden office. A board with *Fazenda Rio Largo* printed on it hung on the blue door, and inside an unreliable telephone and a couple of hammock hooks. He and Ari had built the hut to be in touch with the outside world when they came to town. Often, he had stayed overnight swinging in his hammock, waiting for a call that might never come.

'I'll find a bus for you girls,' he announced.

'I'm not leaving,' Idenea said, her contented smile fading. Leaving where her Zoni might be and away from this man who strode about with such confidence. No.

The blue door banged open. Ari stepped out, a welcome grin all over his face.

'Good to see you, Chefe. A telegram for you.'

Bobby read, 'Report soonest Head Office for urgent discussions. Alistair.'

'I have to go immediately.' He chose his words. 'My boss wants me back in London.'

Saying he would find a bus had been a ruse to see whether she wanted to stay or leave. Her look of disappointment told him. How could he send her back to that motel and those men? What was it that had penetrated the cold reserve that he'd built up these past three years?

179

Ana pulled a reluctant Idenea into the bus. He kissed her forehead and stroked her neck. She raised one hand to his elbow and held it there without looking up. That was all. Neither spoke. As the bus pulled away, she didn't acknowledge the waving Bobby.

The bumps and the heat prevented any sleep. When she recognised a place where the family had stopped, she pressed her nose against the glass for a better look. She smiled ruefully at the memory of her Hope game. If it hadn't been for the debt and the trickery, they would have made it. And here she was going back to that shithouse of oversexed men, to earn money quick and it had to be quick. She tightened her hands in her lap. At least the two hundred dollars from him would help. Him? Oh, *Meu Deus*, Him, just gone like that.

Three days later she was sipping Coca-Cola with Ana in the Perfect Peace Motel. Ludo had greeted them eagerly saying many clients were asking for them. Her tummy had tightened.

'I really cannot do this any more,' she was saying to Ana. 'Maybe I can work as a waitress again, two shifts a day. You saw where Zoni might be, Ana, so please tell me what to do?'

'Don't leave me, Idenea, please.' Ana sucked on her straw and smiled weakly out of her dark brown eyes. 'You and your crazy plans. Listen, here's not too bad. Any money's good for me.'

'Pshaaaw.' Idenea grimaced, 'You like doing it then, huh?'

Ana sucked noisily. 'I can't even read or write so why don't you teach me, *tá bom*? You can help me change.'

Idenea liked Ana's simple trust and friendship and, although she was alone in the world, she was always smiling as if being kind to everyone would help her along.

'Well you never know,' Ana teased, 'that foreigner might come back and whisk you away. I saw you two looking at each other. Well then?'

'Don't you see that I'm only a simple girl who can only just read and write?' Idenea smiled her twist of a smile. 'But he did make me tell everything about myself.' She put her chin in her hand and leant on the table. 'Why did I bother? I don't hope for anything any more.'

'Aaaah,' Ana sighed, 'I never did.'

'Lucky you.'

That night she ignored the Indian on the wall. Even after three days of bouncing up and down and aching limbs, she could not sleep for fear and fuss.

Bobby raced through London airport.

Red double-decker buses belching black fumes splashed through puddles. Black taxis queued at traffic lights, rivulets of rain dripping down their sides, screen wipers waving back and forth.

He had wired his parents before leaving, he hadn't seen them in three years and he longed to see his son, Michael. As to Beatrice, he couldn't make up his mind what to do.

As he climbed the bare wooden stairs of the Atkinson offices, the old cage lift was out of order, to the fifth and top floor of the Victorian building he couldn't stop imagining how Idenea would be earning money at that moment. On that bed with some rough lout. He hesitated on a landing. Could he have shown any commitment? Stepping on, he vowed that once back on the ranch he would stop tormenting himself with self-doubt. Buoyed up by this resolution he bounded forward.

Alistair Atkinson was waiting for him.

'Hello, Cowboy,' he boomed. 'You're fit, not even puffing? Come on in. Good trip? Good, good.'

Alistair never minded when the lift was out of order. On the contrary he enjoyed the discomfort the many breakdowns caused, thus obliging all comers and especially his managers from overseas, to climb the five flights of polished boards. Showed if they were fit, he'd joke. His father, also an Alistair and the previous Chairman, always said that he could judge if they were on the booze by the colour of their faces and by how much they puffed. Hands on out in the field, that's what he liked to know.

This Alistair slapped his artificial leg. 'Bloody Boche.' Never a day passed without him slapping his leg and swearing. He'd lost a leg in a tank battle in the western desert. When the lift was out of action for a second time in a week, he'd say that if he could climb those stairs so could everybody else. Some of his staff, who'd lunched too well on a Friday, didn't agree with him. Each flight took him three minutes, the full climb a good quarter of an hour. He grunted loudly as he thumped upwards arriving at the top in a muck sweat. He would keep fit to show those Hun buggers he wasn't beaten.

Underneath this bluff display there was a tough operator who was fighting to drag his old company into the modern world. Due to his name of Alistair Atkinson, some of his staff referred to him as AA or Brmm Brmm after the national Automobile Association. He ushered Bobby into his office.

'How's the golf?'

Bobby smiled as he remembered Alistair, on a quick visit to the ranch, taking a golf club from his bag and bashing a ball up and down the beginnings of their first clearing. He'd insisted that Bobby join in and soon balls were slicing into the jungle. They didn't bother to look for them. He wondered how a jaguar would react to a white ball whizzing past its nose.

'I trust the clearing's bigger now. We can't go on losing balls like that, can we? How are the cattle, how's the new grass and Ari and the men?' For quarter of an hour Alistair quizzed and even, 'Got yourself a woman yet? There must be dozens of your old flames who'd love to go out for a holiday, eh?'

Bobby shook his head and to himself, 'Well, did he have a woman?'

'Now, young man, to business.' His false leg banged the side of the table. Bobby wondered what it would be like to lose a leg. He touched the wound in his own leg.

'How are the partners in São Paulo?'

'Fine.' Bobby nodded. 'They turn up sometimes. It's usually the guy with the big hat, you know, LG, the difficult son. I humour him.'

'Do you think they've got any extra money?'

'Can't answer that one. LG seems to booze it up pretty good if that's any indication.'

Alistair spoke slowly. 'Well, Robert, the nub of it is this...' Bobby felt impending importance as Alistair rarely called him Robert. 'Our company Atkinson and Co. for the first time in 200 years is short of money. Crop failure and weak prices world wide are all biting. So, we can only support your operation at half-mast. We have to find another partner. Now, can you or your family plug the hole? Of course you'd be co-owners with us and the São Paulo bunch but management would stay with us. You'd be your own boss. Well, what do you think?'

'Well, Sir.' Bobby's strict upbringing made him call Alistair 'Sir' before slipping to the familiar. He felt a tingle of expectancy.

Bobby's head ached with detail and fatigue. He didn't mention the problem of land title. The Colonel would sort that one out for him. In short, the Company needed £300,000 to support Rio Largo's three-year plan.

'I'll talk to my parents...' He faltered. He didn't want to explain the difficulties he had with his father. 'I'll let you know in a few days.'

Alistair shook his hand at the top of the stairs. 'This could set you up young man, put things right for you again.'

He stayed with Perry, his friend from school and the army. He drank too much, researched on malaria and on Indian tribes in the Amazon. In one book there was a photograph of a smiling Indian standing beside a river. He slumped back in his chair, closed his eyes and heard the whirr of Idenea's canoe. He held that page open for some time.

He found Michael with his mother, Alice. Beatrice had left him for the day. He was relieved not to see those eyes which he had loved so much and which had haunted his dreams so often. He didn't ask after her. Michael nagged him for news of Ari and Leonidas. They romped about pretending to be jaguars and piranhas.

He spent a whole day talking to his parents. His red brick childhood home, Abbey Hall, smelled of wood smoke and old curtains. The branches of the cedar tree at the end of the lawn bent in the wind. The stairs creaked as he climbed up to his old bedroom with the blue wallpaper.

His father occasionally asked a question. Bobby, aware that his father felt that he had let the family down by leaving the army the way he did, waited for the inevitable from the old General.

'My boy, consider this please,' his father said on the last day, his tone sharp and without affection. 'Is this plan of yours a sustained vision or is it just an adventure? I always challenged my officers with that.'

Bobby searched for a sensible answer. 'It's a chance for the future, Dad. Remember how you always encouraged me to be positive.' His mother liked what she heard. As he left for the station, she gave him an envelope with a cheque inside. He hugged her. To the rhythmic clicking of the train's wheels, he read,

—*I am quite well off and can spare you this money. Do as you wish*

with this £100,000. Your project sounds extraordinary.
Don't take any notice of Dad, he'll get over it all one day.
I'll keep a watch over young Michael and Beatrice. Your
loving Mother.—

Underneath in his father's hand writing, '*Mind you don't lose it. Dy.*'

Alistair breathed his thanks. 'So you'll have ten per cent of the enterprise and with the São Paulo partners matching yours and you as manager we should be tickety-boo for the next five years.'

Bobby pinned a map of the ranch on the wall. They poked their fingers at it: landing strip here, pastures here, coffee seedlings there, sawmill over there, corral here.

Outside, November rain drizzled onto grey pavements where black umbrellas jostled for space.

'Here.' Alistair handed over a brown packet. 'Some mail for you.' He shook Bobby's hand. 'I must go, so good luck and be in touch.' He thumped off downstairs chuckling in satisfaction that the lift was out of action again.

Bobby sliced open the packet and unfolded the Rondônia Newspaper, the Alta Madeira. On the front page in large unsteady letters, 'For you, Chefe'. Ari had dog-eared the second page:

The unrecognisable body of a young woman was found two days ago at the mouth of a previously unknown river that flows into the Jaci river. Fisherman Benedito dos Santos said that he was exploring for new opportunities when he saw the remains of a body caught in the branches of a half sunken tree. Thinking of the family, the good-hearted Benedito brought the semi-decomposed and half eaten remains back to town. There was no identity card on the body, just a necklace with a wooden cross. Please contact the news desk if anybody can help.

Bobby felt the blood rise to his cheeks. He stopped breathing and stared into the street. The gutters below ran with water. A body floating in that river. He could see it circling in the current, piranhas attacking from underneath. The floodlit dome of St Paul's, a dull hazy yellow in the fine rain.

'Oh, sweet Jesus.' He groaned so loudly that Alistair's secretary looked up from her typewriter.

He cursed himself for not knowing the telephone number of the Perfect Peace Motel.

He grabbed the telephone and dialled the airline, 'For God's sake change my ticket for tonight. It's urgent.'

Above the north Atlantic Bobby read the Alta Madeira from cover to cover; when Rondônia might become a State, new roads, finds of alluvial gold and then a short interview with José Magalhães saying, 'Our agency is sure that several uncontacted tribes live within the Territory's jungle. Please, any rubber tapper, rancher or miner, be in touch if you come across signs of Indians.'

Zé was grinning out of the photograph with his hat pulled down to his ears. He must have made that contact. There was an interview with Colonel Delgado, the Territory's Governor, appealing to all settlers and the agriculture agency, to cooperate to avoid disputes and in particular over illegal squatting.

He rolled the paper into a tight tube and held it across his knees with both hands. He willed the aeroplane onwards bending his legs back and forth as if riding a horse. He found himself praying, something he hadn't done since he had thrown religion out of his life three years ago. 'Dear God, don't let it be her, please...okay?' His favourite hymns and psalms came back to him like summer swallows. He fell asleep with 'Fool that you are' in his head. He woke stiffly with a blue sea and yellow sand below.

He stepped down into the heat of Cuiabá. He told the taxi driver to step on it.

The driver, wearing dark glasses even though it was night, sniggered. 'Starved of it are you? Don't worry, my old banger will do her best.'

'Just get me there, will you.'

'*Sim Senhor.*'

'Keep the change.' Bobby said abruptly as the headlights picked out the entrance of the Perfect Peace Motel under the flashing pink tubular hearts.

He dumped his bags in the small lobby and ran into the bar. Couples sitting at tables, cigarette smoke, the television on the wall showing more of the same soap. But no Idenea. He bumped against tables as he ran.

'Heh, heh, steady on young man. Why such a mad hurry?'

Bobby stopped outside No 5. He leant one hand on the door frame and knocked.

'Idenea?'

He knocked again, louder this time. 'It's me, Bobby, are you there?'

Silence. No movement from within. Nothing.

He knocked again. He gazed up into the night sky. He heard the pulse of his blood against his skull. Maybe it was the barking of a dog or a burst of laughter from the bar that muffled the sound of the door opening behind him.

'Bobinho...I never expected to see you again.'

She was framed in the half open door, her hair sticking in dirty strands to the sides of her face, her eyes heavy and wet.

She gestured with one arm. 'Wait for me in the bar. You can't see me like this.'

He advanced impulsively towards her. 'You, you're not...'

186

'Go to the bar,' she said and shut the door.

Bobby sat at an empty table, his heart slowing. He knew what he was going to say to her. He'd rehearsed every word high above the Atlantic.

Ten minutes later she walked in. He jumped up, skidding his chair backwards on the concrete floor. She had showered. Her hair hung loose down her back. She was wearing her old long-sleeved shirt and her wooden cross. She did not return his smile. She held another wooden cross in her hand.

'You're safe,' he stammered.

She sat down.

'Ari sent this to me in London.' He opened the Alta Madeira. 'I was sure it was you. But the wooden cross in your hand? Ana? What happened?'

Idenea sloped back in her chair, chin down on her chest and dropped both arms limply to her sides.

'I had to try again.'

She looked up at him with remorse in her eyes. 'I was sure those Indians I saw with you and Zé had taken Zoni.'

'Ana, bless her golden heart, said she wouldn't let me go alone, so brave of her. We hired a motor canoe and said we were going fishing.' She forced a rueful smile. 'We found that river, by luck really. I steered too close to the bank. The branch of a fallen tree knocked her into the water. I never saw her again. For hours I circled round and round shouting for her. Poor, poor Ana, trapped under water, my only friend in all the world. And all my fault...'

Idenea struggled with her breathing. 'I spent several days asking for help. They said it was too far away. I gave up. I arrived back here only a few hours ago.' She lowered her eyes to the table.

He pushed across a glass of rum and coke. 'Well, this newspaper took notice, didn't it?'

They sat in silence, her eyes on her glass turning it round and round. He stared at the top of her head, his prepared speech draining away.

187

Minutes passed. Not a word. Others in the bar stumped out bidding goodnight. Alone under the bare fly-blown bulbs, moths fluttering in circles. Silence.

He said, 'Look at me. Go on.'

She raised her eyes. There was a flicker of enquiry. He smiled hesitantly. She smiled back, one second melancholic the next reproachful.

He sought her hands. 'It's all crazy isn't it?'

'Stop,' she said softly, 'You thought the body was me...and you came as quickly as you could, just for me?'

'Yes.'

'I—' his confidence rushing back, 'I—I have come to take you away with me. That is, I want you to be with me? I have to leave in the morning.'

He'd said it. He sighed with relief.

'Where to?' Her eyes widened, a mixture of doubt and surprise.

'Back up there. I have a five-year contract. We can start afresh *together*. Make new lives for ourselves. You and I. Well? Please say yes.'

'But don't you see I'm married, you silly boy, my Bobinho.' She twisted her hands within his.

Hearing that teasing nickname again made him care so much words stuck in his throat. 'He's not around is he, I mean your husband Valdo? Anyhow I'm married as I told you, so we can deal with that later.'

She was no longer smiling. 'You see it's difficult for me to do anything positive or happy at the moment.'

She stood up and walked over to the wall, her back towards him. Her hands tightened into fists. She pushed them down her thighs. 'My guilt for Ana, my guilt for my baby boy. How can I live with it?'

'Living here is hard, Idenea,' he said quietly. 'Accidents happen all the time. Ana's not coming back, is she? And as for your baby, you'd be nearer to where he disappeared up there rather than down here and I'll help you find him.'

She didn't answer. With appeal in his voice he said, 'We go tomorrow, that is if you say yes. There's so much to do and your experience will be worth gold to me.'

'Worth...worth gold to you?' With a quick step she was beside him. She kissed him full on the lips. She was laughing, she was sobbing, she was giggling as if she couldn't decide how to be: happy, miserable, ashamed?

She took his hand and pulled him to his feet. 'First we go to my room. And you tell me who you are. I only know of that bullet wound. You are going to tell me all, *tá bom*?'

In the white square of room number 5, lying side by side with the Indian watching over, he told her about himself, something he had never told anyone in such detail before. Telling Zé to bugger off was the closest he'd got. He spoke fast. His telling or rather admission of his past life and her close attention deepened their growing intimacy.

She stroked his shoulder and his forehead murmuring, 'Aarrh, so that is why.'

He put one hand on hers. 'It's late and I am going to fall asleep even with you beside me.'

She rose on to one elbow. 'There's much more, isn't there? Promise to tell me the rest tomorrow. You haven't told how you got this yet.' She touched his bullet wound. 'Wow, Jesus in Heaven, my Bobinho of the bullet.'

'Things are different for me now.' He squeezed her hand.

'How do you mean?'

'It's that I don't want to leave you. I love the way you strive to do things. You're like me. I just hope you will come with me?' His new-found confidence ebbed as he waited for her reply.

She continued to stroke his shoulder for several moments. 'Yes, it's true, you are something good in my life. But I am in such a muddle myself, I don't know what I feel, whether it is love or something else for you. You know how things have been for me. How long it might last I don't know.'

She kissed his cheek. 'But what I feel right now is for you. I will try for you. That I will. It's a chance for us both. And you're right

189

I'll be closer to Zoni and you'll help me find him, won't you? Go on, promise.' She pinched his arm. 'And I can't help Ana any more.' She hesitated. 'Call it love if you like.' She laid her head on his shoulder.

He kissed one eyebrow, then the other. 'These have done too much crying and I don't want your lips twisting in that sad smile any more. From now on I'm going to make them laugh.'

Even though the light of the coming dawn was upon them they loved each other, touching as if for the first time, shy and tentative. She hid nothing from him, even her scars. All the while they smiled into each other's eyes. At the end, she wouldn't let him go. Thus tied, they snatched an hour of sleep.

'So, where are you two off to today?' Ludo said in surprise as Bobby checked out.

'We're leaving.' Bobby shook Ludo's hand. 'And this time together. You're right, they don't make the likes of her anymore.'

Ludo's smile dropped. 'You can't just take her like that, she's part of…' His chin jutting out. 'She's part of…well, you know. It's my business.'

'Yes, he can.' Idenea pushed forward unsmiling. 'You can't stop me.'

Bobby fumbled in his pocket and laid some notes on the counter.

Ludo brushed them roughly to one side. 'Go on then, off with you. But young man, I do congratulate you. She's a rare one.'

Idenea placed her hand on Bobby's shoulder.

Ludo nodded approval at this gesture of support. 'You're going to need more than luck where you're going.'

Idenea handed over two necklaces with wooden crosses. 'Ana will never come back.'

'Gone back east, huh?'

She shook her head and walked quickly to the door and out.

She carried a cotton bag. In it was everything she owned, a few clothes, her wooden doll and her notebook, now very dog-eared.

Before shutting the door of No 5, she'd put her hand up to take the picture of the Indian with her, but instead she'd murmured, 'You'll have to look after yourself from now on, you old bugre. When I find my little boy, I'll let you know.' And had left it on the wall.

In the taxi she said excitedly, 'I've never been in an aeroplane before.'

'It's quicker, you'll see.' Bobby laughed. 'An hour and a half instead of your five weeks.'

'Here.' She thrust two ten-dollar bills into his shirt pocket. 'That's all I have left. They're yours anyhow.'

He put his arm around her shoulder and whispered in her ear, 'Does that mean I can do whatever I like with you now?'

She bit his ear. 'Just you try, my Bobinho, just you try. But first you tell me how you got that bullet hole in your leg.'

Settling into their seats in the Boeing, Bobby took her hand. She was looking down at the jungle slipping away below.

'I liked him too much. That was my problem.'

With difficulty she took her eyes off the jungle and turned to him.

'You mean you loved a man?'

'No, not like that. Perry is my greatest friend from school-days and I persuaded him to join the army with me, like a couple of Athenians off to war. We talk about everything together. He's short and awkward and no good at football.'

Bobby smiled as he thought how Perry always looked perpetually surprised with a wild look about him as though life inside his head was more exciting than the real world outside.

'What do you mean, a couple of...who did you say... off to war?'

'In ancient Greece, young men used to go to war as a couple.'

She looked back down at the jungle, now a green carpet far below.

'Go on, tell me. All of it. I want to know.'

'It's not easy for me. I've never told anybody before.'

'It wasn't easy for me either so on you go.'

'There was fighting on the beautiful island of Cyprus.

My friend had been captured by guerrillas. My commanding officer had let me go to help find him because I knew where he was. Keep out of any fighting. It was an order.

I was kneeling behind a wall outside a small village. All was quiet as if nobody lived there. It was hot and dusty.

Thump and a bullet hit the wall near the soldier next to me. I saw where the shot came from and there was a hand on the side of a shutter at the end of an alleyway.

Then I heard a high-pitched voice, "Tommy, Heh, listen here. You let three of our brothers go or your man dies." Then a throaty scream. It was Perry.

By the way just so you know, Tommy means a British Soldier.

Then the same shout. "Tommeee, see, we mean business." And the scream again. I can never forget that scream. Dear God, Perry.

Again the screaming on and on.

I was trained to fight and in front of me was my best friend in agony. The wonderful talks all flashed before me. Nothing else mattered. I had to fucking well do something.

I shut my eyes, dreading the next scream. I willed him to have faith in himself and to hold on. He has faith in God, you know. And then the scream again, longer and more full of pain.

Everything happened so quickly. My orders not to fight, but my friend in agony.

As I grabbed the rifle off the soldier beside me, there was another crack and he tumbled over, hit in the shoulder.

I sprinted across to the first doorway in the alley. Bullets flew over my head.

I hid behind the door frame. Suddenly all quiet. I waved at the soldier who'd fired over my head. I was safe behind the door frame. But Perry wasn't.

Again; "We kill one, we kill two, you'll see. Give us our three brothers. This shit of a man, still alive...just."

I didn't move. If I went forward, I'd be shot, if back Perry would die. And it would be ages before help arrived. Like it or not, I was alone. I couldn't breathe. There was a lump in the bottom of my stomach. I was afraid.

I was shivering with cold as I tried to understand this new feeling. I'd never been afraid in front of the enemy before.

That terrible voice, "Tommy...we know where you are." More screaming.

I threw myself into the open towards those screams. Bullets cracked over me.

I was close to the door below Perry's screams when I was hit in the leg. I crashed through. My leg wasn't broken but I knew I'd be bleeding soon enough.

I ran up some stairs. There was a man in a beret with a knife at Perry's throat. Perry was between his legs and a gun close by.

"You see, Tommy," the same voice. "I kill him with knife, huh? Or you let my comrades go, okay?" He spat at me. "You attack me, I kill him and then I kill you too. Your choice, Tommy."

I saw Perry open his eyes. I saw the guerrilla struggle to hold him. I threw myself at him. I hit his jaw with my rifle, knocking him senseless.

My brain was still clear in spite of everything. Where was the guerrilla who'd shot me? Perry groaned for me to watch out. I edged towards the only other door. There he was trying to get out of the window. I shot him twice. He crashed over backwards.

I saw tiny stars of dust shining in the sunbeams through the gaps of the splintered shutter. Perry was holding his right leg and moaning. I reckoned the artery in my leg was cut.

Perry thanked me for coming. There was blood all over his right knee and bright red rings around his forehead with blood in his eyes. His leg was at a horrible angle. They'd shot him in the knee to stop him running away.

Bastards. They'd tightened a wire around his head and twisted his leg to make him howl. He said he was sorry that howling wasn't a very sporting thing to do. I told him that our men would be with us soon.

The guerrilla started to move, spitting blood through his broken teeth. He said he was a simple man and begged me to let him go.

There are moments in all our lives aren't there, when everything, light, sound and your mind stops, a lapse in rational thinking? Blood surges into your throat and into your eyes in a blinding flood.

Whichever it was, when the guerrilla pleaded that he was a simple man, my leg stabbed pain and I went mad. I kicked him in the stomach. But my kicking was weak due to my wound.

I saw a bundle of staves, which the local farmers use to bind their crops onto the backs of their donkeys with. I grabbed one and began to beat the man who had so hurt my friend. I lashed him everywhere, on the legs, on his back, everywhere. I wanted revenge. He begged for mercy. I didn't give it.

I remember Perry shouting at me to stop. Tears of rage poured from my eyes, mucous and spit dribbled from my mouth. I was unstoppable.'

Bobby stopped talking for a moment, struck his forehead with one hand and stammered.

'I heard footsteps stamping up the stairs. A sergeant told me to stop.

I didn't.

He pinioned my arms.

He said my leg was bad.

My boots stood in blood.

I slumped across his arm.

He dragged me.

Propped me up beside Perry.

My legs trailed their blood with them.'

Idenea interrupted. 'If you speak so fast, I can't understand you.'

Bobby sighed, 'Sorry, yes, yes.'

'As I lost consciousness from all the blood, I heard a voice saying what a mess I'd made, a man wounded because of me and a prisoner nearly beaten to death. So how was I going to answer to that? Gone too far.'

Idenea wasn't looking out of the porthole any more. She was holding his hand ever more tightly.

'How terrible,' she said softly. 'So, then what happened?'

'I was taken to hospital. I'd lost over a litre of blood. Perry's leg was cut off above the knee. I tried to see him but he was sent home. The guerrilla had his jaw mended and was thrown into gaol. And then the local press got hold of it in spite of press censure. Shame on British Officer who tortures patriotic brother, was all over the place. My name in black and white.'

Idenea put her arm around his shoulder. 'And then?'

'My rank was held. I should have taken that guerrilla prisoner not beaten him nearly to death. I had no future in the army; to be the greatest general like my forebears.'

He turned towards her. 'What would you have done? Saved your greatest friend or obeyed orders and done your duty?'

'I don't know. I can't imagine it.'

'My ambitious wife abandoned me for shame and my father has difficulty talking to me as he says I let the family down.'

'How did you come here?'

'I stayed in the army wandering about for several years. I often heard the word unreliable said about me. Then I saw an advertisement for a manager for a new enterprise in the Amazon. I'd served in the jungle, so was sure I could do that and remake my life away from scandal. My shame, my guilt won't leave me.'

'But your friend is alive and you're here now.'

He'd turned to one side so she couldn't see that he'd shut his eyes.

'And that's how I came to the Rio Largo,' he murmured, 'and to you.'

5

ROBERT JENNEY

Fazenda Rio Largo.

Three years before.

> *Like one who on a lonesome road*
> *Doth walk in fear and dread,*
> *And having once turned round walks on,*
> *And turns no more his head;*
> *Because he knows a frightful fiend*
> *Doth close behind him tread.*

When Bobby walked out of his old barracks for the last time, a mistle thrush was singing its heart out at the top of a tree. Looking up he thought, 'Here I go to find my own clothes.' He opened a bar of Fruit and Nut chocolate.

Perry telephoned to wish him luck and to say he was walking with a stick now. He told him to start laughing again like his sister, Fran, does.

He told his father that he hadn't forgotten what he had to do for the family.

His mother, Alice, said, 'We'll keep an eye on Michael and you know that Beatrice is a very good mother.'

Beatrice had agreed to bring Michael along to the airport. Bobby hugged him.

'Maybe you can come and visit me amongst the monkeys.'

'Are you going to turn into a monkey, Daddy?'

'Probably.' He ruffled Michael's hair. 'Just like you.'

Their divorce proceedings were dragging on. He could barely look at her as he hugged the wriggly little person they had made together. This wife who thought him a failure. Her hair was down onto her shoulders and her lips were freshly painted. He scowled to himself that would be for some wretch she'd be fucking later that day.

She raised a hand to cover her eyes. He saw, for the briefest second, her eyes shining with tears that would not fall. He didn't look twice.

'You might come out one day as well?' he said.

'Yes, yes.' Michael shouted, jumping up and down.

'Michael, let Daddy go.'

The day after the planning meeting in São Paulo, Bobby bought a brand-new Ford Willys jeep and set off to the untouched rain forest, some two thousand six hundred kilometres to the northwest.

Alistair's comment: The game's set now, the cards dealt. So that was it, all up to him now. As he drove through kilometres of coffee, sugar and orange plantations, his anxiety changed to elation. He started to sing and chant, 'By God I'll stride the world again'. At night, instead of checking in at a motel, he curled up in the back of the jeep. And that fleeting moment, when Beatrice had looked him in the eyes as if she had something more to say.

In Cuiabá he told a barber to leave only an inch of hair all round, en brosse and different for his new life.

The last one thousand five hundred kilometres to Porto Velho were along the potholed BR 364. No rain and he drove to within ten kilometres of the entrance to Rio Largo, just short of the village of Mutum. He left his jeep in a one-man garage. Luiz Antonio da Costa had told him that Ari Nascimento would be there. They shook hands cautiously.

They rode their mules for two hours up a narrow track into a small clearing. Trees towered over. The only light came from a square of blue sky. There was a small hut with walls and a roof made of palm leaves standing amongst burnt branches. The white of a hammock stretched across the dark interior.

'There you are, Chefe,' said Ari, 'your home, look, *casa sua*. I built it with these. It was hard going.' He held up his hands and roared with laughter, hissing through his toothless gums.

Bobby loosed off the rawhide reins. He pushed back his hat and slapped at a mosquito on the sweaty skin of his neck. He said quietly in English, 'God in Heaven, my home.' And to Ari without smiling, '*Obrigado*.'

'Here.' Ari said cheerily handing over a white cotton bag. 'Some food till I get back.' He pointed to beyond the hut. 'There's a stream over there. Sorry to abandon you but I have to round up the men.' He trotted off with, 'I'll be back in a few days.'

Bobby swung his leg over to the ground. Slower than usual, he took off the saddle and fondled the mule's ears. 'There we are Big Ears, just you and I.'

Five red and green macaws flew over cackling one to the other. He stepped tentatively into the hut. He touched the white hammock and sat down on an upturned log beside a table knocked up from planks and bamboo. In the middle were a blue primus stove and a couple of saucepans.

Shadows were forming in the falling light. He bundled up some leaves for his mule. He walked to the edge of the clearing, a short twenty paces. He stood still. He could hear his breathing. Once or twice he spun around as if someone had tapped him on the shoulder.

That evening, he stood in his white underpants in the stream that Ari had pointed out. As he splashed water over himself, he realised how much the heat had bothered him. He'd left his shirt open at the top. He fingered the irritation of the swellings on his neck. He swore for the innocent idiot that he was and splashed more water.

He eased into his hammock. He stretched his feet to the end to make sure he fitted and arranged the mosquito netting. Swinging gently from side to side he breathed quietly knowing that sleep was close.

He looked out through the opening in the palm leaf wall. Outside the black trees stood very still. He had never been so alone. Always before his sergeant was close by. He laughed mockingly into the dark, 'My military career. My married life.' He liked the cries of the night. Nothing frightened him, not even Ari telling him that there might be Indians close by. That's fine, he'd make friends with them. And there was no alarm clock, no bugle.

Next morning, as the rising sun glowed pale green through the leaves of a sucupira tree, Bobby swallowed cold rice and beans. He smiled at a flight of green parakeets. He could see into the jungle. The larger trees rose up, slender-leafed saplings, caught by the slightest gust of wind, waved back and forth in the shade. Creepers fell to the ground entwined together like a mass of twisted rope.

He held out one hand as if wanting to part this tangle of forest with such a simple gesture. How puny he felt. Thirty metres in he looked back at his new home picked out bright orange in the sun. He leant one hand on a nearby trunk. Thus, quite still, not a thought in his head. Nothing. Just looking. A pulse of instinct, maybe of self-preservation, pulled his eyes to his hand on the tree trunk. A finger width away, a pencil thick brown skin stretched about thirty centimetres up the trunk. It was not part of the tree's bark and encircled the trunk like a woollen rug. Hundreds of hairy brown caterpillars lay tight side by side. This rug moved, not up or down the trunk but within itself as if breathing. He jerked his hand away and had to look closer to distinguish where the edge of the caterpillar rug began, so similar it was to the colour of the bark.

The first thought of the day crossed his mind. 'That's them. That's me.'

Later Ari told him he had been lucky, as one touch of those hairs and his hand would have turned into a lump of swollen red with days of burning pain.

Blue butterflies as big as his hand winged up and down in front of him. He thought of that jungle in Borneo on the other side of the world where any mistake could have brought the ripping of machine-gun bullets. He ate sun-dried meat, rice and beans. He scribbled letters to his mother and Perry and wondered how long they would take to arrive. The single kerosene flame twisted shadows into tortured shapes around him.

He strode about deciding where to build the men's dormitories and workshop. To begin with pissing was to be five metres into the jungle, anything bigger ten. He placed a couple of foolscap pages on the table and drew up a plan. The work soon settled easily on his shoulders.

Sometimes with a task so big and difficult for the mind to embrace, imagining where to begin seems impossible. And again, another task can be so small and intricate that failing to concentrate through soft idleness lets success drift away. Bobby didn't trouble himself either way. Nothing was going to be too big or too small. A tightening in his heart, his choice, his life. He didn't say it, didn't even whisper it but deep inside he knew it was his last chance.

Ari rode in three days later.

'I've found ten men,' he announced grinning broadly, 'And no girls, huh? They work for two weeks, and if good they come back. *Tá bom*, Chefe?' He smiled proudly. 'And I bought an old tractor. The seller needed the cash.'

'Any ruffians?' Bobby questioned. 'We can't have fights.'

'Up to you, Chefe. I get 'em, you control 'em. Plenty more poor bastards around.'

Later that day an old Massey Ferguson tractor, black fumes puffing up from a vertical exhaust that rattled and swayed on top of the engine, chugged in pulling a wooden trailer with ten men in the back. Some were grizzled and grey, others were boys in their late teens, a few black-skinned, some brown, some pale. They jumped down with a '*Bom Dia*' to Bobby. All wore a t-shirt, shorts and flip-flops, one or two sported peaked caps.

Bobby shook each man's right hand saying '*Bem vindo*, Welcome' and with his left he deftly frisked over and into belts and bags. By the end there was a small heap of knives, machetes and one pistol. Bobby gave back the machetes but kept the double-edged knives and the pistol.

'I'll give these back when you leave,' he said. 'I don't want trouble, okay?' One or two complained at the unexpected body search. Others smiled in relief.

'That was quick work, Chefe.' Ari chuckled approvingly. 'Done it before have you?'

'Many times, amigo.' Bobby smiled in satisfaction at Ari's praise, 'I had to protect myself and others.'

'Good for you, Chefe. This area's full of desperate drifters.'

Bobby addressed the men. 'We can't have trouble. *Tudo bem.*' As he spoke, he pulled up his trouser leg until the knobbly pinkish scars of his bullet wound clearly showed. 'If there are fights and I find somebody hurt I will do this to the aggressor or to both.' Bobby clenched his right fist in the shape of a pistol and mock fired at his wound. 'You see, I know how to do it.'

'*Tá certo.*' A tall sinewy man with shiny dark-brown skin, called Leonidas, shook Bobby's hand again. 'We'll keep order won't we, everybody?' There was a general murmur of consent. A hawk mewed from a tree. Close by a screaming piha whistled, noisy and unseen.

Leonidas told him his father had come over from Bahia as a Rubber Soldier during the big war. After that, the local economy had collapsed. He'd never known his mother. He'd fished in the rivers to eat, sold a few and tapped for rubber.[8]

Bobby realised he was beginning to fall for the charm of these different people. They lightened his soul. They laughed with him. He laughed with them.

'Men,' he said, 'I'm here to work with you, I'll do what you do. Let's make camp.'

'*Tá certo, Chefe,*' came the quiet ripple of replies.

By nightfall ten hammocks were swinging between the trees close up to Bobby's hut. Pots of rice, beans and dried shaki meat bubbled over a fire. There was laughing as the men smoked around the fire seeking protection from the swarms of mosquitoes.

Ari squeezed his hammock in beside Bobby's. Their bodies touched. From the folds of his hammock Bobby said, 'Have you done anything like this before, Ari?'

'I'm a simple cattleman. What about you, Chefe?'

'Yes, some. We have a farm back home.' Bobby didn't want to admit to his right-hand man that he had never cleared jungle in

201

his life before. 'I have certain guide lines agreed at the meeting in São Paulo.'

'Okay, Boss, but I want to buy cattle. That's me.'

'*Paciência, amigo*. Look, there's nowhere to put them yet is there? Tomorrow we'll get going.'

Outside the men were still mumbling over never-ending stories. It was probably then, while the chat flowed back and forth around the fire, that Bobby's nickname was put together; *Perna de Bala* and *Perna Furada*, Bullet Leg and Punctured Leg. Soon his reputation as the foreigner with a bullet hole in his leg spread into the bars and bus stops in the big town and far around.

Ari started to snore. Bobby watched the dancing patches of orange on the palm leaf roof lit by the flicker of the dying fire. Smoke wafted in and tickled his nose. All day his spirit had been high, but as he closed his eyes there was Michael asking if he was going to become a monkey and there were Beatrice's eyes glistening with tears. A sadness crept into his chest.

Ari shifted roughly in his hammock and bumped against him. They swung together.

Close by frogs and toads croaked, birds and insects whooped and chirruped. On the ground ants burrowed down into their nests, feeding their queen.

Bobby's white t-shirt stuck to his chest and back. White, well, it had been white but that had been at 6 a.m. Now it was around midday and the fire was raging a hundred metres away. Burning leaves and bits of twigs flew high into the air to mix with plumes of white smoke.

Sitting around their makeshift table, he and Ari had planned how they would fell, burn and sow the first 100 hectares; how many men, axes, chainsaws and when to burn. The year's target was five hundred hectares.

The first one hundred were blazing in front of him.

Ari and Leonidas, with a team of fifty, had taken two months to knock down the first hundred hectares. They had slashed and levelled the undergrowth with axes and machetes and then with chain saws had felled the bigger trees to land on top of the drying brushwood. This leafy, twiggy base would help ignite the heavy denser trunks that lay over.

'Well I don't know, Chefe. It'll work out you'll see.'

Bobby recognised Ari's 'It'll work out you'll see' as admitting he had no more idea than he had himself. To Ari he said, 'No big fields, no bad land to be cleared and we'll keep away from rivers. I don't care what Luiz Geraldo wants, we're not going to have big open spaces like others with nothing left in the soil.'

'Tá bom, Chefe.' Ari patted his pot belly and drained his glass of pinga. 'All I know is, fire first then cattle to stamp the seed in. But then I'm a simple cattleman as you know.'

'Yes, yes I know. You'll be getting some of those four-legged beasts once the grass gets going.' Bobby liked Ari's easy-going jokey manner coupled with his knowledge of cattle. And Ari liked Bobby's concentrated dedication that was so different to his own haphazard approach. And there was that endearing feel about this boss that he couldn't quite make out; a vulnerability he hadn't seen in a strong man, who walked with such measured steps. And they laughed.

Bobby had striven with the men to ensure that their first burn would be a success. He had run from flaming torch to flaming torch, as it swept slowly over the higgledy-piggledy layers of horizontal trees and brushwood. He needed a good base for sowing grass seed, no inaccessible pockets of un-burnt ground.

He hadn't noticed how much he had sweated, how red his face. His t-shirt was black and grey from ash and sweat. The drying sweat stuck the cotton to his skin. His short spiky hair was caked white. His trousers hung, tube like, into his boots, rigid with ash and sweat. He was a ghoulish grey all over. Where the smoke did not reach over, the sky opened out brilliant and blue. The temperature around him, depending on the wind coming from the blaze, was between 45 and 50 degrees. He breathed in short regular pants over a leathery tongue. He had stopped sweating. He knew from his army training that dehydration was close to weakening him.

Unable to think straight, he walked quickly towards his hut. He saw Ari some two hundred metres away, a blurry figure through the shimmer of heat waves and smoke. He waved. Only then did he feel the pain in his lungs and the burning of his skin. In the hut he grabbed a bottle of water and with a trembling hand raised it above his head. He lifted up his chin and poured. Water splashed down over his face and hair, some of it mixing with ash and sweat slopped into his mouth. Most of it ran onto his t-shirt and trousers. As the water entered his blood and dehydrated flesh, he began to sweat again. His skin felt as if he was pulling a shirt over sun-dried skin after a swim in the sea.

He watched the leaping of the flames.

'Well, Ari, my friend, it's working.'

He gulped down more water and splashed more onto his face. The flames were gaining strength and height. Small rodents escaped to one side. Hundreds of flying insects and a multitude of two-inch long grasshoppers flew vertically up only to be caught in an upsurge of heat and to fall back into the flames with their wings singed and their bodies boiled. There were no vultures circling above, no hawks mewing from treetops only the sharp crack of explosions from the inferno in front of him. He took another gulp of water.

The ever thickening and growing columns of smoke merged and slowly drifted down wind. Several kilometres later this deep front of smoke joined in with columns of smoke from other burns forming a dense cloud that stretched from horizon to horizon.

All around axes struck and chainsaws ripped as trees toppled over followed by the earth trembling thuds mingled with the men's shouts of triumph.

A split branch impaled one man through his chest. Chain saws cut him free. No identity card was found amongst the few belongings that lay in his hammock. He was known only as Xerxes, pronounced Shershees, and was fair-skinned with blue-red marks of early skin cancer. He had no front teeth. All the men walked behind the trailer and rough board coffin the ten kilometres to the village. There were fifteen other new graves in some uneven ground beside a wooden chapel. Some showed names chiselled into simple wooden crosses, others were a mound of red gravel with no name. From then on either he or Ari were present before any tree was finally toppled. He couldn't lose another man.

Bobby and Ari were standing at the edge of that first burn waiting for the light aircraft that was to broadcast the elephant grass seed.

'All this reminds me,' Bobby said quietly, 'how old battlefields of a great war in Europe must have looked nearly sixty years ago, when my grandfather was killed.' He pointed at a blackened stump with a splintered top.

'Here only bandits and squatters and Indians fighting over land,' said Ari.

'You're lucky. We have wars and I was taught how to fight them.'

Ari, his hands still on his hips, was chewing raw tobacco that he had cut from a dark brown sausage-like roll in his pocket. He spat out black globules. 'You weren't there, were you Boss, in a big war?'

'No, no, only in small ones.'

Ari spat out another black glob. 'Aaah well, you're an old soldier then, eh Boss?'

'For the love of God, Ari, I'm not old yet.'

Ari hissed his laugh and patted his belly, 'Well, you were grey all over the other day. You were too close to the burn, Chefe. Be careful, listen to old Ari.'

A rough whirring and a white Cessna flew towards them, waggled its wings in recognition and banked around to run along one side of the burn. The pilot throttled back and dipped down to just below the tops of the trees. The Cessna glided silently like a great white gull. The side door opened and out poured the seed. The airstream from the propeller broadcast the seed in a cloud of millions to settle on the ash-covered earth and on those burnt trees that a distant sawmill had rejected as useless. Fifteen minutes later the plane flew off for a refill in the big town 150 kilometres away.

By the end of the day the first hundred hectares were seeded, a few small heaps in some places but overall the spread was even. There had been no wind.

'Let's hope for rain now, Chefe.'

'Next year, Ari, we'll have our own airstrip and we'll do this ourselves. It'll be fun, okay?'

'You can fly, huh?'

'Sure.'

They turned towards the hut, so satisfied with progress that each put an arm around the other's shoulder.

Bobby became a bit of a recluse. He rarely went to the big town of Porto Velho. He stalked around the ever-growing clearing as the trees crashed to the ground around him. He held ropes and worked saws. He joked and drank with the men on a Saturday night. The more they drank the more his nickname varied from Perna Furada to The Gringo or just Inglesinho. Sleep came easily after one of those evenings.

'Watch out, Boss!' Ari would twist his mug of pinga between his fingers. 'Too much of this aguadente won't do you any good.' And then, 'We need girls up here, don't we?' And he'd stick his hand between his legs and roar with laughter amidst raucous cheers from the men.

'Come on, Ari, you've got a wife and I'm losing one. Besides I'm not having any fights over sex.'

'Only a thought, Boss.' And he stuck his hand between his legs again and hiccupped.

When he did go to town and before they'd built their own town office, he stayed in a cheap simple wooden hotel. He never glanced in the mirror and kept his hair short. Sitting on a log, Ari would cut it for him once a month with a cheerful, 'See, Boss, what an artist I am'. Bobby whistled in appreciation. Every now and then a pang of homesickness stung his belly.

He managed to persuade Beatrice that Michael would be safe with him. She said on the telephone. 'Our divorce process is taking time. What do you want to do?'

The echo of their voices back and forth on the line confused their voices. He replied without thinking, 'You do as you want.' The divorce could look after itself.

Michael arrived, pale-skinned, with packets of anti-malarial pills and Elastoplast. They fished for piranhas, rode mules and played with the men. Leonidas carried him on his shoulders and plucked at his white skin with his fingers. 'My little white boy' he laughed. They slept in hammocks, everyday an adventure. They imitated the chattering of parrots and the calls of the monkeys. Bobby bought him leather boots and held him firmly on the pommel of his saddle. After a downpour Ari showed him the imprint of a jaguar's footpad in the mud. Excitement grew each day.

Michael had thick black hair and at every glance reminded Bobby of Beatrice. They never mentioned her. They hugged and hugged on parting. Michael's skin had turned that reddy-brown the tropical sun burns onto pale skin. He counted his scars and bites with pride.

When he wasn't buying or organising, Bobby talked to people. He chatted to Reynaldo, the bank manager, and watched as Reynaldo counted one and ten cruzeiro notes with mechanical speed, flick with his forefinger, flick flick one hundred, flick flick two hundred. Soon the wads of hundred notes bound by an elastic band mounted on the desk like bricks for a child's castle.

'You might get a tube of toothpaste with that lot if you're lucky.' Reynaldo looked up at Bobby with a mischievous grin and then on flick flick.

Luiz Geraldo, or LG as his friends called him, came up every two months. As he swaggered towards him across the new 1000 metre airstrip they'd just finished, Bobby couldn't help remembering the first time he had met him at the planning meeting in São Paulo.

When Alistair was introducing his care of the jungle paper and Luiz Antonio da Costa, LG's father, was saying they were similar to his government's guide lines, LG was glancing through a couple of magazines. One page showed a football whamming into the back of a net and another a half-naked girl leaning over a Chevy. He wore an open necked denim shirt, jeans and high-heeled leather boots. At twenty-four, he was four years younger than Bobby and some inches shorter.

LG walked with his legs slightly apart and with his arms curved at the elbow and held away from his sides. Playing football on the beach had thickened his calf muscles. Every day he and his friends exaggerated their prowess with women. At fifteen, an older cousin arranged for a prostitute to introduce him to sex. The next day, he'd boasted how he had shown her a thing or two and how grateful the girl had been. He had a dark complexion and combed his hair straight back like his father but that was where the similarities ceased. He developed an unprovoked antagonism towards blacks and browns. Not to employ anybody from above latitude 14 was a common theme of his. That meant anybody from the state of Bahia. His father argued that since the country was well over sixty per cent black or brown, you'd exclude millions and that wasn't right for the future. LG liked the certainty of army rule and supported the exiling of poets and unproductive intellectuals as he called them.

He didn't hide his disapproval of his father's wish to engage a foreign partner in the Rio Largo enterprise. 'But, *Papai*,' he'd say, 'this is a bad idea.'

'Spread the risk, my son. Use their knowledge.' Luiz Antonio would reply. 'But if you want to go and live up there, on you go.'

No, LG had never wanted to live in the interior. God forbid. But yes, he would visit in his high-heeled boots that would increase his height and his authority. He'd tell people gruffly what to do even if he had no idea himself.

All da Costa men had Luiz as their first name. Luiz Antonio, fifty-five, spoke good English and French. He was dressed in a beautifully tailored English cut suit, a polka dot tie on a light blue shirt with gold cuff-links engraved with his initials. He could trace his family back four hundred years to the early Portuguese and would often remind people that he was a Quatrocentenario.[9] He wanted his children to be part of this new Brazil: the excitement of Brasilia, the Bossa Nova, the band of new novelists and the anti-military-government songs, naughty maybe, but he liked them.

Well, as he'd admit, his own ruling class and other powerful businessmen had influenced the Military to take over in 1964 after so many years of political turmoil. The Left called it a coup but he thought of it as a Political Rearrangement. At least the Military would root out corruption. And the generals promised to hand back to democracy. But when? Meanwhile he had built up the family business and now he wished to invest its tax credits in this Amazonian project and follow the call of President Getulio Vargas in his famous speech to develop the Amazon.[9]

He had met the affable one-legged Alistair at a trade fair in London and invited him to Brazil to show him where the future lay. He always sent a hand-written message asking after Bobby's health and complimenting him on progress.

LG's visits to the ranch were flyers, in for the day, a quick look around and out.

'Faster, faster,' he pestered Bobby, 'I want more cattle. How can you achieve results with so many black and half-caste workers, huh?'

Bobby had not met such racism before. He couldn't see any difference between the output of Leonidas or any other of his men. LG strode about. He pushed his reflector sunglasses so far back into his eyebrows the sweat from his forehead ran down over the lenses.

'We need more progress. I'm sending some big machines up to speed things along. You'll see the difference. More profit for us and more for you maybe.'

'Big machines? What are you suggesting?'

'That's my decision. I'll tell you when they're coming.'

They were standing in front of some young pineapple plants. Bobby was rather pleased at how well they were growing.

---

9 Quatrocentenario; a Brazilian who claims four hundred years of ancestry in Brazil.

'Why waste your time planting fruit? No money in that. Plant some soya. Now that would be intelligent.'

'Fruit is good for the men.' Bobby replied, 'Good eating helps fight malaria.'

'Squatters?' LG demanded every time he came. 'Found any yet?'

'Difficult to know,' Bobby said carefully, 'I keep asking for our title verification at the Ministry but get nowhere. It's as if we were an odd case. I'm going to try the army soon and see if they can help. I met the Colonel on Independence Day. You never know, something might come of that.'

'Squatters are a plague.' LG hunched his shoulders. 'Get rid of them. They reduce the value of the land.'

Bobby was relieved when he left. Ari bared his gums in a false smile.

Bobby asked, 'What if we do find Indians out the back, what do you reckon we do?'

'Indians?' LG turned slowly round, 'Indians? Look here. Bang bang.' And in a tone of aggressive authority. 'Understood?'

Bobby frowned. 'The Government says to inform the Indian Protection Agency and compensation will be a similar amount of land somewhere else where there are no Indians. I agree with that. I know the local FUNAI agent quite well and...'

'I don't believe a word of that.'

On leaving LG said to the pilot, 'Vamos! Why do I need a bloody foreigner? Brazil is for Brazilians don't you think? There must be a way.'

'For what, Chefe?' asked the pilot.

'Without that foreign gringo.'

The propeller kicked. The Cessna climbed, its undercarriage missing the tops of the trees by ten metres.

'Have you done this before?' yelled LG.

The pilot didn't answer. A few minutes later LG shouted, 'Looks like bad weather coming up,' and pointed at a vertical screen of white about half a kilometre in front that stretched from right to left.

'That's smoke,' the pilot shouted back.

'What?'

'Burning forest.'

Moments later the white cloud engulfed them, no visibility, only waves of white streaming over the windscreen. The pilot steered sharply to the left. 'We're going back.'

'No, keep going straight.' LG shouted.

'No, I'm going back,' the pilot insisted.

'I said go through. I'm paying.'

'*Tá bom. O senhor que sabe.* You know best.'

The pilot gestured at the white. 'I can't see a thing.'

LG leant forward. 'We'll be through shortly.'

The pilot. 'I'm on instruments.'

'What do you mean?'

'I've never flown blind before so must follow them.'

'Give me the controls.' LG, his forehead moist and panic in his voice grabbed at the joystick.

The pilot tried to push him away. 'You don't know what you are doing!'

The plane swerved, dived and climbed straight upwards. The engine whined. It dived again.

'Let go, you idiot,' the pilot screamed, 'We'll stall and you'll kill us both.'

The Cessna, one wing up vertical, one wing down vertical, sliced like a knife through the smoke throwing LG onto the pilot's shoulder.

The pilot, 'Get off me or I'll shoot you.'

LG jerked back, took his hand off the joy stick and levered himself back to his side of the cockpit.

The pilot fumbled in the door pocket and pulled out a ·38 Taurus pistol. He pointed it in LG's direction as he steadied the joy stick. LG slumped into his seat and took off his dark glasses. Sweat dripped onto his trousers

The Cessna suddenly emerged into the clear, missing the top of the trees by thirty metres.

On landing LG said, 'How dare you threaten me. I'll never use you again.' He half-walked, half ran to a waiting taxi.

The pilot jeered at the scurrying figure, 'At least you'll know what burning jungle looks like next time.'

LG had given Bobby a packet of letters. 'From your Boss in London,' he'd said with a casual gesture

Dear Robert, the first letter began. That was odd Bobby thought, something serious from Alistair.

He smiled at the short military style of his boss congratulating him on being on target, the small fields, keeping malaria down and telling how his other directors felt that the title problem threatened their investment. And how there wasn't any money for LG's bulldozers.

Then:

> *I admit that I am working more than hard to keep this old company alive. So here's a proposal: I have no children, probably due to my losing a leg to the damn Boche! Watch out for them in Paraguay, won't you! I'm told there are dozens of them down there. So why don't you come back and join me as a partner? You are the best manager we have. Think about it. I can't leave my desk due to money trouble so won't be over for some time. I look forward to your next report. It only took three weeks this time, and I hope to have a positive answer to my proposal.*

Bobby folded the pages carefully and looked across towards the green of the nearest pasture. So that was the reason for Robert and not Bobby. How flattering to be asked. He continued to gaze at the green for some time. No, not yet, any move would have to wait till he was sure of success.

Amongst the other papers was a red envelope with his name typed in large black letters on red paper. Inside,

'WE KNOW ROBERT JENNEY THAT YOU CUT DOWN THE FOREST OF THE WORLD. BEWARE, WE WILL NOT FORGET OR

FORGIVE YOU, YOU KILLER OF NATURE.'

Some nutter who forgets that every year we have a few million more people to feed on this planet, Alistair had scrawled on top. Bobby screwed the letter into a ball and threw it in the bin. That night in bed — he'd discarded his hammock six months before after he and Ari had finished the ranch house — he felt the return of that familiar melancholy worry at him again. Was he really a killer of nature?

He sat up, chose a packet of sleeping pills from among the many other packets on the shelf beside his bed, and swallowed one noisily with a glass of water. No longer was he carefree about cuts and bruises, they took ages to heal in the hot damp anyhow. He looked after himself with close attention, pills for this, ointments for that. A big toenail had recently fallen off due to burrowing worms. He'd taken days to poison them out, poking with a needle and dabbing with alcohol that left him with a swollen stub of a toe. Ari admired the red of the stub. After that, the shelf soon filled with colourful packets and tubes.

When Ari went south to visit his family, to be with *meu povo*, my people, as he put it, he did miss him. Then the heat and damp pressed in on him, even the calls of the birds that he so liked rang tiresome. He worked in frantic bursts of unstoppable energy. Some days he felt a numbing sadness sap at his strength and with it a sudden desire to escape, not slowly but in a rush, to jump on a horse, catch an aeroplane. Anything to get out.

Next day he flew down to Cuiabá to buy cattle with Ari in the Pantanal. As he gazed down at the moss-like tops of the untouched rainforest dotted with purple Ipé flowers, he thought of that red letter. Surely with Ari's good sense things would be all right.

Seven days later Bobby and Idenea make love under the picture of the staring Indian in the Perfect Peace Motel. Three weeks later, she goes back north with him. Bobby drives his jeep up the red access road to Fazenda Rio Largo. Idenea sits beside him.

6

PALACE IN NOWHERE

Bobby led Idenea, hand in hand, into the newly built ranch house. The walls smelled of freshly sawn wood, the floor of red painted concrete, the roof of fresh palm leaves. There was a recently planted bougainvillea on each side of the entrance door.

'Come into my Palace in Nowhere, Ari and I built it with wood from our mill,' he said with pride. 'I used to live in that.' He pointed to a tiny thatched hut where a couple of hoes leant against one side.

'Bobinho, you've been so alone.' She mimicked hardship with her shoulders and tossed her hair back over one shoulder.

'That's all over now.'

She pulled open the netted entrance door, sprung on the inner tube of an old bicycle tyre. She was wearing a new pair of blue jeans tucked into short leather boots, a white t-shirt and a straw hat.

'You'll see how my orchard and maize will grow. And milk and goats and guava and caju and mango and bananas and...Aaah.' She stopped with an excited laugh.

She walked into the kitchen with its bottled gas cooker and stainless-steel sink propped up on bricks.

'*Puxa, que maravilla!*' she exclaimed and opened the door into the sitting room with its cane chairs, sofa and a couple of homemade wooden tables. 'What luxury. *Que luxo!*' she repeated over and over again. Into the bathroom with bucket shower and on to Bobby's bedroom with the double bed, mosquito net, shelves with his books and his collection of pills and lotions all in a neat row. He was close behind. She stepped nimbly up onto the bed and turned to face him smiling broadly.

'Catch me.'

She threw herself straight at him, her arms outstretched, her legs spread wide. So unexpected that he only just caught her in midair. She wrapped her arms around his neck and her legs around his waist.

'You crazy idiot!'

In gleeful enthusiasm she bit his ear. 'Listen. You'll help me find my Zoni, won't you? Remember you promised?'

He nodded.

She whispered. 'And then we make a baby in this Palace in Nowhere. What do you say?'

He laughed. 'Remember I have a job to do. And no more tears from you, *tá bom*?' His grip around her waist started to slip.

She bit his ear again, 'It's all your fault for turning up at the motel.'

They collapsed onto the bed.

Ari, seeing the jeep arrive, had ridden over to greet and share news. Instead he heard the sound of the lovers. He discreetly turned his mule away.

Within a week Idenea had marked out her orchard and begun to hoe into the hard, red earth. Two men helped her. One was Leonidas who had become Ari's assistant. He had built himself a hut a hundred metres away and brought his family in. His wife was as black as him as were the older two of his three children. The youngest had browny-fair hair.

'Where's that from?' Bobby asked ruffling his hand through the boy's curls.

Leonidas laughed, 'Well, Chefe, I expect from somebody like you some time back.'

'Well, there you go,' Bobby thought, 'Black and white.' And those two Indians he'd seen with Zé. Brown, black and white, that's this frontier. And me a killer of nature? These two wouldn't be here if it wasn't for the likes of Ari and me.' He rode off towards the sound of axes and saws.

On their first Sunday, Idenea moved a cane chair into a corner of their sitting room and put her wooden doll on a cushion in the middle. She picked fresh green palm leaves and made an arch around the chair. 'Look, Bobinho, see how comfortable Zoni is. I'm going to make clothes for him. That'll make us look for him, won't it?' She stroked the doll.

Bobby looked away towards the jungle and wondered where to start looking.

'And, Bobby, have you got an old shirt so I can make some trousers and a t-shirt?'

'I'll have a look. They'll be rather old.'

She blew him a kiss. She was still fondling the doll.

She dressed Zoni in blue trousers and a white t-shirt made from Bobby's old shirts. She painted brown the little eyes that her father had so carefully chiselled. She arched more palm leaves over the chair and its precious image. She stuck a candle in its own wax and lit it every night. She lifted him off the cushion, hugging and smelling him.

She started to sing, more of a humming than a singing, '*Ciranda, cirandinha, vamos todos cirandar...*'

She stroked the tufts of wild cotton tree fibres that she'd glued to its head and had painted brown like the eyes. 'Mama will find you, yes I will.' Some days she sang, '*Ciranda...*' others, '*Boi boi boi da cara preta ...*'

Every evening Bobby pushed the shrine back into its corner.

One day, Leonidas brought Idenea a fledgeling toucan.

'I found him on the ground. He must have tried to fly too early, lucky he wasn't gobbled up.'

She stroked the coloured feathers on its head murmuring, 'How beautiful.' and 'What a lucky bird you are. No, we're both lucky.'

The toucan snapped nervously at her fingers with is long heavy bill. She knocked up a box from bamboo and placed it in one corner of the kitchen and settled him inside.

'Your home from now on.'

When Bobby arrived, she said, 'Let's call him Toco because that's what he is, a real Toco, don't you think?'

Soon Toco was competing with Bobby's dog, Massby, for scraps and never left Idenea for one moment. You could tell where she was by the sound of Toco's *pad-pad* of a hop behind her. She had to shut him up at night to keep him out of their bedroom. Later she built a perch but Toco preferred to be right beside her.

'I think it's time we went over to your plot 921 to see what's going on,' Bobby said casually as they were forking into midday rice and beans. 'I have to check out whether it's within our boundary. There could be a title problem.'

Seeing her dismay, he said kindly, 'I have to check. Please understand. My bosses are on my back. If I don't get this matter of title sorted out this whole project could fail.'

Idenea put her face in her hands.

'I can't. Bosco who...I think of that terrible time so often.'

'I know.' He took her hand. 'But I'll be with you.'

'Why do you think that would be any better?'

'Because I will look after you.'

'No, I'm not coming.'

'Well, then, I'll have to go on my own. It won't be easy for me as you know the place.' He continued firmly, 'And if that bastard Bosco is there, I'll...'

'Shoot him?' She brightened.

'If I must.' He reached over and placed his other hand over hers. 'And Romi might be there.'

She smiled bravely, quiet for a moment. '*Tá bom*, I'll come, just for you and for Zoni. But you are not to leave me alone for one single moment.'

'I promise. We'll go tomorrow.'

217

They left before first light. The new fence posts shone white in the headlights as straight as an avenue. In the back, Massby lay curled up on a pile of hammocks beside a box with enough food for three days. Bobby was taking no chances. Idenea was dressed in jeans, t-shirt, boots and straw hat, her lips freshly painted.

'I want to be smart for you,' she'd said as she swallowed her daily malaria pill at Bobby's insistence. She'd left Toco with Leonidas.

Five hours of bumping and lurching. Idenea showed the way for the last fifteen kilometres.

'*Meu Povo*, my people,' she exclaimed. 'And my land. Has Romi come back? I can start looking for my Zoni again. Even that son of a whore Bosco. I hope he's dead. And Chico? Maybe he's found his way back. Aaah, my people.'

As he drove up the final two hundred metres, she said quietly, 'Nothing has changed.' Another hundred metres and her excitement had melted into soggy dread. 'Stop, Bobinho, please. I can't face it.' She leaned her head onto his shoulder and closed her eyes.

The last time she'd been on this track, she'd been running for her life.

The jeep turned the last corner and stopped twenty metres from the two huts. Idenea sat forward.

'Look, there's Bolo. There's Zoni's monkey. Somebody must be here.' Her voice faltered with emotion, '*Olá*, Romi, Carlito, Chico?' She called out, 'It's me.' She pushed on the horn. She jumped out and strode towards the main hut.

Bobby remained discreetly at the wheel and wondered how he would react if Bosco was there.

She continued shouting and waving her arms. 'Everything's the same. The cooking stove is alight.' Bolo stretched, wagged his tail and sidled up to her legs. She stroked his head. The monkey ran up and down its pole chirruping loudly. She turned in triumph to Bobby. 'There must be somebody here. *Olá*! Anybody about?'

A girl in her late teens with dark eyes and brown skin pushed aside the beaded curtain to her parents' old room.

She peered closer. 'Carmen?' she said softly, 'is that you? It's me, Idenea, remember?'

Carmen stepped slowly out. 'Idenea? You? Still alive? My mother, remember? She washed your wounds and reckoned you might have died of them. But look at you, so smart. I heard your jeep approaching. I was nervous. The men are out working. I didn't want any trouble so went in out of the way.' She looked shyly towards the jeep and raised her eyebrows in admiration.

'My friend Bobby.' Idenea beckoned at Bobby. 'Come over and meet Carmen.' And to Carmen, 'Who else is still here?'

'Juca, Carlito, Bosco.' At the mention of the last name, Idenea's smile vanished.

'And Romi and Chico?'

Carmen shook her head. 'I don't know.'

It was close to midday. The shriek of the cicadas was beginning to wear itself out. Bolo wandered into the shade of the hut and lay down.

'And you, Carmen, what are you doing here?'

'I'm with Juca now.' Carmen smiled sheepishly and passed a hand over her bulging belly. 'My father's very happy I live here. Juca is a good man.'

'Bobinho, come over here.' Idenea called over her shoulder. 'This is the place I told you about: my place.'

As Bobby walked over, three men came up the path between the small pastures where a few head of cattle stood motionless in the heat. Bobby recognised Juca from the aborted trip up river with Zé. He was carrying a chain saw on his head padded on his cap. He was topless and his mahogany-coloured body gleamed in the sun. The other two, the limping Bosco and the cousin, Carlito O Lentão, matched Idenea's description and were clad in ragged jeans. They carried axes and machetes.

Bobby shook hands with Juca. 'Good to see you again, Juca. How are things?'

'Fine, *tudo bem*, thank you. We heard the horn.' Juca smiled recognition through toothless gums. And to Idenea, '*Olá*, Idenea, what a surprise to see you here again.'

Bobby shook hands politely with the other two. Bosco reluctantly took his hand with exaggerated up and down pumping.

Idenea put her hand on Bobby's shoulder, grimacing awkwardly. He heard her sharp intake of breath and felt her fingers dig into his shoulder.

'That's him.'

Bosco grinned at her. 'You *are* smart, aren't you?' He leered, 'and with a foreigner too? I thought you were dead.' He feigned horror at the scars on her arms. 'Even more tasty than before. Where's Valdo? A new man, huh? That was quick.'

'Fuck off, Bosco,' she hissed.

He smirked, 'Just worried about you that's all.' Then he shrugged as if to say, *Well, that's life for you.*

'Where's Romi?' she blurted. 'Where's Chico, and where's my baby? Gone. It's all your doing, you bastard, Bosco.'

Bobby was making every effort to look calm but his hands tightened into fists. 'If it's all right with all of you,' he began, 'I run a ranch as well not far away and would much like to compare notes.'

Juca, sensing the tension, heaved the chainsaw off his head, leant on a post and bared his gums in a humourless smile. 'Carmen, *meu bem*,' he said, 'please be kind and put some food on the table.

Welcome Idenea, Welcome Senhor Bobby. Tell us what you've been up to. Please, let's sit down.' He pointed to the rough table and chairs.

Bobby looked down at the stained surface of the table. So, this was where she gave birth. He glanced sideways at Idenea to make sure she really did exist.

Nobody said much as they ate rice and beans with bits of dried meat mixed in. Bobby sat at the table with Carlito, Carmen and Bosco. Juca, still leaning against the post, scooped at his bowl with a spoon. Idenea, tin bowl in hand, paced back and forth, stabbing noisily at her plate with her fork. 'Carmen, you cook so well.'

When Bobby spoke, they regarded him with deference. At the slightest suggestion of a joke, they laughed aloud except Juca, who watched from the side. There were long awkward silences. Bosco, intent on provocation, continued to leer at Idenea as Bobby asked politely about the cattle and maize. Although he already knew the answers from Idenea, he was determined to approach everyone as if all was new to him.

'Who do you sell your logs to?'

'Carmen's father in the village and our rubber as well.'

'Is the land good here?'

'*Mais ou menos*, more or less. Not much good soil.'

'How's the grass and maize?'

'*Mais ou menos.*'

After a sweet cafézinho coffee, Bobby unfolded a map on the table. Images of an umbilical cord appeared in front of him as he spread it flat.

'Our Fazenda Rio Largo lies within this line.' With his finger he traced round a boundary line marked in black ink. 'And this is where you are, here.' He pointed inside the same black lined boundary.

Bosco, leaning over, spilled coffee on the map. 'You're joking, right? The land is ours, my land.'

'Yours?' Idenea butted in, '*Merda*. You liar. The shit you talk.' Her voice rose hysterically. 'It's *my* land!' She waved her arm over the baked red earth of the yard towards the graves. 'Father and Mother are dead and with Romi not here, it is mine. The titles say so. You know that, you *filho da puta*.'

'What titles, you bitch?' Bosco shouted back. 'Where are they?' His jaw jutting, gone any angelic look. 'Show them to me.'

'I will.' Idenea suddenly calm. 'I'll get them back from that Captain Dias you'll see. Then you can get out of my sight for ever. To that Hell where you belong.'

Bosco sniggered mischievously at her. Bobby swallowed an urge to punch him.

Carlito O Lentão stammered, 'No titles...taken from us...some time ago.' He looked sadly at the map.

'Quite.' Bobby returned to studying the map. His fears confirmed: their plot was on Rio Largo's land. He folded his hands.

'So we both claim this land do we?' Juca said quietly smiling his toothless smile, still leaning against a post.

He'd guessed this gringo would bring trouble, when he'd met him up that river with Zé. He had to tell the Boss. And now with Carmen pregnant, surely the Captain would help him claim some land? He'd promised.

Nobody answered. Carmen stopped washing the tin plates. Outside, Bolo, smelling another dog, had ambled over to investigate a possible friend. Massby, as ever, wouldn't leave the jeep. The cicadas quiet in the midday heat.

Bosco, outside in the sun five metres away, was striding about looking one moment at Bobby, the next at Idenea. He was shaking his head and swearing, '*Merda*, *Puta*. It's my land, mine.' He'd have to tell Bébé or all would be lost. Of course he had as much right as Juca and Carmen.

Bobby, uneasy that there was no reassuring feel of a pistol or a knife in his belt, twisted around. He took a deep breath.

'Let's see if we can sort this out. I am a small shareholder. The big ones are far away down south, so let's try and agree without a row, *tá bom*? I don't want problems and I'm sure you don't either but we must resolve our boundaries even in this wilderness.' He crossed his arms.

'I offer you, that is whoever are the true owners or whoever are the true squatters and...' He found Juca's eyes and held them as if to suggest who the real people of the land were. 'We can offer a cash

222

buy out or a share in our company. I prefer to pay cash because it's clean and done with. Also, I don't know if you have any squatters' rights at all?' He glanced from one to the other.

'Yes we do.' Bosco shouted from outside, 'I do.'

'Liar,' Idenea shouted back at him. '*My* family does.'

'You left, bitch. We stayed. We worked.'

'I worked, remember that Bosco, while you boozed it up in the village. And you lost Chico.' And beside herself with fury, 'I left for fear of you, you disgusting...'

Juca, no longer smiling, shifted his weight from one leg to the other against the post.

'Be that as it may.' Bobby began again, forcing his voice to remain steady. 'There's good work on our ranch which would clear out your debts.' He glanced at Juca, wishing for a nod or some gesture of recognition. 'So, whatever we agree to do, Fazenda Rio Largo will have definite and agreed borders and you with no debts.'

Juca pursed his lips. How did this stranger know about their debts? The silly bitch must have told him. Were they plotting to drive him off? He stood onto both feet.

Idenea pointed at Bosco. 'Him? Never. He can't stay.'

'Or,' Bobby tried again, sweat uncomfortable in his arm pits, 'you can remain where you are and my partners down south will challenge you. However, I suggest that seems a drastic measure with so much land about.' He finished with a thin smile. 'Let's talk about it.'

Idenea wasn't listening. She was walking in small circles mumbling to herself. She couldn't be near Bosco. She turned defiantly to Bobby for support. 'You can't offer Bosco anything. He's evil, *maldito*. He has no title. It's me who does.'

'I did say the rightful owners. That's what the bosses down south will consider.'

Bosco raced over shouting, 'No! No! We are, it's us who work here and have done for the last seven years.'

Juca licked his lips. So, Bosco was going to try to claim that one, was he? Seven years? What a lie.

Dragging his leg, Bosco advanced on Bobby. 'Who are you anyway?' His mouth contorted in hatred. 'Think you can come here and take our land away, you bastard? Look at me.' He put a fist on his chest. 'I've got real claims, you'll see.' He was two paces from Bobby, his voice rising hysterically. 'And I am ready to fight for them with this.' He snatched at his belt and pulled out a heavy skinning knife. 'Ha-ha, you'll see that I will.' And thrust it towards Bobby's stomach. His face reddened. He jabbed forward. 'Go away, this is ours. I mean mine. And I'll use this.' He rotated the knife handle in his hand. 'I'll get you, gringo, taking my land and stealing my woman.' He gestured at Idenea.

Bobby dropped both hands to his sides. How could that angelic look change so quickly into one of such evil? One step more with that knife and he'd strike back.

Idenea edged half in front of Bobby. 'Leave him alone you idiot, he's trying to help.' Bosco swung his knife arm at her.

She screamed, 'Use your knife again, would you? Remember the last time, you coward?'

'Why don't we sit down and talk?' Bobby said firmly. Sweat began to run down his breast bone.

Bosco, lunging his knife towards Bobby and Idenea, growled, 'I'll get him and then I'll deal with you.'

'Stop it right now, Bosco.' Juca had moved unnoticed and with a quick grab wrenched the knife out of Bosco's hand, 'Fighting gets us nowhere.' The knife thudded to the ground.

Idenea laughed sharply, 'That's right, nowhere.'

'Juca, you?' Bosco yelped in pain. 'I thought you and me? Together?'

'Not with knives, we're not.'

Bobby tried again. 'Why don't you go and talk to someone like a lawyer who specialises in title problems? And I'll talk to my partners and come back and see what we can do.'

Idenea gripped Bobby's elbow. 'Take me to Porto Velho right now. I'm going to get our titles back off that thief of a Captain Dias right now.' And to Bosco. '*Seven years*? You liar Bosco. We've only been here four years and by God you know that. All you three here...'

224

She pointed at the three men, 'are squatters. Without Father and Romi, I'm the only rightful owner here today.'

To Bobby's surprise, Juca offered his hand. They shook.

'I don't know what to think, Senhor Bobby, but thank you for your offer. I have a baby on the way.' He smiled at Carmen and she smiled sweetly back at him. 'Yes, let's discuss soon.' He had to talk to the Boss.

Idenea ran into her parents' old room and burst back out smiling. 'They're still here.' She held up two framed photo pictures, one of her father and mother, the other of her grandparents that she had packed so carefully before coming north. 'And they're coming with me,' she said and climbed into the jeep.

Juca waved. Carlito shook his head in bewilderment and carried on staring at the table where the map had been. Bosco pretended to laugh. Bolo followed the jeep for a few metres with his tail down as if saddened that Massby had ignored him.

'Ah, seven years what a damned lie!' Idenea swore. Then sharp and angry at Bobby. 'Are you with me or not?'

'Of course, I am.'

Bobby turned onto the gravel road towards the big town. The wheel jerked.

'I hate to say this, Idenea, but I don't think your Plot 921 officially exists. It's a funny number. All the others have sensible numbers like 30 and 31.'

'You mean, our titles are false?'

'Could be.'

'Baby lost. Land lost. Brother lost.' She began to cry softly. 'I have to get them back.'

He gave her his handkerchief.

She looked out of the window at the passing jungle. A deep hole threw the jeep into the air and both were laughing. She looked at him sideways through the folds of her hair. Yes, she could see why she was with him, he treated her like an equal. And he would find

Zoni, she was sure of that. He caught her eye and put his hand on her knee until the next lurch demanded both on the wheel.

He dropped her at the Ministry building where she'd stood for so many hours three years earlier. They decided that she should go alone. He said he'd arrange to see Colonel Delgado and he'd pick her up in a couple of hours.

Due to the respectability that her new clothes gave her, she was admitted through the main gates but after saying she wanted to see Captain Dias, she was abruptly told to wait. She paced about watching the hands of a clock turn a full hour. Unable to wait any longer, she banged on the door. The same assistant opened.

From inside rough voice. 'Find out what she wants.'

She pushed at the door. 'It's Idenea Saladini from Plot 921, Fazenda Boa Esperança, remember? I've come to get our titles. You promised, and I won't go away till you give them back!'

'Tell her to go away. Tell her that I will contact her when I'm ready.'

The door shut flat in her face. Two armed security guards escorted her out of the building. As they pushed her towards the exit door, she shouted over her shoulder, 'I'll keep coming back till I get them.'

What she didn't know was that Captain Dias was smiling.

A few streets away, Colonel Fabio Delgado, Commander of the West Amazon Frontier Regiment, CEFAR, Porto Velho, Rondônia, switched on a brand-new air conditioner. He patted the shiny new top of the metal casing and, after a few rumbles and gurgles, delicious cool air fanned into his face.

'Finally, I can work in comfort,' he said aloud.

He liked to talk to himself. It was as if there was a friend beside him to share his responsibilities in this lonely world of the Interior.

He looked out through the only window at the expanse of the great Madeira river flowing on and on to the Amazon. His office was the only room on the first floor; the rest of the barracks lay spread out below.

'Quite right.' He chewed on the ends of his long black moustache. 'Up here, I'm above everybody as I should be.'

A green-uniformed soldier crossed the drill square below. How was he to control 1,500 kilometres of frontier, dense forest and inaccessible rivers with only a thousand raw recruits, like the one below? He needed true authority but those bastards at the Ministry of Agriculture down the road ignored him. They never stopped making trouble.

Irritated, he wheeled around and saluted first the national flag and then his regiment's flag. Both hung on shiny brass rods angled out from one corner. He saluted them every morning. He glanced up at the large photo-portrait of his old friend, the President of the Republic. The stern face of authority stared down at him from humourless eyes. Colour retouching had made the President's military uniform and bejewelled sash of state stand out.

'*You won't find it easy up there in Rondônia, Colonel Fabio. Land trouble, Indians, drug traffickers, crazy people.*' His old friend had said.

He was proud of his friendship with the President, that dated back to well before the 1964 military takeover, or, as the Military liked to refer to it, the sensible political adjustment. Those had been the days of decisive action. Nowadays it was hard to know what might happen. Dictatorships, however benign, were unpopular abroad. And he and the President both agreed that the army was the only true protector of the country's sovereignty.

'My army,' Colonel Fabio would say emphatically, 'is different. It works for the people.'

Two young beady-eyed cadets, Colonel and President had joined up in the 1950s, full of patriotic pride, following Gaûcho tradition. Now things were on the move. There were those who said it was the American trust in the military government that had given Brazil confidence. God bless America. What would have happened without their help? Russia? China?

God spare us, please.

President de Gaulle's '*Brésil n'est pas un pays sérieux*' still stung. Nor did they want to be called monkeys from the north by those loathsome Argentines. That really was a truly nasty military dictatorship. Who did they think they were anyway? Spanish, Italian, British? At least here there wasn't any killing. Well, not that he knew of. He was too far away to know of any torture or of the exiling of dissidents. It must be the Portuguese blood, a bit dour at times but more peaceful than the Spanish. He and the President just wanted their country to be part of the modern world.

He dropped his saluting hand. He was immaculately dressed; green uniform, open at the neck with a row of medal ribbons on the upper pocket and smart button-down straps on his shoulders. Of medium height, broad shouldered, darkish skin with dark eyes and he would curse the shortness of his legs every time he dismounted from his horse. He'd never be a great rider with those.

Sometimes he thought he should have been a general. Damn it.

But he was proud of his work, building roads, opening up the great interior, maintaining stability. Even in the heat amidst the tangle of conflicting political ambitions, he was sure everything would end up all right, especially under the steady hand of the Military. He glanced at the large national flag with its distinctive green background and yellow globe in the centre and the motto, '*Ordem e Progresso*'[10]

'Progress, yes.' He stroked his neatly clipped moustache. 'With the Army.'

He opened the folder on his desk.

For the personal attention of Col Fabio Delgado,
Commander of the frontier regiment, CEFAR, Rondônia.

Below the printed logo of the head of a jaguar baring its teeth was the regiment's motto; '*Foi bom que voce veio.* It was good you came.'

He ran his eye over the agenda for the meeting he was to chair that morning.

—Security, murders, robberies 0900 hrs.
—Land and title problems 1000
—Indian matters 1100

—Incidence of disease, latest Malaria count. 1200

—LUNCH 1300

—Problems of current immigration—Disease and Starvation.1430

—Construction and road projects. 1530

Usual stuff. With a sigh, he looked out of the window. Thank God for Construction. At least that was progress.

Below the agenda in small type was,

—Meeting with rancher, Robert Jenney, at 16.30.

Bloody foreigner. What did he want? He had noticed plenty of their kind around in the south but not up here. Well, at least it was that British Army fellow. They could discuss horses and real soldiering. He rubbed his right arm, massaging an old broken bone.

Underneath that day's agenda sheet lay a thick brown envelope with; 'To be opened personally by Colonel Fabio Delgado' and a large rubber stamp with FORÇAS ARMADAS, in blue across his name. The Colonel clicked his tongue. This was from the high command. He'd look at that after the meeting.

At lunch the conversation had been about the arrival of as many as two thousand immigrants during the current week alone. Lieutenant Bentes reported that last week there had been over five hundred reported cases of malaria and a hundred of hepatitis.

To his left was a row of locked filing cabinets with TOP SECRET written on the top. There was a file on that bastard Ananias Barbosa, the ringleader of that cursed protest march in 63 that had ended with him busting his arm when his horse Negrone had fallen on hundreds of marbles that had been thrown in front of his troop of mounted police. But he'd had the satisfaction of feeling his truncheon whack into the softness of a human body. He had brought that file with him as a sort of token of revenge. And where was the brute now? Down the road as a manager in the Ministry of Agriculture meddling about in rural affairs. Army intelligence had informed him of his presence, but the photographic identity image was so blurred it could have been anyone. He often wondered which son of a bitch he was.

He pulled a thick document out of the envelope. In the top margin he noticed the handwriting of his old friend the President.

Dear Amigo Fabio, I am sure you know this Decree Law but even so please go through it again carefully. I am nervous of unrest in your area. Remember we are responsible for the sovereignty of our country. I send you a strong embrace, Your President.

Colonel Fabio nodded at the portrait on the wall.

He poured boiling water onto maté tea leaves in a small silver-rimmed coconut bowl set in a silvery tripod on his desk. As a traditional gaucho he preferred maté to coffee. He sucked noisily through his silver straw. Sure, he had read the Decree Law 4504 and The Statute of the Land sometime before, all thirty-four pages of it. He started to read:

Social justice: How in God's name was that going to work? The powerful thought in one way, the poor and the landless, and God knows there were plenty of them, thought in another.

Confiscation of land in the interest of social interest: Oh dear, in Heaven's name what did that mean? He sucked at his silver straw.

Here we go again. Another well-intended but impossible-to-put-into-practice piece of legislation put together by those incompetent politicians. Would any big landowner give up land without a fight? Ha! He stood up with a jerk and strode over to the window and stared out over the river. A couple of dolphins flicked their scimitar curved tails out of the water. He folded his hands behind his back.

'Ha!'

There was a knock at the door and Lieutenant Bentes announced Robert Jenney.

Colonel Fabio had met Bobby or rather had ordered a meeting with him about two years previously, after the annual 7th September Independence Day parade in the old town square. Some teenager had let off a firework right in front of him as he stood to attention on his new young horse taking the salute as his regiment marched past. His horse had reared and, because he was busy saluting, he'd nearly fallen off. A fair-haired young man with a foreign accent had stepped forward and with steady confidence had calmed his horse in seconds. Now that was a cavalry man.

Colonel Fabio pushed his chair back.

'How are you my son, *tudo bem*?' He strode forward, a broad smile on his face, hand outstretched. More than twenty years older than Bobby, he liked calling him my son.

Bobby's smile exaggerated the lines on his sun-burnt face. His mud-covered shirt and jeans contrasted sharply with the Colonel's neat uniform. He clasped and unclasped his hands.

'Good to see you, Colonel. How lovely and cool in here. How's the arm?' He always asked after his arm but hoped not to hear the broken-arm story again.

'Sit down, my son, you look a bit rough. Me too with trouble here and trouble there. So, tell me, what brings you to me?'

'Colonel, I need your help.' Bobby leant forward and drew a deep breath. 'I wouldn't ask for a favour unless I really needed it...'

'Go on, out with it.'

'Our land titles.'

'What about them?'

'Our land is not fully registered. The lawyers in São Paulo said they were good but they aren't. There are plenty of others like us but I must have them otherwise we are working illegally.'

'Illegally?' Colonel Fabio forced a laugh. 'Ha! What does that mean around here? I just try to keep order as best I can.' He shrugged his shoulders as if all his responsibilities were too heavy for him, especially after the morning discussions with his fellow officers.

Bobby pressed on. 'I'm asking whether you could tell those people at the Ministry and in particular Captain Dias to give me a hearing. I've asked many times. He refuses to meet me.'

Colonel Fabio raised his eyebrows, 'A Captain Dias in the Land Reform Agency. I don't know anybody of that name. Is he ex-army?'

'You'll know the guy, big and heavy with a large nose. Albino-like on one side of his face and dark on the other. He's always shouting at every one. I met him once with Zé, my Indian scout friend. Apparently, they knew each other before the Military took over.'

Colonel Fabio sat back and looked up at the ceiling. Albino-like on one side dark on the other. That's rare. Not possible. Could it really be the same bastard leader of that march all those years ago? He rubbed his bent arm. So, he called himself Captain Dias these days, did he?

'You're upset and angry, my son, aren't you?'

'Yes I am.'

'Here, have a drink.' Colonel Fabio pushed over the maté tea. 'Suck away. That'll calm you down. I've always got time for an old soldier.'

Bobby wondered if he'd ever acquire a taste for the bitter green maté. How he longed for a bar of Cadbury's Fruit and Nut. They passed the tea back and forth, sharing the single straw as Bobby talked.

An hour later Colonel Fabio stood up. 'Supper calls. My wife, Orlanda, needs me.' He showed Bobby to the door.

'I'll try to pull a string or two but they're a fiendishly tricky lot especially with us army. It could be months before I receive an answer. And I mean months. I'll be in touch.'

Secretly he was pleased that Dias or whatever his name was, might be close by. He would find out more, his President had warned.

Bobby found Idenea sitting on the ground outside their wooden town office, her arms around her knees. She didn't look up.

'What happened?'

She told him, her eyes to the ground.

'I haven't been very successful either,' he sighed. 'The Colonel might help but we can't be sure of anything. So, let's check into that new hotel for the night.' He said in a comforting voice, 'There'll be air conditioning and we can cool off. Ari will look after everything. Hopefully tomorrow we'll get answers to the telegrams I sent today.'

So many people. Only one room free with a single bed. 'We can be close as well,' he said laughing.

232

She didn't smile, didn't reply. When she came out of the shower, he slipped her towel off and hugged her to him.

'No, Bobinho,' pushing him away, 'I can't. Let me be, so much to think about.'

They lay head to toe on the narrow spongy mattress. After a couple of hours with her toes a few inches from his nose, he slipped to the floor and slept with his head in the crook of his arm.

Next day, he picked up three cables in the new Post Office. Idenea was waiting in the jeep. He opened the door quickly, the handle too hot to hold. Inside the cabin, the heat pricked at their skin. She watched him intently as he read aloud.

'From Luiz Antonio in São Paulo: *Try to buy them out so no trouble in future - Will provide name of good lawyer to help - Try to firm up our own titles at the same time - Good luck. LA.*'

'From Alistair in London: *You must do a deal with them - Discuss with Luiz Antonio - Good luck. AA.*'

'From LG in São Paulo: *Get them off do you understand - Use force if necessary- Will come up to check – Don't fail - Luiz Geraldo da Costa.*'

He gripped the wheel and watched a dog limp across the road. She held his elbow. 'So now, what do we do?'

Months later.

'You are here because I say so.' Captain Dias on his feet, tall behind his desk in the heavy heat of his cramped office.

The previous afternoon a soldier from Colonel Delgado's regiment had driven up in a VW beetle and delivered a sealed envelope. Colonel Delgado had written in his own hand;

Dear British Cavalryman Roberto,
I have arranged a meeting for you with Senhor Dias [I assure you he's not a Captain] for tomorrow at 9 in the morning. Don't miss this opportunity. I cannot do this again. I used the argument of cooperation. He replied that

land titles are a big problem. Do not quote me.
Sincerely Colonel Delgado another Cavalryman.
P.S. My arm is well. Come and visit me soon or I'll come
out and see what you are up to.'

'True to his word.' Bobby said as he read the message to Idenea.

Bobby jumped into the jeep. Idenea put a bowl of cold rice, beans and stewed beef on the seat beside him. She kissed him, hands on both his cheeks.

'Keep your eyes and ears open for my baby won't you and don't forget my land title as well?' He nodded and drove off into the dark for the eight hours of mud and pot holes.

Now in Dias's office, there were two chairs, one behind Dias, the other in a corner. Dias did not offer a seat.

The old electric fan clattered in the corner. Every now and then it slowed, barely turning but then with a noisy metallic ticking picked up speed again as if the effort of propelling the heavy air was almost too much for it.

'Good to see you again, Captain Dias,' Bobby began. 'You may remember that we met in the Suspendido Bar with my friend Zé Magelhães. How are you?' He offered his hand.

Just as Idenea had described, there was the squint, the wall-eye, the scar on the cheek.

'Yes, yes, I remember.' Dias ignored his hand. 'Now. What do you want from me? I have little time.'

'Colonel Delgado said he'd arrange a meeting with you to discuss...'

'Yes.' Dias barked his interruption. 'I agreed for reasons of, take note, unavoidable necessary cooperation within government. Do you understand? Now then what is it you want? Speak up!'

Bobby closed his feet together and stiffened. He began slowly, 'I need help, Senhor. I understand you are responsible for the legalisation of land titles in this territory and...'

'Yes, I am.'

'Well, although we bought our land in good faith, I cannot get full registration.'

'*We?*'

234

'My São Paulo partners, my London partners and me.'

'You are foreign.'

'My accent?' Bobby smiled, trying to lighten the conversation.

'No matter.' Dias lowered his bulk into his chair.

The fan buzzed noisily with a surge of unexpected energy. Bobby spread out his map of Fazenda Rio Largo but the heaps of files prevented it from lying flat. Dias listened in silence.

'I would also like to ask that you look into Plot 921 at the edge of our land. The settlers there say their titles have been taken away from them and that they are the rightful owners. This sounds most irregular...'

'Why do you care about them?' Dias snapped.

'Their plot 921 falls within our boundaries. They came in good faith and like us work hard.' Images of Idenea hoeing in her orchard flashed before his eyes.

Dias glared at him. 'Who are you talking about?'

Bobby smiled, thinking he was getting somewhere.

'They're called Saladini and believe passionately that the land belongs to them. It came to them under a government programme.'

'What sort of deal are you thinking of?'

Such was his squint that for an instant Bobby imagined that Dias was addressing the rumbling fan in the corner.

'You can register the title in their names or incorporate the land into ours for a good price.' He paused. 'My partners say they are definitely squatters and that I must remove them... ' He paused. He was talking too glibly.

Dias stood up roughly, his belly pushing over the edge of the desk. 'That's enough. I will consider your situation and inform you of my decision in due course. Now, please leave.'

Bobby realised that he was being thrown out. For a moment the two men held each other's eye: Dias hostile, Bobby determined. Without a handshake, Bobby saw himself out into the white sunlight.

With a sharp, 'Don't disturb me', Captain Dias shut his door, sat down heavily and crossed his arms. He had reckoned that this Senhor Roberto would be just another big landowner doing nothing with the land but instead he had a big landowner and a foreigner who would actually do something like clear squatters out. How very nice of him! He started to write;

> Dear Pedro, Remember what our course leader in East Berlin said to us, 'Be negative to cause unrest'. Well, I have an opportunity. I planted several seeds some years ago. One of them is likely to bear fruit and come good very soon. I never expected this area to be invaded by so many thousands thus giving me so much power. I will keep you informed. Your old friend and fighter for the Cause. Ananias.

But he thought better of it and tore the letter up. No, he'd deal with this one on his own. If intercepted it could compromise both Pedro and himself, and upset Mercedes, his wife. He whispered to the ceiling, 'Like that' and 'Yes, it could work.'

Outside, Bobby sat in his jeep. He'd talked too much. That bastard Dias had got him talking. Damn, Damn. He'd been weak. And Zé had warned him.

He badly wanted a shower. The barking of dogs echoed down the streets. A mule and rider ambled past. He'd leave in the morning; he couldn't face all the mud that night. How could he confront Dias alone? There was that acid feeling of failure back in his stomach. Alone? Nonsense. They'd fight together. He and she, of course they would. How he missed her. He thought of the pleasure on her face tomorrow when he jumped out of his jeep. She would scold him for being away for so long before throwing her arms around his neck. He bought some of her favourite soap.

Before going on home, he took the long turning off to Plot 921. He'd promised Juca he would keep him informed. He and Carmen would help surely. But he'd have to watch out for that brute Bosco. Why didn't he carry a pistol?

Back at Rio Largo, his eyebrows stiff with dust and under the bucket shower, Idenea asked, as she soaped him down, 'Well, how did it go?'

'Dias said he'd look into it. He was very aggressive.'

'And on my place, what did they say?'

'Bosco ranted and raved, Carlito said nothing as usual, Carmen suckled her baby. And Juca, well, he just ogled their baby. And I said we needed their support and didn't want any trouble and that they could all, and by that I mean all of them, own some land one day if we all work together.'

'And me?'

She put the soap into his hand and made him wash her down before all the warm water ran out of the bucket.

'You? Of course, you have the strongest claim as your father's heir. But we can't evict them can we, even if LG wants that? We have to find a solution.'

With water trickling down her cheeks she said, 'Juca's strange isn't he? Maybe it's because he's half Indian.'

'Funny you should say that. As I was leaving, he said thank you to me. For what I asked? He just smiled that toothless grin of his. But I admit, I did feel pleased.'

He dried first himself and then Idenea, 'God, I hope it works, my future's in it.'

'Mine too.' She drew their bodies together.

'What shall we do when we're not working in this Palace of Nowhere?' Bobby asked one late Sunday afternoon. He was poking at a big toe with a needle and bathing it with raw alcohol. He gasped at the sting.

'How are your toes?'

Idenea looked up from the old fashion 'magazine' she was flicking through, studying a picture of a model in a fur coat standing in deep snow. She was lying beside him on the cane sofa.

'Damn worms. Sorry, not very pretty. Why don't they bother you?'

'I don't know. You must be more tasty than me.'

'Well, you haven't answered have you?' He stood up and looked down into her eyes. 'What shall we do when we are not working...?'

'Work hard for a better life,' she said with a playful smile, 'and make a baby Adam.' She dropped her smile. 'And find my Zoni.' She glanced towards the shrine with its wooden doll.

'And after that?' Bobby was gazing out through the mosquito netting that was their outer wall. The creep of the lengthening shadows was turning the red earth into shades of dark purple and deepest brown. A Nellore cow coughed in the nearest field. Leonidas's children were chasing chickens with shrieks of excitement.

'For God's sake, it's been three months since I saw that man and still we're waiting for our damn titles. Dias thinks he's God around here.' He roughed his hair. 'Well, I've ordered an electric piano up from the south. You can teach me your childhood songs.'

Idenea was staring sightlessly towards the jungle. The two black and white photographs of her parents and grandparents tinted with colour hung on a post. Toco sat beside her on the floor.

'My childhood songs,' she murmured folding her hair under her chin, '*Meu povo*, My People, so far away.'

'Your people?' he snapped. 'They abandoned you.' And accusingly, 'Your people indeed. *Meu povo, meu povo*? Where would you be if I hadn't turned up? I saved you, mind you remember that.' He ended with a rasping in his throat.

She jumped up and pointed a forefinger close to his face, her eyes wide with anger.

'Heh, you, *Bolas*. It was me who saved *you*. You were the mess, your whole life a failure. It was me who put you together.' She bit her lip. Her eyes shone. 'How dare you think you did more than me.'

Bobby was sweating. Memories of the last time he'd lost control in that dusty loft full of spent cordite rushed back. He shouted at her retreating back.

'You mended me, huh? You were the runaway. I healed your sadness, I...I...' He spun around, still shouting. 'There are times when I want to escape from this alien world where nobody delivers and to... to have a hot bath. Chaos. Talk about a mess.'

With her back to him, she said, 'That's what it's like here. Haven't you learnt that yet?' And to comfort herself, she stroked Toco's head.

He lifted his heavy black and yellow bill. 'I'm the true saviour, you old bullet leg, *Perna de Bala*. Don't you see, *Me*!'

'Please come over here,' he said quickly, 'For God's sake, please look at me.'

She came. He smiled, his lips in a shy curl, 'You were so vulnerable, so wounded.' His voice slowed.

'And you?' she replied also softly, 'Don't tell me you weren't lost and sad just like me?'

He lowered his eyes.

'We were the same then,' she said. 'Maybe that's why I came with you.'

Bobby sucked at a bottle of water, sat down at the table and pulled out a sheet of paper.

Fazenda Rio Largo, Amazon.

Dear Perry,

I have to write to you.

There is a brooding of black clouds outside. It's going to rain lead nails. I've just lost my temper with my wonderful girl. I'm very cross with myself.

The only sound out here similar to home is from a woodpecker. I used to love it here, not so sure any more. Amazingly at times, in spite of the heat, all my energy seems to drive out any doubt about what I am doing.

Sometimes, I feel all that education rotting away, my old resolve evaporating. Am I just a result of that teaching? Do I approach people with any kindness, as old Doggard used to say was all that mattered? Do you, my one-legged Perry, you with your gift of Faith as you call it? I'm here wanting to KNOW.

I look out at my hard work, or rather the destruction, at the green grass, the cattle fattening. AND, swinging in a hammock is the bravest girl in the world. But is she of my people as she's always saying, as if she doesn't want to be with me any more? Is she too different to build a new life with? She wanted to escape like me. She hopes I'll help her find her baby whom she's convinced some Indians stole. It probably fattened worms long ago.

*I was called a killer of nature in an anonymous letter—me
a killer?*

*I've got an electric piano arriving soon so we'll have fun
with that.*

How's your leg?

He stopped writing. He'd finish it later when his temper had
passed.

That night he said, 'I'm sorry I lost my temper today, Idenea. I
want you to be happy. I want us both to be happy. We must try to
think how to find your Zoni.'

Outside the air throbbed with the rhythmic croaking of frogs,
more like a crisp chatter than a croak. Night birds belled and
whooped. Their calls were so regular that he could anticipate a
particular boom or whirr before it came.

Lying on her back, naked like him, beneath their domed
mosquito net, she touched his hand.

'I didn't know you had a temper like that.' She took his whole
hand in hers. 'Yes, you gave me new life. Yes, you showed me love.
I still don't know if I know what that is. But I taught you how to
stand tall again.'

He squeezed her little finger.

She rolled onto her side towards him, her body inches from his.
'Since I met you I've become a new woman. We're both new people,
aren't we? Sometimes, no, often, I think of my family and the cool
south. I can't help it. But remember, I came up here for a better
life and to help my father.' Her eyes white in the semi-dark. 'One
day when we've found Zoni we'll make *our* baby, *tá bom*, and we'll
call him Adam to mark our beginning.' She sighed with a resigned
sadness. 'But I don't think we'll ever find my Zoni...Aaah?'

He stroked her damp shoulder. It was a particularly hot night.
'Yes, you're right we are born again and you gave me hope.' He
smiled. 'And I thought I'd got over losing my temper. It didn't do
me any good before.'

He touched her eyebrows one after the other. 'And we'll find
Zoni, you'll see. Then we'll think about Adam.'

She put a hand on his shoulder. 'I've been thinking...'

'About what?'

'Leonidas's wife, Cida. She's got three children.'

'They're happy, aren't they?'

'Cida wants to educate them. She can hardly read or write herself and asked me to start a school. There are six other children on the ranch. She says the government might help with books and things for writing and maybe some money.'

'You have no teaching experience.'

'I was good at school and I was doing well with Zoni before he was...was stolen. I can teach reading and writing.' She closed her eyes as helping Zoni to shape letters came to her.

He rolled onto his back. 'I like the idea and I'm sorry if I was short with you. If the government won't back you because you are unqualified, I'm sure the shareholders would be delighted. Except LG of course.'

'Oh, Bobinho, let's start right away.'

'Let's sleep now,' he said. Starting a school could take her mind off looking for Zoni, he thought.

The next day they attacked their work with a renewed determination. She had taken to wearing a skirt again but kept to her leather boots. Enthusiasm bounced in her step. In two weeks they had built a school room with benches and tables out of their own wood for ten children. There was a thatched roof and a notice on the door, 'Escola Fazenda Rio Largo'.

Often, she rode out with him to inspect the cattle and check the fence lines. When done, they'd race home, their mules neck and neck, shouting and laughing. Ari trotted behind and, on arrival, he'd ask who'd won. He could never be sure.

On Sundays she always cooked a special meal. If they had slaughtered a young bullock or pig, then it all had to be eaten within two days except for the thin slices of red flesh drying in the sun as *Carne Seca*. She never told him what she was cooking and teased him to guess. Oh, not again, he'd say pulling a face but they ate every mouthful; any scraps to Toco and Massby.

He gathered red seeds as large as his thumb and carved small chunks of dark Sucupira wood into hollow rounds. He fashioned a necklace and hid it under her pillow. Feeling the roughness, she pulled it out and with an excited giggle put it around her neck.

'How clever of you, Bobinho.'

She tried sleeping with it on but the hard nobbles kept her awake. Instead she wore it every evening.

After a day with the cattle he laid the sofa cushions end to end on the floor, stretched a sheet over and placed two pillows at one end.

She smiled at him. 'Before supper?'

He nodded. 'Why not? I'll shower first, I'm all sticky.'

She pushed Toco into its cage. 'Be still, you silly bird.'

Minutes later he was back, his hair slick with water. He held a towel in front of his body. She wasn't there. Not in the bedroom either. He heard a humming from outside.

Her naked body gleamed in the moonless dark. She was looking upwards at the tops of the trees. No wind clattered the leaves.

He came up behind her and put a hand gently on her shoulder. 'Mosquitoes?'

She crossed one hand over her shoulder and took his hand, 'They don't bother me any more.'

He pressed his full length against her. She whispered, 'Be gentle with me, won't you?'

A mutum whoomped and whoomped from the jungle floor.

'We're together,' he said.

Her smile faded. 'Are we?'

He gripped her hand. 'Of course, we are.'

He pulled her gently but firmly towards their hut but she kept looking back over her shoulder at the jungle.

'You can't stay out here,' he insisted, 'naked like this.'

'Why not? It's me. It's all around me.'

He tugged at her hand. 'I'm being bitten.'

Lying side by side on the cushions, his fingers lingered on her scars. For him they were beauty spots.

'You're beautiful, Idenea, like the jungle. I'm a lucky man.' He kissed her eye lids.

'I'm lucky too,' she said without a smile.

She cried out, not a cry of pain but of alarm. She pounded her fists on his chest like she had in the Perfect Peace Motel. Then had been in panic at his leaving her alone, now she beat at him as if wanting to expel him from her body. Tears slipped down her cheeks.

He faltered. 'Are you cross with me?'

'Bobinho,' she murmured.

He disentangled himself. She clung to his arm as he stood up. 'I'm sorry, my Bobinho, I can't make love today,' and pulled the sheet over herself. 'It's all around me, all around me.'

Bobby collected the electric piano in Porto Velho and picked up a bundle of mail. Amongst the business and the official were letters from his parents and Beatrice. Beatrice told him about Michael and hoped he was safe. Her letter was longer than usual and he read it twice before screwing it up.

That evening they pulled the piano out of its box and connected it to the 5 hp generator outside.

'And now,' he beamed, 'Brazilian or British?' He kissed her on the cheek.

'Brazilian,' she said firmly. 'We'll start with songs that me and my friend Rosie used to sing.'

'I'll do my best to accompany you. If we can manage one song today, we'll be doing well.' He spread his hands above the black and white keys and held them motionless with fingers curled as if the keys were unbearably hot. He hadn't played for more than four years. Bending his head forward and spreading his fingers, he pressed down hard.

'Glorious,' he exclaimed.

He looked across at Idenea. She nodded encouragement. He smiled back. No more rows. He would try with all his heart to make these two worlds mix. He'd help with the school. Already such a success that, with her enthusiasm, the children were soon forming squiggly-shaped numbers and letters. They never missed a class for fear of losing her attention.

Every evening, after their bucket shower together, he played from memory or from the sheet music that his mother sent. Sometimes he played for her to sing songs from the south, her reserve gone when she realised that the monkeys were her sole audience. She asked the children in and they all sang together. Other times he played for himself. Out at work under the burn of the midday sun, he longed for the feel of his fingers on those black and white keys.

'I'm in touch again,' he said one night in bed.

A single candle flickered on her side. Mosquitoes whined beyond the white dome of netting.

'*O que*, what?' she asked sleepily.

'The person I once was.'

'Hmmm? You mean *saudades*, nostalgia, for your people like I have for mine?'

He rolled to one side. 'At least I have the piano.'

'Well, I don't like that duh-duh-duh stuff you keep playing. I like songs and dancing. And what's more important, when are we going to find Zoni? You promised.' She poked him irritably in the ribs.

'Soon. Don't do that. It hurt.'

He heard despair choke her voice. 'We've got to look for him.'

He reached for her hand but she pushed him away. Instead of less rowing, they quarrelled more often.

'It's the heat,' he'd say.

The sun, an orange sickle against the pale purple of early dawn, rose up over the rain-soaked greens and browns, dispelling the moonlight as it grew rounder and brighter. The trees, their leaves heavy with rain drooped and dripped. Lightning flickered. Thunder banged and rippled in the distance. A filmy mist hung over the tops of the trees lacing white amongst the sodden branches. Soon this sun, that ogre of the tropics, would blaze in full triumphant glory out of a hard blue sky.

An open jeep with two men, both in t-shirts one red one blue, slipped and squelched along the mud track. Steam rose from the red surface of the track. The driver was a weather-beaten white man of around forty, the passenger a mulato of about twenty-five. Both wore army fatigue caps over dark glasses and a revolver belted around their waists. They passed a small wooden board with *Fazenda Boa Esperança* painted in faded rain-washed letters. The driver thumbed up his right fist.

They had spent the night in the jeep on the main road. The driver had no wish to be caught in a downpour on this boggy track. They hadn't eaten since the day before. The driver was certain there'd be some rice and beans shortly. The jeep skidded and slithered around the final bend.

In the open-sided living room of the main hut, Bosco, Juca and Carlito sat eating cold rice, beans and sun-dried beef; cold because Carmen and her baby had left the day before in the mule and cart to be with her mother and father in the village. Bébé had sent an urgent message asking her to make sure she came that same day. They were discussing the problem of land titles. *Would that gringo really be able to help*? Bosco was shouting and banging the table. Juca quietly urged patience. He was thinking of his girl Carmen and their baby and how he must marry her soon. Carlito said nothing, he rarely did and when he did, he took so long to explain himself that the others didn't bother to listen.

Zoni's monkey panted in the shade. Bolo lay stretched out in a corner. Juca stopped chewing. 'Listen, are we expecting anyone today?'

Bosco fork in the air. 'I can't hear a thing. And as I was saying that damn Ministry should...'

'Stop.' Juca raised one hand. 'Listen, you fool, there's somebody coming and they're just around the bend.'

Bosco stopped chewing. 'Yes, you're right, look it's a jeep.'

Carlito mumbled something unintelligible. Juca, at one end of the table stood up for a better view. Bosco and Carlito, behind the table, also stood up.

The jeep accelerated rapidly and skidded to a stop five metres from the table. Juca was running before the jeep had stopped. Something about the two pairs of dark glasses under similar caps and clean t-shirts had unsettled him. As he sprinted across Idenea's abandoned orchard he heard,

'Quick! Quick! Get 'em! I'll take the two here, you get the runner. MOVE!'

Bosco's voice in panic, 'Stop. We're just simple...'

Two shots. Bosco screamed. Two more shots. Juca ran. He was already twenty metres away, and would have Idenea's hut between him and his pursuer and then into the trees. He felt a violent sting in his right shoulder and then another in his right thigh that shattered the bone. The force of the two bullets in quick succession propelled him onto his face. His dark glasses snapped off. 'Keep still,' he said to himself, 'It's your only chance.' He heard Bolo bark, another shot and a yelp.

Again the voice of command from the hut, 'Is yours dead?'

'There's blood on his back.'

'Good, these two are finished. Search for the others, a girl and her baby. Look everywhere. We must get them all. Eh, eh now, what's this? One of them not dead huh? I'll see to that.' He drew a knife from a canvas sheath in his belt and leaned over the groaning Bosco and yanked his head up by the hair.

Juca lay quite still. He could hear his pursuer rushing and stumbling about. A minute later the voice of his appointed executioner gasped, 'I've looked everywhere. There's nobody else. No mule, no cart, nothing.'

The voice of command, 'Merda! Bastards! And there're only three plates on the table. You're right, she's gone, but she could be back any moment. Are you sure yours is dead?'

That voice, Juca thought as he held his breath. Lightning flashed. Juca counted, One, Two, Three. Thunder exploded into a thousand pieces above him.

The voice of his pursuer from some way away. 'I can see a shit load of blood and the black bastard hasn't moved.'

'Okay then, quick, let's get out of there. Vamos, into the jeep.'

The monkey hadn't moved. The six vultures, who had been waiting on the roof of Idenea's old hut for scraps from the men's lunch, had flapped up into the air at the first shot and were circling up and up, their wait nearly over and now with an added interest below. The jeep revved and spun around in the mud and headed down the track.

Heavy rain splattered onto Juca's bare back and thigh mixing with his blood. He opened one eye, barely able to move, and spat out red earth jammed into his mouth by the fall. He raised his head. That voice, he thought. And I'm not black. I'm half Indian, you murderous bastards. Stay alive. For Carmen, for my baby.

He dragged himself with one arm and one leg towards the shade of the hut leaving a line of red on the earth behind him. The rain splashed grit onto his skin. Ten minutes of struggle later, he propped himself up against one of the hut posts. The monkey silently bared its teeth. Bolo lay a couple of metres away with tongue hanging out of open jaws. Bosco and Carlito's bodies sprawled over the table, blood from Bosco's throat dripping into a pool below the table.

The jeep skidded along the track, wheels spinning one moment to the left, the next to the right. Several times the driver ordered the mulato to get out and push. The rain caught them, splashing onto the bonnet and into the open jeep, water swilling around their feet. Their t-shirts stuck to their backs. The driver shouted, 'Go on! Push you, *filho da puta*, or we'll get stuck.' His blue t-shirt soon a reddy-brown.

They reached the bigger road. The driver accelerated. He turned to his mud-covered companion and through clenched teeth, 'Job done. The Boss will be pleased.' He pulled his cap down to the rim of his dark glasses.

Carmen was trotting back to Fazenda Boa Esperança in the cart. She held the rawhide reins in one hand while holding her baby in her other arm.

As the jeep approached, the man in the blue t-shirt pointed. 'Look, there she is. And look, there's a baby. Let's get them. Then we'll get a hundred per cent reward, right?' He rose up out of his seat, his hand on his revolver. The mule and cart were only twenty metres away. The driver slammed his right hand across and punched down the hand with the gun.

'You idiot! Someone might see us. Besides, she could be the wrong one.'

Carmen slowed to a walk as the jeep swerved past her. She waved a greeting. Neither of the two men glanced in her direction.

Bobby had much to do that day. First, several head of cattle had broken out over night and had to be rounded up. Second, he was to supervise the largest felling programme yet attempted on Fazenda Rio Largo. LG had ordered, 'To drive his Big Yellow Babies to the limit'. Bobby needed Ari and Ari was late.

Idenea had packed him a lunch of pork fat mixed with manioc flour plus a ripe papaya from her beloved orchard. To drink he had a small packet of guaraná powder to mix with water from a stream, that is if he could find any water sufficiently clear of ash to be drinkable. He rode out on his favourite mule.

She called after him, 'See you at sundown. I'll be in the orchard with Leonidas, he's helping me today. And then I'll be in the school with Cida.'

Bobby found Ari on his mule walking unusually slow. Behind him, attached by a rope to his saddle, skidded two long dark green tubes.

'Ari, what are those?'

'Snake, Chefe. anaconda.' Ari spluttered and laughed. 'Your Ari nearly ended up in that monster's belly, if it hadn't been for this.' He hoisted his machete into the air. 'You wouldn't have old Ari to protect you any more.' He sliced downwards with his machete.

Bobby chuckled. 'That would be a shame, old friend. Tell me about your brave deed.'

'Well, Chefe, I was fishing for piranhas and pácu[10] when this monster wrapped itself around me, its foul head banging against the back of my head. Its tail was coiled around a tree.' Ari gasped heavily. 'It wanted to crush my ribs and then drown me. But, Chefe, luck was with old Ari. My right arm was free and Ari with a machete is dangerous! You've seen me clear paths in the jungle, like this.' And he sliced his machete up and down with such force that his mule shied.

'So, Chefe, I hacked and I hacked.' Ari's mule by now was fairly skittering about, 'And, and...with the fifth blow I cut the brute in half. I had to fight to squirm out of its grip. It bared its jaws right in front of my face. God in Heaven did it stink! It can't have eaten for ages. Come to think of it, otherwise why would it have gone for an old rum-sodden cowboy like me, huh?' Ari grinned at this confession. 'I watched it thrash about before it went the way of all things that attack Ari...to Hell.'

'Were you afraid?'

'You bet, Chefe. Imagine choking to death with other half-digested things in that brute's stomach. I once saw one as big as this one cut open and inside was a rotting body with shorts and shoes still on, all slimy and shiny, the poor bastard.'

Bobby chuckled. 'But for that right arm of yours, I'd be without you. Then what?'

'Dunno really, Chefe.'

'Come on, Ari, leave those horrible bits of reptile, we've got to find those runaways.'

They rode along the side of the three hundred metre fence line, their mules carefully picking their way over the remains of half-burnt trees. Bobby looked out across the two thousand hectares of grassland where over a thousand head of cattle were grazing. He had left substantial areas of forest where the soil was weak and fragile, roughly like a chequer-board, the weak soil left alone and the good soil partially cleared as Alistair had recommended and Luiz Antonio had agreed, all contrary to LG's wishes who demanded every tree to be on the ground.

---

10 Pacu; a fruit-eating piranha.

They stopped where the fence lay flattened. Two posts were snapped with the wire and the attached wooden stringers on the ground leaving a gap of about fifteen metres. A dead cow lay inside the fence.

'Jaguar?' said Bobby.

'No, not this one. Only vultures. Keep looking.'

They tied up their mules. Ari slashed into the jungle.

'Over here,' he hollered. He was standing beside a young calf with its head and breast half eaten. 'Big cat, look at the ripping of its claws.' They knelt for a closer look. Some of the calf's front teeth had been pulled out and lay beside the head. 'You see, Chefe, this cat probably stalked up in the night behind some cows and their young. Keeping down wind, he rushed in, possibly missing with his first charge. Panic and a stampede against the wire. Some scrambled over crushing the one back there. In the panic, this tasty calf was easy for him. I'll come with my gun and wait for the bastard. He'll be asleep somewhere near. Good meat here though, we can't waste it. I'll slice off some steaks.'

He drew his knife.

Bobby glanced behind him and imagined the rush and the pounce of the beautiful spotted cat, its sharp claws out.

'Up you get, Chefe, or we'll never find those runners and they'll go wild.'

An hour later, cattle rounded up and fence line mended, they rode on. From about half a kilometre away, they could hear the sound of a heavy cracking and splitting that reminded Bobby of tank and artillery fire; not the same crash or thump but the intensity of the sound. Only once had he heard such a noise with similar regularity and that was when ten tanks had fired their guns at short intervals at an imaginary enemy. Every soldier had worn ear protection. Here, the sound of crashing assaulted everything, the trees, the animals, even the blue of the sky, with flying debris and continuous explosions. As the two rode closer they had to raise their voices. A hundred metres on and they were shouting.

Bobby bawled at Ari, 'You take a look to the left and I'll go to the right. And watch out.'

Ari wheeled away.

Two yellow Cat D8 bulldozers were crawling through forty-five-metre high rain forest. A fifty-metre-long ship's anchor chain trailed between them. In the middle of the chain rolled a three-metre diameter steel ball filled with concrete. For the ball to roll forward without twisting the chains, there was a steel rod within a tube cast through the middle with rings strong enough to take the pulling strain of the two bulldozers. As they ground inexorably forward, their tracks biting into the topsoil, the chains cut through the undergrowth and toppled over trees of every shape and size. If a tree should stubbornly resist the initial thrust of the chain, the ball rolled up the trunk pulled by the horsepower of two times 280hp until the tree gave up the struggle and fell over.

Bobby winced as a tree crashed to the ground sending shockwaves up his mule's legs and through his saddle. Was this the fastest method of felling yet devised by man, he wondered? There had been no time to measure the quality of the land underneath or check the flow of the streams. Several months before, he'd argued with LG.

'What's the difference between clearing land by axe and saw and mowing with machines like these?' had been the sharp reply. 'I'll tell you what, more cattle and more profit. Your annual target quicker and more money for me and more money for you. So why resist new ideas? Thanks to these yellow babies, next year will be much bigger. I've persuaded my father, so get on with it. Or if you don't like it, you can always leave.'

At the beginning of the dry season the two bulldozers with the ball and chain had arrived with a note from LG.

—*Make sure you have the engines in good working order when I get there. A friend of mine with a huge ranch in Pará and thousands of head of cattle and much soya showed me how. LG.—*

Bobby had learned to ignore these commands. Thankfully LG's fear of malaria kept his visits infrequent and Ari's cynical laugh cheered him up.

251

At dusk in the ranch house with a long drink to hand, a short one for Ari, the three of them agreed that destruction was destruction whichever way you looked at it.

'At least some trees have been sold,' Idenea said.

'It'll be over soon, Chefe,' said Ari, 'and then I'll have many head of cattle fattening on good grass. That must be good.'

Bobby always ended with, 'This level of deforestation is without care. It will create a wilderness.'

One night, after a day of clearing forty hectares, Bobby dropped his head into his hands. 'I could leave the ranch couldn't I or rather we could? LG would like that.'

'No, no,' said Idenea, 'what would happen to us? No land. No money. We've worked so hard.'

Ari, for once quiet and thoughtful. 'What's the matter, Chefe?'

'It's not as we planned, is it?'

He swept his arm towards the jungle.

A jeep and an enclosed van were parked outside the ranch house when Bobby returned one evening. Both cars had PM in large letters on their side doors.

'What's this?' he said to his mule as he tethered it to the veranda rail, 'Policia Militar? Whatever next?'

Two uniformed men sat in the front seat of the van.

Ari was still out with the cattle. The sun had dropped below the level of the palm leafed roof. The magic hour of six o'clock was half an hour away. Bobby was longing for a good shower, his customary rum and tonic with Idenea and a happy time at the piano. What would they sing tonight?

Bobby raised his hand in greeting. They didn't acknowledge. Perhaps they were after a runaway prisoner? There had been a few of those around looking for work on ranches as remote as this. He pushed open the door to the living room. Idenea was sitting in one of the cane chairs, alarm in her eyes. This was odd from his steely girl. A uniformed policeman stood on each side of her.

'Bobinho, thank God you're here,' she blurted out. 'These brutes won't say why they're here. I was doing the office paperwork when they walked in.'

She gestured to her left. 'He's Lieutenant Bentes. I know him. He's the one who interviewed us all when Chico disappeared. I don't know what they want and...'

'Well Senhores,' Bobby took over, 'what can we do for you?' He walked towards the lieutenant with an outstretched hand.

'We're doing a regular check on firearms.' Lieutenant Bentes ignored Bobby's hand. 'There have been too many shoot-outs around here. You have a gun, don't you?'

They were all a bit nervous, Bobby thought. No greeting, no niceties but then they were your typical clumsy police. And aloud, 'Yes, of course. Doing your duty, eh Lieutenant? I am glad you're catching up with the baddies. Yes, I have a Taurus ·38.'

'Please, can I see it? I have to make a note of the serial number.'

'It's in the bedroom. I'll fetch it. As it happens, I've never used it.' Bobby opened the door to their bedroom.

The Lieutenant followed. Bobby rummaged at the bottom of the cupboard for the old pair of boots that served as the hiding place for his revolver. The two men from the van outside entered the living room.

'Bobbeee!' He heard Idenea cry out. 'Come here quickly. They've got guns.'

Bobby jumped round, his revolver in its holster in his hand. The Lieutenant barred the doorway.

'Anything wrong, Lieutenant?'

'Your revolver please,' the lieutenant said politely.

Bobby handed it over. 'It's licensed and unloaded. I'll look for the papers, probably lost though. I'd like it back please. You never know at night, snakes, jaguars.'

'Bobby,' Idenea cried again. 'Come here quick.'

Through the doorway he faced three policemen with drawn revolvers. Idenea, panic in her eyes. A belt of frost around his gut. He wasn't afraid, he'd faced guns before. But there was something awkward about the men in front of him. One looked at the other.

Another glanced furtively around the room. It was as if they didn't quite know what they were doing and that was dangerous.

'What's all this about?' Bobby said calmly.

From behind; 'Senhor Jenney!'

Bobby turned to find the Lieutenant also pointing his gun at him. Bobby's brain flashed for a second and then floated as if in a dream. Four revolvers pointing at him at once.

'I am here to arrest you for the murder of three people two days ago on Fazenda Boa Esperança belonging to the Saladini family near Mutum.'

The Lieutenant pulled out a piece of paper. 'The murdered are, Senhor Bosco Saladini and Senhor Carlos Saladini, and the wounded is Senhor Juca. You will come with us.' He gestured to the four behind Bobby. 'Handcuff him and put him in the van.'

'This is nonsense,' Bobby heard himself say.

'We'll see about that later,' said Lieutenant Bentes.

'You're wrong, very wrong.' Bobby's voice came as a whisper.

'*No*,' Idenea groaned, 'leave him alone. Those are my family. He'd never kill my family. He was here all day. Leave him alone.'

'These murders happened at midday. There was plenty of time for him to be back here by sundown.'

'You liar!' She was screaming now.

Bobby felt both his arms pinioned, his wrists yanked behind his back and handcuffs clipped on. 'This is a terrible mistake' was all he could mumble as he was rough handled out of the door.

At that moment Ari rode up, harness jingling, dragging the two lengths of anaconda. 'Chefe!' he cried out, leaping off his mule. 'Wait, I'm coming.' In one movement his machete was in one hand and his revolver in the other. 'Stop, all of you, or I shoot.' He strode forward brandishing his weapons. 'Chefe, Bobby. Ari's here.'

At the sound of Ari's voice, the Lieutenant, who was trying to fend off Idenea's fists, barged through the hut door. Things were going wrong. He hadn't expected this girl to fight. Weals on his neck showed where her well aimed blows had hit and now this mad cowboy threatening to shoot his men. He fired two shots over Ari's head. A group of parrots squawked.

'Stop where you are or I'll arrest you as well, you stupid cowboy. We need to question your boss about a murder.' He hesitated. He had to get away fast.

Ari halted in his tracks, suddenly unsure. Idenea stumbled out of the house and past the lieutenant whose revolver was levelled at Ari.

'Ari! Don't! It's all a mistake. Don't shoot. They'll kill you.'

Ari spat to the ground in anger. The back of the van opened and at the Lieutenant's 'Quick now', Bobby was hustled in and the door slammed. There were no windows, only a small vent in the roof. Intense heat mixed with the smell of human excrement and fear. Bobby struggled to kneel.

From outside. 'Bobbeee.'

And, 'Chefe. Don't you worry, Ari will get to you.'

The revving of the engine drowned their cries.

Bobby tried to wedge himself with his feet and shoulders between the iron side benches. Every bump triggered a shout of pain. Finally, he sat with his shoulders pushed into a corner and his back to the driving cabin.

Laughter from the cabin. 'He'll be in for a long time.' More laughter. 'Gringo murderer.'

Three hours later in the early evening the bucking stopped. Two policemen dragged him into a small courtyard towards a row of gated cells. Hands and arms hung out through the bars. Shouts and jeers as two armed gaolers grabbed him by the arms. Lieutenant Bentes released the handcuffs. One of the gaolers unlocked a cell gate, shoved him in and clanged the gate shut.

'Gringo murderer,' sneered the Lieutenant, 'we've got you now. This will cause some fun.' And to the gaolers, 'Mind you look after this *sem vergonha*. No escaping, huh?'

When the cell door had opened, four men had scrambled onto the four available beds, that is if you can call rough wooden planks on brick pillars, beds. The smell from an open bucket in the corner sickened Bobby's stomach. Heavy silence. He sank to the floor, his arms around his knees and squeezed his body into a ball. A heavy hand grabbed his shoulder. The grip was violent. He balled up as tight as he could, knees to chin. Hands wrenched beneath his armpits and tried to lift him. Bobby rammed his heels against the wall.

'What have we here? A voice said. 'No sleep for you, my beauty.'

'Hey Whitey, look at your pale arms.'

'Get him up. Let's fuck him. Let's bugger the precious little bastard. You go first. I'll hold him down. I haven't had white arse before.'

'Come on, little Whitey, we're going to have some fun with you.'

From the dim light through the iron grill door, Bobby could see two other men lying on their rough beds and laughing.

'Leave me alone.'

The hands pulled harder. And then there were Ari's and Idenea's shouts of encouragement and strength surged back into his body. With a violent thrust of his legs he propelled himself across the floor to the opposite wall.

Facing his assailants, he raised his hands and in a hoarse stammer, 'Together, you bastards can kill me, that's clear. But I swear by God I'll take one of you first, understood? So, choose which one of you it's to be.'

The two attackers hesitated. The lookers-on stopped laughing.

'Against four, how can you manage that, idiot?'

'I said one of you.'

'How can you be so sure, little Whitey?' The two advanced a step.

'It was my job.'

'Your job, huh?' The attackers stopped two paces in front of Bobby. A sense of unease infected the cell. 'So tell us, why are you here?'

'For a murder I didn't do.' Bobby managed across a dry tongue. 'I'm innocent.'

'Aren't we all?' Rough laughter.

'Let him be. We'll talk in the morning.'

The night gaoler came running. 'Leave him alone. He's a big catch and it'll be the worse for you if you fuck him up.'

Bobby sank to the floor. The four rolled noisily about on their wooden bunks. A few goodnights and a cough-filled silence. Bobby curled foetus-like on the concrete. By the first show of daylight through the small barred aperture at roof level, Bobby had pushed away the scratchy feet of three or four rats and brushed a good score of cockroaches off his face. He could hardly breathe for the same feeling of self-doubt that had haunted him before meeting Idenea. A flood of loving swept through him.

Yes, she had given him new life. And he was going to fight like she would fight. She would get him out of here, of course she would.

After a bowl of rice and beans, a policeman handcuffed him and pulled him to a jeep. Lieutenant Bentes drove him to the new court house where, in a clean side room with cool piped air, he was formally charged with murder.

'Did you know these people?' demanded the Prosecutor.

'Yes.'

'Did you kill them?'

'Impossible, I was nowhere near.'

'Who discovered the crime, Lieutenant?'

'A girl called Carmen, daughter of the owner of the bar in the local village fifteen kilometres away. She found the two dead bodies and her companion, Juca, bleeding to death. They have a baby together. Her father fetched the two bodies back to his bar.'

'Lieutenant, is there a murder weapon?'

'Yes, here is the gun that he...' The Lieutenant pointed at Bobby, 'used to kill and wound these innocent settlers.'

The Prosecutor addressed Bobby. 'Is this yours?'

'I don't know. All Taurus ·38s look much the same.'

Lieutenant Bentes picked up the plastic bag with the revolver in it and handed it to Bobby who took it out and held it in one hand.

'As I said they all look the same to me.'

He gestured at Lieutenant Bentes. 'This Lieutenant asked me to hand over my gun. He said he was checking firearm licences. A useless thing to do in this lawless territory. There are hundreds of unregistered guns all over the place.'

'I wasn't asking for your opinion.'

Lieutenant Bentes smiled as Bobby handed the revolver back to him. 'This is the prisoner's, I took it from him,' he confirmed to the Prosecutor.

'It will be needed for forensic analysis,' replied the Prosecutor. 'Have you retrieved any bullets from the bodies, Lieutenant?'

'Yes sir. My sergeant extracted them.' The Lieutenant handed over another small plastic bag with four spent bullets inside.

'Have you any from the wounded man?'

'No, my sergeant couldn't find the wounded Senhor Juca. The owner of the bar said that his daughter Carmen and the wounded Juca took their baby into the forest. He's half Indian, you see, sir, and full of mumbo jumbo. We're still looking for him.'

The Prosecutor addressed Bobby.

'Did you fire these bullets with this gun?'

'No, I've already told you, no.'

'The lieutenant says you did.'

Bobby croaked through dry lips, 'He's a liar. Let him prove it.'

The Prosecutor to the lieutenant, 'Why would this foreigner kill innocent men, Lieutenant?'

'Because he thought they were squatters on his land.'

'I see.' The Prosecutor raised his eyebrows.

'Rubbish,' protested Bobby, 'We discussed how to solve their title problems at the same time as our title problems. I told Captain Dias of the Ministry all about it.'

'Are there any witnesses?' The Prosecutor turned to the lieutenant.

'Not yet, but we're still investigating.'

The Prosecutor faced Bobby. 'I'll take the gun and bullets for forensic analysis. I will set the date for your trial when all the evidence has been collected. The forensics may take some time as may a full, written report and the assembling of a jury. You have the right to appoint your own lawyer. The judge will be his Excellency

Proensa Tancredo.' He leaned forward. 'I remand you in custody until trial. Take him away.'

'What?' Bobby protested, reddening with fury. 'This is madness. To hell with you all. I've had nothing to do with this. This is not right.'

'Take him away.'

Handcuffs yanked at his wrist.

Outside, Idenea and Ari were waiting. She shouted, 'Bobby, we'll save you. I'll find witnesses to swear for you. I love you.'

'Be calm, Chefe. Trust in Ari.'

He mouthed *Te Amo* to Idenea as his guards bundled him into the police jeep.

Two days later he was moved to a different cell, this time with his own plank of a bed. There were rats and cockroaches but at least he could lie off the floor. The guard, intrigued by this foreigner with the funny accent, liked to chat through the bars. Every morning Bobby told him about the rats but his answer was always the same, that there would be a new prison soon and that the Territory would be a State before he would be let out. 'Now gringo, tell me about London, Liverpool football club and the Beatles. And please, who is this Jimmy Hendrix?'

The three other prisoners in his cell were; Negão, Big Black, he'd knifed a man in a bar fight; Neginho, Little Black, who had killed another diamond prospector and Vermelhão, Big Red, a hefty older man with crusty red skin who snored heavily at night. He had strangled his wife over money. They nicknamed Bobby, *Ratão*, Big Rat, because he dared to complain about the rats.

'You are a good man, *Ratão*.' Neginho said, 'We must help each other.'

Four days after Bobby's arrest LG arrived in his usual hurry. He paced about in high heel boots, his Stetson hat firmly pressed down and sunglasses wedged tight. With him was defence lawyer Senhor Clodoaldo Aranha.

'My father knows his father.' LG introduced him in the stifling heat of the prison's visitor room. 'He will defend you. I hope you're not a murderer. Imagine the trouble for us. Being a foreigner won't help much either. I never could understand Father agreeing to employ a foreigner. Do you realise that I've had to sign a statement declaring where I was on that day with witness support? Me a suspect? How dare they? It's all your fault.'

He rubbed his hands and slapped the lawyer on the shoulder. 'See to it, Clodoaldo. Let me know how things go.' Then he was out of the door with, 'God damn heat,' and, 'Cattle and soya, that's the way forward.'

Clodoaldo Aranha stroked his greying moustache, shifted his heavy body on a small cane chair and ran his hand over the few strands of hair on his head. His belly protruded over the edge of the chair. He was sweating profusely.

'I have some questions,' he began.

Bobby smelt alcohol on his breath. They talked for an hour. Bobby repeated over and over, 'I was out checking fence lines and counting cattle on my own as I often do. I returned home at sundown as usual.'

'But how do I prove it?' Clodoaldo Aranha scratched his head and lumbered his big frame out through the door.

Big Red, Vermelhão, was condemned to eighteen years with hard labour. In his place a dark elderly man with curly white hair sat on his bunk staring at his hands and didn't say a word for two days. Even the gaolers didn't know why he was there.

'Eighteen years!' Bobby shook his head. He pestered to see Clodoaldo Aranha but always the same; they had to find witnesses.

A week later Bobby was down with malaria. His cell mates complained of his delirious moaning. Negão asked, who were Idenea and Beatrice and who were Perry and Ari? He never, never stopped mumbling about them.

Idenea brought him pills and letters. He learned his father's heart was in bad shape and so neither his mother nor Beatrice could come out. Alistair had a cash crisis but for Bobby to know that he was in daily touch with the head office in the south.

The edge of the wooden slab-of-a-bed dug into his back. Beatrice had finished off her letters in her familiar way of before, 'Thinking of you, Your B'. What was she up to, having made his life a misery and now signing her name as if the past had never been? As he tossed and turned in malarial fever, sweating one moment, shivering the next, he saw her coming up the aisle in her wedding dress. *I do. I do.* Those vows.

And walking out of church under a roof of shining swords held by his officer friends. Perry, Best Man. She still had white roses in her hair when they'd walked into their hotel in Paris, bright-eyed and flushed from their day and there, on the ceiling of the lobby, was a Goddess in a golden chariot pulled by two cheetahs smiling down at them. How they'd wanted each other that night.

And, yes, he'd sworn that day in church to worship her with his body so that was what he would do even though she kept pleading for him to wait for another day. When she'd seen him naked, she'd exclaimed, 'I made this nightdress myself. It's my surprise for you, twenty-two buttons for your age and twenty-two for mine, so be gentle, won't you? I worked all night and my aunt told me that you would slice me like a knife and leave me wounded forever so please, please, be gentle... can't we wait a bit?'

Would he just? Grim and tight-lipped, he'd inserted the fingers of both his hands under the top button just below her chin and ripped sideways to the left and to the right. The tiny buttons hit the ground like spent shot. He would never forget that sound.

'Bobby!' she'd cried out. 'Are you mad?' as he'd slipped the buttonless nightdress over her shoulders. He'd wondered adoringly at what he saw underneath. But then the pants.

'Oh God,' he'd groaned, 'after all this and you've got pants on. They're coming off now or we're lost.'

'Yes, yes, sorry, sorry,' she'd flustered and slipped them off. She'd wanted to please him so badly. They'd kissed and fumbled. Then everything from him had gone everywhere, on the sheet, over her belly, everywhere except in the right place. Appalled, she'd pushed him away. How embarrassed he'd been. She'd flushed to the roots of her hair. He calmed her and begun to caress her with his hands

261

and with his lips paying gentle attention to every part of her body. His strength returned.

'This time I take control,' he'd said without inhibition. She let him. She swallowed her pain without a sound.

In each other's arms, their eyes liquid with laughter. 'We're not virgins any more, not you, not me, hoorah.'

Living the memory, in spite of the smell of the latrine bucket a couple of metres from his head, his mind rambled on. He groaned so loudly that Negão stopped snoring.

They'd met at a formal party at the end of his first year at Sandhurst. All officer cadets were dressed in their dark blue and red. A band played old-fashioned waltzes one moment and rock and roll the next. The air was heavy with cigarette and wood smoke, the smell of wine and the scent of women.

She danced so correctly. She'd placed her left hand on his right shoulder and smiled upwards into his eyes. She was a good three to four inches shorter than him.

And he smiled now. All that certainty. What *was* he doing here?

Up the steps into the British Museum. You're a different sort of soldier, she'd said with her tinkly laugh, we're not exactly in bang-bang country so is there something else behind that stiff reserve of yours?

And the bust of the emperor Hadrian with his funny ear; the statesman, poet, soldier who'd led men through the impossible. She asked ironically if he was his role model? He'd said yes. And you're going to the top like him, aren't you? He'd said yes again. Me too, she'd said quietly.

Shaking his head with feverish red behind his eyes, he saw her leading him into the Wigmore Hall declaring that it was her turn to show off. She'd run up onto the stage, played some Beethoven, some Britten until the caretaker stopped her. She said that Myra Hess was her role model. She told how her youth had been so difficult, her mother dead, her father away, and living with her maiden aunt where fun never came through the door. At least there'd been a piano. He said he played the piano as well. He'd sung to her then and he sang and hummed out loud now,

'The water is wide, I cannot get o'er
and neither have I wings to fly—'
Negão shouted at him that it was time to sleep not to sing.
'Oh give me a boat that will carry two
and both shall row, my love and I'
Neginho shook him till he shut up.

Now able to sit up and talk coherently, his unshaven face gaunt, his eyes yellow, he was told that his trial was to be in fifteen days. Bobby pestered to see Clodoaldo Aranha but always the same answer; they had to find witnesses.

Clodoaldo shrugged. 'Why should anyone have a grudge against you?

Judge Proensa Tancredo reckoned that two days in court would be enough for this case. After all, the evidence showed that the accused had killed two people and there was no evidence to the contrary. And the motive: land, nothing new in that. But it had been difficult to find men and women reliable enough to serve on the jury. However, since this was a case of murder and had the added interest of a foreigner, he hoped that all members would attend in full for both days.

Judge Proensa Tancredo was a delicately built man of medium height in his fifty-fifth year with waxy pale skin. He combed his grey hair straight back with no parting, giving him the appearance of an inquisitive bird. The constant bobbing of his head, like a bird pecking after an early worm, had earned him the nick name of *Passarinho*, Little Bird. He wore a fawn-coloured, hand-tailored linen jacket. Only very occasionally in intense heat did he remove his jacket and tie. His fingers were long and delicate and he visited his personal barber once a fortnight. Trained in the law in Rio, he considered himself educated and civilised and, like the majority of his peer group, was disappointed that the Military seemed even more entrenched in power than ever. He told his family that this position was new and different and, furthermore, the frontier states needed enlightened government.

Intrigued by the murder case of the Englishman, he was looking forward to the preliminary out-of-court interrogation when he could take a first impression of the man. He had judged several foreigners in the past, simple ruffians and clever swindlers, who had come to his booming country to make a quick buck but never before somebody from such a disciplined background.

Idenea brought Bobby clean clothes. He notched his belt three holes tighter. Shaving for the first time in two months, he took care not to cut his skin where new furrows had formed.

A large ceiling fan whirred in the small interview room beside the newly-built court room. Judge Tancredo addressed the seated and handcuffed Bobby.

'How did you come to be here?'

Bobby drew a deep breath. 'Your Excellency...'

Judge Tancredo listened. Occasionally he bobbed his head. He had specifically refused the presence of the Public Prosecutor and had instructed to be left alone with this Senhor Jenney and his defence lawyer in order to try and understand the motive behind the murders.

Bobby decided to explain everything to this intelligent man.

When Bobby had finished, Judge Tancredo said, 'I have attended trials in America, France and your own country. I admire the stability of your institutions. I wish we had them. After all, you British invented the Jury system.' He paused. 'But I don't understand why you would want to come all this way over here. You have everything in Europe. What is it you like about this country and, in particular, up here?'

Bobby smiled faintly. His first smile for weeks. 'Well, your Excellency, the wilderness. I like a challenge, although I don't agree with everything we do.'

'And the women?' Judge Tancredo's eyes smiled boyish enquiry. He had once sat on an advisory panel that had examined evidence of an agency that organised sex holidays out of Germany into the north eastern states of Bahia and Pernambuco.

264

'Yes, I live with a very special woman who has had a harder life than me.'

'Her name is Idenea Saladini, isn't it? What did she say when you were accused of killing her cousins?'

'She didn't believe it of course. We think alike. She's a great girl.'

'Anything else you can tell me which might help in your defence?'

Bobby looked into the heavily hooded eyes of the man who would judge him.

'Yes, well, your Excellency, I work hard and there's so much to do.'

'Even to murder?' Judge Proensa ventured in a soft voice.

Bobby tried to stand up but the guard, to whom he was chained, dragged him down. 'Excellency, I don't kill innocent people.'

'But you're taught to kill, aren't you, now? Your dossier tells me much about you.'

Bobby swallowed hard. 'Yes, that was different, I was a soldier trained to serve my country.'

'Be that as it may,' Judge Proensa continued quietly, 'apparently the knife-cut to the throat of Senhor Bosco looked like the work of a professional. The evidence against you is pretty compelling, Senhor Jenney. Let's see what the jury thinks. You have powerful accusers. I will see you in court in three days' time.'

Back in his cell, Bobby sank into memories of his childhood, his education, his training. And that farewell by the headmaster at Winton College. 'You'll find old boys from this school in palaces and prisons all around the world.' And here he was in a damned prison. During his daily half-hour exercise, round and round the prison compound with the other prisoners, he didn't talk to anyone. He watched his feet as he walked or looked up at the sky, black vultures circling above.

Under the gush of water from an open pipe protruding from the wall that served as the prison shower, he let the stream of water pour directly onto his forehead. Dear Perry, everything so easy for him. And his mother saying that there were other people in the world. And there was Ari and his cattle. And Idenea? A better life.

And Beatrice's eyes demanding, 'Go on Bobby. Go on for us. If you won't, I will.' What was that? Be the best and leave the devil behind. Goddamn it.

At night, struggling to sleep on the flat wood, he tried to think who could wish him ill. Even the cockroaches left him alone or more likely he didn't notice them.

Bobby looked around the new courtroom thankful for the air conditioning. Beside him sat Clodoaldo, sweat marks already staining his shirt. He scrutinised each one of the seven members of the jury: short, tall, fat, thin, black, brown, white, even Japanese. So these were the people to decide his life. By chance, he made eye contact with the Japanese member who surveyed him long enough to make up his mind that there was something out of place about this haggard-looking foreigner accused of murder.

In the restless silence, fingers pointed at him with whisperings of 'Murderer' and 'Go Home'. He searched for the reassuring faces of Idenea and Ari. They weren't there; must be something urgent on the ranch. Of course, she'd come to be with him but where was she?

He noticed the heavy presence of Captain Dias and Lieutenant Bentes on the seats reserved for witnesses. Beside them, to his surprise, sat Bébé. A few moments before the Judge was due to enter, Colonel Fabio Delgado dressed in a clean pressed uniform, strode in with a sergeant behind him. Silence all round. He exchanged a quick remark with Lieutenant Bentes then glanced across at Bobby but gave no sign of recognition. General chatter resumed and people started to point at Bobby again.

'All stand.'

His Excellency Judge Proensa Tancredo was ushered in.

He faced Bobby directly. 'Senhor Jenney, you are accused of the murders of Senhor Bosco Saladini and Senhor Carlos Saladini and the attempted murder of Senhor Juca. The Public Prosecutor has shown me the gun you are accused of using and the bullets taken from the bodies. Forensic analysis shows that these bullets were fired by this gun and...'

Bobby leaped to his feet, pulling the policeman up with him. 'Your Excellency. Impossible. I was nowhere near.'

Judge Proensa raised his hand; 'Senhor Jenney, sit down. Your opportunity will come.'

As he sat down, Bobby glanced across at his two principal accusers. Did a flicker of a smile cross the faces of Dias and Bentes?

Judge Tancredo looking directly at Clodoaldo Aranha; 'And we will see what counter evidence the defence will present.'

'I now ask the Public Prosecutor to explain why you are accused. Public Prosecutor, Sir, you have two hours to substantiate your case.'

The Public Prosecutor, a middle-aged lawyer who had reluctantly taken this posting, despite the heat, hoping it would better his career, was conscious of potential media attention both local and international. He cross-examined the witnesses one by one. For Bobby these questions and answers merged like water running down a river bank during heavy rain, every now and then a clear patch would emerge but otherwise it was a swirl of dark water. At times he sat up and listened keenly, at others he slumped forward with his head in his free hand.

'Who discovered the bodies?'

Bébé was giving evidence. 'My daughter Carmen,' he said with an ingratiating smile at the judge.

'Who brought them to your bar?'

'I did, in my jeep.'

'Where is your daughter now?'

'I don't know, your Excellency. She disappeared after the murders with her baby and wounded boy friend. They're getting married. He said he wanted to cure himself in his own way. You see, your Excellency, he is very Indian so you can see what I mean?' Bébé spoke as though he was trying to offer the judge something special that only he could provide.

Slimy Bastard, thought Bobby, but he noticed that Bébé was looking nervously around the courtroom as if he was frightened of being recognised.

Lieutenant Bentes gave evidence. Bobby paid close attention.

Public Prosecutor; 'Why did you suspect the accused?'

Lieutenant Bentes indicated the bulky frame beside him. 'Captain Dias here, of the ministry, said that the accused had every reason to clear these settlers off their land because he considered them squatters and therefore to be removed by force if necessary. Obviously, your Excellency, that's illegal and criminal, especially as they had been there for over seven years. I put two and two together and went to investigate. I discovered that nobody had seen him on the day of the murders. I made him give me his gun and arrested him on suspicion. I'm right, aren't I?'

Silence.

Judge Tancredo leaned forward towards Clodoaldo Aranha, 'Senhor Aranha, aren't you going to say anything?'

Clodoaldo shook his head.

Judge Tancredo; 'Well then I will do some of the questioning if you won't. It's not standard practice for a judge to intervene but I'm curious.'

'How are you proved right, Lieutenant?'

'The bullets match the gun don't they, your Excellency?'

'How do you know he pulled the trigger? Nobody saw him.'

'No, Excellency, I agree, but who else could it have been? And, your Excellency, there was another curious aspect to one of the murders.'

'Yes?'

'Well, it's the sergeant. He extracted the bullets from the bodies as they lay waiting to be buried that afternoon. They were already three days dead so burial was essential'

'Yes, yes. Go on.'

'He said that the throat of Senhor Bosco had been cut in a distinctive way.'

'And?'

'Excellency, the way my sergeant described the manner of the cut to the throat made me think it had been executed by someone trained in close combat hand-to-hand fighting. The accused, as we've heard, was trained in his country's special forces and has seen action.

Now that is more than a coincidence, don't you think?' Lieutenant Bentes finished with one hand pointing at Bobby.

A sigh passed round the courtroom. Everybody stared at Bobby.

The next witness was Captain Dias. His eyes squinted around the room. He answered the questions in a loud voice.

'Senhor Dias, why do you suspect the accused?'

'Because he,' pointing at Bobby, 'asked me to help him register his company's land titles. They are working on unregistered land. He considered the murdered as squatters who could question or threaten his entitlement. He told me that he was under pressure to resolve the situation from his head office. He feared for his job.'

'But to commit murder,' Judge Tancredo interrupted, 'to kill his girlfriend's family on her family's land? Very strange don't you think, Senhor Clodoaldo?'

Clodoaldo Aranha shuffled his papers. 'I agree it is very strange, your Excellency.'

The Public Prosecutor stood up. 'Senhor Dias please explain to the court who the land belongs to where the victims were found?'

Bobby smiled grimly to himself. Explain that one if you can.

'Well, it's like this,' Senhor Dias began.

When, an hour and many questions later, nobody in the courtroom was much the wiser, Judge Tancredo interrupted him, 'Are you saying you don't know whether the land at plot 921 belongs to the Federal Government, to the Fazenda Rio Largo or to the Saladini family? So, if there is this much doubt regarding ownership, why did you place the Saladinis on this plot? You are supposed to be in charge. And can you explain why the plot has such an unusual number? 921 is very odd, is it not?'

Dias pursed his lips. The back of his shirt stained down to his belt. Because of his squint Judge Proensa was unsure as to whom he was directing his answers.

'I thought I was acting in the interests of the people, your Excellency.'

'Well now, you've got two murdered men on disputed land and you yourself don't know who the legal owners are.' Judge Tancredo

269

glanced at his watch, 'We adjourn for lunch. After, will the defence please present their case.'

Clodoaldo did not accompany Bobby back to the court's holding cell. He'd had enough of the lack of support from Luiz Geraldo da Costa; it was as if he wanted his client to be sent to prison.

'Members of the jury,' Clodoaldo began after lunch, 'Leniency, gentlemen, and lack of any credible witnesses, that is how we plead. There is little I can say to counter the forensic evidence but I can say without fear of contradiction that nobody saw the accused fire that gun on the table in front us today and the only witness has vanished into the jungle.'

He spun out his questioning of the witnesses for as long as he could. He read out the good character references from José Magellan and a statement copied from Ari's emotional words.

'In my mind there is much doubt as to his guilt,' he finished lamely. 'I therefore ask for leniency.'

Judge Tancredo leaned forward, 'Are you agreeing that the accused is guilty?'

Clodoaldo shifted his heavy body from one foot to the other, 'Excellency, I cannot refute forensic evidence, can I?'

Bobby held his head in his hands. If his own lawyer couldn't defend him, what chance did he have? He looked at the judge in resigned despair.

Judge Tancredo; 'The Court is adjourned until tomorrow.'

A hubbub of excited chatter followed him out.

'I'll plead for early release after six years,' Clodoaldo mumbled as he shuffled away. 'It's the best I can do.'

Neginho pressed for news. 'How did it go? Are you guilty?'

Bobby lay on his bunk and in between short spells of sleep began to contemplate six years in prison. And there was the bloodied face of that guerrilla in the dusty Cyprus attic grinning at him through broken teeth. That'll teach you it seemed to say. How could he ever say sorry?

'You'll know tomorrow,' said Neginho.

Bobby smiled feebly, 'I've got a child', and clasped his head between his hands.

Neginho put his hand on Bobby's shoulder. 'I don't know how many children I've got. Maybe we will spend some years together and you can teach me English.'

In the morning the gaoler pushed the local paper and two telegrams through the bars. Neginho passed them to Bobby. 'Look, you're famous.' The headlines in big black letters declared, *Foreign landowner murders squatters in grab for more land–facing 18 years*.

Neginho sighed. 'They're after you, poor old Ratão. Are you sure you didn't do it?'

Bobby scanned the two telegrams but the Good Luck's and Thinking of You, Your B, failed to rally him. All he could see was the face of Judge Tancredo.

Crowds stood shoulder to shoulder for this second day. Dias and Lieutenant Bentes sat side by side as before. They were talking and joking together. Colonel Delgado marched in a minute before the judge, his eyes to the front. When seated, he began to study the profiles of Dias and Lieutenant Bentes. Lieutenant Bentes nodded recognition. The Colonel did not acknowledge.

Judge Tancredo signalled for silence.

'Members of the jury, I have discussed this case in private with the jury and there seems little doubt that with the evidence put forward by the Public Prosecutor and due to the few arguments provided by the defence so far, we have a case of straightforward prime facie murder for motives of financial gain or shall I say for land grab. I shall be asking each one of you to cast his or her Yes or No vote in the special urn in front of me. We shall then be able to see if we have a majority decision.'

He stopped and looked across at Bobby.

Where were Ari, LG, Zé? Where was Idenea? Had she left him, changed her mind after their row the other day, gone away, fallen out of love? She had to come, she couldn't leave him now. He started to hum 'Hang down your head Tom Dooley'. Then he noticed the faintest of smiles on Judge Tancredo's lips. Obviously pleased to be getting this one over and done with quickly, so he could go for an early lunch.

'You may or you may not have noticed,' Judge Tancredo began again with two bobs of his head, 'that I said evidence provided by the defence so far, Yes? *So far*.' He glared at Clodoaldo Aranha. 'I have just received a call advising me that four people, and I can add, with a baby as well, are hurrying here to lay more evidence in front of this court. Please remain seated and be silent. Thank you.' He sat back and folded his hands on his lap and looked over to the main door with bemused anticipation. An armed policeman stood guard by the door.

Bobby groaned again this time out loud. 'More cussed lies, more rubbish.'

A minute or two passed. Bobby pushed his forefinger into the small keyhole on his handcuff so hard that a tiny white imprint marked his skin. He noticed that Captain Dias and Lieutenant Bentes were no longer smiling but staring at the door. Loud whispers around the room.

Judge Tancredo, 'Quiet please.'

From outside a woman's voice shouted, 'Let us in. *Pelo amor de Deus*, let us in.'

Bobby leaped to his feet, dragging his guard up with him.

At a signal from the judge, the policeman opened the double doors. First, Idenea ran in followed by Ari waving an envelope in the air. A few paces behind hobbled Juca with one arm on Carmen's shoulder and the other bent over a handmade crutch. Carmen was clutching their baby in her arms.

Idenea, her hair in straggly tangles onto her shoulders, saw Bobby and cried out, 'We've found it. You're saved. See, Bobinho.'

'Chefe,' shouted Ari. 'I told you to trust Ari. It's here.' He waved the envelope higher.

Judge Tancredo, 'Silence both of you. Please explain yourselves.'

Ari bursting with excitement. 'Can I come forward, Excellency? '

'Yes. Let him pass.'

Idenea pushed her way through the crowd towards Bobby. 'It's your gun licence and the sales receipt,' she shouted. 'I remembered I had come across them when I started to organise the mess in your office.'

A protesting guard tried to hold her back. She yelled, 'Go and burn yourself in hell!' And struggled past him.

The tittering in the courtroom had risen to a noisy gabble. Someone started to clap.

Judge Tancredo, 'Silence everybody. The envelope, please.'

Ari handed him the envelope and then stumbled in his heeled boots over to Idenea and Bobby. The guard had relented at the threat of burning in hell and let him pass. Ari hugged them both in a single wide embrace.

'We drove all night.'

Bobby tried to smile. What if they were wrong?

Idenea was laughing and jumping up and down. 'Not you, Ari, it was *me* who drove all night. You shouted at me as if I was your horse. I couldn't believe our luck when we ran into Juca in the village. We told him everything. He said to take him with us. He hasn't said a word since, just sat in the back of the jeep with Carmen and their baby.'

A rasping whisper behind them, 'You...You.'

Juca was hobbling over to where Captain Dias and Lieutenant Bentes were sitting. His left thigh was wrapped in a Capibara skin and supported by short bamboo staves strapped with twisted leaves. He was pointing at Lieutenant Bentes with his crutch.

'I recognise you,' he whispered between toothless gums. 'It was you who interviewed me when Bosco was accused of murdering Chico and it was your voice that I heard when I was bleeding on the ground, wanting to know if I was dead. The same voice. I had to make sure it was you. And it is you, you murderer! Look at you sitting there.'

Lieutenant Bentes half rose from his seat. Captain Dias brushed away the accusing crutch.

'Please,' Judge Tancredo interrupted, 'can everybody sit down and be quiet, otherwise I shall close the court.' The courtroom hushed. 'Public Prosecutor Sir, I will read the content of this envelope and then ask you to come forward and examine it.'

As Judge Tancredo opened the envelope, Juca began to chant, the words floating around the silent room.

'It was you, you, you...'

Juca spun around to face the judge. 'Here's your murderer, Excellency, right in front of you. I will never forget that voice, never, never.'

Judge Tancredo bobbed his head. 'Please be quiet, young man. You can talk when I have seen what's inside this envelope. Be seated.'

All eyes on the judge. 'Public Prosecutor, Sir, there are two documents here, one a licence for a Taurus ·38 revolver and a receipt for the purchase of the same. They are in the name of Senhor Robert Jenney, care of Fazenda Rio Largo. Please check that the serial number on these papers is the same as the serial number on the gun on the table with which the accused allegedly murdered two innocent men.'

The Public Prosecutor picked up the revolver and examined it. He read the papers the judge had given him. With furrowed brow he rotated the revolver in his hand, scrutinising it carefully, and rereading the papers.

The only sound, the banging of a door.

'Your Excellency. I am confused. The registration numbers are different.'

A chorus of gasps.

'Tsssssh!' Judge Tancredo through his teeth. 'Now, isn't that interesting? Are you sure? Please give the gun and papers to the leader of the jury.'

He addressed Juca, 'Now you, sir, with the crutch, what have you to say?'

Bobby collapsed onto his bench. Idenea pressed close to him.

Juca banged the floor with his crutch. 'Where is that *filho da puta*, in God's name where has he gone?'

Lieutenant Bentes, unnoticed in the excitement, had slipped away. The guard at the door, rank prevailing, had saluted and opened the door.

Judge Tancredo to Juca, 'Face the court, young man. What is your name?'

'Juca.'

'What have you to say, Senhor Juca? I am glad to see that you are alive.'

'He's gone. The murderer,' exclaimed Juca glaring towards the open door.

'I put you under oath to tell the truth, Senhor Juca. Turn around and face me.'

Juca limped forward, put his hand on a Bible, not that it had anything to do with his god, and swore to tell the truth.

'Excellency, the lieutenant who has just run away from here, killed my two companions Bosco and Carlito. The second gunman nearly killed me as you can see. They came in a jeep. I ran as fast as I could. Bosco and Carlito were shot down by that Lieutenant. The other chased me and shot me in the shoulder and thigh. I pretended to be dead. I recognised the voice giving the orders. When I heard the jeep start up, I opened one eye and saw him, that lieutenant. And here he was today in front of me. You must catch him, Excellency. I can help. I can track in the jungle and...'

Idenea cried out. 'That lieutenant must have swapped Bobby's gun for his when they arrested him.'

Judge Tancredo, 'Please be quiet, young woman, or I'll have to send you out. Now, Senhor Juca, why do you think Lieutenant Bentes, an officer in the army, would wish to kill and murder innocent settlers?'

Juca shook his head.

Judge Tancredo, 'Public Prosecutor Sir, we must find Lieutenant Bentes. Please contact the police immediately.'

He stood up and addressed the jury, 'Members of the jury, do you agree that the gun that killed the settlers is *not* the same as recorded on the registration papers belonging to the accused? And therefore, the accused is innocent of all charges?'

The seven members nodded Yes.

General clapping.

Judge Tancredo, 'Will the prisoner and his guard please stand up. Public Prosecutor, do you consider that you still have a case against Senhor Jenney?'

'Your Excellency, in the circumstances.' He smiled at Bobby. 'No.'

Judge Tancredo, 'I congratulate you, Senhor Jenney, you have true friends. As for myself, I am pleased. There was always something fishy about this case as you would say in your language. Forensics said that your finger prints on the pistol were fresh and probably left when you handled the gun in front of the Public Prosecutor. That shouldn't have been allowed of course. There were no other prints. I suspect the gun had been well cleaned. However, I am determined to find the criminal. You are free to go.'

As he pushed himself up from his chair, Judge Tancredo addressed Dias who was staring at the ground, head in hands. 'Senhor Dias, please come to my office. I demand that you help me immediately.'

He left the court without another word.

Idenea threw her arms around Bobby and kissed him passionately on the lips.

'It really was me who saved you this time,' she whispered in his ear.

He could only smile his thanks, his throat thick with emotion. 'I thought you weren't coming.'

Ari patted Bobby on the back. 'Didn't I tell you, Chefe. You can always trust good old Ari? That's what I always say. Let's go home.'

Bobby insisted on going back to the prison to say goodbye. He grasped the hands of Neginho and Negão through the bars.

'You lucky bastard.' Negão smiled ruefully.

'I'll never see you again, gringo.' Neginho said, his eyes glistening with sadness. 'We'll never spend all those years telling stories to each other.'

Bobby held onto their hands through the bars. 'I won't forget you either, I promise.' A feeling that he didn't recognise came over him. A sense of deep affection touched him as he held their hands. It was as if the whole world was no longer just for him.

'We're all part of it and I won't forget.'

Neginho clung to Bobby's hand. 'Part of what, Ratão?'

'All I know is that we can be part of whatever it is.'

'Come on, Chefe,' Ari said impatiently, 'we must get going.' And putting one arm around Bobby's shoulders. 'Chefe, you've a kind heart, haven't you?'

Idenea drove. The holes didn't bother. They sang samba songs. Ari drummed the rhythm on the side of the jeep. They thumbed up at everyone they passed.

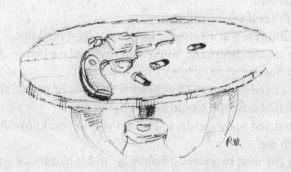

7

BELOVED COUNTRY

Arriving at the ranch house, Idenea dragged Bobby under the bucket shower and filled it to the brim with warm water. She wrinkled her nose.

'Heavens, you stink.'

As the water ran down his chest, she tapped his ribs one by one.

'Like playing your piano.' She slipped off her clothes and stepped in beside him.

'Let's see if you're still strong.'

He didn't feel at all strong. He'd lost at least ten kilos.

She smiled cheerfully. 'You've never refused me before. Another time, *tá bom*?'

He kissed her on the forehead. 'I thought of you all the time and worried how you would be managing here.'

She dried his shoulders. 'I'm not stupid you know. And Ari was with me.'

For the next two weeks, Bobby lay in his hammock watching the tiny geckos and listening to the staccato bellows of the Nellore cows in the distance. At meals he ate as much rice and beans as he could force down. He spoke little. Idenea told him all about what she was doing; how good the tomatoes were and how well the children were doing in school. Sometimes he would look at her intently and say in English,

'Are you sure?'

'What are you saying?' she'd ask with a frown.

'But are you sure of this, of everything?' He cast an arm at the jungle.

'Don't start that again. I miss my Zoni and I'll never give up hope. Why don't we dance and sing together like we used to?'

'Oh well,' he'd finished in Portuguese, 'that's not what I was saying.'

This exchange became regular.

It took a week for her to succeed in seducing him. 'Come on,' she said, 'don't let us forget making our Adam.' But he was clumsy, his touch lacking its former passion. She was so attentive that he felt ashamed. Afterwards, they lay apart, not curled up together as before.

With sleep annoyingly just out of reach and in the black behind his eyes, Bobby saw those cockroaches, those rats. He heard the sighs and curses. Who had set him up?

Idenea lay on her side, eyes wide open. Only when she heard Bobby's breathing slow, did she relax. She thought of all the fun they'd had, racing side by side up the track on their mules, herding cattle, singing silly childhood songs. How she had managed to teach him to dance a little samba. Thank you Clara Nunes[11]. Their crazy love. She smiled in the dark and gripped the edge of the bed at the memory. If only they could find her Zoni, all would be perfect. And then Adam would surely come.

Ari came by every day with news of the cattle and another jaguar attack. 'Bastards are getting bolder, Chefe.'

'Ari. How can I repay you for what you did?'

'Help me brand some young stock tomorrow. *Tudo bem*?'

The next day Bobby rode out with Ari. He'd been looking forward to getting back in the saddle and to the smell of singeing cow hide. Despite the sheepskin padding, his backside felt hard in the saddle. He cheered at Ari's skill with the lasso. Together they wrestled each animal to the ground and rammed the red iron downwards with a sizzle of burning. The sharp bellow of pain. They admired the RL burnt into its shoulder for the rest of its short life. Next year they would build a modern corral with a branding trap and gate. Then there would be no more struggles.

---

11 Clara Nunes; probably the most famous singer of samba and popular songs in the 60's and 70's. When a faulty operation killed her, the whole country mourned.

A Cara Cara hawk on the top branch of one of the trees mewed, his red head gleaming in the sun. On the horizon, thunder clouds bulged up like great soaked sponges ready to be squeezed.

'Well, Chefe, good to be back, eh?' Ari slung the rawhide of his lasso round his neck as they walked towards their mules. He puffed from exertion. 'I love the smell of cattle and the smell of burning hide and dung drying in the sun. It's real, don't you think?'

'I'm getting there, Ari.'

'I'll make a true cowboy out of you yet, Chefe.'

'Okay, *tt*, let's see who can be in the saddle first.' They sprinted and were astride in seconds.

'You're getting better eh, Chefe?'

Trotting beside Ari, Bobby said, 'The Colonel sent a message. He wants to see me urgently tomorrow and Idenea has things to do as well. We'll be back by nightfall on that new road.'

Ari pushed his hat back. 'Yeargh, that new road is progress, isn't it? We'll get our cattle in and out quicker eh, Chefe?'

Branding with Ari had invigorated him. He must find Idenea and show her. He strode into the orchard remembering how he used to pull her towards the ranch house, she complaining she had to finish the hoeing but at each gentle pull her protests softened until they were running hand in hand. He found her, fully dressed lying in bed, her back to him. His closing of the door woke her. She rolled over.

'*Olá*, Bobinho, I was only half asleep.' In the crook of her arm lay her wooden doll, her Zoni.

'Why have you brought that doll into our bed?' he exclaimed, his desire frustrated. She smiled sleepily. 'I want him close. Come and get in with us.' She patted the mattress beside her. He pointed at the doll, 'You love that piece of wood more than me. Why can't it stay in that shrine you made for him?'

The door snapped shut behind him. She clutched her wooden Zoni tighter and shut her eyes.

'Send the Colonel my personal greetings.' Ari quipped as they drove off the next day.

Idenea went to see if there were any replies to her *Disappeared Wanted* advertisement for Zoni and to chase after her land titles. Now that only Juca and Carmen worked on Fazenda Boa Esperança, she was even more determined to prevent a claim either from them or from someone else.

'Sit down, my son.' Colonel Fabio was looking out over the great river, his hands clasped behind his back.

'This affair,' he spoke slowly, 'and those murders have come as a big shock for me.' He turned around. 'I'm sorry you had such a terrible time. I couldn't answer your letter asking for my support. I might have prejudiced your case. I hope you understand.'

And then in a tone that Bobby hadn't heard before, such was the menace in it. 'Now listen very carefully.' Colonel Fabio spread his feet wide apart. 'Two days ago your accuser, that Captain who I call Dias, was found dead in one of our regiment's jeeps about fifty kilometres from here. The jeep was on its nose in a river gully beside a bridge. At first, it appeared like an accident, his neck broken, bruises on his body and so on but...' The Colonel advanced on Bobby, hands still behind his back. 'But, he was found in the *passenger* seat. The driver must have jumped out before the jeep crashed down the bank.'

'How odd, Colonel.'

Colonel Fabio raised his arm for silence. 'Now listen to this, young Roberto, it's not so simple. First, we discovered a letter in Dias's pocket signed Pedro. Second, Lieutenant Bentes didn't report for duty after your trial. He too has disappeared. Gone. He was always rather unsatisfactory and quite old still to be a Lieutenant. I never understood why until now.' He sat down and sucked aggressively at the silver straw in his maté tea. 'Listen to this. It's handwritten in pencil with no heading, no date and no address.'

Comrade, Thank you for your phone call. In future be careful when using the phone. I am glad that at last you have a golden opportunity to promote the CAUSE. Yes, you're right we were taught, —Be negative to cause unrest—Those were the good old days. As it happens I have a man, or rather the Cause does in your

region. If you need any help he will be there. I have told him to make himself known to you, discreetly of course. Always in hope, Pedro.
'Now, *who is* this Pedro, what is the Cause and who is their man in this region? We have no clues except this.' He held up the envelope. 'See, it was sent by regular post and look, franked with an official stamp from Brasilia. So, this Pedro works in central government, at the heart of one of the more socially sensitive ministries. The bastard. I'm going to find him if it's the last thing I do.'

His voice rose in anger. 'When I saw that Dias in court, I had a suspicion. I went to the morgue yesterday to have a closer look. That scar on his face was the wound that I inflicted on him when he was an ugly mulato youth and member of a left-wing protest group all those years ago. Military Intelligence had told me the bastard was around here but I had never actually seen him before. How could a communist *Sem Vergonha* be in a responsible position inside our progressive government?'

Colonel Fabio nursed his crooked arm. 'It was Dias who did this.'

'*Meu Deus*, really?' Bobby said, remembering the broken arm story but never before with a name mentioned.

'After that riot the press accused us army of unnecessary violence. And the next day, I saw a photograph in the newspaper of an ugly face with a big bruise and hoped it was from my blow. Since I had never actually seen this Dias face to face before, I'd never made any connection. Now I am certain it's the same brute. I can't forgive anybody who hurts horses. My beautiful Negrone was lame for six months.'

He sat down on the front of his desk and smoothed his trembling moustache with his thumb. 'I'm going to get to the root of this matter for all our sakes. So let's consider the facts. A possible solution is as follows.' He jabbed a forefinger at Bobby.

'One. The Cause is Communism.' Jab.

'Two, the man in the region is Lieutenant Bentes. That's why he stayed in the army so long refusing promotion, even doing special forces for a time, keeping a low profile, all to promote the Cause. Your Indian friend is right, he is the murderer.' Jab.

'Three, Dias is not the dead brute's real name but an assumed one.' Jab. 'And it was him who sent Bentes, his co-conspirator, to kill those two unfortunates and then to arrest you.' Jab.

'Four, Pedro is a mover, an organiser of this Cause, this Communism, here in my beloved country.' Jab.

Colonel Fabio was close to spitting.

'Five, Pedro and Dias probably trained together in Cuba or East Germany.' Jab.

'Six, Bentes swapped his gun for yours in order to set you up.' Jab.

'Seven, the whole affair with that false land registration number 921, how ridiculous for God's sake, all through to the murders, was a scheme to cause maximum trouble.'

Colonel Delgado was breathing heavily as he lowered his jabbing hand. 'Unless it's all a coincidence and I'm inventing everything and the murderer was a passing bounty hunter and your Indian is mistaken. But I am convinced that it all fits with Bentes running away after getting rid of Dias in a deliberate crash in an attempt to hide his own detection.' Colonel Fabio puffed out his chest. 'And all under my very nose.'

Bobby leaned forward. 'Communism, Colonel, up here?'

'You fool,' Colonel Fabio barked, saliva edging over his lower lip. 'Why do you think we Military took over in 1964? For the fun of it? No, we did it to save this great country from the left and all its horrors. We, in the army, are the only true protectors of the people.' He gestured at the portrait of the President on the wall. 'What do you think he stands for? Chaos? No. Order? Yes.'

'I'm sorry, Colonel, I didn't know how strongly you felt.' Bobby was trying to remember where he had heard before that the army was the only true protector of the people.

'That's all right young man. You see, you could have been very useful to them.'

'Me, how?'

'You were a pawn in a much bigger game. Think of it, a large landowner murders squatters on disputed land is big enough news but a *foreign* landowner? Now, that's a political atom bomb. Look

283

what the Press was saying about your case in spite of my efforts to stop them. I wish we still had the power of censure.'

Colonel Fabio shook his head.

'Yes, this certainly would have been a case of be negative to cause unrest, as that son of a whore Pedro says in that letter. I can see people marching with machetes and guns. And you, my son, were the chosen victim. A stroke of luck for them. How they must have itched with excitement at the smell of success for their accursed Cause.'

'Colonel, I see some of your argument but how...?' Bobby faltered.

'Don't worry. I'm going to find out everything, even if I am only a Colonel. Now, young man, I want you to do me a return favour this afternoon, *tá bom*?'

'Of course, Colonel. I owe it to you.'

'That Dias, whatever he was, is to be buried this afternoon and I want you to come along and be a sorrowful mourner but really to see if you can recognise anyone who might help my enquiries. It's been advertised. When you asked me for help, remember how I persuaded Dias using the argument of Unavoidable Necessary Cooperation? Well, that's what I'm saying to you now, cooperate. Understood!'

'But Colonel?'

'No buts. Listen to me.' Colonel Delgado made a fist around an imaginary plum. 'Everything must look normal while I hunt down this traitor Pedro. In my position, I shouldn't really be going to such a funeral but I will be seen to be caring and can hide my real intentions. To crush.' He squeezed his fist over the imaginary plum. 'Bring your woman and anybody else you want like your Indian agent friend. The press will think the whole thing was a cock-up and Dias's death yet another accident on that merda of a road.'

Bobby stood up. He was shaking with as much emotion as the Colonel.

'I can't believe what you're asking me to do, Colonel. Dias wanted me in a rat-infested hole for eighteen years. He made the Saladini's life a misery on purpose. And he wanted to use me as the scapegoat. And now you want *me* to pretend to appear sorry for him at his funeral. I would rather swim in a piranha-infested river.'

Face to face, half a metre apart.

'I am not mad, my son.' The Colonel drew himself up close to Bobby, their faces inches apart, 'But I will drive this Communism out of my beloved country.' He drew himself up to his full height. 'As your superior officer I command you to appear at the funeral this afternoon.' A mischievous smile flickered across his face.

'The devil you are.' Bobby's eyes widened, a short laugh and he saluted.

Colonel Fabio saluted back.

That afternoon a battered Chevrolet pick-up pulled into the town cemetery. In the back lay a plain wooden coffin. Two official look-ing cars and a VW taxi followed behind. Colonel Delgado and his soldier driver sat in the car with the military markings while in the other, a rather old rust-covered jeep with Fazenda Rio Largo in faded letters painted on the doors, sat Bobby and Idenea. A few metres away stood a mule, its single rein looped to the ground. Its rider, the gravedigger, leaned on a shovel beside an open grave.

Devils of red dust twisted and danced amongst the graves. Some were simple mounds of gravelly earth while others were marked with wooden crosses and brightly coloured plastic flowers. Pinned to the crosses were photographs of the dead, staring out through transparent envelopes.

A short procession approached the grave. Colonel Delgado, in his dark green uniform, swore, 'God it's hot. But here we go, Senhor Bobby, we're in business, out you get.'

A priest in a long white surplice embroidered with a black cross walked up to the grave. The gravedigger cursed loudly when the coffin didn't fit. 'You never told me he was such a big brute,' he complained as he hacked out a further twenty centimetres.

About a dozen others, all men, eased out of their cars and strolled over. Some from the Ministry, others out of curiosity. When they saw the Colonel, they halted at a polite distance.

Colonel Delgado said loudly so all could hear, 'Big brute of a communist traitor.'

The gravedigger didn't wait for the priest to open his prayer book and started to shovel. The gravel rattled on the coffin.

Colonel Delgado and his driver stood on one side of the open grave, Bobby and Idenea on the other. A dark mulata woman in a red dress that hung loosely around her slender frame came up beside Idenea. She wore a red headscarf that matched the colour of her dress. She was holding the hand of a child. She was crying.

Idenea eased to one side to make room for the two of them. As she did so, she looked down. The little boy glanced up. She held his eye for a quick second. She dropped to her knees as goose pimples chilled her skin and blood rushed to her face.

'Zoni?' she whispered, 'Zoni? Zoni *meu querido*.' The little boy smiled timidly, amused by her attention. She jumped to her feet.

Following the Colonel's instructions, Bobby was examining all those standing round the grave.

Idenea burst out with, 'Bobby, it's him.' She pointed at the boy. 'Bobby, please look. *Pelo amor de Deus*, look! It's *him*!'

'What's wrong, Idenea?'

She fell to her knees again and clasped the boy to her bosom. 'Zoni you're safe,' she crooned, swinging him from side to side. 'I thought you'd been stolen by Indians. Oh, Zoni, my beautiful boy.' She started to sob, then to laugh and then to sob again, tears streaming down her cheeks. She kissed the boy's fatce again and again.

'You've grown so much. Look, it's Mama.'

Bobby impatient. 'Idenea. Please, what is going on?'

Colonel Delgado called across the grave, 'Be quiet, woman. This is a serious matter.'

Idenea in tears. 'No, I won't...'

The priest ceased intoning. 'Quiet please,' he said.

Everybody was now staring at the woman squeezing a small boy to her breast and shouting as if the whole world wanted to hear. The small boy wriggled and started to cry stretching out an arm towards the woman in the red dress.

'Mummy, *Mãezinha*...' he whined.

'No, Zoni,' said Idenea overjoyed, 'She's not your Mummy, I'm your mummy. Don't you recognise me?'

At this, the mulata woman in the red dress lunged at Idenea.

'Give me back my child, you crazy woman.'

'No, never.' Idenea moved a few paces backwards. 'Who are you anyway, you baby snatcher?'

'I'm Mercedes Dias, his wife.' She pointed into the grave. 'And this is our boy. Give him back to me now.'

'Never! He's my baby. You thief, you...' Idenea backed away from the advancing Mercedes.

She began to laugh shrilly. 'Bobby, look, he's alive!'

Bobby could only mutter, 'Idenea, please...'

Mercedes began tugging at the boy's legs. 'Give me back my Ananias, or else.'

But Idenea tightened her arms and the little boy yelled even louder, looking first at Mercedes and then at Idenea.

'He's mine and he's called Zoni not Ananias.'

Colonel Delgado marched over.

'What's going on here, Senhor Bobby?'

'No idea, my Colonel.'

This was ridiculous. It couldn't be Zoni. But part of him was thinking how wonderful this would be for her if this little boy really was Zoni but the other part of him was wondering how such a triangle would work. It had been bad enough with that doll in their bed.

Mercedes Dias had managed to wrench off one of the boy's shoes. Idenea, through gritted teeth, was fighting to wrestle it back.

'Bobby, stop this baby-snatcher. Quick!'

'*Order!*' Colonel Delgado, hands on his hips, took control.

He ordered Idenea to hand the boy back to Mercedes and that the matter would be dealt with immediately and that he would place two guards on the Dias house, front and back.

'Zoneeeee.' Idenea cried hysterically. Bobby had to restrain her forcibly.

'I told you we'd find him,' she said, and kissed him on the cheek.

'I don't know why I'm doing this,' the Colonel grumbled as he stumped off to his jeep bellowing at his driver to follow. Maybe it was because he felt responsible for the subversive plotting he had discovered so close to him or maybe it was that he had a hunch that Dias's wife could lead him to the leader of the Cause, Pedro.

Two days later, the director of the Protection of Minors Agency, Doctor Ignacia Perreira, ordered Idenea and Mercedes Dias to come to her office, a suite of rooms within the new Ministry of the Interior. Ignacia, a lawyer and unusually for the time a career woman, had recently been appointed to head up this new agency. She was in her mid-fifties and with four grown-up children of her own. Her husband had run off with a younger woman so what better way to flee her past than in this new world. She'd tell her children how mad São Paulo was. How the city government wanted it to be twenty million.

And shaking her dark wavy hair would often say, 'All those poor forgotten children.'

Whereas in São Paulo, she had spent ten years struggling with child abuse, street children, child murderers, illegal trafficking of kidnapped children, split families and cases of domestic slavery, here her job was to attempt to manage the rapidly increasing problem of children whose parents had died or disappeared into the vastness of the jungle. She had the reputation of being tough but kind.

'The boy's birth certificate, please,' she said to Mercedes and Idenea.

From Idenea she also asked for a letter describing at least two distinctive marks on the child's body. She ordered both parties to hand in their evidence within two days. Colonel Delgado, true to his word, had asked her to solve this case quickly. The pile of files on her desk would have to wait.

Idenea did not have a birth certificate.

'I never found time to register his birth,' she explained to Bobby as he drove as fast as the ruts would allow back to Mutum. 'Juliana must help.'

After her parent's burial, Juliana had wisely given her a statement signed by herself as witness—*Amazon Saladini was born to Idenea Saladini on March 15th 1973 at Fazenda Boa Esperança, near kilometre 175 on the road BR 364.* But Idenea had forgotten to put this into her one and only bag when she had fled from Bosco. Would Juliana still have her copy? Her luck was in.

'There you are,' Juliana said handing over a yellowing piece of paper with fold marks.

Outside the bar, a truck accelerated away.

'Is that Bébé?' Idenea asked.

Juliana shrugged. 'He's been all over the place since your Senhor Bobbi was let out of prison. The police want to talk to him.'

Idenea hugged her. 'We'll be back soon and then we'll be a proper family.'

As to body identification marks, Idenea wrote with glee—*on his left big toe a scar from a poisonous caterpillar, on his back 18 dark brown moles.*

'There you are,' she declared in triumph to Bobby, 'I know him like the back of my hand.'

Mercedes, meanwhile, had produced a fully registered birth certificate naming her dead husband and herself as the parents of Ananias Liberdade Dias born in Rio de Janeiro.

Ignacia Perreira interviewed each party separately. A policewoman cared for Zoni in a side room.

First, she called in Idenea. 'When your baby disappeared, why didn't you report him missing to the police?'

'I did, but when I said he'd been taken by Indians, they laughed at me. I was living rough and had no money.'

'Well, you are right about the scar and the moles.'

'Of course I am, he's mine.'

Idenea described how she had heard Zoni screaming, how she'd run and how she had been sure he'd been stolen by Indians.

'How very difficult for you.' Ignacia took her arm and accompanied her to the door. 'I am going to interview the other party. Please wait outside.'

Ignacia addressed Mercedes Dias. 'This birth certificate looks genuine. Now please explain to me *why* he is so different, with his fair hair, to you and your husband. I need an explanation.'

A long silence. Mercedes wrung her hands and looked out of the window. Her lips quivered.

'I am waiting for your explanation,' Ignacia demanded.

More silence.

'Senhora Dias, answer me!'

'I am a proud woman,' Mercedes began quietly. And with a heave of her chest. 'I stand for my rights as well as for those of others.' Tears began to slide down her face.

'Rights?'

'Understand this, Senhora. I wouldn't have come to this godforsaken hole if my husband Captain Dias hadn't promised to find me a child, a bribe, you see. I love children. We couldn't have babies together.' Tears welled. 'I didn't know how he had found the little boy. I thought everything was genuine. My husband was very powerful.' Her sobs prevented her speaking coherently. Eventually she said, 'I can't go on like this. The boy isn't mine, but I love him as my own.'

Ignacia not unkindly. 'Yes, I can see that and so does his real mother. Didn't you realise you were breaking the law by accepting a baby that wasn't yours?'

'I didn't know. I thought I was doing the child a favour. My husband said that terrible things happen every day. He preferred to have a false birth certificate rather than adoption papers because he said I would feel closer to the baby.' She fell silent and rubbed her eyes.

'I'm leaving.' She pushed her chair back with a jerk and stumbled over to the door.

Ignacia, also on her feet, reached for the telephone. 'Wait! This needs proper investigation. I forbid you to leave.'

But Mercedes didn't wait. She elbowed her way to where Bobby and Idenea were sitting. She tugged at Idenea's arm.

'Out, out, come outside before they get me.' She pulled Idenea roughly out into the glare of the street. A determined look had replaced her crying. 'I have two minutes at the most before they arrest me. I have a taxi waiting. So listen to me.'

Mercedes spoke fast, her mouth close up to Idenea's mouth. 'All night I worried what to do, but I am an honourable person, not a baby-snatcher.' She squeezed Idenea's hand. 'I can see you are his true mother. I am happy for you. You seem kind. He is a sweet boy and I loved him and he called me *Mãezinha*. We had lovely times together.' She rubbed her eyes. 'My husband told me that an Indian friend of his had found an abandoned baby boy in a bar, far away.'

'Tell little Ananias that I love him.' She ran to a waiting taxi.

As she opened the passenger door, she shook her fist. '*Land for the people, not for the few. Power to the people, not to the rich.*' She slammed the taxi door and was gone.

Idenea had wanted to hug Mercedes but instead, she barged into Ignacia's office. Ignacia was on the telephone.

'Don't arrest her, please! She thought she was helping an abandoned baby. Please.'

Ignacia hung up.

'You're right. Let the poor wretch be. At least the boy's with his real mother now, more than I can say for most of these.' She gestured at a heap of files in front of her. 'Please sign here and I wish you every good luck.'

Bobby drove to the ranch. He was wondering who Dias's Indian friend was. Surely not Juca? Idenea was clutching the startled Zoni on her lap, one moment he was crying, the next smiling.

Later, Bobby recounted these events to Colonel Delgado. He vowed that he would find the bitch and he was sure she was part of the Cause.

Mercedes Dias was never seen in the Territory again.

'The Board of Directors wants three thousand hectares this year, the double of last.' Bobby gestured at the two Caterpillar D8 bulldozers parked nearby. Scratches and dents marked their yellow paint. 'No cleared area to exceed a hundred hectares. At least we won that one.'

They are inspecting progress. Ari on his mule, Idenea and the others had driven up in the jeep. Black anu birds hopped amongst the fallen branches. Hawks circled searching for the wounded.

'Soon there won't be much jungle left,' Idenea said quietly. 'Remember how it was, the trees full of dark mystery and full of...' She hesitated, frowning and searching for a word, '...of other knowledge. And now all we see is smoke.'

A broad straw hat cast a shadow over her face. Beside her, Leonidas held Zoni's hand. Leonidas wore a much-thumbed peaked cap. Shorts and flip flops accentuated his skinny legs. It was after school and there was the threat of a stifling afternoon.

'Progress, isn't it?' Bobby smiled encouragingly at her. 'That's what we hoped for, wasn't it?' He placed both hands on the back of his head and spread his elbows like a butterfly's wings. 'Won't be long now will it, Ari?'

'*Tá certo*, Chefe, and then phleeup, flames and lots of cattle.'

'Fire, fire.' Zoni piped up. 'That'll be fun won't it, Mama?'

She stroked his hair. 'And here I am with the two best men in my life.'

Bobby put a hand on her shoulder and squeezed Zoni's arm. 'Keep him safe. I'll be back before we start the fire.'

'Back from where?' she exclaimed.

'Yes, sorry. I've been so busy.' He shuffled his feet in embarrassment. 'A telegram came this morning with the supplies. My father has died. I must go to my mother.'

She took his hand. 'I'm very sorry. Why didn't you tell me before?'

'I had to think what to do. It was a shock.'

'Of course, I know what it's like to lose a parent but why didn't you tell me before?' There was hurt in her voice. 'Don't you trust me any more?'

She grabbed his elbow. 'What's wrong with you? You're like a stranger. What's happened to all those promises?'

She walked off to the jeep pulling Zoni behind her.

He followed. 'I'm not sure if I understand you?'

'Yes you do. *Yes* you do.'

They talked little and avoided each other. Zoni followed her everywhere. He insisted with constant crying that his bed be beside theirs.

'Why can't he sleep on his own?' Bobby demanded irritably.

'Try to understand. He's afraid of losing me again.'

On the morning he was to leave, as the rim of the sun arched over the trees, they faced each other beside the jeep. He said gently, 'Hold the fort. It's only a week.' And kissed her lightly on the lips.

She nodded, her eyes moist.

'You're happy to be going, aren't you?' The old twist back in her smile. 'I've never seen you like this before.' She put her hand to his cheek. 'I'll miss you.'

He kissed her again. 'What you said about the knowledge that lies in the jungle bothers me as well, you know.'

She walked away towards the ranch house, her hair swinging from side to side over her shoulders.

'Seven days, I promise.'

Zoni skipped after her. 'Mama wait for me.'

She'd been right, he had been pleased to go. And now, seven days later, true to his word, he was looking down at the yellow sand of the Bahia coastline.

Every hour of the past six days still wormed about in his mind.

His mother Alice's hug. His father's dead face. His short address beside the coffin in church. He regretted so much that he hadn't been able to tell his father how he had succeeded in opening up the Rio

Largo. The family house with its creaking stairs. And he'd slept so well in that old soft bed of his.

Perry's false leg as good as new. They'd talked for hours. 'You've changed old warhorse, haven't you?' Perry had said. 'No longer that blazing desire to be the best.'

He'd mumbled a reply that maybe it had been the prison, maybe Idenea, maybe the jungle, maybe all together. And Perry and Fran were to marry. His sister and his best friend? Fran had proudly shown him her ring.

'Look who's here. Come on in, Beatrice, please,' Alice had announced, opening the front door on the morning of the funeral. He had stiffened awkwardly, the moment he'd been dreading... 'Daddy, Daddy.' Michael was running towards him. 'Tell me about Ari and Leonidas? And the jaguars?'

He couldn't make out the expression on her face, framed as she was against the light from outside. Her black hair down on her shoulders, different from the tight aggressive bun she'd sported four years ago. Her lipstick a quiet rouge, not the scarlet of before. Her soft coloured clothes hung loose, not neatly cut over her body as when he'd last seen her.

'You look older and yellowy,' she'd said with a quick smile and the familiar tinkle and nervous laugh.

'Both of us do,' he'd said.

As he said 'Both of us', he'd felt the same feeling that, at first, he didn't recognise, it was so unfamiliar. But there it was, the same as when he'd said goodbye to Neginho at the prison gate. It was as if the world had become more peaceful. He smiled at her, this time with confidence. She held his eyes with a gentle boldness that dispelled any reproach that he might have still held against her.

He strokes Michael's head. He tells how Ari cut the anaconda in two. Michael wriggles with excitement.

'I hear you've been a success,' she'd said. 'I'm happy for you. Would your old role model, Hadrian, be pleased? Remember?'

His mother drives him to the airport. 'Your girl out there in the jungle is good to you, isn't she? How do you pronounce her name again?'

294

'It's like this.' He says slowly, 'Id–en–ea.'

And Alistair is shaking his hand goodbye. 'Quite an achievement, young man. Congratulations to have got so far. Why the hurry now?'

'The men are waiting for me. I thought you knew about this year's plan.'

'Yes, I do. The scale of it does worry me though.'

At the top of the stairs. 'And don't forget my offer to come back and help me out.'

The plane tilted over in its final curve before landing in Rio and he flew on to Cuiabá and Porto Velho. Under its wing he could make out Coshipó and the Perfect Peace Motel.

Bobby arrived at the Bar da Amizade in a cloud of dust. He had to start sorting out the title problem before going on to the Rio Largo. He would be quick, Idenea would be waiting and he longed to be with her. He pushed through the beaded curtains into the bar. Two truck drivers were playing pool next to some balls of latex.

'Where's Bébé?' he asked Juliana.

'Not here,' she said without her usual smile. 'He's in the big town nowadays. Some say he's been shot. Not surprising really with those methods of his. The police called it slavery. I'm not sorry. So, I'm in charge now. With the new road coming through, business should get good.'

'Is Juca here?' he said happily, 'I must talk to him.'

'Juca,' Juliana shouted and went through to the back without another word, no goodbye, no smile. That was odd, he thought.

Juca came in bare-chested in shorts and flip flops. He smiled his inscrutable toothless smile.

'Juca, good to see you.' They shook hands. 'The big burn starts in a few days. You are coming to help, aren't you?'

Juca nodded.

'I want us to settle this land problem once and for all. We must act together. There's a good chance, now that Dias is no longer in charge. Since you and Carmen have lived and worked there for so long, what do you think about being your own boss? I'll try to get the partners to agree and we can cut a track through to avoid the two-hour round trip.'

'Thank you Senhor Bobbi, that would be good for us.'

'See you in a couple of days, then.'

Juca walked back to the bar without a wave.

What was wrong with those two? He drove faster than usual, hitting some holes far too hard.

He skidded to a stop outside the ranch house.

'Idenea. I'm back,' he cried, jumping out. 'See, seven days as I promised.'

He saw a hoe leaning on a papaya tree. Had she missed him as much as he had missed her? The monkey's stand was empty.

He shoved violently at the door. It smacked back on his foot. He hurried from room to room. A few clothes here and there. A folded sheet of paper on the kitchen table.

Dear Bobby,
You silly boy
I woke up and thought I was wrong to be here
You happy away I was sure
I don't think you should be here either
Zoni was ill. I think it is malaria. I cannot risk losing him again
I do not think you love me like you used to
I do not know what I feel anymore because of that
I am always thinking about you and about the wonderful things we did
I have gone south to be with my people to find my brother and to cure
Zoni
I don't think our land title will ever be sorted out
I took some money
The company owes me wages. I gave the rest to Ari
He is very sad. I am sorry. Things are different now. You

are different
I am different
We do not understand what we are doing
I know this is quick You know I am like that quick is better
Leonidas will look after Toco and Ari will Massby till you
get back
Cida will be in the school. She says the government will
send a
teacher
We took the monkey Zoni couldn't leave it
You know the name of the town where I come from
It will be easy to find me if you want to
IDENEA

He sat down. He stood up. He sat down. He barged at the door. The shadow of the afternoon moved out from the house in front of him.

'Ari,' he yelled, 'Ari, where are you for God's sake?'

Only the lunatic screeching of the cicadas answered him. He saw quite clearly the colony of yellow-backed orioles in the tree above the roof, their hanging nests sharp against the sky and although they were quarrelling as usual, he didn't hear them.

He jumped into the jeep. He veered from right to left along the fence lines, wheels spinning. He found Ari checking out the firebreaks.

'Ari, what did she say? Why?'

Ari dismounted and put a hand on Bobby's shoulder, '*Calma*, Chefe.'

'I need to know, Ari, now!'

'She told me that what we're doing isn't right and that she was going back to her people. She said he can follow me if he cares enough.'

Bobby kept his hand on Ari's shoulder. Everything around him appeared in exaggerated sunlight or the darkest shadow, and all seemed so quiet.

'I'm sorry, Chefe.' Ari raised his eyebrows knowingly. 'Women, you know. My woman and I live apart. It suits us, at least it does me.' He slapped his belly. 'You wouldn't have me here otherwise, would you?'

'Ari, everything was going so well. And there's good treatment for malaria now in the big town so why's she gone?'

'Work, Chefe, the best cure for all. We have the big burn in two days.'

'Ari, come back with me and talk to me, please.'

Bobby tripped as he clambered into his jeep. That night, they drank one shot after another. Ari fell asleep in one cane chair, Bobby in the other. The next morning, Ari, rubbing his forehead and groaning, left to organise the men while Bobby counted out wages. What was there to keep her down south? He couldn't stop himself looking out towards her orchard, at her papaya trees and at the big waving green leaves of the banana trees.

Should he go after her? He couldn't, he had to be with the men tomorrow. Of course, she'd come back. This place was progress after all. Zé wasn't always right. Massby rubbed against his leg.

Leonidas arrived to hoe in the orchard.

'Did she tell you the name of her village?'

Leonidas shook his head.

That night he stared at his unshaven face in the mirror. He flopped into a cane chair. Ari was right, he must keep calm. Tomorrow would be rough. In the dark with a candle flickering beside him, he tried to think. His work a success, even Beatrice said that. And now Idenea saying it was wrong to be here. He could smell her in the air.

In the pink light of dawn, he went outside with a mug of coffee and a stale rusk of Idenea's corn bread. Of course, everything was going to be all right.

He shouted. '*Our doubts are traitors, and make us lose the good we oft might win, by fearing to attempt.* Look, all of you, Shakespeare understood.' He looked defiantly about him and gulped at his coffee.

Ari rode up leading Bobby's mule. 'Chefe, the men are here. The torches are ready.'

'*Tá certo*, Ari. Off we go.'

'You look wild today, Chefe. You're wearing the same clothes...'

By eight o'clock Bobby had positioned himself in the centre of a seven-man line stretching out two hundred metres. There was a good breeze behind. Each man clutched a burning torch. Although difficult to see in the bright sun, flames flared up from the kerosene-soaked sacking wrapped around the top of each stick. Ari was on his extreme right, Juca on his extreme left. A few palm trees still poked up out of the morass of broken trees.

He brought his torch down with the violent flourish of a chequered starter flag. 'Okay, men. Vamos.'

Each man ran to and fro dipping his torch to the ground. The wind, in differing strengths and directions, caused some of the fire to run forward faster, forcing the men to recoil from the heat in one place and concentrate on an unlit spot in another.

Within half an hour an orange wall of flame some three hundred metres long spat and raged. Here and there the line of fire bulged but on the whole the wall of flames was straight. The crackling of dried leaves and the exploding of moisture, trapped in the trunks, obliged him to shout.

'You can go now, men.' His face scarlet red. 'I'll stay and watch over.'

'Success, eh, Chefe?' Ari and Juca were at his side.

'I'll stay. No need for you two as well.'

'Sure, Chefe, see you later.'

On the spur, Bobby decided to check out where the fire had faltered. He clambered over trunks and brushwood towards the left-hand firebreak. The sheets of orange were rampaging forwards well to his right. Idenea not with him. 'To Hell, to Hell,' he shouted hysterically.

As he jumped and clambered along, he dipped down the head of his torch. Flames sprung up. He scrambled on. After a hundred metres he climbed up onto a spiky stump about shoulder high, left by axe and saw and surveyed full circle around him. Fire to his left, fire to his right, in front, behind. He was surrounded. As each second passed, the unburnt area, and he was roughly in the middle of it, shrank.

'Shit, Damn.' He jumped to the ground, thought better of it and climbed back up. At least up here he could see. The wind blew a wave of intense heat over him. He swore again, he couldn't die like this, stupid idiot. He peered through the approaching smoke and flames. Only fifty metres separated him from the firebreak. Beyond was a strip of jungle left as a protective barrier beside one of the smaller rivers. Another wave of scorching heat enveloped him and dried the sweat in his shirt in a second. He gasped with sudden fear.

He spotted a taller palm tree with yellow fruit at its top, spared by the bulldozers, in the direction of the firebreak. Hurriedly he yanked off his boots, dragged his trousers down and slipped off his underpants. He took a deep breath and with a concentrated effort emptied his bladder onto his pants. Not much, he thought as he pulled them partially wet over his head and face, adjusting to see out through a leg hole. Trousers and boots back on, he jumped down and stumbled over the short distance to the palm tree.

Smoke stung his nostrils, breathing hurt. He rammed his knife into the palm trunk as a step and levered himself upwards. Somehow, he wedged his body amongst the lower branches. He wouldn't be able to breathe soon. He laughed sharply. What a way to go, burnt by his own destruction. What an Auto da Fé. His underpants were nearly dry. He'd pissed too early, the fool. His sergeant had been right, never do anything in a hurry. The sun hammered on his head.

The flames were ten metres away. He slid to the ground. He judged where the fire was weakest, took a deep breath, covered his eyes with his hands and bludgeoned his way forwards. He could see the edge of the jungle and safety. His heart lifted. But he tripped and fell onto a tangle of burning branches. His right foot wedged fast. He pitched forward, the left-hand side of his face and neck landed on a smouldering branch. He knew he was burning. His fall had altered the position of his foot. He pulled and was free. He rolled to one side and staggered the few metres to the firebreak.

He'd felt no pain when his head had hit the burning branch but now there was a hard, relentless smarting to his left cheek.

'*Water, I must have water.*'

He ran into the shallows. He sighed as the water cooled his legs. He tore off his boots and the black-stained cloth that had been his trousers, careful not to touch the burnt skin, and splashed water over his face.

He glanced behind him.

'For the love of God, it's still chasing me. Oh dear God, where can I go?'

He turned back to the river in desperation. Out in the middle, a half-burnt log with a branch on each side was drifting in the current. He swam out to it. Slipping and grappling, he pulled himself astride.

'To Hell with the piranhas, they can have me grilled.'

He heaved himself, face down, along the trunk and laid one arm out sideways on a branch. To hold his balance, he stretched his legs out behind. He groaned in pain. He lay still, fearful of rolling into the water, but after drifting a few metres, he realised that the side branches acted as a stabiliser and the log floated steady.

Looking down he saw the outline of his head and face on the surface of the water reflected against the sky above. Flying ash hissed into the water beside him. A tall tree, leaning over from the bank, trailed creepers over the log and its human cargo in a temporary embrace. It was too early to pull in, the fire would still be following. Soon, facing downwards became too painful for his cheek and neck. Unable to control his groans, he twisted his body round inch by inch until he lay prostrate on his back, his arms spread out either side on the two branches as if on a crucifix; the rest of him naked except for his blackened shirt.

Nausea of utter disillusion crept over him. He blinked up at the sky and began to sing, more of a chant than a song, 'On my own, on my ooooown, between the heavy sky and the heavy wooorter. I must be the first man on this whole earth, the first, the first, ever, ever...the very first.' His chanting dropped to a murmur. Images of Idenea. Images of that sword of honour glinting in the sun and he was marching in full dress uniform in front of his men.

'Yes,' he shouted, 'such a fine line between hope and ambition. Who said that?'

'Quiet, you fool. Don't disturb the monkeys. See where I am now, Perry. You and your Faith.' He started to sing again, 'My true love said to me...and a partridge in a pear tree.' He laughed hoarsely, 'Oh yeah. Where is the eye of God? Dead. Me and my feeble Hope.'

The log swung slowly in the current, drifting down river and away from the falling ash. He tried not to think about Idenea but there she was as real as if she was kneeling beside him on the log. Was it her or was it Beatrice? Then a voice.

'There isn't any hope, not for you and not for me up here in this jungle.'

And another voice.

'Remember, Hope's all right but don't expect anything from it.'

'Who's talking to me?' He cried out and twisted his head from side to side.

The sun hung blood-red in the fog of smoke. He stared up through the rolling clouds of smoke. More drifting. A sharp tap and a bump.

'*Damned cayman, I suppose.*'

Instead, a splash and, 'Senhor Bobbi.'

Juca was pulling the log into the shallows, chatting as he waded.

'Here, put your arm around my neck. Hooup, there we are. Look, I said to Ari, he's gone too far, the fire will get him. I said your only chance would be the river. I ran, I swam. Ari thought he could ride his horse to find you. Silly cowboy. I heard you shouting and singing. I thought you'd gone mad.'

In a husky voice Bobby said, 'Good to see you Juca. Mad? Yes. I mean I don't know...'

Juca laid Bobby down on his back beside a tree. 'I'm going to find something for those burns.'

Night was upon them, when Juca crouched beside him crushing a greeny-brown mixture between the palms of his hands. He gently spread the mixture over the black and red of the wounds on Bobby's left jaw.

'Grip my arm tight. It may hurt.'

Bobby yelped like a puppy.

'It's too dark to go back tonight,' Juca comforted. 'We'll get you to a doctor tomorrow.' Juca wrapped the remainder of the greenish balm in a leaf. 'For later,' he said reassuringly.

Juca took a leather pouch from his pocket. 'I never go anywhere without this.' He unrolled a length of nylon with a hook at the end. He peeled the bark off a rotting log and fingered out a white grub. A few minutes later two piranhas lay flapping on the bank.

'They were waiting for you, Senhor Bobbi. Better we eat them than they eat you.'

He built a fire upwind and fanned the smoke over Bobby. Juca's face shone from orange to dark brown in the light of the flames.

'You're a strange one, Juca, aren't you?' Bobby said, grimacing with every chew.

'Like you, huh?'

Juca arranged a mat of broad leaves on the ground for a bed.

'You were quick to find me, weren't you?'

'Wondering why, huh?'

'Yes, I've been intrigued about you ever since you and Idenea wrecked Zé's Indian contact.'

Juca sat on his haunches, his back against the tree. He laced his arms around his knees. The moon cast a sheen of silver on the surface of the water.

'You like the jungle, Senhor Bobbi, don't you?' He pulled out a roll of twisted and sodden black tobacco about an inch and a half thick and began to chew at it with his back teeth. 'I always wanted some of my own. My Indian ancestors did. But for a half-caste Bugre like me, it's not easy. My Indian mother coughed her lungs out.'

Juca spat brown tobacco. 'I ran into Bébé a few years back. He sucks the blood of poor innocent settlers. I tried to help the Saladinis. Only the mother realised what was happening. Even your Idenea fell for it.'

Juca laughed a short snap of a laugh.

'I also helped your friend, Zé. We met real Indians, not tame ones like me. I picked up a few words.'

Juca was kneeling now, spreading his green herbal mixture onto Bobby's face.

'I met that Captain Dias in Bébé's bar. He promised jungle for myself. I called them both Boss. I believed they would help me.'

Juca fell silent.

'Then me and Carmen got together. She likes the colour of my skin and we laugh a lot. Bébé said we might get Fazenda Boa Esperança in spite of its trouble. So I squat there with her.'

'And the day when the boys were banging pots to scare away Indians, the silly idiots, I wandered off to get away from that nonsense. I saw fresh tyre tracks. I reckoned someone who knew their way in had stolen that baby. I kept quiet. I wanted land not trouble.'

A fish broke the surface of the river.

'Dias,' Bobby said.

Juca nodded and spat noisily. 'And then you turned up, Senhor Bobbi. I thought you were trouble. But I should have realised that Dias was the real trouble.' He fingered the bullet scar on his leg. 'And that lieutenant called me black, the bastard.'

'So why did you come and find me today?' Bobby flinched with the effort of speaking.

Juca chuckled. 'Because you might get me some land and also to help your Idenea. You have friends. Try to sleep, Senhor Bobbi, I'll watch over.'

He settled his back against the tree.

Ari and Juca drove Bobby to the airport. Ari's boots echoed clumsily on the hard floor of the smart new terminal,

They embraced carefully.

'Thank you.' Bobby repeated, 'Please, Ari will you look after Massby and Toco? I know Idenea would want that.'

'Don't worry yourself, Chefe, Massby likes my scraps. Tell Idenea the government is going to send a new teacher to the school. As for

Toco, he hopped about everywhere looking for her. Then I found him dead. I reckon he'd died of a broken heart. She was his life.'

'Now what, Chefe?' Ari asked anxiously.

Bobby didn't answer for several moments and then in pain. 'LG will send orders. He won't come up. You'll be all right.'

'And the land titles?' Juca demanded raising his voice.

'Yes, I know. I'll talk to Luiz Antonio. He listens to me. Even the local Press will be on your side.'

'Chefe, here take this.' Ari handed over a small piece of paper. 'Leonidas thinks it's Idenea's home town.'

Bobby tucked the chit of paper into his shirt pocket.

A tannoy announced Bobby's flight.

'Go and find her, Chefe.'

'I'm not going back. I don't care what you say. It's not right.' Idenea was shaking her head.

Bobby had tracked her down to a government-built village near the town of Londrina. He'd wandered up and down the straight lines of identical red-bricked and red-tiled houses.

He saw the blue wooden train he had carved so painstakingly for Zoni a year ago.

At his knock she'd thrown open the door and run forward. 'It's you, Bobinho, I'm so, so happy.' And stopped with a gasp.

'Bobinho, your face. It's so red?' She touched his cheek.

Embarrassed, he gently pushed her hand away and kissed her on the cheek, inclining the pink skin-graft on his left cheek away to one side. She gripped his shoulders with both hands for a better look.

'You crazy man. Come in and tell me. I'll make coffee. I want to hear everything. Why have you come?'

He looked out through the window at the lines of red tiled houses.

'To find you, that's why. That letter of yours couldn't be the end of us.' He hesitated.

She lowered her eyes. 'I'm sorry, but I was right.' She looked back at him defiantly.

'And I wanted to tell you about plot 921, your Fazenda Boa Esperança.'

He took her hand across the table. She stroked his fingers. The smell of her body and the soft fragrance of her breath brought the jungle rushing back.

'It was as if a single raging demon...' There was a desperation in his voice that she hadn't heard before, 'was chasing me, forcing me to face up to what I, or, let's say, what we were doing.'

Unsure he said, 'I wanted to see if you...' His smile froze at a spasm of pain in his cheek.

He grasped her hand tightly.

'What if,' he paused, 'if I took you to that island we flew over? We forget big Rio Largo. I mean, just you and me.'

She looked away. He was losing the argument and he knew it. She pulled back her hand in quick irritation.

'I'm not going to die of malaria, thank you. I stay here. And I like teaching.' She smiled the smile that he had missed so much, not the sad old twist but a big generous smile full of affection.

'But...' Her voice tender, 'you could stay here with me and we could make things work together?' She reached for his hand. He stared out of the window at the house four metres away. Two tom cats were fighting and screeching in an alley close by. A couple of women were shouting at each other.

'Heh, are you doing your washing today?'

'Not now, later. *Agora não, mais tarde talvez.*' They hollered back and forth discussing in ever louder cries the wayward activities of their husbands.

'I don't know,' he said. 'I simply cannot let shareholders and everyone else down.' He didn't recognise ever being so unsure of himself or admitting that he didn't know.

'But it was wrong up there, wasn't it?' she insisted.

He stared back out of the window at the monotonous line of red roofs. 'I can't stay here. This is not for me.'

Her eyes wouldn't leave his, a tinge of sadness in the grey. They stroked each other's fingers.

'Yes, I understand.' Her voice soft again. 'That's why we used to quarrel.'

The women's voices seemed far away.

'Where now, Bobinho?'

'Do you remember Luiz Antonio?'

'The big boss in São Paulo, right?'

'He's sorting out the land titles and will make a cash offer to you and Romi. Juca will be looked after as well. Not rich, but safe.'

'Bobinho, you're not so silly. Maybe one day I can buy a place of my own. I've sold one or two of my jungle drawings already. People are becoming really interested in the Amazon.

'Come, that's enough.' She stood up. 'I want to see how badly burnt you are.'

She led him into a tiny room open to the tiled roof. Two simple beds, the only furniture, crammed against the plain brick walls. In that sudden closeness he knew he had found her as she should be. What surrounded them as well as love was the compassion that he had felt for Neginho, for Perry and later, without understanding what it was at the time, for Zé and Ari. And again, when he and Beatrice had smiled at each other over the garden gate.

Idenea was close. 'You came to find me?' She took his hand smiling shyly. She placed a hand on his shoulder. 'I'm so happy you are here, even with a red face.' A dimple of a smile touched the edge of her mouth.

The only sound was the harsh mewing of the cats.

'So you want to see my scars?' He smiled as best he could.

'Yes. Go on. I bet you haven't got as many as me.'

With short words of surprise, they took off each other's clothes one by one. 'Look at that for a scar!' and 'Oh God that must have hurt!' She examined each new scar and ran her fingers over his discoloured skin.

'Horrible, aren't they?' he said as she touched a knobbly skin-graft on his collarbone.

'Why should I mind?' she whispered. 'Mine never put you off, did they?'

He touched one of hers that he had known so well, now just a ragged white stripe.

She began to laugh softly. 'At least today we are whole people, you and me. We did help each other didn't we, you for me, me for you?'

'How right you are, you clever, beautiful, Idenea.' He laughed as they had always laughed. 'Yes, we did help each other. Come with me—I don't know where but somewhere.'

'I'm not beautiful, Bobinho, you know what a lie that is.' Her smile faded. 'But this house is my home. I cannot leave.'

Of an instant, scars and pain forgotten, she put both her hands on his shoulders and with a tease in her voice. 'I am more beautiful than the jungle, aren't I?'

They lay down and with intense tenderness they loved each other. Bobby held her as if she was more delicate than anything he had ever held before. She was a different Idenea, a quieter more receptive Idenea. She didn't rush him along or pummel at his chest demanding a baby as so often before. She let him be. She laughed into his eyes, kissed his wounds and enfolded him in her arms and legs as if she would never let him go. She so wanted him to see how settled she was, to show him how ready she was for him now, that is if he wanted to be with her.

He whispered, 'More beautiful than the jungle.'

Later, as he was leaving.

'Good luck be with you,' he said as he walked away. 'I will always...'

'*Vai com Deus*, Bobinho,' she said quietly at his retreating figure.

TEN YEARS LATER.

Bobby sits alone in the kitchen at Abbey Farm, a half glass of wine within easy reach. It's close to midnight. The November wind rattles the windows and bulges the curtains through gaps in the frames. He is trying to write. Balls of screwed up paper on the floor are the first result. He tries again.

—The jungle is never far from me. That fire chasing me. Those pictures.

She's asleep upstairs with Eva, Zoni as well. She can never leave him—never could, the little brat sleeping in our bedroom on the ranch. She always spoilt him. Octavia and Eva of much the same age get on well, Michael and Zoni don't. Zoni's always in a sulk.

She's grown quite thick and heavy around the waist, like us all, and looks at me from those big round eyes as if to say, 'We're all right now, aren't we?' She's a headmistress and teaches English and Art. She bought a shop with money from the sale of her Plot 921. Romi sells car parts and she sells hammocks sent by Ari's wife plus her own pictures. She's famous as a jungle artist. She's brought some of her new work with her this time and *that's* what did it.

Beatrice says that I must write out why I'm so churned up, do me good. It's ODD!

So, no milk or wheat yields today.

No money in my eco-farming. Thank Heavens for Beatrice's physio clinic and piano lessons. She might even become a concert pianist one day. She said she'd explain why we had fallen for each other again, especially with my plum-coloured face. She still hasn't.

We've changed. She doesn't need to be put on a pedestal any more. I don't need to be the best in the world. She says we had the giddy gift of beauty and it was a curse that helped in our downfall. I tease her about the holes in her sweater. We soon had our Octavia in spite of her fear of pain. Our marriage has stuck in spite of her long affair with some brainy lawyer and my time with Idenea.

Perry took ages to see what I'd seen in those grey eyes in the Perfect Peace Motel. He does now, and always comes over when she does.

Beatrice even thanked Idenea for what she did for me. And when Idenea said in a practical way, 'You are of him, I am not', I could see tears on Beatrice's cheeks. How typical of Idenea, just like when she left me, all quick and done with.

Zé is important now in the National Indian Foundation. I speak to him on the telephone. He tells me about plans for two hydroelectric dams on that great Madeira River that will cause so much destruction. But he's still positive for his Indians. I ask how many of them are left.

Ari hasn't been home for more than two years, probably trampled by stampeding cattle or swallowed by an anaconda. My good friend.

Carmen sends Idenea photographs of all her children. They are trying to start up a new Indian tribe. They are thinking of calling themselves the Burning Wonder Tribe, named after me apparently. Much better would be the Juca Tribe. They have a baby every year but the mosquito has robbed them of more than one.

Valdo killed himself in a motor bike crash.

At supper today, Idenea told us of a dream that won't leave her. It's that bastard Dias. He bugs her dreams demanding she helps him find his wife Mercedes. He says he sees her body floating down the canal in Rio riddled with bullets. Probably shot by the notorious Esquadrão da Morte, if Colonel Delgado had anything to do with it. We exchange Christmas cards. He's always complaining about the democratic movement. I tell him to give them a chance.

The SHOCK.

Idenea showed us her pictures. The first was of two huts with jungle behind with the title, The Beginning of Fazenda Boa Esperança, Plot 921.

'Look Eva,' she said, 'there's the tiny hut I lived in before you were born and your grandparents in the big one next door. I can't draw enough of these they sell so well.'

Draw enough? What passes through her mind as she shapes the hut where she'd given birth and then, dear God, been raped? How can she do that? But then that's why I loved her. Walking away from her was a terrible wrench. All that we had done together.

The second drawing, Our Palace in Nowhere was of a long, thatched hut seemingly built within the overhang of the jungle. I blurted out that Ari and I had built that and I could walk right in there now. Beatrice said, 'Well, you can't, can you?'

In front of the hut were four figures, a man, a woman, a boy and a little girl.

Idenea said, 'Look Eva, I've never shown this to anyone before. It's my very favourite. I will never ever sell it.'

Eva pointed at the picture. '*Mãe*, that's you isn't it?'

'Yes. Look at my smart boots and big hat.' Eva's finger moved sideways. 'And that's Uncle Bobby?'

Yes, it did look like me.

Idenea smiled at me the open smile that I had loved so much and which I flatter myself I gave her instead of that miserable twist she'd had, when I first met her.

'Yes. Look how scruffy he is.'

Eva went on. 'The little boy, that's Zoni isn't it?'

'Yes, you clever girl.'

'Who's the little girl, *Mãe*?'

'The little girl? Well?'

'She looks a bit like me. But I was never there, was I?'

Idenea hesitated and I saw a faint flush on her cheeks as she answered, 'I always thought you'd look beautiful in the jungle, my baby.'

What a shock! My blood tingles as I think of it. So Eva is *my* blood! Beatrice, clever as she is, always said Eva was mine. Look at her chin, look at her hair she'd say. For me she was Valdo's child. And the name Eva, of course how stupid can I be? Idenea had yearned for an Adam to mark our beginning in that wilderness. Of course Eva was just as good. I hugged and kissed her.

Perry and Fran and their two kids stayed for supper eating a Feijoada that Idenea had cooked. Much pinga as well.

There was such harmony around the table, the joy of being together. I thought of little Neginho when I'd said goodbye to him through the bars of that filthy prison. The same feeling. Old Doggard was right and neither Perry nor I had chosen Charity for that school essay all those years ago. Funny word Charity, Compassionate Love much better. But I do still hope that my two-year-old steer will win a prize at the County Show.

I must go to bed. I know those pictures will bug my sleep.

I try to sleep.

I see tall trees and palm leaves waving in the wind above my old hut and the flashing colours of toucans and macaws, of cackling parrots and of the sobbing cries of the capuchin monkeys. And there's Idenea's pet toucan hopping across the hut floor and there's Massby curled up in the back of my old jeep.

And then everything darkens and I see a wounded land of majestic trees felled like slain giants, hundreds of fires burning like funeral pyres, thousands of hectares of grass that yellow every year as the thin layer of topsoil surrenders what little good it ever had.

No birds, no animals not even a whining mosquito.

Dried-up rivers, that harbinger of a red desert with twisters of red dust chasing each other about and stinging my eyes.

END

ACKNOWLEDGEMENTS

I thank Sparsile Books and in particular Lesley Affrossman, Alex Winpenny, Jim Campbell, Madeleine Jewett and Stephen Cashmore for their enthusiasm and support. Talking with them is a pleasure and I always know that their opinions are carefully considered.

In Brazil, Antonio d'Andrada de Almeida and Nicholas Reade made sure my information was correct.

In the UK, special thanks to David Inman for his publishing and marketing advice. And to Janine Edge, Mary Allen and Julia Gurney Hoare for patiently going through my early efforts and suggesting cuts and eliminating repetition.

I am also grateful to Peter Khoroche for listening to me .

Endnotes

i Londrina; literally meaning Little London named by or after British entrepreneurs and engineers who built the railways for the export of coffee. It is the second largest city in the state of Paraná.

2 Rondônia became a State between 1983 and 1984. Named after Marechal Candido Rondon, possibly the greatest Brazilian of all time and certainly of the 20th century.

3 The pull north. In the mid 1960s and 70s some in authority in the Brazilian Government and especially in the Ministry of Agriculture spread the rumour that the Americans were on the verge of taking over the Amazon. This rumour was the result of the Hudson project, a study by the Hudson Institute, which proposed the internationalisation of the Amazon and the creation of a huge inland lake. However impossible such an idea, there emerged a propaganda cry aimed at the general populace, 'Occupy so as not to hand over', 'Colonisar para não entregar'. This encouragement to populate the Amazon was easy to spread because of some inherent nationalistic resentment, justified or not, against multi national companies who were, more often than not, perceived as American. This perception was not exclusive to the uneducated but equally held by the rich and the landed. So 'Colonisar para não entregar' appeared in the national press, on the radio, the television and in particular in local newspapers of the southern coffee growing states of Paraná, Rio Grande do Sul, São Paulo and Santa Catarina. Frost had struck the coffee groves over more than one year, destroying millions of coffee trees. The resultant social impact was hunger, anger and widespread unemployment. The growth of large agribusiness that displaced many small farmers added to the fire of resentment. Since the military Government of that time influenced both the local and national press, it was able to target destitute people, only too eager to escape their misery with offers of free land, money for seed and working capital in the Amazon region where

the majority of the land and forest still belonged to the federal government. Offers of up to a thousand hectares were common. The Government believed this policy would solve two problems at the same time. First, it would help relieve the appalling conditions on the frost struck coffee plantations and secondly would move people to the Amazon, creating settlement and employment thus dispelling any mythical or actual interference from the outside. Around 1972 the then transport minister, Coronel Andreaza, in support of the construction of the Trans-Amazonian Highway said, 'With this great enterprise we will bury the Hudson lake.' Others declared, 'A road that joins nothing to nowhere - Uma estrada que liga nada a lugar nenhum, and, To take men without land to land without men - Levar homens sem terra para uma terra sem homens'. Even though it has never been completely paved it has opened up for huge soya bean planting and caused the elimination of Indian tribes. And, of course, the destruction of wildlife habitat. The BR 364 from Cuiabá to Porto Velho, when paved in1983/84 with World Bank funding was described by one environmentalist as the single most destructive piece of engineering in the world.

4   Debt Bondage, known as Devendo ao Patrão; a practice, still around today in remote areas of the interior, whereby an employer, very often a rancher, or shopkeeper drives or tricks an employee or unknowing low-paid customer into permanent debt. It is against the law and the courts pursue the perpetrators vigorously.

5   Capital of Brazil. The seat of government and so the Capital was transferred from Rio to Brasilia in 1960. Ministries followed over the next few years. The people of Rio, known as Cariocas, who had to accompany them, hated the move.

6   Bolivia had lost a nasty war and access to the Pacific. An international treaty demanded railway access for Bolivia to the Amazon and the Atlantic. Years later in 1911/12, and only then after threats of sanction, the railway was built, known as the

railway of death with the legend of a dead man for every sleeper. But from stolen seeds, world rubber production moved to the Far East and the Panama Canal opened. Trade on the railway collapsed. No dividend ever swelled the bank accounts of the original investors; the many trusting widows in Brighton and Philadelphia.

7 Squatter, Posseiro; It was generally believed that if you occupied empty land, even if it belonged to the state, for seven years you could claim title. In law difficult to prove but used by some landowners to increase their ownership by simply occupying land whether there were Indians there or not. Armed fighting was and is common. Some ranchers train cowboys to kill both Indians and any invaders.

8 Rubber Soldiers. When Malaya and much of Indonesia fell to the Japanese in the Second World War, the Amazon became a major source of rubber again. Known as Soldados de Borracha, many unemployed and famine- struck people emigrated west from the northeast to tap for latex. Many were black descendants of African slaves. The USA took about six hundred thousand slaves while Brazil took six million, the majority of whom ended up in the states of the northeast like Bahia.

9 1940. On the 9th October in Manaus President Getulio Vargas declared in what became known as the River Amazon Speech, 'I came here to see at first hand the conditions for the resurgence of the Amazon plan. All Brazil looks to the north with a patriotic desire to help in its development. And, not only Brazilians but also foreigners, technicians and businessmen will come to collaborate in this project applying experience and capital.'

10 Ordem e Progresso on the national flag comes from the beliefs of Positivism, a philosophical and semi religious belief started by the Frenchman, Auguste Comte, in the mid 19th century. It became very popular in Brazil and its principal temple still stands in Rio, sadly in a state of extreme disrepair. Marechal Candido Rondon was a firm follower.